The Lost Daughter *of* Liverpool

D0931981

ALSO BY PAM HOWES

Fast Movin' Train

Short stories
It's Only Words

The Rock n Roll Romance series
Three Steps to Heaven
Til I Kissed You
Always on My Mind
That'll Be the Day
Not Fade Away

The Fairground series
Cathy's Clown

The Cheshire Set series
Hungry Eyes

The Lost Daughter *of* Liverpool

Pam Howes

Bookouture

Published by Bookouture
An imprint of StoryFire Ltd.
23 Sussex Road, Ickenham, UB10 8PN
United Kingdom
www.bookouture.com

ISBN: 978-1-78681-103-5
eBook ISBN: 978-1-78681-102-8

Dedicated to the memory of my much-missed, lovely friend,
Geoff Barber. 1950 - 2015

Chapter One

Knowsley, Liverpool, July 1946

Dora Evans breathed a sigh of relief when the dinner-break bell rang out, gloriously loud and clear. Peace descended as the hum from twenty machines ceased, punctuated only by the loud voices of the factory girls as they dithered between eating in the canteen, or sitting outside on the grassy knoll at the back of Palmer's factory with their pack-ups.

Dora and her friend Joanie Lees brought their dinner from home each day, except for Fridays, when it was their favourite Spam fritters and chips in the canteen. They hurried outside into the bright sunshine and sat down on the wall that skirted Old Mill Lane, just under the now-faded factory sign that boasted *Palmer's Ladies Fashions of Distinction.* The decorative black and gold cast-iron railings that had previously graced the top of the sandstone wall had been removed a few years ago to be melted down to help the war effort. Now, wild flowers grew in their place, cascading down to the ground, giving the wall colour and a place for butterflies and bees to frequent.

These days, there were no distinctive fashions made at Palmer's. At the beginning of the war, the factory had been commissioned to make uniforms for the troops and nurses. But since the war had ended and old Gerald Palmer had passed away, to be succeeded by his son-in-law, George Kane who, according to the loyal workforce, hadn't a clue about the rag-trade, the company had struggled to make ends meet. The only contracts so far this year were for men's shirts that were sold in Littlewoods stores and catalogues.

Dora and Joanie had been classmates all through school and were best pals. Joanie was the only girl in her family and, with four younger brothers who drove her mad with their brawling and noisy games, had spent most of her childhood playing at Dora's house, where they'd spend hours making dolly clothes from scraps of material that Dora's mam had given them. The pair were as close as sisters and shared a special bond and all their secrets.

They'd joined Palmer's in 1941 when they left school, just after their fifteenth birthdays. Both enjoyed working in the business, though they daydreamed about making pretty dresses and skirts, rather than spending all day stitching collars and cuffs onto shirts. The nearest they'd come to making any dresses at all had been the plain cotton ones that were sent out to the nurses serving abroad. Still, they'd been helping the war effort and it was a decent enough job. They were grateful for the training they'd received, and their supervisor said they were exceptional seamstresses.

'What you got in your sarnies today?' Dora asked taking a greaseproof-wrapped package from her bag and smiling at the jam and margarine filling. She had two ginger nuts for afters too.

'Dripping on toast, *again*.' Joanie pulled a face.

'Here, swap for half of mine, and give me half of yours.'

'Thanks,' Joanie said. Dora's mam's home-made bread and jam was always delicious.

The pair tucked in, enjoying the welcome warmth of the sun after being cooped up all morning. After they finished their dinner and shared a bottle of lukewarm corporation pop Dora had dug out of her bag, they dropped down onto the patch of grass below the wall to sunbathe. Dora hitched up her faded wrap-over pinny, exposing her bare legs slightly, and Joanie did likewise.

'Look at my legs! What if Frank can't get me any stockings for the wedding? We need to spend time on the beach at New Brighton to get some more sun on them,' Dora said. 'Might ask Joe if he'll take me across on the ferry at the weekend.'

Dora was excited about marrying her fiancé, Joe Rodgers. They were teenage sweethearts and had always been inseparable at school, but then the war had forced them apart. After years of anxious days and nights, and love-letters that took months to arrive, Joe returned safely home. He'd immediately proposed, and Dora, who'd dreamed and hoped for that moment the whole time he'd been away, had accepted.

She knew she was lucky that her Joe had come home safe and sound from the war, and apart from being a lot skinnier, he hadn't changed too much in his years away with the army. Several members of his platoon were never coming home, including young men from their village, who'd left behind heartbroken wives and girlfriends. For some, it wasn't all Vera Lynn, bunting, and finger sandwiches on VE Day, as Dora's mam reminded her whenever Dora got too carried away with her fancy plans for the big day.

She'd never have got through those long and lonely years without Joanie by her side, offering comfort when the postman didn't bring a letter from Joe for weeks on end and she'd feared the worst, helping her to keep her spirits up, and always encouraging her to think positively.

'Isn't he playing with the band next weekend?' Joanie asked, tucking a straying curl under her turban.

'Yes, but only on Saturday this week.' Dora smiled as she thought about how handsome Joe looked when he played the alto saxophone in Murphy's Dance Band. He had been part of his regiment's brass band, and when some of the lads had suggested forming a dance band after being demobbed, he'd been happy to join them. 'Maybe he'll take me on Sunday. You and I need to work on Saturday anyway, if we're going to get the bridesmaids' dresses finished.'

Dora's own gown was hanging in the small wardrobe in her bedroom, covered by a sheet. White lace over taffeta with lace sleeves; made and designed by herself and Joanie, with some help from Mam. It was the type of dress she'd thought she could only ever dream of wearing, as fabric and money were in short supply.

Dora got to her feet and stretched. 'Let's go inside and grab a cuppa before it's time to go back upstairs.'

In the canteen they collected two mugs from the trolley and joined some of their co-workers at a table near the window. Peggy, a girl with unruly red hair and a voice as loud as a Mersey foghorn, was flirting with Len, one of the packers, who'd rolled up his shirt sleeves and was flexing his muscles outside the open window in an attempt to impress her.

'Call them muscles?' she yelled as he raised an eyebrow. 'Maude 'ere's got bigger muscles than youse. Show 'im, Maude.'

The girls laughed as Maude, a plump girl in her late teens, rolled up her sleeves and flexed her muscles in his direction. 'Beat that if you can,' she said with a giggle.

'How's yer wedding plans coming along, Dora?' Peggy asked, flicking cigarette ash onto the quarry-tiled floor. 'Youse finished making yer dress yet?'

'Yeah,' Dora replied. 'We're onto the bridesmaids' dresses now. They should be finished this weekend, and then we can relax a bit.'

'Not long now, eh, gel? When is it, six weeks?'

'End of August.' Dora took a sip of her rapidly cooling tea.

'And then yer freedom'll be up the Swanee, queen; especially when a babby comes along. Have youse found anywhere to live yet?'

'We're staying with Joe's mum for a while, until something else turns up,' Dora said with a half-smile, thinking about her freedom or the lack of it once married.

Starting a family wasn't in her immediate plans, and the thought of living with Joe's mother filled her with dread. She wasn't the easiest woman to get along with and a bit over-possessive where her only son was concerned. She'd so far shown no real interest in the wedding plans either, which suited Dora and her mam, as they preferred to do it themselves. She wished there was room for her and Joe to live with her parents, but there wasn't, so her future mother-in-law's it had to be.

'Right, gels, let's get back to work.' Peggy jumped to her feet and stubbed the end of her ciggie out. The workers were not allowed to smoke anywhere else in the factory. The bales of fabric and boxes of completed shirts piled up everywhere were deemed a fire hazard. 'The sooner we start, the sooner it'll be the next tea break.'

Dora swallowed the last of her brew and followed the other girls out of the canteen and up the wide wooden staircase to the first-floor workroom. She sat down on her chair next to a window overlooking farmland in the distance, and switched her machine back on. Joanie settled at her machine next to Dora's. The box of shirt collars they were working on was sitting in front of them and they each reached out and grabbed the next collar in the batch.

'There's nothing more boring than this,' Dora muttered. 'No colour, no fancy bits, just plain old white. It's driving me mad.'

'Me too,' Joanie agreed. 'Chin up, girl. Just keep thinking of the future.'

The wireless played in the background, broadcasting the end of *Workers' Playtime* with the show's producer announcing his usual, '*Good luck, all workers.*'

'Pity they never choose Palmer's for a broadcast,' Peggy shouted above the general hubbub. 'Not much chance of that now though. It's always one of them big London factories.'

Dora trimmed the thread and threw the collar back into the box where it was picked up by Peggy, who snipped the corners, turned it inside out and passed it over to Maude for pressing. Dora sighed and reached for another. She hated piece-work and they never got to see the finished garment. There'd been a time, before war broke out, when their factory had been as busy as any in London, and the floor above them had also buzzed with the noise of machinery and happy workers. But that floor was now silent, closed except for storage, and only twenty of the factory's forty machines were still in use.

Surely there would be a time in the not too distant future when money wouldn't be as tight, and ladies would want to wear pretty dresses and smart suits again, and not just for church on a Sunday or to a dance. Dora thought of the bridesmaid dresses. If she and Joanie were to have any hope of starting up their own business they needed those dresses to be the talk of the town. At the moment it was just a pipedream: girls like her and Joanie didn't own businesses anyway.

Chapter Two

Dora ignored the loud wolf-whistle from one of the packers as she and Joanie rode their bicycles out of the factory yard and turned onto Old Mill Lane.

'Cheeky devil.' Dora smiled as the gentle summer breeze blew her long honey-blonde hair around her face. She loved the feeling of release after it had been secured all day under her turban. Joanie still had her hair tucked inside hers, but her unruly curls were starting to stray and dangle down into her eyes. She stopped pedalling and rang her bell. Dora, a few yards in front, braked too and turned around. She laughed as Joanie whipped off the red and white checked scarf, shoved it into the basket on the front of her bike and ran her fingers through her mousey brown hair. Both girls chose *not* to wear the metal hair curlers that some of the factory girls had on under their turbans. There was no need - Dora's hair was naturally wavy, and Joanie's was a mass of corkscrew curls.

'Freedom, eh?' Dora said. 'I hate that sweaty feeling; makes my scalp all itchy. You definitely coming over later?' she asked as they set off up the lane again, riding side by side. 'Then we can see about tea-dipping that lace our Frank got us. Hope it works, otherwise it'll be ruined. And then what?'

'It should be fine, and a nice contrast to the dress material,' Joanie said.

When they reached the cottage on Sugar Lane, Dora's dad was in the front garden. He doffed his cap at the girls and carried on weeding the flower beds.

'See you 'bout seven,' Joanie called as she went on her way to her home on nearby Knowsley Lane.

'You okay, Dad?' Dora climbed off her bike, parked it beneath the window of the terraced cottage and retrieved her handbag from the basket. 'How's your leg?'

'Playing up a bit, chuck,' Jim Evans said, turning towards his pretty daughter who looked so much like her mother, with her blonde hair, big blue eyes, trim figure and a wide smile. 'Bloody shrapnel.' He rubbed his thigh. 'It'll never be right, but at least I've still got it, not like poor Len down the road. And I'm quite capable of doing a bit of work, so I'm not grumbling.' Poor young Len had lost both legs in Normandy at the D-Day Landings, but still managed a smile and a cheery wave when his mother pushed him out for a bit of fresh air each afternoon. Dora's dad, who'd been stationed with the Home Guard, had lost part of his thigh muscle as well as breaking his leg in several places during a bomb blast in Liverpool in the Blitz. It had been touch and go, and although his leg was stiff with the metal pins holding it together and much weaker than before, he coped well enough. 'Yer mam's inside. I'll be in meself in a few minutes when our Frank gets home. I'll see he puts your bike in the shed, if you've finished with it for today.'

'I have, thanks, Dad.' She frowned as he turned back to his gardening, coughing and spluttering as he did so. His chest had never been right since the war, all that poison he'd breathed in during the horrendous fires of the Blitz on their city. But he was stubborn, refused to go to the doctor's, and there was no point in arguing with him about it.

Dora let herself in and wiped her feet on the mat in the tiny vestibule, where the staircase, with its worn, red-patterned runner, held in place with old brass stair rods, rose steeply in front of her. She loved the little cottage she'd been born and brought up in and was glad that her dad was still able to do his gardening work at Knowsley Hall nearby. The rent-free cottage was tied to his job and it would break his heart if he lost it.

She pushed open the door to the front room where her mam was resting on the sofa; feet encased in blue slippers and stretched out on the colourful rag rug. In spite of the open window, the room felt stifling as Dora walked in, the range in the exposed brick chimney breast still glowing from an earlier fire. Mam used the side ovens for bread-making, and Monday was always her baking day, so the whole house would feel like a furnace tonight. It was cosy on cold winter days when fingers of ice clung to the windows and the heat rose up the chimney to the rooms above, but a nightmare in the warmer months of the year. Mam's eyes were closed and her glasses had slipped down her nose. Unusual for her to take forty winks, Dora thought, especially at tea time when they'd all be coming in from work, Dad from his part-time gardening and her brother Frank from his labouring job down at the docks.

Mam had been born into quite a well-to-do family in Hoylake. Dora had never met her maternal grandparents. She'd been told that her grandmother had fallen on hard times following the death of her husband during the First World War, and she'd passed away not long after the war ended. Mam had met Dad when she'd come to work in service at Knowsley Hall, needing a job and a roof over her head, and they'd married soon after. She'd managed to hold on to her gentle Cheshire accent and had instilled in her children a nice way of speaking. Dora had often been teased at school for sounding posh, but was glad now that she could adapt her way of speaking to suit any situation, although her older brother Frank's accent had strong overtones of guttural Liverpudlian. He'd told their mam he couldn't do posh in front of the dockers, he'd be laughed out of town.

Dora shook her gently by the shoulder. 'Mam, Mam, it's me. Are you okay?'

Mary Evans opened her eyes and smiled. 'I wasn't asleep, chuck, just resting my eyes. I've been on my feet all day.' She struggled upright. 'Come and see what I got today.'

Dora followed her into the kitchen at the back of the cottage. On the scrubbed pine table stood the fruits of her mam's labours; a few plain scones, enough small loaves for the week and a Victoria sponge, sandwiched together with jam made from hedgerow blackberries and apples from her dad's wartime Dig for Victory efforts. Most back gardens had been turned over to growing vegetables and fruit for the families and her mam had taught Dora how to feed an army on scraps. Nothing ever got wasted in their household. There was always a decent meal after a long day at work, even if it was just a meatless stew, like today's Blind Scouse.

Mam picked up a brown paper bag from the table and opened it. Inside were a good handful of glacé cherries, fat raisins and chopped walnuts.

Dora gasped. They had a bag of currants in the pantry that Frank had brought home a few months ago, which they'd been saving towards the wedding cake. Her dad's chickens would provide the eggs, which were so much nicer than using the powdered substitute that tasted nothing like the real thing. They'd been saving up their sugar rations, Dora and her mam substituting connie-onnie for sugar in their tea and porridge. The meagre butter rations had been eked out, so there was just enough with this week's supply for the cake. Frank and his mate had commandeered a sack of flour down at the docks.

'How did you get these?' Dora asked.

'Joanie's mam gave them to me,' Mam said, tapping the side of her nose. 'She did a favour for Cook last week. I gave her a couple of loaves in exchange.'

Dora smiled. Their mams had met when they both worked at Knowsley Hall. Joanie's mam was a part-time housekeeper there, and was friendly with Cook who nearly always paid for a favour with a bit of food.

'That's really kind of her,' Dora said. 'We'll have the best wedding cake this village has tasted for years.'

'We'll have the best wedding, never mind cake,' her mam declared. 'In fact, it's the first wedding since the lads came home. Well, apart from Sadie Jones's rush-job.' She folded her arms, lips pursed.

Dora thanked God she'd managed to keep Joe's amorous advances at bay. She thought back to last Thursday night's dance at the village hall when he'd walked her home and they'd taken a short cut through the nearby woods. They'd stopped to kiss beneath a large oak tree, fuelled by a couple of drinks. It was getting harder to say no when his kisses were so passionate and demanding. She felt she deserved a medal for her efforts in restraint. She loved him so much and was desperate to belong to him, but she wouldn't cause her mam and dad any grief now, even with Joe's little diamond ring on her finger. They'd just have to be patient for a few more weeks. Their pals, Sadie and Stan, had been so relieved to be back together following his safe return from Egypt that they *couldn't* wait, and were now the proud parents of a beautiful baby.

The front room door opened and Frank and Dad walked in. Mam shook her head as they trod dried mud onto her spotless, varnished floorboards. 'How many times have I told you two to use the back door? Look at the state of my floor now.'

Frank winked at Dora as she made to escape up the stairs. He dug into the old army rucksack in which he carried his dinnertime sarnies and bottle of tea, and pulled out a jar of brown gloopy stuff. 'Got this today.'

'What is it?' Dora asked, frowning.

'Molasses. Sugary treacle for the cake. It'll give it colour and help sweeten it too. A cask split down the docks and a bloke said it was good for cakes.'

Mam took hold of the jar and stared at the contents with a suspicious eye. 'Where did the jam-jar come from?'

'A fella on board ship. And yes, I washed it, before you ask. He kept his maggots in it for fishing,' he teased, ducking as Mam reached out and clipped him around the ear.

'Ouch! I'm joking. It's clean, I promise you.' He laughed and gave her a hug, his blue eyes twinkling mischievously. 'Right, if nobody needs the carsey, I'm off down the garden.' He tucked the *Liverpool Echo* under his arm and strolled out of the kitchen.

'Don't take all night,' Mam called after him. 'I'll be dishing up in a few minutes.'

Dora sat down on her narrow bed in the large front bedroom she shared with Frank, a curtained partition hung down the middle to give them some privacy, and she fingered the length of lace that he'd brought home last week. If they tinted it with leftover tea it should end up the perfect colour to trim the edges of the sleeves of the bridesmaids' dresses.

The dresses were cut from a bolt of pale green silk that Frank told her came from France, along with the leftover white lace and taffeta that her own dress had been made from. He said he'd got it at a good price from a merchant who supplied the more exclusive draperies in Liverpool city centre. She hadn't questioned the fact that the material had arrived on his back, on the motorbike, bundled up in an old, but thankfully clean hessian sack, rather than in the fancy paper a receiving draper would expect to see… and it had a peculiar odour that she'd tried *not* to put a name to. But once her mam took charge and cut it into lengths, a few days of hanging outside in the garden in a nice fresh breeze had lifted the smells. The leftover fabric had been cut into strips to dress the village hall with swags and bows that would be decorated with some of her dad's pretty summer flowers. Her bouquet would be cut from Dad's prize pink rose bush too, and tied up with white ribbons.

Joe had his navy pinstripe demob suit to wear for the wedding and a white shirt and navy tie, and he'd managed to arrange for Murphy's Dance Band to play. Dora knew it was going to be a day to remember.

All the scrimping and scraping and planning and organising was coming together. She was lucky that she could turn her hand to anything with a sewing needle, and had even made the rest of her trousseau from some parachute silk her brother had brought home. French knickers and a camisole for under the wedding dress; and a pretty nightdress for the honeymoon, trimmed with ribbon and white lace. Her friend Agnes had found a lovely blue garter in a gift shop and had given it to her for her last birthday. All she needed now were stockings, fine silk ones, if possible, and Frank was on the look-out for those. Hopefully there'd be no need for the usual gravy-browned legs with a seam drawn up the back.

Her mam said she'd wager a bet that not even the Princess Elizabeth would look as nice as Dora on her wedding day. As far as she knew, the princess and her fiancé, Philip, hadn't set a date yet. She and Joe had beaten them to it for the wedding of the year.

Joanie moved the poncher up and down in the dolly tub where the lace was steeping.

Dora brought two cups of tea outside and tipped what was left in the pot into the tub. 'Mam said we can't have any more tonight or she'll have no tea ration left for the rest of the week.' She dashed back inside and brought out a small plate with a scone split in half and spread with jam. The girls sat down on a couple of old deckchairs by the back door and enjoyed their supper in the warm evening air. The scent from nearby flowers and a neighbour's freshly cut grass wafted over them in the gentle breeze. It was a pleasure to enjoy the garden again without the sounds of planes droning overhead, air-raid sirens, and the bombings in Liverpool centre, followed by the stench of burning, and the feeling of overwhelming fear. Sitting night after night with her mam and the neighbours in the nearby Anderson shelters during the blackouts, she'd felt that the war would *never* end and she wouldn't see her beloved Joe or her dad and brother again.

'Sorry there's no butter, it's been saved for the cake,' Dora apologised, pushing thoughts of the war away. It was bad enough waking in a cold sweat at night on occasion, without the memories invading a peaceful evening.

Joanie licked the jam from her fingers. 'Your mam's scones are a treat, no matter what's on them. They're even better than Cook's up at the hall. It's nice that your mam's doing the wedding buffet.'

Dora nodded, pushing the last morsel of scone into her mouth. 'It is. And Dad's grown loads of stuff for salads,' she said, pointing to a makeshift greenhouse near the bottom of the garden where tomatoes and cucumbers were growing. 'And over there, he's got spring onions, lettuce and radish. We're so lucky he's green-fingered. I'm really excited, I can't wait.'

Joanie laughed. 'Bet you can't. And I bet Joe can't either.'

Dora rolled her eyes, feeling her cheeks warming. 'Well yeah, but you know it's for different reasons. I want to walk up the aisle like a princess, and Joe's desperate for the honeymoon! Typical man.' They both laughed and turned their attention back to the lace, which was taking on a dark creamy hue. 'Shall we rinse it now? It's been steeping for long enough and we don't want it to go orange. We'll dry it on the line and then sew it to the sleeves tomorrow night.'

Joanie smiled. 'Once the village women see what we've made, they'll all want something. I reckon we could get out of Palmer's and work for ourselves by next year.'

'Me too,' Dora said. It hadn't been too bad during the war when they felt they were helping the war effort in their own little way. But now, well maybe it really was the right time to try something new. 'As soon as I'm back from my honeymoon we'll put a card in the paper shop window, and maybe one on the notice board in the village hall, see what happens. Joe will be working a couple of nights a week with the band, so it will give me something to do. We need every penny we can save for our own place. I really don't want to live with Joe's mum for too long. Can you imagine? She'll be listening to every little noise we make.'

Joanie laughed and her cheeks flushed slightly. 'Where's your Frank tonight?' She lifted the lace from the tub, not quite meeting Dora's eye as she squeezed out the excess tea.

'Out for a drink with his mates, but he said he'd be back early enough to walk you home.'

'I'll be fine walking back on my own. He doesn't need to spoil his night out.' Joanie blushed a deeper shade of pink. She went inside, dropped the lace into the sink and turned on the tap to rinse it.

Dora smiled as she followed her. 'He enjoys walking you home, you know that. He's not bothered about leaving his mates early. Anyway, I thought you liked him, I mean, *really* liked him?' Dora knew Frank was sweet on Joanie and she wished her friend would admit she felt the same. But apart from walking her home from the dances at the village hall and on nights when she came over to help with the sewing, Frank was yet to ask Joanie on a date.

'Um, yes, I do…' Joanie muttered, bundling the lace into a chipped enamel bowl. 'There, all done. You can peg it out now.'

'Stop changing the subject! You could do worse than our Frank.'

'I'm not really looking for a boyfriend.'

'Well *he's* looking for you; you know he is, so think about it. Then maybe we could go out on double dates.' She winked at Joanie in encouragement.

Dora knew her friend was shy and she was hoping the wedding would be the right time to get them together. With a few drinks and romance in the air, Joanie might just respond to her brother's charms. Frank was a good-looking lad with his big blue eyes and shock of blond hair; they really would be the perfect match.

Joanie stumbled and caught the heel of her shoe in a rut on the dirt pavement. She held her breath as Frank reached out and grabbed her arm to save her falling head-first into the road. It was dark on the lanes and he'd borrowed the lamp from Dora's bike to light their way. As he shone the light into her face and smiled, she felt the flutter of butterflies in her stomach.

'Whoops!' He grinned. 'Better hold my hand. Don't want you breaking your neck or our Dora'll never forgive me.'

She looked away from his teasing blue eyes as his hand gripped hers and he pulled her along. She really liked Frank, but was never sure if he was serious or just messing around. In spite of Dora telling her that he enjoyed walking her home, she wouldn't allow herself anything beyond a daydream that his feelings for her were more than just friendship.

The tiny terraced cottage where she lived with her family came into view, the upstairs windows ablaze with light, and she tried to pull her hand away in case one of her brothers was peeping through the curtains, but Frank held on tight and gave hers a squeeze.

'Are you coming to ours tomorrow night?' he asked as they drew level with the gate.

'Probably.' She nodded. 'We've got to sew the lace on the sleeves.' She could feel her cheeks heating as he looked at her and she glanced towards the front door to avoid staring into his eyes. 'I'd better go in. Mam will wonder what's keeping me.' Why did he make her feel like such a blushing, dithering wreck in his presence? He'd never ask her out at this rate and he probably still thought of her as his little sister's friend whose pigtails he used to pull.

He lifted her hand and dropped a kiss on the back. 'See you tomorrow, then.'

Joanie stared after his retreating back and raised her hand as he turned on the corner and waved. She sighed and hurried up the garden path. No doubt Frank had plenty of girls after him, with more sophistication about them than she had. He was always out with his mates, so wouldn't be short of admirers. Ah well, there was always tomorrow.

With her parents in bed, Dora had a strip-wash in the kitchen. She slipped her nightdress over her head and put a pan of milk on the stove to boil. She'd make a jug of cocoa for when Frank got back from walking Joanie home. Mam and Dad always went to bed early, and on nights when she wasn't seeing Joe, she loved the half hour before bedtime, chatting in the kitchen with her brother. He made her laugh with his tales of dockside labouring. It was a hard job, but he seemed to enjoy the camaraderie.

Frank was a clever lad and never one to miss a trick. He'd passed the eleven plus exam, but with no spare money to buy him a uniform and books, he'd forgone the opportunity to go to the grammar school. He'd never borne their hard-up parents a grudge for his missed education, but as soon as he could he left school and joined the army to see the world, and then war broke out. Since being demobbed he'd gone straight to the docks, even though Joe told him he should try to get a job at the Royal Ordnance Factory in Kirkby, where Joe had been employed since his demob. But Frank said he'd stay where he was. He'd heard rumours that the ROF would soon be closing now the war was over. No need for munitions factories any more.

Dora really hoped he was wrong about that, because Joe needed the job, and had told her that once they were married,

Chapter Three

Joe grabbed Dora by the hand as the pair ran along the waterfront towards the ferry boarding point. He bought return tickets at the booth and they hurried on board the *Royal Daffodil*. Up on deck they breathed in the salty tang of the Mersey as the ferry pulled away, leaving the river foaming in her wake, the seagulls swooping and diving for titbits in the murky waters.

'That was close,' Joe said, reaching into his jacket pocket for a packet of Woodbines and matches. He lit up, threw the spent match overboard and took a long drag, relaxing as he inhaled the strong nicotine. They stood side by side and leant on the rail, looking back at their home city, damaged so badly during Hitler's seven-day Blitz in May 1941. Some of the waterfront buildings were amazingly still intact. They scanned the skyline, admiring the Royal Liver Building, with its two mythical Liver Birds standing atop the clock towers, one looking out across the river and the other keeping a protective eye over the city. The Three Graces had been such a welcome sight for all the troops of Liverpool as they'd arrived home from their wartime battles abroad. Joe always felt a lump in his throat when he looked at the buildings. The very fact that they still stood proud after Hitler's wave of destruction was proof enough to him that Liverpool could triumph over anything.

'We should have a good few hours in New Brighton now we've caught the early ferry,' he said, taking another drag on his ciggie. 'Might even get some dancing in too with a bit of luck.'

Dora smiled as he slipped his arm around her shoulders and she leaned into him.

'I'm not really dressed for dancing, Joe. And I want to sit on the sands and get some sun on my legs, they're too pale!'

He raised an eyebrow and grinned. 'They look all right to me, *and* you look good enough for dancing later.' Her pretty short-sleeved cotton dress, with red and yellow flowers on a white background, and white peep-toe sandals, looked as nice as anything he saw other girls in the dance halls wearing. Dora always looked lovely, even though she made and restyled most of her clothes from jumble sale finds. She was clever that way and he was proud of her resourcefulness.

He felt he was the luckiest man in the village that she'd waited for him, even though sometimes he'd had to wait weeks and months for her letters to reach him and often they came in threes. When she'd written that she'd been to a couple of dances at the American airbase in nearby Burtonwood with Joanie and their friend Agnes, his heart had been in his mouth in case the next letter was a 'Dear John'. A few of his comrades had lost their girls to the American airmen, but not him. Dora had been there on the dockside waiting when his ship berthed. She'd run into his arms and he'd vowed never to be away from her side again.

The cinders crunched beneath their feet as Dora and Joe strode around the New Brighton fairground. They shared a stick of fluffy pink candy floss as the steam organ on the Gallopers ride belted out 'Blaze Away'. They'd spent a few lazy hours sitting on a couple of stripy deckchairs on the beach. Joe treated them to ice-cream wafers after they'd eaten their Spam and salad sarnies, packed up for them by Dora's mam, and they'd bought a jug of tea from a stand near the prom. Children rode up and down the sands on donkeys, laughing and giggling as the lad in charge made the animals run.

A Punch and Judy show on the promenade had attracted a large audience, and childish laughter floated down. It was good to hear kids enjoying themselves again. Some of them had no doubt been conceived on a weekend pass from the barracks, and then arrived while their fathers were billeted away. Dora thought of the children that had been evacuated from Liverpool and the surrounding areas in the early war years, and packed off to Canada for safety on the *SS City of Benares* steamship that had sailed from their own dockside in 1940. While far out in the North Atlantic, the ship had been torpedoed by a German U-Boat. It sank, taking eighty-seven precious little lives with it, as well as many adults, leaving devastated families to cope with more than Hitler's bloody bombs.

On the way to the waterfront, they'd walked down from Lime Street station, through several streets of bombed-out properties, now under demolition, blackened and damaged houses, schools and shops. Some of the families living in those slum streets had been wiped out, children who hadn't been evacuated as well as adults. But many were still living there in appalling conditions. It had brought it home to Dora just how lucky her family had been that, although affected financially, they'd suffered no loss of life or damage to their home.

Thank heavens the war was finished before she and Joe brought any children into the world. God willing, their family would be welcomed into a secure home and loved, without anything bad happening to tear their young lives apart.

'Big wheel?' Joe said, breaking her thoughts and leading her over to join the queue for the Ferris wheel.

When they took their seats the lad in charge clanged the bar shut across their thighs and the wheel rose slowly into the air, stopping at the top to let passengers off below. The view across Liverpool Bay was breathtaking and Dora could see a large ship on the horizon, belching steam from three red funnels and heading towards the Irish Sea.

'That's the *Queen Mary* on her way to New York,' Joe said, squinting in the bright sunlight. 'One day, gel, we might be doing something like that. Off to a new life in a new country.'

The wheel started up and they had another full spin around before it was their turn to alight. After wandering around the penny arcades and taking a ride on the steam-powered swing-boats, Joe suggested fish and chips for tea. Dora clapped her hands. It was a rare treat, and they shared a wrapped parcel, sitting side by side on a lawn in the floral gardens, devouring and enjoying every last morsel of the crispy fish batter and delicious golden chips.

Joe drew Dora into his arms and kissed her. She felt safe in his arms. It was where she belonged. He was kind and hard-working too and she knew he'd always look after her.

She dug into her handbag for her compact and lippy. 'I've had a lovely day,' she said, pouting in front of the small mirror as she applied a slick of Tangee and smacked her lips together. She powdered her nose and then ran a comb through her hair, tangled from the sea breeze. 'Thank you, Joe.'

'Me too. It's been great. The last free Sunday the band has got until after the wedding. So I'm glad we've spent it together. We've got full weekend bookings right through now. Still, it's a bit more money towards our Southport honeymoon.'

'Do my legs look any browner though?' Dora laughed.

He grinned. 'Not really, but you've caught the sun on your face. You've got a little red nose.' He leant over to kiss her.

Chapter Four

August 1946

Dora lifted her arms as Joanie slipped the wedding gown over her head and supported the skirt as it fell to the floor. She did up the back zip and Dora turned towards the full-length mirror to take a look. She could see Joanie and her other bridesmaid Agnes standing behind with their hands over their mouths.

'Does it look okay?'

'*Okay?*' Joanie said, a tremor in her voice. 'You look fabulous, Dora. You really do.'

'You look wonderful,' Agnes agreed.

'Wish I could stop shaking though.' Dora held out her hand. 'Look at that. I'm so nervous I feel sick. And does my hair look all right, pinned up like this?' She patted the back of her hair into place and smoothed her fringe to one side.

'Your hair looks lovely. And it's only wedding nerves you've got,' Joanie said reassuringly. 'I'm sure every bride feels the same. Sit on the bed for a minute and relax while we finish getting you ready.' Dora sat down and Joanie picked up the net veil with the headdress attached and placed it on top of Dora's head, fluffing the net out and arranging it around her head and shoulders. 'I'll drop it over your face when you're down the stairs. Don't want you missing your step and falling.'

Dora held out her right foot as Agnes slipped her white court shoes on. She got to her feet and took several deep breaths.

'Feeling better now?' Agnes asked.

'I think so.' She stared at her reflection in the mirror and chewed her lip as a little icy feeling ran down her spine. She shook herself. 'What if he doesn't turn up?'

'Who?' Agnes frowned.

'Joe, of course. What if he's changed his mind?'

'Oh, Dora.' Joanie rubbed her arm. 'Don't be silly. Of course he'll turn up. Why wouldn't he? He loves you and he's waited as long as *you* have for today. He'll be there, believe me.'

'Thank you, for always being there for me while he was away. I couldn't have got through it without you. And you too, Agnes.'

Joanie smiled. 'That's what friends are for. And you're always there for us.'

Dora gave her a hug and stepped back. 'Shall we do it then?'

Joanie and Agnes nodded.

'The flowers are in the sitting room,' Joanie said. 'We'll go down first and tell your dad you're ready. Make sure he's not dropped ash all down his suit or your mam will give him hell.'

As her bridesmaids left the room, Dora drew a deep breath and took a last peek in the mirror. Of course Joe would be there. What was she thinking? He'd never let her down.

Joanie was calling for her and she walked out of her bedroom for the last time as a single girl. Her dad's face was a picture as he stared at her from the lobby at the bottom of the narrow staircase; she'd never forget the proud look in his eyes.

When she reached his side he took her in his arms and planted a kiss on her cheek. His voice husky with emotion, he whispered, 'I'm feeling that made up right now, chuck.' He led her into the sitting room where Joanie and Agnes were waiting.

'I need to fix your veil,' Joanie said and dropped the net down over Dora's face, arranging it neatly. 'Now Agnes and I have to go to the church with your mam, she's waiting in the car. Here's your bouquet.' Joanie handed Dora the pink roses, tied up with white ribbons. 'Mr Jones will be back for you both in a couple of minutes.' She squeezed Dora's arm. 'See you very soon.'

Joanie hurried outside, leaving Dora alone with her dad. She blinked back tears as she looked at him, all dressed up in his best suit, his grey hair neatly brushed and his blue eyes shining with pride. His tie was slightly askew. She reached out, straightened it and brushed the ash from the front of his jacket. He squeezed her hand and smiled.

'You look beautiful, my little queen. I'm that proud of you.'

Not only had Mr Jones, their neighbour, cleaned and polished his black Morris Eight so that it gleamed in the bright morning sunshine, but his lovely wife had tied white ribbons to the bonnet, and laid some pretty blue and white flowers along the back shelf. It looked like a real wedding car. Dora felt like royalty as they pulled away from the gate and drove slowly down the lane towards St Mary's, the attractive sandstone parish church near the village hall. She waved at several neighbours, who waved back and smiled as the car passed.

She could see Mam waiting anxiously by the entrance, looking smart in her lilac dress and jacket that she'd made herself. Her little pillbox hat, borrowed from a neighbour, had been titivated with a bow of lilac chiffon. She rushed forward as Dad helped Dora out of the car, and adjusted her veil, smoothed down the lace overlay of her dress, stepped back and smiled proudly. In a rare show of emotion, she pulled Dora into her arms and kissed her. 'You look beautiful, my love, you really do. It's all been worth it, all the scrimping, scraping and sewing; we're a good team when it comes to making the pennies spin out.' She blinked away a tear.

'I couldn't have done all this without you, Mam,' Dora said, a catch in her voice.

'Get away with you.' Mam dabbed her eyes with a hanky. 'Right, I'll go and get seated and give the vicar a nod.'

Agnes and Joanie smiled as Mam hurried away.

'You two look really lovely,' Dora told them. 'That colour suits you so well.' The dresses hung perfectly on their slender frames, the pale green silk complementing both Agnes's wavy red hair and Joanie's mousey brown curls.

Dora linked arms with her dad as Joanie and Agnes took up position behind. Another deep breath and they crunched up the shingle church path. As they went inside the organist struck up with the wedding anthem and Dora felt her nerves fading and her spirits rising as she set off slowly down the aisle on her dad's arm. She beamed at her seated guests, who nodded and smiled as she passed them. She looked up at the sunbeams dancing through the tall stained-glass windows, throwing colourful patterns onto the plain cream walls and arches.

Dora could see Joe standing by the altar. A proud smile lit up his face, and the rush of love and relief she felt as he looked at her was overwhelming. He was there just as Joanie had said he would be, his best man, Frank, by his side. The pair, identically dressed in their de-mob suits, sported white carnations from Dad's garden in their buttonholes. She didn't think she'd ever seen Joe looking so handsome.

The vicar nodded as Dora took her place beside Joe. He reached out and squeezed her hand reassuringly and she squeezed his back. Dad lifted her veil and pecked her on the cheek. Feeling more relaxed now, Dora handed her bouquet of pink roses to Joanie and turned her attention back to the vicar and the solemnity of the marriage service.

When Joe was instructed to kiss his bride, a murmur of congratulations rippled through the congregation and Joe squeezed her hand again.

As the church bells pealed, Dora and Joe led their wedding party down the aisle. Outside she leant against her new husband

and gripped his hand tightly. 'I can't believe we've done it,' she whispered. 'I'm so relieved it all went well.'

'Me too,' Joe said. 'Just the photos now and then I can get a pint down my neck!'

As Dora opened her mouth to reply, little Kenny Holt from one of the cottages across the lane came running over. He stopped in front of Dora and Joe, wiped his snotty nose on his tattered shirt sleeve and with a proud flourish produced a slightly battered silver horseshoe. He handed it to Dora with a gap-toothed smile.

'Me mam's patched it up wiv silver paper from a chocolate she saved at Christmas,' he began, his wide smile lighting up his grubby face. 'She sez to tell yer it was given to 'er and me dad at their wedding and it brought 'em good luck 'cos he comed 'ome safe from the war. She 'opes it brings you good luck, too.'

'Oh, thank you, Kenny.' Dora bent to kiss the little lad's cheek and Joe ruffled his hair.

Kenny blushed and wiped the back of his hand over his face. 'You looks just like a real princess, Dora,' he said, and ran back across the road to his home.

'And he's right, you do,' Joe said, a catch in his voice. 'You look gorgeous. I can't wait for tonight.'

'Shh,' Dora said, suppressing a giggle as the photographer, who was a pal of Frank's, organised everyone into groups and proceeded to click away with his camera.

'I got one of the little lad giving you the horseshoe,' he told them. 'Too good to miss, that was.'

Laughing, the bridal pair dodged rice and confetti as they made their way across the green to the village hall. Dora looked around the room with pride. The sun blazed though the large windows, filling the room with natural light. The neatly draped swags between the beams were decorated with small bunches of scented summer flowers, tied up with white ribbon, and they filled the room with a pleasant perfume. Mam and some of her friends had laid out all the food on trestle tables and the make-shift bar was stocked with bought-in bottles of ale and sherry and the home-made brews and fruit cordials, donated by kind friends and neighbours.

One of the members of Murphy's Dance band had brought along a gramophone and records. Joe suggested he play some-thing as the guests filed in and found seats at the tables around the room. While the boys sorted out the music, Dora and her friends helped her mam take off the wrappings from the plates of sandwiches and bowls of salad.

Joe jumped up onto the stage and announced the refresh-ments were ready and for everyone to help themselves. Drinks were poured and the guests toasted the bride and groom. After much cranking of the handle, Glenn Miller's 'In the Mood' crack-led from the gramophone, filling the room with sound.

When every last crumb had been devoured, and the cake cut, sliced and handed out, wrapped in paper serviettes, one of Joe's band clapped for silence.

'Would the bride and groom please take their places on the floor for the first dance, thank you.' Everyone sang along to Vera Lynn's 'Anniversary Waltz' and a few couples joined the bridal pair.

As Dora waltzed in Joe's arms she couldn't stop smiling. She'd never felt happier in her whole life and this was just the start of it.

'I love you so much,' Joe whispered. 'I'll never let you down.'

'I love you too,' she whispered back, looking into his eyes as the song came to an end.

'We'll have a wonderful life, you and me,' he promised.

'It's time to play a spot with the lads now,' Joe said. 'We'll just do an hour and then me and you are off to Lime Street station, Mrs Rodgers.' He dropped a kiss on Dora's lips and hurried over to the small stage where the rest of Murphy's Dance Band was about to start warming up.

* * *

Joanie came dashing across to Dora. 'You two looked so lovely on the dance floor just then,' she said. 'And there are loads of people asking about our dresses,' she carried on excitedly. 'I told them we made them, it looks like we've got our first order for a wedding ensemble and a couple of summer frocks for the honeymoon! I promised the bride-to-be that we'll be ready for business in a couple of weeks.'

'Oh that's wonderful, Joanie!' Dora exclaimed. 'What a great start.' As Dora gave her best friend a hug, Frank tapped them on the shoulder and asked Joanie to dance.

'Go on, he won't bite you.' Dora gave her a friendly push and she got to her feet, took his hand, and he led her onto the floor as the band struck up with The Andrew Sisters song, 'Don't Sit Under the Apple Tree'.

Dora winked at Agnes, who was sitting opposite with her boyfriend Alan. He'd missed the wedding due to work, but had joined them for the reception. She crossed her fingers on her lap as Frank and Joanie jitterbugged, laughing and singing along. Her brother hadn't taken his eyes off her friend since this morning. Joanie had downed several glasses of old Mrs Hayward's elderberry wine, which had given her rosy cheeks and an air of reckless abandon. That home-made wine had probably been fermenting since before the war and packed a punch. Judging by Joanie's wide smile, she was really enjoying herself. Joanie and Frank looked like Knowsley's answer to Fred Astaire and Ginger Rogers tonight. Dora smiled to herself as she watched them jigging around.

She caught Mam's eye and waved her over, nodding at her brother and Joanie.

''Bout time eh, Mam?'

Mam laughed. 'I'll say. That pair have been pussyfooting around for months. Even a blind man could see they're sweet on each other. Don't know what's took them so long. Joanie's mam just said the same.'

'Well let's hope something comes of it,' Dora said, clapping when the song came to an end.

As the band played a few Glenn Miller numbers and the crowd on the dance floor thinned a bit, Dora spotted two young women she didn't recognise. They hadn't been at the church, or here for the buffet earlier; they certainly weren't from Palmer's factory or the village. Dora felt a shiver run down her spine as she noticed the shorter of the two staring at Joe on the stage. Throughout 'Pennsylvania 6-5000' she watched his every move, swaying her hips from side to side, in time to the music. She clapped loudly, called his name and blew him a kiss as the song ended.

As Frank brought Joanie back to the table and went to fetch her a glass of water, Dora beckoned him to one side. 'Who are those two women who just came in?' She nodded towards the pair, still standing near the stage, still looking at Joe.

Frank turned to look. 'They work in the ROF canteen. Joe must have asked them along. Ivy Bennett, the shorter one, is the cook and her mate Flo helps her. I've seen them around town.'

Dora frowned. 'He didn't tell me he'd invited anyone else from work, other than the people I knew about.'

Frank shrugged. 'Does it matter? They're not really doing any harm, are they?'

Dora sighed. 'I suppose not. But he could have at least said something. There's nothing left for them to eat.'

'Not your problem, Sis. Joe'll be off stage in a minute and then the pair of you will be going on your honeymoon.'

She nodded and gave him a hug. 'Look after Joanie, Frank. And no hanky-panky. She's too drunk to know what she's doing. Don't you be taking advantage, or else!'

'As if I would,' he said, his blue eyes twinkling. 'I'll see she gets home safe, don't worry. I'll get her sobered up a bit or her mam will think it's my fault she's tipsy.'

Dora gave Joanie a big hug goodbye. 'Thank you for all the help, especially with making the dresses. You never know, yours might be next.'

Joanie laughed, flushing bright red and looking at Frank, who was grinning broadly.

Dora joined Joe and they made their way around the room, saying goodbye to everyone. They stopped beside the two women from the ROF, and Joe introduced her to them. 'Thank you for coming, Flo and Ivy. May I introduce my beautiful wife, Dora?'

'I love your dress, Dora,' Flo gushed, shaking her hand. 'And congratulations to you both.'

'Thank you, Flo,' Dora said, shaking her by the hand.

'Congratulations,' Ivy muttered and stood back, offering no handshake.

'Thank you,' Dora said, frowning as she observed the unfathomable cold look in Ivy's pale blue eyes. There was something about her that made Dora feel uncomfortable. She was glad when they moved away to say their last goodbyes.

'She's a miserable one!' Dora whispered to Joe.

'Who is?'

'That Ivy, from your works.'

'Is she? Can't say I noticed, really.'

'Hmm.' Was he blind? The woman was more than sweet on him and she wouldn't trust her as far as she could throw her. But she wasn't going to let her put a dampener on their lovely day, which had been everything she'd hoped it would be. Joe was hers now, and they had the rest of their lives to look forward to.

Chapter Five

October 1946

Dora's dad pulled a face as the door-knocker went again. It was the third time tonight. Bloody women calling to order new frocks and him being sent upstairs or outside while his daughter and Joanie set to with a tape measure and cups of tea. He felt invaded lately, as though his home wasn't his own. Mary had told him to stop moaning as Dora and Joanie were on the verge of getting their business off the ground and he should be proud of them. Well that was all well and good, but when the only peace a man could get was sitting in the carsey for hours on end, it was a bit too much. Time Joe got them a place of their own. His bloody mother wouldn't put up with *her* front room being all messed up with pins and needles and what-have-you. He'd trod on a pin in his stockinged feet last week and it was still painful.

'Sorry, Dad,' Dora said as she showed a tall young woman into the front room. 'Can you just give us ten minutes while Mavis tries on her dress for size?'

'I suppose so,' he muttered, getting to his feet, making sure his slippers were on firmly. He limped into the kitchen and sat down at the table with the *Echo*. Mary was at her fortnightly WI meeting in the village hall and wouldn't be back for another hour. That bloody sewing machine Dora was using was as old as the hills now and had been his mother's before she gave it to Mary. The clattering and rattling drove him mad. What Dora needed was one of them new-fangled things that you turned a hand wheel on.

He'd seen some advertised in the newspaper with an electric motor attached, that you could plug in. He'd love to treat her to one, but he simply didn't have the money to spare. The treadle was too big to be easily transported anywhere, and anyway, there was no way Joe's mother would have it in her precious house.

He lit a ciggie and blew a cloud of smoke into the air, coughing and spluttering as he did so. His chest had never been right since the war, not that he'd been sent abroad like the young lads, but he'd seen his share during the Blitz and choked on smoke and flames, breathing in them bloody poisonous fumes. Mary nagged him about giving up smoking, but the damage was done and it was one of his only pleasures.

Dora knelt on the floor as Mavis stood in front of her in the new dress. The white cotton fabric, with a bright red poppy design, was ideal for the strappy sundress with its fitted bodice and slightly flared skirt: the little matching bolero set it off nicely and covered the tops of Mavis's arms, as she'd requested. Dora had adapted a ready-made paper pattern to her own design and it had worked out well. She hoped to make her own patterns once she and Joanie had got the business up and running properly. Joanie handed the pins over as Dora measured the length and pinned up the hem. 'Do me a little twirl, Mavis,' Dora said. 'Then I can see if it's level.'

Mavis obliged and Joanie nodded her approval. 'It's spot on, Dora. And Mavis, it looks lovely.'

'We'll have it finished by the end of the week,' Dora said as Mavis slipped the outfit off and put her own clothes back on. 'I'll drop it off for you on Friday night after work.'

Joanie saw Mavis out and came back into the front room followed by Frank. 'Mavis is dead happy.' Joanie grinned. 'She says she'll tell all her mates about us.'

Dora laughed. 'Smashing. Fingers crossed she does.' She popped her head around the kitchen door. 'We're nearly done for the night now, Dad; just packing away then we'll leave you in peace. Our Frank's going to walk me back to Joe's mother's house and then take Joanie home.'

Dora placed the sewing kit in the footstool, put the machine into its case and pulled the wooden top back into place. She put the doily and vase of flowers on top and looked around to make sure nothing had been left out while Joanie checked for any dropped pins in the rag rug. After the fiasco last week, Mam had warned them not to let it happen again.

'I'll take Mavis's outfit home and neaten the seams,' Joanie said, getting up off her knees. 'Shall I do them with my pinking shears or stitch the edges down with a narrow hem?'

'The pinking shears should be fine,' Dora replied. 'The material's cotton, so it won't fray. As soon as we can afford it we'll invest in an over-locker.'

'I thought about that the other day,' Joanie began. 'When I went upstairs in the factory to get something, I noticed there are still three over-lockers up there doing nothing. I wonder if Palmer's would let us buy one cheap from them?'

'No harm in asking.'

Frank popped his head around the door, making them jump. 'You two ready to go yet?'

'We are,' Dora said, dropping Mavis's new outfit into a bag and handing it to Joanie.

Dora waved goodbye to Frank and Joanie as they left her at the door of her mother-in-law's house on Ormskirk Road, and walked away holding hands. They seemed to be getting along really well and had been on several dates since the wedding. She was keeping her fingers crossed they would soon be making a wedding dress for Joanie.

She sighed and opened the front door. Although it was still early, Mrs Rodgers was ready for bed, her pink nightdress and matching housecoat swamping her bird-like frame. She was sitting in her neat-as-a-new-pin lounge that was twice the size of Dora's parents' front room. It would be ideal for sewing in with all that floor area to cut out on, and there was a spare alcove next to the chimney breast where the treadle machine would fit perfectly. Her mother-in-law didn't seem to like sharing, but she had no choice other than to let her son and Dora live there for the time being. Dora knew that his mother felt Joe had married beneath him. His late father had worked in banking, and hers was a gardener. Thankfully, Joe wasn't a snob like his mum. He was friendly and treated everyone he met with the same respect. The war had been a good leveller for the majority, with the exception of Ida Rodgers. She would have to let him go soon enough though, Dora thought.

Joe was anxious to start a family, but she wasn't comfortable about doing that here. They had hardly any time to themselves and privacy was a problem with Ida's bedroom being right next to theirs. Dora couldn't relax and enjoy lovemaking like she'd done on their honeymoon. She had visions of her mother-in-law with a glass pressed up against the wall listening to them. Joe had laughed when she'd told him that, but he knew it made her nervous of making any noise.

'If you're going to use the bathroom, will you do it before I go to bed, please?' Mrs Rodgers said; a pained expression on her face. 'It disturbs me, you running water and flushing the toilet late at night.'

'Of course.' Dora went slowly upstairs and put her coat and bag on the bed she shared with Joe. Late at night? For God's sake it wasn't even half-nine yet. She'd been hoping to take a bath tonight, but there was no chance: it would only cause an argument if she asked for permission. A strip-wash it would have to be. At

least the toilet was in the small room next door to the bathroom
and not down the garden like at home, and the water was always
hot from the tap, no kettle-boiling necessary. A small mercy, but
a nice one all the same. She reached into the wardrobe for her
wash-bag and pulled out her soap and flannel. Pears' soap, a bit
of luxury she'd treated herself to. She held the bar to her nose
and breathed in the scent. A little thrill ran through her as the
smell reminded her of the wonderful time they'd had on their
honeymoon.

As she came out of the bathroom and crept across the landing
she heard the front door open and Joe calling out that it was
only him. Thank goodness for that. His mother would clear off
to bed now and they could enjoy a cuppa together before they
also turned in. She slipped her nightdress over her head and ran
barefoot down the stairs and into his arms in the hallway.

He held her tight and kissed her, running his hands down her
back, until his mother coughed loudly and excused herself to go
upstairs.

'She been giving you *the look*?' he asked with a grin.

'No, just complaining about us making a noise in the bathroom when she's in bed.'

He shook his head, led her into the lounge, closed the door
and pulled her down beside him on the sofa. 'How did the fittings
go tonight?'

'Just the finishing touches left to do now. We can drop them
off on Friday when the girls get paid.' She sighed and twisted the
hem of her nightie between her fingers.

'What's up, sweetheart?'

She shrugged and looked around the room. 'My poor dad
tonight had to keep going outside or in the kitchen when we
were doing the fittings. It's not fair. But now we've got a few regular customers, I don't really want to stop, because we might lose
them.'

Joe took her face in his hands and kissed her again. Then he fished in his jacket pocket and handed her an envelope. 'Read this.'

Dora unfolded the headed letter, her eyes widening as she took in the words. Tears filled her eyes. She couldn't believe it. They'd been offered a prefab bungalow on the Belle Vale estate. Her dream home, and it was closer to work for Joe, and not too far from her parents' place in Knowsley.

'Happy now?' He tilted her chin with a finger.

'I don't know what to say. And we can have the keys next week?'

He nodded. 'Yeah. And there are two bedrooms!'

Happy tears ran down Dora's cheeks. 'Joanie and me can use the second bedroom to sew in. This is exactly what we need if we want to get more business.'

He rubbed her tummy through her nightgown. 'You can use it, until we need it for the little ones.'

She smiled. 'Well that won't be for a while yet. Once we're settled in we can maybe think about starting a family.'

'Talking of Joanie and families, how's the great romance going?'

Dora laughed. 'She really likes him, drops his name into conversations as often as she can, and Frank has never looked happier. He takes her to the pictures on a Friday and they go for walks and to the dances at the village hall. It's still early days though, I suppose. But they do seem keen, so we'll have to see. Would you like a cuppa or some cocoa?'

He shook his head. 'Let's go to bed and celebrate getting a new home.'

She pulled away from him and chewed her lip. 'Joe, you know I worry that she might be listening to us through the walls.'

'Aw, come on, Dora. We've hardly done it since we got back from honeymoon.' He cocked an ear. All was quiet. 'She'll be asleep by now.' He pulled her back into his arms. 'What about down here on the rug then?' He unbuttoned the front of her nightgown, slipped it back off her shoulders and kissed her, breathing in the scent of her body. 'Mmm, Pears' soap. You know how much I love that smell.'

She smiled and responded to his kisses and caresses, helping him out of his clothes. They slid down onto the rug in front of the fireplace and made love with the passion of newlyweds, lost in their own special world.

Dora looked around the small sitting room of her new home. It was perfect. There was a tiled fireplace and a back boiler that heated the water. It would be so cosy in the cold months.

The kitchen had an enamel sink unit with a wooden draining board, and two pale blue wall cupboards above; a copper boiler like her mam's for doing the washing, a gas cooker, and a refrigerator. No one that Dora knew, except for Joe's mother, owned a refrigerator. It was a real step up in the world. There'd be no throwing milk away because it had turned sour, or butter when it melted to rancid oil. Having an indoor toilet that they didn't have to share with anyone else felt like a luxury too. She would invite her mam round for a nice bath one day. Filling a tin bath in front of the fire on a Friday night and taking turns as the water cooled would be a thing of the past. She felt so lucky.

'Happy, Mrs Rodgers?' Joe asked as she wandered around, thinking how she would make it their own little place in no time.

'Very,' she said. 'Finally a place to call our own and we'll have it all fixed up in time for our first Christmas.'

'We will.' Joe put his arms around her and nuzzled her neck. 'You know, I think you should give up work soon.' He smoothed her hair back from her face. 'It's further to get to Palmer's from here and I hate the thought of you riding that bike along the dark lanes when the weather's really bad.'

She looked at him and frowned. 'But we need the money, Joe. How will we manage?'

'I'll do more overtime and I've got my band work. We'll be fine. And you've got this place to build up the business now. You'll have all day to work, instead of having to do it at night. Then we can have more time together when I get home and Joanie won't always need to be here. *She* can spend more time with that brother of yours instead.'

'I know, but I don't want to decide anything until after Christmas at least. And I can always get the bus to work if the roads are that bad.' She liked the idea of not going into Palmer's - especially in the winter when the factory was freezing cold and the roads were icy - but she didn't want to leave just yet. There was still so much they needed to save up for, including equipment for the workroom. There was lots to be done in the house; good job both she and Joe had been saving up hard since they got married. She was about to make short work of every penny they'd put away.

As Joe led Dora out he waved at a man who'd come out of a gate a couple of doors down. 'That's my mate Eric Parker from the ROF. His wife's called Dolly. They've a couple of little ones. Come on, I'll introduce you and then we'll get the bus back home. Are you coming with me later? We're playing a social club over in Woolton. Should be a good night.'

Dora couldn't have been more relieved. 'I can't face sitting in with your mum again.'

'Slippery slope once they start ordering you to give up your job,' Peggy said, flicking ash onto the floor from her ciggie as, a week later, Dora told the girls at work about Joe's suggestion. They were sitting in Palmer's canteen, warming their cold hands on mugs of early morning tea before the first shift of the week. 'And you can always get the bus in like most of us do.'

'Joe's not really ordering me to do anything,' Dora said with a frown. 'It was just a suggestion he made because winter's coming and it's a long way to go. We need my wages at the moment anyway so I can't see it happening just yet.'

Joanie chewed her lip. 'There's no way I'll be able to leave work. Not unless things really take off. I'll have to keep coming over at night to your place at night like I've done at your mam's. I'm sure Frank'll give me a lift on the bike.'

Dora thought back to the conversation with Joe about them spending time together in the evenings without Joanie there. But she knew that things were tough for Joanie and her family: Joanie gave almost all of her wages to her mam and she barely ever had anything left for herself. 'It doesn't matter, Joanie. I'll do the cutting out and machining and then drop things off at yours for the hand-finishing. That way, we're both doing a similar amount of work.'

'If you're sure?'

'I'm positive. We're moving in this weekend. I'll be up to my eyeballs after we finish on Friday night so you could come over and give me a hand if you're not too busy? Frank'll be there on Saturday afternoon too. He's borrowing a horse and cart to load up with our new furniture. God help us!'

Joanie laughed. '*That* I'd love to see. He told me he was helping you move in, but he never mentioned the horse and cart. They'll have women running after them with arms full of rags, wanting donkey stones for the steps!'

The bell rang for the start of the shift. They finished their tea and Dora followed the others up to the factory floor, all the time wondering how the heck she was going to cope with working full-time as well as working at home, and making sure Joe didn't feel neglected. All she could do was give it a try and see how she managed. If it all got too much she'd leave Palmer's in the spring, but for now Joe would just have to put up with Joanie being around on the odd weeknight while they got on top of things.

Chapter Six

December 1946

Dora handed Joanie a mug of tea. She sat down on the sofa next to her friend while they waited for Joe and Frank to come back with the horse and cart, having picked up the treadle sewing machine and a few pieces of bedroom furniture that Mam was giving them. Joe had lit a fire before he left and Dora looked around her new sitting room with a feeling of pride.

As though reading her thoughts, Joanie put down her mug and smiled. 'It looks lovely in here, Dora, and you've done a really smashing job with the curtains. Maybe we could offer to make curtains as well as dresses?'

Dora nodded. 'Yes, good idea. I'm so excited about all this, Joanie!' She stopped as the sound of clip-clopping hooves and loud neighing broke the peace. An excited shout went up from the gang of lads who were playing football in the street. 'Sounds like Dobbin and our boys with the rest of the stuff.'

She opened the front door as Frank and Joe struggled up the path with the treadle machine and manoeuvred it onto the step. They carried it, huffing and puffing, through to the back bedroom.

'Just put it under the window for now,' Dora instructed. 'We'll decide where everything's going once we start working in here.'

'Make us a brew, chuck.' Joe grimaced, putting his hands on his back. 'Bloody hell, that thing weighs a ton. We'll bring the other stuff in, have a quick break and then take Dobbin home.' He and Frank followed Dora into the sitting room. 'The kids are feeding him carrots and he's in his element. Just dropped a load and the fellow across came over with a bucket and shovel. Said he'd put it on his garden!' He paused, looked around and smiled. 'Looks a treat in here, gel. You've got a good eye for putting things together. It's a little palace.'

Dora smiled. 'Well, it's not much, but it's ours and I know we'll be very happy here.' She reached up and kissed him. She couldn't wait to be alone with him later. The first night in their own home, and the beginning of the new life she'd been so looking forward to.

Frank hurried out to the cart and rushed back in carrying one of her mam's old shopping bags. He handed it to Dora. 'Dad's sent some veg and half a dozen eggs. Hope I've not broken them. Mam's shoved a couple of loaves and a cake in there as well. She said you'll have been too busy today to get to the shops so that's to tide you over until Monday.'

Dora looked in the bag but could see no evidence of broken eggs. 'Tell them thanks very much when you get home. I haven't given food a thought, to be honest.'

'That's exactly what Mam said. She'll be that busy with her frills and furbelows, she won't stop to think about feeding poor Joe.' He mimicked their mam to perfection, right down to the folded arms and pursed lips.

Dora laughed and gave him a friendly shove. 'Cheeky. Why don't you and Joanie stay for tea? I've got a tin of corned beef in, so I can do us a hash.'

Dora knelt on the floor and stacked the patterns, boxes of threads and all the other paraphernalia needed for the business of being a seamstress into a tall, free-standing cupboard. She filled the two bottom drawers with parcels of leftover fabric scraps, pads and pencils, and got to her feet. Joe was busy cleaning an old drop-leaf table that had been given to them for cutting out on. It would fold neatly away when not in use and would be ideal to stand the new machine on when they got it. She looked at the corkboard that he'd fixed to the wall and smiled with glee at their current workload, which was pinned to it in date order. She and Joanie were going to be very busy in the coming weeks.

The other day they'd persuaded their foreman to part with an adjustable size dressmaker's dummy from the unused first floor at Palmer's. It had been standing around doing nothing for years, alongside many others and, once the cobwebs had been brushed away, was as good as new. They'd christened it Florence.

Getting her back here had been tricky and Dora grinned as she thought back to the other night when they'd brought her home. Their foreman had hidden Florence away from George Kane's eyes, and presented her to Joe in two pieces.

'It's as good as new,' Jack said. 'But you didn't have to buy me a packet of fags to persuade me. It's my pleasure to help you girls where I can, in any little way. I wish I could do more, but you know how it is.'

'Thank you,' Dora said. 'And you're welcome to the ciggies. We're very grateful for your help.'

''Ere, Joe, you carry the body out,' Jack had called as Joe parked his bike at the front of the factory building. Joe struggled outside and sat the dummy on the back of the bike while Jack brought out the stand.

Dora and Joanie giggled as they watched Joe trying to tie the unyielding body to the seat with garden twine. Florence was a dead weight and insisted on leaning backwards as Joe tried to persuade her to sit forward.

'You can't ride through the lanes with her stark naked,' Joanie said, dashing outside to drape the dummy in one of her mam's old nighties and a cardigan that she'd thoughtfully brought with her, anticipating Florence's undignified ride home.

'She's not bloody real, you know?' Joe rolled his eyes and again adjusted Florence so that she sat upright. Joanie tied an old scarf around the stump of her neck while Joe fixed the base to his back pannier.

'Right, she'd better not fall off when I go round the bends. And I hope no one thinks I've got another woman,' Joe quipped as he got ready to ride away into the night with Florence tied to the seat behind him.

Joanie and Dora waved goodbye to Jack and followed Joe home on their bikes, stopping every few yards to wipe their eyes, unable to control their fits of the giggles. When they reached home Florence was still sitting in position on the bike parked on the road and Joe was inside the bungalow, helpless with laughter on the sofa.

'Why haven't you brought her inside?' Dora asked.

'Two fellas from down the road walking their dogs gave me right funny looks,' he said. 'Then they crossed over and kept looking back over their shoulders. So I thought I'd better wait until you two got here in case they thought I'd kidnapped a headless old lady. *You* can explain if the police turn up.'

Now Florence stood in pride of place, draped with a length of brightly coloured cotton print that would soon become a dress for a customer's daughter.

Joe finished his cleaning. 'Cuppa?' he asked, breaking her thoughts.

'Please, love. What do you think?

'Yeah.' He nodded his approval. 'It all looks really good. Is that treadle okay now I've tightened the belt and given it a good oiling?'

'It's fine. Just need to make sure all the excess oil is absorbed before we use it again.'

He slipped his arm around her shoulders. 'I have such a good feeling about this, gel. It's going to be a great success for you and Joanie.'

She smiled. 'I hope so.'

As they enjoyed five minutes with a brew, there was a knock at the front door. Joe got up and let in Frank, who dropped his jacket onto the floor and sat down in the armchair opposite Dora. Joe went to pour him a cuppa.

'Everything okay, Frank?' Dora asked her brother. 'You look a bit flushed. Is Joanie all right?'

'Yes, everything's fine.' Frank accepted the mug of tea Joe handed him. 'I want to ask you something, to see what you think. You know your opinion means a lot to me, Sis.'

Dora tucked her legs and feet up on the settee as Joe sat down beside her again.

'Ask away, we're all ears.' She frowned. Frank looked a bit nervous as he sipped his drink. He put his mug down on the coffee table and laced his fingers together.

'Well, we're only three weeks off Christmas now, so I've been thinking.' Frank nervously cleared his throat. 'On Christmas Eve I'm going to ask Joanie to marry me.'

Dora stared at her normally unflappable brother, whose cheeks were crimson, his hands shaking. 'Frank, that's wonderful news.' She jumped up and kissed him on the cheek and Joe got up to shake him by the hand.

'Congratulations. Joanie's the best. I'm sure you'll both be very happy.'

'Do you think she'll accept?' Frank stammered. 'I mean, what if she says no?'

'Why would she? She loves you, you know she does. She'll be thrilled, Frank. And so will Mam and Dad. Has Joanie really got no idea?'

He shook his head. 'Settling down's not something we've ever really talked about. But she knows that I love her, and I want to spend my life with her. She's the only girl I've ever felt this way about.'

'Then I'm sure she'll accept your proposal. She'll be really excited. What about a ring?'

'I've been saving up and I've got enough put by to get a nice one. But how will I know it's the right size, and what have you?'

'Ah, well,' Dora said, 'when Joe gave me my engagement ring, Joanie tried it on and it fitted her perfectly, so if you get her one the same size it will be fine.' She sat back on the sofa as an idea popped into her mind. 'Would you like me to come with you on Saturday morning? You can choose something you think she'll like, get it sized to fit, and then pick it up nearer the time. Unless of course it's the right fit and you can buy it there and then.'

'Oh thanks, Sis, that's great. As long as Joe doesn't mind me stealing his missus for a couple of hours.'

'I tell you what, Frank, why don't you propose on Christmas Day?' Dora suggested. 'You're both out with us on Christmas Eve at the dance in the village hall, so it'll be really noisy and busy. If you wait until the day itself, it will be so much more romantic. We're doing Christmas dinner here for you and Joanie, and Mam and Dad. It will make the day really special for us all.'

Frank smiled. 'Good idea. You can tell I'm not very good at this sort of thing, can't you? I've not thought it out properly.'

Dora laughed. 'Well it's not every day you ask someone to be your wife. It has to be just right. You'll remember the moment for the rest of your life, and so will we.'

'Do you think I should ask her mam for her hand first? But what if she lets something slip to Joanie by mistake and spoils the surprise?'

'Joe didn't ask our mam *or* dad until after he'd proposed to me,' Dora said. 'It's up to you, Frank. I can't for one minute see Joanie's mam putting up any objection. She likes you, and she's our mam's best friend, so we'll all be one big happy family.'

* * *

Dora called out the measurements and Joanie wrote them down. Marlene, a neighbour from the prefabs, wanted a new dress for the ROF dinner dance. There wasn't much time, Dora had told her when Marlene knocked on the door having seen the postcard in the paper shop window offering their services. But she didn't want to turn business away, so they'd squeeze one more appointment in somehow. The paper bag lying on the table contained a length of royal blue satin for the dress. Marlene's brother had got it for her last year, but she was rubbish with a needle and thread, she told Dora, so it had been sitting in the sideboard cupboard until today. The blue was the exact same colour as Marlene's eyes and would look lovely with her blonde hair, but the style of dress she'd requested was going to be a problem as there wasn't enough fabric. Dora sat down at the table and sketched a design that was similar to the full-skirted affair Marlene had described, with a sweetheart neckline, but the skirt was less bulky and would look so much better on Marlene's generous figure.

'The New Look's all the rage now,' Dora told her. 'We'll create the illusion of a full skirt by cutting the fabric to flare over your hips and finish just above the knee. What do you think?' Dora said, encouragement in her voice. It *would* have to be flipping satin fabric; there was nothing worse for fraying. This dress would take ages as they'd have to hand-stitch a small hem along all the raw edges to neaten them. Just what they didn't need when they were so busy.

Marlene nodded. 'It's perfect,' she gasped. 'I'll look dead slim in that. Youse two should have a posh shop in town. You're really good at this guessing what looks nice on people malarkey.'

Joanie smiled. 'We do our best. We'll let you know as soon as your dress is ready for a fitting, Marlene. It'll probably be towards the end of next week, but it will definitely be ready in time for the dance.'

'Will *you* be at the dance, Dora? It's a big night. And it's so nice to have something to look forward to where I can get all dolled up to the nines.'

'All being well,' Dora said. 'Does everyone on the staff go; office, works, and er, canteen?'

'Oh yes, everybody. You must come. Your Joe's band's playing, so you should be there to support him.'

Dora nodded. 'I'll do my best. Yours is the last dress, so hopefully I'll be free that night.'

Joanie puffed out her cheeks. 'Don't forget we've got a couple of outfits to get ready for New Year's Eve.'

'I know, and we'll have them finished in time.'

'Right, ladies, I'll love you and leave you.' Marlene put her coat on and picked up her handbag. Dora saw her out and went to put the kettle on. She made two mugs of Camp coffee and together she and Joanie sat on the sofa.

'I hope we *will* get them all finished,' Joanie said, sighing loudly. 'God I wish we could give up working at Palmer's, I'm so bloody tired.'

'Me too, but it'll all be worth it.' Dora eased her shoes off her aching feet. It had been a long day and the roads had been icy, riding home on her bike. She'd have to start taking the bus as soon as it snowed. She thought about the ROF works do: she wouldn't miss it for anything. She wanted to make sure that the woman from the canteen, that Ivy, remembered Joe was a married man. She saw the way Ivy had looked at him when he was on stage at their wedding. She hadn't mentioned it, not even to Joanie, as it would make her sound like a jealous wife for no good reason really. She didn't think for one minute that Joe would get up to anything behind her back - he loved her too much. It was Ivy she didn't trust, not her Joe.

Chapter Seven

Dora looked up from her work as Peggy shouted across the floor over the sound of Christmas carols being played on the wireless.

'Jack, big boss wants you,' Peggy called to the foreman, who was lifting boxes of shirts for a completed order onto a large table.

'Right you are. Keep at it while I'm off the floor, you lot,' Jack called cheerfully. 'Bet he wants to tell me he's upping the annual bonus this year.'

'Yeah, right,' Peggy muttered, shaking her head as Jack sauntered away. 'And pigs might fly. Who's he kidding? You do realise that once this order is completed, we've only one more for next year and that's it.' She looked around at the girls, who stared despondently at her.

'He might be telling Jack that we've got more contracts coming in,' Dora said, optimistically, trying to sound cheerful. Two weeks to Christmas and they didn't really need to hear any bad news.

'I doubt it. Anyway, you and Joanie will be all right, you're raking it in with your new business.'

'I wouldn't say that,' Dora said, frowning. 'We're building things up slowly and we work really hard for what we earn. It'll be ages before we're up and running properly.'

'If the worst comes to the worst, you could start making clothes on your mam's machine at home too and earn a bit extra that way,' Joanie suggested.

Peggy shrugged. 'She'd never put up with the noise. No, it's not for me. I've not got a business head like you two. I prefer to be out during the day, working with people. It'd drive me mad being stuck in all day with me mam. If we get laid off any time soon

I'll probably try for a job at Tate & Lyle's in town, or Littlewoods pools or something. I'll get out of the rag-trade, it's not like it used to be and the jobs are few and far between in Liverpool. Most of the north's clothing factories are in Lancashire and I'm not moving up that way.'

Dora nodded and rubbed a hand across her eyes. She had a banging head and felt off colour. She wasn't looking forward to riding home along the icy lanes and then having to cook tea for Joe and sit up half the night sewing, either. All she really wanted to do was sit in front of a nice warm fire and put her feet up. But unless Joe arrived home first there would be no blazing fire to greet her and she'd have to keep her coat on for a while to get warmed up. Much as she loved going back to her own home, she missed her parents' cosy little cottage and her tea on the table when she got in.

Joanie patted her hand and smiled. 'You still feeling a bit iffy?'

Dora sighed. 'Think I'm getting a cold or something. I feel shivery and sickly.' The afternoon break bell rang out and she got to her feet. 'You ready?'

The pair followed the rest of the girls down to the canteen and helped themselves to mugs of piping hot tea and a lemon puff each from the trolley.

'Let's sit over near that radiator.' Joanie led the way. 'Bloody hell, it's stone cold,' she said, leaning against it. 'That's unusual. No wonder we can't get warm, they were cold upstairs as well. Bet the janitor forgot to stoke the boiler.'

Peggy and Maude joined them, both shivering. Maude pulled her old cardigan around her body.

'Has the boiler broken down or something?' Dora said and wrapped her hands around her mug, taking a sip of tea.

Peggy shrugged. 'I'll find out from Jack when we go back upstairs. Wrong time of year for that to happen. We can't be expected to work in cold conditions. They'll have to get it fixed or we'll walk out.'

They were joined by Alice, one of the packers, who had brought her coat down with her. 'S'not bloody right, this. Expecting us to work when it's so damn cold.'

'Maybe they've arranged to get it fixed for tomorrow,' Joanie said optimistically.

'Fixed! Huh, youse can't fix something that's not broken, gel. If Kane paid the bills the coalman would deliver more coke for the boiler.'

Dora frowned. 'Is that what's wrong? They've run out of coke?'

'So I've heard. Kane hasn't paid for the last few months so the coalman's refused to deliver any more until he settles his bill. I tell you; since old Mr Palmer died this place has gone to the dogs. No bloody work, and now no heat either. We'll all be down with pneumonia by Christmas at this rate. It's not right.'

'Well I'm putting my coat on when we get back upstairs too,' Joanie said. 'If they don't like it they can lump it.'

Jack Carter called all the girls together when they came back from their break. He cleared his throat and Dora saw him grit his teeth, as though preparing for the onslaught that she felt sure was to come. Something was very wrong and she had a feeling she knew what he was about to tell them.

'Gerron with it then,' Peggy called. 'Is he getting that bloody coal bill paid? We can't work in a freezing factory.' As she spoke her breath puffed out in little clouds that hung in the air.

'I'm sorry, girls, but there's no easy way to say this,' Jack began, his voice cracking with emotion. 'As you know, since the end of the war we've not been getting the orders coming in, apart from the shirts, and that's not enough to keep us going. So unless we can get some new clothing contracts in early next year we'll be closing the factory down. Your jobs are safe for now and you *will* be paid, so don't worry about that. But I'm afraid there'll be no festive bonus in this year's Christmas pay packets.'

A cry went up as the women took in the news. Most of them relied on that extra few shillings to put a Christmas dinner on the family table. Everyone began talking at once; shouting at Jack. Dora pulled on Joanie's sleeve and nodded for her to go to her seat. She glanced towards poor Jack, who, red-faced, was trying to placate the angry women. He looked as though he might cry himself as they pushed and pulled him towards the door, demanding to be taken to George Kane's office.

'What the hell are we going to do now?' Joanie was on the verge of tears. Her mam had five mouths to feed on Christmas Day. 'Mam's ordered a turkey and was expecting my bonus to pay for it. She'll go mad.'

'Don't worry. We'll manage. We've got some money to collect in for the Christmas orders; and you can take a bit extra from it for the dinner. We'll still be working in the New Year for now and we'll just have to work as hard as we can at home, *while* we can.' Dora frowned as the sound of the bell that usually summoned break time rang again.

Jack stood on a chair and took control. 'I suggest we stop early for the day. You've all had a shock and I know it's too cold in here to work. Go home. Hopefully by tomorrow I'll have sorted out some coke to keep us going. But come in bright and early, well wrapped up just in case, and let's show that we can get this order finished on time. Palmer's have never let a customer down yet and we're not going to start now.'

Jack Carter saw the girls out and locked the door behind them. He lit a cigarette as he wandered around, switching off lights. He'd been with the business since he left school and would miss the place if and when it closed. He hadn't a clue what he'd do and his wife would go mad when he told her. That bloody daft, work-shy son-in-law of Gerald Palmer's was a waste of time.

He'd been warned again and again they needed representatives to visit the stores up and down the country that were still trading. Palmer's customer list had been extensive and the place should be blossoming again. But Kane had ignored all the advice he'd been given, trying to save money, and now it was too late. Good for Dora and Joanie that they'd had the sense to start their own little business. They'd got good heads on them, those two girls, and he'd be proud to see them grow and maybe in time have their own factory. But heaven help the others who weren't so lucky. They'd end up doing some sort of unskilled work, just to put food on the table, no doubt like the future he'd be facing himself at this rate.

He put on his coat and cap and let himself out of the building. His motorbike was standing by the back wall and he made his way across the yard. He'd call at the coal merchant's place on his way home, to see if they'd deliver a couple of bags of coke tomorrow to tide them over. If they billed him rather than Palmer's he'd see they got paid somehow. He couldn't have his girls working with freezing hands for another day. He wouldn't blame them if they all walked out, but they knew they'd lose pay and none of them could afford to do that, and certainly not at this time of the year. Kane had told him to prepare for a meeting at half-nine tomorrow. The coward had cleared off pretty sharpish today. Jack sighed, threw his leg over the bike, started the engine and set off down Old Mill Lane towards Knowsley village.

Chapter Eight

Dora groaned and snuggled deeper under the blankets as the alarm clock shrilled the start of another working day. Joe slid out of bed yawning, and shut the door quietly on his way out. She heard him use the bathroom and then water running as he filled the kettle in the kitchen. She'd swear that clock was getting louder and more vindictive as the days went by, and six am was far too early, unless you had feathers and wings. She closed her eyes again and tried to drift back into her fading dream.

'Wake up, sleepyhead.' Joe shook her gently by the shoulder and put a cup of tea on the bedside table. 'Would you like some toast?'

She sat up slowly and shook her head. The sickly feeling she was unable to shake off overwhelmed her as soon as she was upright. She flung back the bedcovers, ran to the bathroom and dropped to the floor, retching over the toilet bowl. Joe followed her and stood in the open doorway looking worried. As she sat back against the side of the bath, breathing deeply, he flushed the toilet and wiped her clammy face with a damp flannel. He smoothed her hair from her eyes and dropped a kiss on top of her head.

'Come on, back to bed with you.' He helped her up from the floor and led her into the bedroom. 'This tummy upset is lasting ages. Perhaps you should see the doctor.'

'I need to get ready for work,' she mumbled, flopping down onto the edge of the bed, knowing full well that going to work was the last thing she felt like doing. 'But my head's banging and I ache all over.'

'You're going nowhere,' he said as she opened her mouth to protest. 'I'll ring Palmer's as soon as I get to work, let them know you won't be in.' He helped her into bed, tucked the blankets around her and propped her up with the pillows. 'Drink this while it's still hot.' He handed her the cup of tea and dashed out of the bedroom, coming back with two aspirins. 'Take these and I'll call at your mam's on the way and see if she can come and look in on you later.'

'I'll be fine,' Dora said. 'She'll be busy helping at the village hall for Saturday's Christmas Fair. And I really *should* go in to work; I don't want to let them down. We've got that last shirt order to finish and I need to pick up my wages.'

'They'll give them to Joanie. I'll try and catch her before she goes in, and ask her to get them for you.'

'But, Joe - '

'Never mind, "But Joe"! You've struggled in all week feeling rotten. You need to rest or you'll be laid up over Christmas, and then you won't be fit to get your own orders finished. Palmer's couldn't give a toss about you girls. The way they've treated their workforce is shit, letting you all down like that and after you've worked so hard and kept the place going during the war. And that bastard George Kane repays you with no festive bonus and threats of closure. I bet *his* family won't be going without on Christmas Day. The idle sod's been sat on his fat arse, or buggering about at his golf club, without putting any efforts in to secure more orders. He's pathetic.'

Dora handed him her empty cup and sank back against the pillows. He was right. She'd lose a day's pay, but she'd got some work to finish here. Later on, when she felt like getting up, she might do some hand-sewing. She really didn't have the energy to ride her bike this morning and the thought of getting the bus made her feel even worse.

Joe left the room and she heard the sound of him raking out the grate and getting the fire ready to light. Good, at least she'd be warm; sitting comfortably on the sofa while she worked.

'I need you well for next week,' he said, coming back into the bedroom and pulling on his work clothes. 'It's the works do and I want to show off my lovely wife on that dance floor.'

She smiled. He always knew how to cheer her up. And anyway, she *wanted* to be there, to keep an eye on Ivy. Not that the woman's name was ever mentioned, but still. 'I'll be all right, love. Just been doing too much I think. It's hard work, balancing two jobs *and* looking after the house.'

Joe leant over and kissed her. 'Let's see how it goes in the New Year. If they close, they close. Right, I'm off.' He pulled on his jacket and scarf, wrapping it twice around his neck. 'The fire's lit and it's burning nice. When you feel like getting up, put a shovel of coal on mid-morning and then do the same this afternoon. I've brought the scuttle in and left it on the hearth so you've no lifting to do. Make sure you get a bit of toast or some soup later.'

She nodded. 'I will. Don't worry, I'll be all right.'

'See you tonight.' Dora took a deep breath. Dare she try to get out of bed, or would she throw up again? Usually she felt a bit better after chucking up the once, apart from the queasiness that overwhelmed her when she caught the scent of coffee or bacon frying in the factory canteen. And lately even walking past the chippy made her stomach lurch.

She was in no doubt that she was in the family way, although it didn't seem to have dawned on Joe yet. She'd seen no sign of her monthlies since the beginning of October, and the morning sickness confirmed it. Tomorrow, she'd take another day off work and go and see the doctor. She didn't really know how she felt about it, but excitement was growing within her and she knew Joe would be over the moon. She would tell him as soon as she was sure; she wanted to keep the surprise from everyone else until Christmas Day, for when the family were all here. What a wonderful Christmas present for her mam and dad; Frank and Joanie getting engaged and their first grandchild to look forward to.

* * *

Joanie arrived at tea time with Dora's wage packet and stayed for a brew. Dora was up and dressed, had managed to hand-hem two skirts and had cut and stitched the buttonholes on a top, while sitting with her feet up on the sofa in front of the fire, listening to *Housewives' Choice* and *Workers' Playtime* on the wireless. She felt much better for resting.

'So, how did it go today?' she asked as Joanie sipped her tea.

Joanie pulled a face. 'There's a horrible atmosphere. Mr Kane and Jack Carter were in a meeting for most of the day. Jack put Peggy in charge and she's been a right bossy cow. Give her a bit of responsibility and she thinks she owns the place. She took them a tray of tea in the late afternoon and she said they shut up talking and looked shifty as though they didn't want her to hear what they were saying.'

'Well, they probably didn't. You know what a gob Peggy's got. You can't keep anything private once she gets a whisper. Wonder what they were talking about though?'

'God knows. Getting new contracts in, I hope.' Joanie sighed, finished her drink and put her cup down on the coffee table. 'I'd better be going. Mam'll wonder where I've got to. Are you coming in tomorrow?'

'No.' Dora shook her head. 'I'll give myself another day or two. I should be fine by Monday. They'll dock me two days' pay next week, but I'll do some more bits here and then we can get some money in when we finish the two dresses for New Year's Eve. Pity they're both satin fabric. I wish we could get access to Palmer's over-lockers, and then we could neaten the seams quickly.'

'I've been giving it some thought,' Joanie said. 'There'll hardly be a soul around in that last week, apart from us stitchers. I'll sneak upstairs one night while you're all getting ready to leave and I'll do the seams in no time. Jack usually hangs around checking things before he locks up and he always goes to the canteen for a last brew and a ciggie. Keep him talking while I do it, and if he *does* see me, I'll just say I lost my purse, or something, and was looking for it. I can say I thought it'd fallen out of my pocket when I went to get something from upstairs. I don't know why we didn't think of it before. It'll save us loads of time on future seams if we can get away with it. No point in just asking if we can use them because he'll say no.'

'That sounds like a good plan,' Dora said, breathing a sigh of relief. 'And when we know for sure that they're definitely closing, we can ask if we can buy an over-locker from them.'

Joanie got to her feet and fastened her coat. 'Well at least we've got a future of sorts to look forward to now.'

'We have.' Dora saw her to the door. 'We'll make it work somehow, I promise you.' She gave Joanie a hug.

'I hope you feel a bit better tomorrow. You look so pale.'

Dora chewed her lip. She was dying to say something before keeping quiet drove her mad. 'Can you keep a secret? I mean, you can't say anything to anyone.'

Joanie nodded. 'You know I can. Why, what's wrong?'

'I think I'm expecting!' Dora couldn't help smiling broadly as she said the words.

Joanie let out a yell and flung her arms around her friend, nearly knocking her flying. 'Oh my goodness. You're not?'

'I'm going to the doctor's tomorrow, but I'm pretty sure I am. Joe doesn't know yet, nobody does.'

'I won't say a word. I absolutely promise. Oh, I'm so excited for you. I can help you look after the baby when we're working here. We can take turns feeding it and things.'

Dora laughed. 'It'll be just like the times we shared our dollies when we were little girls.'

'We can make clothes for it. Pretty dresses if it's a girl. It'll be the best dressed baby in Knowsley. Oh, I can't wait to be Aunty Joanie!'

As Dora waved Joanie off, Joe turned the corner and pulled up outside the bungalow. A big smile lit up his face as he dismounted. Dora breathed a sigh of relief that he was home. She hated him riding the motorbike when the roads were so icy and wished they could afford to buy a car. Maybe one day.

Dora's legs turned to jelly as Doctor Owens confirmed her suspicions. She *was* pregnant. He said he would send her urine sample to be tested and the result would be back next week, but all other indications, including an undignified internal examination, pointed to the fact that she could expect a happy event in the first week of July next year. Doctor Owens had been their family doctor for as long as Dora could remember, and he congratulated her as he made her an appointment to see him again following the Christmas holiday.

She left the surgery, head in a whirl. She was dying to tell Joanie that it was definite, but she was at work, and anyway, Joe should really be told first. The little café down the road was open so she popped inside and ordered a cup of tea and a slice of Victoria sponge cake. Taking a window seat, she kept her eyes on the street outside. It was finishing time for the nearby primary school and the pavement was busy with mums pushing prams and dragging reluctant toddlers along on reins as they went to meet their older offspring. She smiled at a harassed-looking mother who caught her eye through the window as she yanked a toddler out of the gutter and sat him on the end of a large pram. The young woman raised an eyebrow and smiled back.

Dora took a bite of the moist sponge cake, picturing Joe's face when she broke her news to him later.

* * *

Dora placed the shepherd's pie and a dish of boiled carrots on the top shelf of the oven to keep warm, and set the table for tea. She drew the sitting room curtains, threw a shovel of coal on the fire, wiped her hands down the front of her apron and arranged a knitting pattern, a ball of white wool and a pair of needles on the coffee table. She'd popped into the haberdasher's on her way back from the doctor's, with the plan of seeing if Joe noticed her purchases when he sat down after tea to read his *Echo*. If he was anything like her dad, the hint would go right over his head. She grinned as she heard his motorbike pull up outside, and ran to let him in.

Joe washed his hands at the kitchen sink while she dished up their meal.

'Thank God it's Friday,' he said, wiping his hands on a tea towel. 'I've got rehearsals tomorrow, and the band's playing tomorrow night and Sunday afternoon, but the money will come in handy next week when *you* get short pay.' He sat down at the table and Dora handed him a plate piled high. 'Thanks, love, smells good. I'm starving. How've you been today? Feel any better?'

'Sort of…' She lowered her eyes and stared at her plate, feeling her cheeks heating. She wasn't really hungry after that huge slice of cake earlier and was dying for him to finish his tea, then she could tease him a little before she told him her news. She played around with her food and was conscious of him looking at her.

'Do you still feel rough? You might feel a bit better if you eat something.'

She made the effort and ate a few mouthfuls while he wolfed his down.

'Shall I finish it for you?' he offered a hopeful expression in his eyes.

She nodded and pushed her plate across the table. 'I've made an apple crumble,' she said. 'I'll just go and make some custard.' She poured two cups of tea and slipped out to the kitchen, pushing the door to behind her. How she was managing to stay silent, she didn't know. But she wanted the special moment to be just right and for them both to be relaxing on the sofa with the wireless playing quietly in the background.

Dora cleared the empty dishes. Joe carried the drinks to the coffee table, picked up his *Echo* and sat down on the sofa. 'Leave them pots, chuck,' he called. 'I'll do them when my tea goes down. Come and sit next to me and tell me about your day.'

She closed the kitchen door, flopped down beside him and snuggled close.

He folded his paper, dropped it onto the carpet and slid his arm around her shoulders. 'You look a bit brighter today. Not quite as pale.'

She smiled. He hadn't noticed her display on the coffee table, or if he had, it hadn't registered. 'I went to the doctor's this afternoon.'

'Did you? And what did he say? Did he give you anything for it? Bet you've caught a bug from someone at Palmer's. Can't be from me.'

She shook her head. 'Well, you did have *something* to do with it.'

He frowned and pulled away. 'How do you make that one out?'

She picked up the knitting pattern and waved it in his face. He stared at the picture of baby hats and booties, his frown deepening, and then a smile began at the corners of his mouth and spread across his face. His hazel eyes lit up and he choked on his words. 'Oh, Dora.' He held her tight and rained kisses on her face. 'I can't believe it. A baby! Apart from being sick, you're okay? Everything's all right?'

'Yes, everything's fine. I'm due the beginning of July.'

'Are you happy about it? I mean, I know you wanted to wait a while. But you can leave work soon anyway, and then you can rest at home.'

She laughed. 'I'm *very* happy, but there won't be much time to rest. I'll be working for a while longer and then I've got a business to build up. I can't let Joanie down. But it'll be much easier for me, working from home. I can put my feet up as and when I need to.'

'The sewing room will have to be sorted out for the baby now. I'll shift everything out.'

'It's months off, Joe. Stop flapping! The baby will be in with us for a while, anyway. We'll sort all that out next year. But listen, I don't want us to tell anyone just yet. Don't say anything to your mates at work. We'll tell Mam and Dad, and Frank and Joanie on Christmas Day. And we're at your mum's on Boxing Day so we'll tell *her* then.'

He nodded. 'My heart's racing. Me a dad! Promise me one thing though.'

'What?'

'No more riding that bike to work. Get the bus for now, please, love. I'll get a sidecar for the motorbike next year and you and the baby can ride in that when we go out, until I can afford to buy us a car.'

Dora rolled her eyes. 'Stop getting carried away. Wait until next year before you start spending money we haven't got on things we don't need yet.'

'I'm so excited. I can't believe it.' He pulled her back into his arms.

She hugged him tight. He was as thrilled as she knew he would be. *She* was too, but there was also an underlying feeling of anxiety in the pit of her stomach and it wouldn't go away. She hoped it wasn't an omen. Things would be fine. She was married to the most handsome fella for miles, he had a good job, they had a lovely home, the new business was taking off slowly, and hopefully Palmer's would be a distant memory for both her and Joanie next year. She and Joe had everything to look forward to with their expected baby. What more could she wish for?

Chapter Nine

Dora glanced around the festively decorated room to see if she recognised anyone. Murphy's Dance Band were up on the makeshift stage, and the ROF Christmas party was in full swing. She was sitting with their neighbours, Eric and Dolly Parker from the prefabs. Most of the people here tonight were from their estate, but Dora struggled to remember all their names. Once the baby arrived she'd no doubt see a lot more of her neighbours and get better acquainted when she went out for walks with the pram. She felt a little thrill run through her as she thought of the future, and sipped her drink. She was sticking to squashes tonight. The queasy feeling would be there again in the morning and she couldn't cope with a hangover on top.

Ivy Bennett and her mate Flo were sitting with several other young women at a circular table, in-between a large, brightly lit Christmas tree and the stage. Dora could see Ivy's eyes fixed firmly on Joe as he leant back during his sax solo, his own eyes closed in ecstasy. He was note perfect. She felt so proud of him, he loved performing. Before the band took to the stage she and Joe had danced a couple of times and she'd felt Ivy's eyes burning into her back. For God's sake, the woman couldn't be more obvious if she'd written 'I Fancy Joe' across her forehead in that tarty red lipstick she wore.

As Dora watched, Ivy dragged Flo to her feet and the pair danced together, wiggling and gyrating as close to the stage as possible. If she thought it would make Dora jealous she had another think coming. Ivy's too-tight, shiny red dress had split near the back zip, but she appeared unaware, until one of the other women called out to her and beckoned her to sit down. Her white bra was on show along with the flesh spilling out above her girdle. Dora smirked as she saw the woman whisper to Ivy, and Ivy's cheeks blushed crimson. Her friend had on a black cardigan and she removed it and draped it around Ivy's shoulders, hiding the gap. Ivy glanced over and stared straight at Dora, who raised an eyebrow, patted her blonde curls in place and smiled sweetly.

'That your friend?' Dolly asked, nodding towards the table of women.

'Er, no,' Dora replied. 'I don't really know her.'

'You want to watch that one,' Dolly muttered. 'Bloody tart. Got her eye on all the men, single or married. Thinks she can win 'em over with an extra sausage at breakfast. Even tried it on with my Eric when we first moved over this way. Cheeky mare, she's got no chance.'

Dora smiled. Eric was a nice man and a kind neighbour, but she'd only ever seen him out in the garden, wearing a stained white vest and a pair of old trousers tied up with a length of twine. Tonight he had on the standard pinstripe demob suit, but the trousers were tight and his jacket didn't quite meet across his chest. He'd probably regained all the weight he'd lost while away with the army, thanks to Ivy's extra sausages. He was hardly a pin-up, but Dolly was happy and that was all that mattered, Dora thought. She'd definitely be watching that Ivy one more closely now. Joe never mentioned her but she wondered if he had contact with her during the day, apart from when he ate in the canteen. From now on she'd be making sure he took sarnies for his dinner and a flask of tea. That way he'd have no need to use the canteen at all.

She turned her attention back to the band. 'Chattanooga Choo Choo' was the last song in this spot. Joe would soon be back beside her and they could have a few more dances to the records the band leader would play on his gramophone.

'Won't be a minute,' she whispered to Dolly. She made her way to the ladies and bolted herself into a cubicle. She heard the outer door open, and a couple of young women clattered in, talking in breathless voices as though they'd just come off the dance floor.

'Did you see that bloody Ivy's frock split apart,' one of them said, laughing loudly.

'Yeah.' The second one giggled. 'Serves her right for making a show of herself. Cavorting around in front of Joe like that. It's wrong when she knows his missus is in the room.'

'She'd gerra right slap round the gob if it were my fella she was mooning after.'

'And mine.'

It went quiet as the two girls locked themselves in the adjoining cubicles. Dora dashed out, hurriedly washed her hands and rushed back to the party. She took a deep breath and made her way towards the table. Joe had just come off stage and he came over and swept her into his arms, dropping a kiss on her lips.

'You all right, sweetheart?' He pulled the chair out for her. 'Would you like another drink?'

She shook her head. 'You get one, though.' More drinks were the last thing she needed, or Dolly might ask her what was wrong when she rushed off again, and then her secret would be no more. She looked across to Ivy's table. The woman had buttoned up her friend's cardigan, leaving the top buttons open, making sure her ample cleavage was still on show. Ivy got to her feet, yanking the garment lower so that it covered the split, and Dora saw her friend nod that it looked okay. She stiffened as Ivy walked across to the busy bar and pushed her way to the front where Joe was talking to a pal while he waited to be served. The brazen hussy. Dora jumped up, marched across the room and pushed *her* way to the front. Elbowing Ivy sharply in the ribs, she slid in beside Joe, who smiled and put his arm around her.

'I've changed my mind. I *will* have another drink,' she said, smiling at his pal.

'You've met my lovely wife, haven't you, Graham,' Joe said.

'At the wedding,' Graham said, smiling back. 'And may I say, you are looking more beautiful than ever, Dora.'

'Thank you, Graham.' Dora grinned as Ivy's face flushed scarlet and she stomped away without waiting to be served.

'Oops, was it something I said?' Graham laughed, raising an eyebrow.

Joe ordered the drinks and they made their way back to the table.

'That Ivy woman,' Dora began. 'Do you see much of her at work?'

He shrugged and she watched his face closely, but he didn't flush or look guilty at all. 'Only in the canteen, or when she brings the tea trolley onto the factory floor. Why do you ask?'

'Because she never takes her eyes off you. I don't trust her, Joe.'

'Don't be silly, love. And believe me, *I've* only got eyes for one girl, and I think you know who that is.'

Dora smiled, feeling reassured. She *did* know. But in the next few months she was going to get fat and ungainly, and probably grumpy as well. What if he went off her? He wouldn't, surely? He loved her. Maybe the insecure feelings were to do with her condition. Hopefully they would pass in time, and once the baby arrived she'd soon get her trim figure back. Joe would never need to look elsewhere.

Joanie sat back in her theatre seat and looked around, feeling excited. They were seated in the stalls at the Liverpool Empire. It was years since she'd been to see a pantomime, and she'd swear she felt as giddy as the little kids sitting close by. Frank had called at her home on his way back from work and told her he was taking her into town for the night. He said it was a surprise and he'd be back in just under an hour to pick her up as they needed to catch a train to Lime Street station.

She'd never got ready so quickly and was worried she looked a bit of a mess as she'd planned to wash her hair tonight and instead she'd had to leave it. She'd smoothed the frizz from her curls with a spray of her mam's home-made lavender water and it had made her hair smell really nice and fresh after being stuck under a turban all day. A sweep of rouge, a slick of bright pink Max Factor lipstick, a dab of Evening in Paris perfume behind her ears, and when she opened the door to him, Frank's beaming face took all her worries away. She grabbed her coat and scarf and slipped them on over the pale blue sweater her mam had made, and a fitted black wool skirt Joanie had made last year from a jumble sale dress that must have belonged to Two Ton Tessie O'Shea originally. There was still a lot of the good quality fabric left over and she'd saved it to make another garment when she found time. She pulled on her warm boots and took Frank's arm, calling goodnight to her family as he led her to a waiting car. His pal was acting as chauffeur to the station in exchange for a pint.

The theatre lights dimmed and a hush fell over the audience at the announcement that *Sleeping Beauty* was about to start, and for everyone to make their way to their seats. Frank laced his fingers through hers and Joanie smiled and snuggled closer to him as the opening bars of 'Once Upon a Dream', the *Sleeping Beauty* waltz, filled the theatre. She felt very lucky that they'd found each other. Maybe one day, there'd be a fairy-tale wedding for *them*.

Frank squeezed Joanie's hand as the interval lights went up and two usherettes made their way to the front of the stage, carrying laden trays around their necks. 'Fancy an ice-cream?'

'Please.' She watched him as he stood in the queue, his blond hair flopping into his eyes. A little thrill went through her as she thought of how lucky she was to have a man like Frank to love her. Hopefully he would continue to love her for the rest of her life.

* * *

On the walk back to the station and with their heads filled with romance and fairy tales, Frank pulled Joanie into his arms in a Lime Street shop doorway. He had the engagement ring in his pocket and he really couldn't wait to give it to her. They never had anywhere private to be alone. He glanced around. The area was fairly quiet so he dropped down on one knee on the frosty floor and took her hand. She stared at him, a half-smile playing on her lips, a puzzled look in her eyes. A few theatre-goers hurried by, looking at them, but for Frank he and Joanie were the only two people in the world. He cleared his throat and began. 'I, er, I was going to do this on Christmas Day, but I can't wait. Joanie Lees, will you marry me?' He got to his feet and held his breath as her eyes filled. He held out the ring box and her eyes opened wide when she saw the sparkling solitaire diamond, nestling in the red velvet interior.

She clapped her hands to her mouth. 'Yes, oh yes, Frank, of course I'll marry you.'

Chapter Ten

Joanie and Dora joined their co-workers and the packers in the canteen for hot roast pork sandwiches and mince pies on Christmas Eve.

Joanie glanced around at the subdued faces and sighed. 'Might as well make the most of this,' she said. 'Jack says it's the nearest we're going to get to a works Christmas dinner this year.'

Dora nodded. 'Count ourselves lucky then, eh? The pork's lovely though. Nice and tender. Mavis has done us proud.'

Peggy, her cheeks bulging, said, 'Mavis's home-made stuffing. You can't beat it.'

Mavis beamed at the compliments. She'd done her best, decorating the canteen with a few paper chains she'd brought in, but there were no crackers to pull or silly hats to wear as in previous years, which meant Len wouldn't be making them groan with the cracker jokes as he usually did. Christmas carols played quietly in the background on the wireless, but the spirit of the season was sadly lacking.

'I'm just annoyed that we're not getting paid early, like we've always done in the past,' Joanie said. 'Talk about having us over a barrel.' They'd been told they would have to come in on Friday the twenty-seventh to help with the shirt order and to collect their pay.

Because of the general feeling of unrest amongst the girls, the completion of the order had been delayed and there was still a fair bit of work to do. In a way it was good for Joanie and Dora as it meant they stood every chance of getting the two dresses for New Year's Eve finished as planned. Joanie had kept Frank's proposal to

herself for now, but tonight they were going to surprise Dora and
Joe at the village hall dance.

Dora and Joanie shivered at the bus stop, wrapping their
scarves tightly around their necks and stamping their feet.
The despondent faces of their workmates made Dora feel sad.
Money was tight enough as it was and without the festive bonus it would be even tighter this year. Maybe in the New Year,
when Joe had gone back to work, and before they were back
in at Palmer's, she'd invite some of them round for a brew
and ask her mam to bake a nice cake and some mince pies to
share. A few, including Peggy and Maude, said they were going to look for new jobs anyway after Christmas and would try
Tate & Lyle's in town. The bus lurched into view and stopped
with an over-exaggerated screech of brakes. It was packed with
women and excited children, who looked like they'd rather
be anywhere than out shopping with their mams on such an
important day. Bulging bags on knees showed there were still
last-minute bargains to be had, probably from Paddy's market.
The girls found seats at the back of the bus and flopped down
with a communal sigh.

'I'm shattered,' Dora said, puffing out her cheeks. 'I half-wish
we were stopping in tonight. I've still got loads of things to do for
tomorrow.'

'You'll be fine after a rest this afternoon. Have a soak in the
bath. I'm wearing my new pink dress tonight. Are you wearing
your new one?'

Dora nodded. 'If I can get the hem finished before we go out.'
She felt a little thrill as she thought of the dress, currently hanging
on Florence in the sewing room. The time spent making it had
had to be squeezed in, in-between the orders. The light blue fabric
brought out the colour in her eyes. With its square neckline and

flared New Look skirt, it draped neatly across her slightly swollen stomach, keeping her secret intact, and finished just above her knees. She still had the silk stockings from her wedding day and luckily they hadn't laddered at the ROF dance the other night. She was excited about getting dressed up for Joe and having him all to herself, instead of him spending half the night on stage. Knowsley village hall had its own resident local band; a piano player, a drummer and an accordion player. The drummer's wife was the singer who also led the church choir, but sang modern popular songs as well as hymns.

'I'm really looking forward to a good dance and so is Frank,' Joanie said smiling happily.

Joe's breath caught in his throat as he looked at his wife when she emerged from the bedroom. Her wavy blonde hair hung below her shoulders in a peek-a-boo style, like the glamorous actress, Veronica Lake. The dress she'd been finishing as he'd come in from work mid-afternoon fitted her slender figure to perfection, with just the slightest rounding of her tummy showing. She was perfect, everything he'd ever wanted, and he loved her with all of his heart.

'Do you think I should wear a girdle?' she asked. 'I don't want anyone to guess tonight.' She rubbed her hand lightly over her stomach and sucked in her breath.

'You can't really tell. Just keep breathing in,' he said, raising an amused eyebrow.

She laughed. 'I'll be glad when it's tomorrow and we can tell people.'

'Me too.'

'Is there anyone else from your work going tonight, apart from Dolly and Eric?' she asked, standing on tiptoe in front of the mirror over the fireplace, and clipping on her favourite earrings,

little blue sapphires with marcasite chips that sparkled like real dia-
monds in the right light. Joe had given them to her last Christmas.

'A few. One or two couples from the estate.'

'What about her from the canteen, that Ivy?'

He laughed. 'I've honestly got no idea, love.'

'Hmm.' She slipped her warm coat on. 'Are the Parkers coming here for the taxi?'

'Yes,' he replied as the doorbell rang. 'That'll be them.'

He let Dolly and Eric in with a blast of cold air and a flurry of
powdery snowflakes.

'It's just starting,' Dolly said. 'Not sticking though, so hopefully it'll stay clear until we get home.' She shook the flakes from
her red curls as the doorbell rang again. 'Here's the taxi.'

Dora picked up her handbag and Joe shepherded them all out
to the waiting vehicle that had seen better days. The shabby interior stank, as though the driver had been transporting animals
in it, which was a possibility as there was straw on the back seat
and floor. But it was better than walking in this cold weather. The
buses had stopped running at six tonight and there was no way
Joe could expect Dora to get on the back of his motorbike when
she was all dolled up. He brushed the straw off the seat and she
sat down, squashed in-between Dolly and Eric. Joe climbed into
the front and sat beside the driver.

Dora removed her coat and waved at Joanie and Frank, who,
along with Agnes and Alan, had saved them all seats at a table
near the makeshift bar. Joe brought drinks across for everyone
and raised his glass. 'Cheers. Here's to a happy Christmas.'

They all clinked glasses and Dora took a quick glance around.
No sign of Ivy and her mate, thank goodness. She relaxed back
into her seat and sipped her drink.

The trio of musicians, standing on stage, waited while the piano player's wife fiddled with the microphone, tapping the end and one-two-ing. She welcomed everyone to the party and started the evening's entertainment with Glenn Miller's 'I've got a Gal in Kalamazoo'.

Frank nudged Joanie and nodded towards the dance floor. Joe pulled Dora to her feet and Alan took Agnes by the hand. Dolly heaved Eric up to dance.

After another couple of songs Dora was ready for a sit-down and Joe dashed away to the gents. Dora finished her drink and frowned as Joanie waved her left hand in the air, grinning broadly. 'Oh my God!' Dora exclaimed. 'You pair of dark horses. When did he give you that?' She caught hold of Joanie's hand and admired the sparkling diamond. 'It looks lovely and fits you perfectly. Congratulations.' She gave them both a hug and a kiss and Joanie told them all about Frank's proposal.

'We wanted to save the surprise for tonight.' She smiled as Dora's mam took a seat next to her, her red Christmas dress covered with her best paisley frilly pinny. It only came out for parties, as opposed to the usual faded floral wrap-over that she never took off except on days it spent on the washing line.

'You all look excited. What's going on?' Mam said.

Dora smiled as Joe rejoined them. 'It's this pair.' She nodded at Frank and Joanie. 'They've only gone and got engaged.'

'Calls for a celebration,' Joe said and he and Frank went to the bar while Mam admired Joanie's ring.

Joanie told them how Frank had surprised her with his proposal on Lime Street after the panto. 'It was very romantic, even though he went down on one knee on the icy pavement.'

'Well, what a lovely surprise,' Mam said. 'And you're so lucky the ring fitted without having to be altered.'

Dora smiled and tactfully kept her mouth shut.

'You still look a bit pale, love.' Mam turned to Dora. 'Perhaps you're overtired. Maybe you'll be giving up Palmer's soon if they close next year.'

'I hope so. And then me and Joanie can work at home. We're hoping we can get more orders as the year goes on.'

'I'm sure you will. Your new frocks are lovely.'

'Thanks, Mam.' Joanie's dress was a similar style to Dora's but in a dark pink fabric. 'See Marlene, over there, in that blue dress?' Dora pointed to the young woman. 'That's one of our designs too.'

Mam nodded. 'Well I never. It's gorgeous. And you've done a good job of making her look a lot thinner than she really is.'

Dora stifled a giggle. Mam never minced words. 'She does look slimmer.'

'Carry on like this and I can see you doing well. Make sure you don't get too bogged down though. You mustn't neglect your Joe.' She got to her feet. 'Right, I'd best go and help get ready to serve up the buffet.'

The singer had just announced the last song of the first spot as Joe came back from the bar, followed by Frank.

'We won't stay too late,' Joe said. 'I bet Eric and Dolly's kids will have them up at the crack of dawn.'

Dolly laughed. 'It gets earlier each year. We had to send them back to bed last year. Four o'clock young Freddie was banging on our bedroom door. Eric told them presents get taken straight back if Father Christmas sees anyone up so early.'

Eric nodded. 'Aye, it did the trick. Didn't hear another peep until half-nine.'

As the evening drew to a close the queue for the phone in the lobby was lengthy and it took Joe ages when he went to ring for a taxi to take them home. The singer had just announced the final song as he came back to the table and he pulled Dora to her feet. They joined Frank and Joanie and Alan and Agnes on the dance floor and waltzed to 'As Time Goes By'. It was one of Dora's favourite songs and she and Joe had seen the film *Casablanca* twice. She used to have a secret crush on Humphrey Bogart, but he wasn't a patch on her Joe. She nestled her head into his chest as he held her close. The love she felt for him was overwhelming and she just hoped she had enough in her to go around for their baby as well, when it arrived.

Joe handed everyone a glass of sherry as they relaxed in the sitting room after Christmas dinner. Dora had decorated the little room with holly and ivy, fastened up with red ribbons. A small pine tree in a red pot stood next to the chimney breast, filling the room with its Christmassy scent. She eased her shoes off her aching feet and sat on the floor in front of the fire next to Joanie. She rummaged under the tree and handed a gaily wrapped parcel to Joanie, and one to her mam.

'Just a little extra bit of something for you both.' They'd already exchanged family presents earlier in the week to be unwrapped at home on Christmas morning. But Dora had been busy with some scraps left over from dressmaking as a surprise for Mam and Joanie.

Joanie unwrapped hers first and exclaimed with delight at the matching patchwork cosmetic and sponge bags in pretty silk fabrics. 'These are lovely, thank you. You're so thoughtful.' Joanie leant over and hugged her. 'I'll save them in case I ever go on holiday now the war's over.'

Dora beamed and watched as Mam unwrapped *her* parcel. Two pretty patchwork cushion covers in shades of pinks and blues fell onto her knee and Mam smiled with delight. 'They're beautiful; just the job to replace the tatty ones on the sofa. Thank you, my love.'

'You're welcome.'

Frank got to his feet. 'That holiday you mentioned, Joanie, maybe we could go somewhere nice next year on our honeymoon.'

Joanie blushed as Frank dropped a kiss on her lips.

Joe smiled at Dora as the pair drew apart.

Dora got to her feet and took his hand. 'Joe and I have something we'd like to share with you all.' She caught Joanie's eye and winked. Her friend was the only one privy to the closely guarded secret, but she'd kept it to herself, as Dora knew she would.

Joe took a deep breath as they all looked expectantly at them. 'Dora is having a baby,' he announced proudly. 'Your first grandchild is due in July.' He laughed as Dora's parents gasped and then cheered along with Frank and Joanie.

Mam clasped her hands to her chest and beamed. 'What a wonderful Christmas this has turned out to be. The best one ever.'

'Aye, it certainly is,' Dad said shaking his head. 'We're getting rid of our Frank at last,' he teased, as Joanie laughed. 'Gaining a new daughter-in-law. And blimey, to top it all, a new babby too. What a smashing year to look forward to, eh, Mary?'

'I'll say. We need a drop more sherry for another toast, Joe. Well, I'll go to the foot of our stairs. That blooming tummy upset was a baby all along.'

Dora laughed. 'It would seem so, Mam.' Joe topped them all up and she raised her glass. 'Here's to a successful new business, a wedding to plan and a new baby to keep us all on our toes. Cheers, everybody.'

Chapter Eleven

Joanie basked proudly in the excited oohs and aahs of her workmates as they took it in turns to admire her lovely engagement ring. She'd just spent the happiest few days of her life as Frank's fiancée, and felt content in the knowledge that she had a lifetime of being loved to look forward to.

Joanie had never felt so important, and couldn't wait to start planning their wedding day properly. She wanted it to be just like Dora's had been, and they'd talked about it last night, making tentative plans to marry in the same church. Frank said he'd look out for some nice fabric for her wedding dress and Dora had offered to help as much as she could, though she'd be too fat to be a bridesmaid. Joanie said because she was now a married woman she could be the matron of honour. On the walk home, Frank had suggested they get married in May, a couple of months before Dora's baby was due, and they could go to Blackpool for a honeymoon. She'd never had a holiday before, just the odd day trip to New Brighton on the ferry before war had broken out. It was all so exciting.

The factory girls were in the canteen on their dinner break and the happy news had cheered them all up, as no one really wanted to work today. It seemed pointless, opening for one day only this week, but with the promise of their wages, there'd been no choice. Up to now the money hadn't been forthcoming and the machinists were getting restless. Jack Carter had kept his distance all morning, after telling them to stop mithering; they'd get paid as soon as the wages clerk had finished doing her job.

Joanie dug Dora in the ribs and smiled encouragingly. 'Dora has some good news to share with you too,' she announced with glee.

All eyes switched to Dora, whose cheeks flushed slightly. She got to her feet and ran her hands over her stomach as eagle-eyed Peggy blurted out, "'Ere, are youse in the family way, gel?'

Joanie smiled. Trust Peggy.

'Well spotted, Peggy,' Dora said, beaming. 'I am, and my baby's due in July.'

She sat back down as further congratulations filled the air and mugs of tea were clinked together.

'Well at least you two have got summat to look forward to next year. Lucky buggers,' Peggy said, laughing.

Jack Carter appeared in the doorway and clapped his hands together to get the attention of his workforce. 'If you're back upstairs in the next ten minutes you can all finish at four. You'll be paid just before you leave. No need to come back in then until the sixth of January.' He turned and walked away, ignoring the indignant shouts of, 'And about time too.'

Joanie shrugged and beckoned to Dora. 'Finishing at four's better for us,' she began, closing the door. 'They'll all be rushing off as soon as the bell goes. We'll get the bus when I've finished the dresses and go straight back to your place.'

'Okay,' Dora said. 'You and Frank can stay for tea if you like.'

Joanie nodded. 'That'll be lovely: it's Friday so we'll treat ourselves to fish and chips. I told Frank to meet me at yours tonight and Mam knows I'm going home with you. We can do some planning for our wedding. I've got an idea for a dress; it's been in my head all day, so if I describe it, you can draw it, seeing as you're better at that than me. Then see what you think and whether we can manage to make it, or something similar. But don't let Frank see it.'

Dora smiled at Joanie's excitement. 'I'll look forward to it. Whatever the style, you'll look beautiful and our Frank will be so proud of you. While we're at it, we'll design a tent for me to wear!'

The afternoon passed slowly, each girl pulling her weight to get the current shirt order finished. Wage packets were handed out and faces screwed up with disappointment when realisation hit that although they'd been told there'd be no festive bonus this year, it was now an actual reality. As the bell rang early, machines were switched off and belongings gathered together in readiness for the mass exit. Joanie glanced out of the window at the already dark fields and the light snow that had started to fall. Heavy snows had been forecast for the last few days but it never seemed to get beyond a dusty-looking sprinkle. Hopefully it would stay that way for the next couple of hours until they got safely back to Dora's.

'I'll go and distract Jack in the canteen while he has his last ciggie and brew,' Dora said as Joanie picked up the bag with the dresses. 'Good luck.' She gave Joanie a hug and hurried off the factory floor with the rest of the girls.

Joanie breathed a sigh of relief as no one hung back. They all seemed to be in a rush to make the most of the extra hour while the shops were still open and they had a bit of money to spend. She dashed up the flight of stairs to the next floor and manoeuvred a lamp into place beside one of the over-lockers at the back of the room. The lamp cast a pool of light that was just enough to see by, but wouldn't be spotted through the windows if someone looked up from outside. She fished in the dress bag for the spools of thread and set about threading up the machine, confident that she'd have the job completed in no time at all. It felt spooky up here all on her own, the lamp casting shadows in the corner of the room, but she kept her eyes down and concentrated, rather than let her mind get carried away with the thoughts of ghostly beings jumping out at her.

Dora caught up with Jack in the canteen where he was seated at a table, hugging a mug, a ciggie dangling from his lips and a weary expression on his face. She parked herself opposite him and waved to Mavis at the counter, who brought her a mug of tea across.

'Hiya, Dora,' Jack said, blowing a cloud of smoke above his head as she took off her coat. 'What's up, gel?'

'I wanted a private word with you,' she said, and took a couple of sips of tea to gain a few seconds.

'Rightio, make it quick then,' he said, flicking ash carelessly onto Mavis's freshly washed quarry-tiled floor, earning him a glare and shake of the mop. 'I've a lot to do before I get off home and I've to ring Mr Kane when I've done my final lights-out check.'

Dora nodded and took another leisurely sip of tea. She could make the time spin out a bit longer by waffling, something her dad had told her she was good at. He always said she could talk the hind legs off a donkey.

'I was just wondering,' she began, aware she was speaking a bit slower than normal. 'Do you *really* think the company will shut down next year? I mean, has Mr Kane said for definite, or has he maybe decided to employ some of the old reps to get us more work in?' Dora chewed her lip, hoping she sounded as though she knew what she was talking about. 'Mind, you, I suppose they've all found new jobs now, those reps that survived the war, that is.' She looked at Jack over the rim of her mug. 'Because if there's any chance it will close, well, it was just that I, er, I'm thinking of the future for me and Joanie and I wanted to ask you something while the other girls aren't around. I don't want to cause any upset or ill feelings with anyone… Would it be at all possible for us to buy one of the over-lockers from the company if they sell the equipment off? As long as it's not too expensive, of course, because we haven't got a lot of spare money.'

He looked surprised at her question and scratched his chin thoughtfully. 'Well, I don't see why not. If they *do* decide to close, and there's nothing definite yet mind, Mr Kane will probably sell all the machines at auction. Let me see what I can do, chuck. I'll ask him in the New Year, and if he says it's okay, I'll make sure one's kept back for you if and when they clear the place out. It's nice that you and Joanie are making an effort to better yourselves for the future. You deserve a chance.'

'Oh, thank you so much,' Dora gushed. She looked up at the clock above the counter. Joanie should have at least one of the dresses done by now. 'It would make all the difference to us,' she continued. 'You've no idea how long it takes us to finish the seams by hand, especially on satin material with it fraying so much…' She looked up as Mavis waved the tea pot in her direction. 'Thanks, Mavis, I'll have a top-up and then I'll get off for the bus.'

Jack opened his mouth as if to say something, and then closed it again. Dora took the opportunity to fiddle with her handbag clasp and accidentally-on-purpose drop something on the floor that rolled away under the rows of tables and chairs.

Jack jumped up and scrabbled around before retrieving her lipstick, buying her a few more seconds. 'Now, hurry up and finish your tea then we can get out of Mavis's hair,' he said, an edge of impatience creeping into his voice as Dora finished her drink. 'She's waiting to go and she'll want to lock up in here.'

Mavis didn't seem in a rush and was leaning on the counter as Dora got to her feet and carried both her and Jack's empty mugs across. 'Thanks for the tea, Mavis. Shall I wash these for you?'

'No, chuck, I'll stick them in the sink.' She went out to the kitchen area and sauntered back, pulling on her coat and a brown woolly hat that she tugged low over her ears. She picked up her bag and rattled a bunch of keys. 'Be careful you don't slip when you get outside. I emptied the mop bucket out the back earlier and the snow was starting to come down a bit heavier. Don't want you falling and hurting yourself, especially now you're expecting. Congratulations by the way. I heard you talking to the girls earlier.'

'Come on now, ladies. I'll see you both out,' Jack said, jigging from foot to foot with impatience. 'I've still to check everything's off upstairs and make my phone call before I can go home.' He practically pushed Dora and Mavis to the front door and manoeuvred them outside. Mavis waved and set off across the front to the lane. Jack waved goodbye and shut the door, leaving Dora standing on the step, still fastening up her coat. Joanie should be with her any minute. She stared at the closed door and frowned. Not like Jack to be so impatient with his workers, and he'd always had plenty of time for her and Joanie.

The uncertainty of all their futures must be getting to him. Hopefully he'd be talking for ages on the phone to Mr Kane, and Joanie would be able to sneak out before she was spotted. There were only three seams on each dress to neaten: they'd already done the bodices by hand, so it was just the skirts, two side seams and a back seam on each one. She huddled in the doorway, stamping her feet and willing Joanie to hurry up. The door creaked open and her friend slipped outside, closing it quietly behind her, a big grin on her face.

'Mission accomplished,' she said, waving the bag with the dresses in the air. She slid her arm through Dora's as they hurried across to the bus shelter on the lane, just as the bus rumbled into view. 'Bang on time as well. Now we've got away with it, I can do that again. I didn't even see sight of Jack. Well done for keeping him out of the way.'

Chapter Twelve

January 1947

Dora stared out of the window as the large snowflakes, thick, swirling and lacy, like heavy net curtains, obliterated everything in her view. It was the second bad snowstorm this week that had kept her trapped inside, with a forecast of more on the way. It was a good excuse not to go out though, and not even bother getting dressed. Joe had lit the fire before setting off for work on foot. Buses, trams and trains had been cancelled and the roads were too treacherous to ride his bike. According to the news on the wireless, the country was virtually at a standstill. Dora flopped down onto the sofa and curled her feet up beneath her. Her mind felt hazy and it bothered her. She'd been plagued with terrible sickness again since New Year and the doctor had ordered her to rest. She'd lost a bit of weight, although her baby bump was growing a bit, and she struggled to keep down anything that wasn't liquid.

She'd been off work now for over two weeks trying to get herself right. The doctor had suggested a very mild sedative to help control the bouts of vomiting but she worried about taking it and planned to tell Joe tonight that she wanted to stop in case it harmed the baby. Almost two weeks of being in a foggy haze was long enough. She didn't like being off work either, but Joanie had been to see her a few times and told her she was better off at home for now as there wasn't much doing. A few staff members had been unable to get in due to the weather. There was still no sign of any new orders, although there was a bit of good news in that George Kane had hired a rep who was supposed to be visiting stores up and down the country, though the weather had prevented him from travelling too far.

She shivered and went back to the sofa and pulled a knitted blanket around her shoulders. The mug of tea she'd brewed earlier had a skin on top and the sight of it made her gag. She took a couple of deep breaths, fighting the need to be sick again. The effort made beads of sweat form on her brow and she sighed, wondering what the heck was causing this nausea. She hoped it wasn't a sign that something was wrong with her baby. The doctor had prodded and poked her and listened to its heartbeat the other day and told her everything was okay.

She remembered a girl at work a couple of years ago who'd suffered a lot of sickness and her baby had been born with a hole in his back and some of his innards on the outside of his body. The poor little man had only survived a couple of days and the hospital had told his mother that he'd developed something called spina bifida while he was growing inside her. No one at work had ever heard of it and speculation was that something in the air from Hitler's bombs must have caused it. Dora lay back on the cushions and closed her eyes, her arms folded protectively over her growing bump. If the roads were passable tonight maybe Joanie and Frank would pop over for an hour or two and cheer her up with their wedding plans. They'd decided on a date, the last Saturday in May, and had already booked the church where she and Joe had married. She'd be huge by then with the baby, but Joanie was still insisting she be her matron of honour.

Joe stamped the snow from his boots on the mat and hung his coat on a peg in the hall. He cocked his ear for the sound of the wireless but there was nothing other than the eerie silence that a snow-filled street brings, and the air in the bungalow felt chilly. He pushed open the sitting room door to see Dora snuggled under a blanket, asleep on the sofa, and the fire on its last legs. The curtains were still wide open and there was no light on. He wondered how long she'd been asleep. She felt cold to the touch and he hurried into the bedroom and took a blanket from the bed. He tucked it around her, drew the curtains and switched on the lamp. He raked the fire and twisted some old newspapers together to encourage the embers and threw a shovel of coal on once he'd got them going. The room soon felt warm again.

Dora stirred and opened her eyes. She looked a bit puzzled, but then smiled with recognition.

'Hiya, darling.' He gave her a kiss. 'Did you wonder where you were? Would you like something to eat? Your mam left a pan of lentil soup yesterday for us. It might do you good to try it.'

She nodded and pulled herself into a sitting position. 'How long have you been home?'

'Only about ten minutes.' He busied himself in the kitchen and heated up the soup. Dora's mam had also left a fresh loaf of bread. He cut a few slices and spread them with margarine, wondering how he'd manage without her mam. She'd been coming most days since Dora had taken ill with the sickness again, to make sure her daughter was okay while he went back to work and to make her drink plenty of fluids as instructed by the doctor, who'd told him that if the sickness continued she'd become dehydrated and would end up being taken into hospital and put on a drip. She wouldn't like that. He'd managed to get a few extra days off work after the holidays, but too long a break would be frowned upon. He couldn't afford to lose his job now as Dora was only paid from Palmer's when she worked and there was no other money coming in apart from his band money.

There were rumours of job cuts at the ROF and that worried him. He didn't know what they'd do if they lost their home. And the weather forecaster on the dinnertime news at the factory had announced the worst weather in over a hundred years was about to hit the country. More heavy snows were due, with freezing temperatures. Dora's mam wouldn't be able to get here and he hated leaving her alone all day. Maybe he could ask Dolly Parker to keep an eye on her occasionally. Joe stirred the soup and sighed. Hadn't they all had enough to contend with the last few years? The bloody war and all that came with it; and now, just as the country seemed to be getting on its feet, weather that threatened to shut everything down. Dora was isolated when he was at work, but what could he do? He couldn't expect anyone to trek over in this and most of their friends were at work during the day, if they could get there.

She was supposed to see the doctor this week about the baby, but there was no way of her getting to the surgery on her own. Maybe if he phoned them tomorrow, they might be able to send a midwife out to see her. He'd rung his mum from work to let her know he was back in but that Dora still wasn't too good. He'd been surprised at how concerned she'd seemed. But then again, Dora was carrying her grandchild, although there was no offer forthcoming to call round and sit with her.

'You need to get a telephone fitted, Joe,' she'd said. 'Then it's there for emergencies. If you arrange it, I'll stand the cost.' She'd been thrilled by their baby news on Boxing Day, which seemed like a lifetime ago now. He hadn't discussed them getting a phone yet with Dora. But he'd do it tonight if she was up to it. At least then he could call her each day at dinnertime to make sure she was all right and to remind her to drink plenty of boiled water.

He poured the soup into two bowls and carried Dora's through on a tray, balancing it on her knees. He brewed a pot of tea, put two mugs on the coffee table, switched on the wireless and joined her with his own tray.

'Will you help me to have a bath and wash my hair after tea?' she asked, taking a spoonful of soup. 'And, Joe, I've decided I don't want to have any more sedatives. I know they stop the sickness but they make me feel so sleepy and I can't think straight. I hate the feeling. I'm also worried that they're not good for the baby.'

'Okay, love.' He wasn't sure if stopping them was the right thing to do without asking the doctor first, but he'd sort that out tomorrow when he phoned the surgery. The fact that she even wanted to get in the bath was a good sign as she'd neglected herself for a while and that wasn't like Dora, who was normally fastidious about smelling nice and fresh and having clean, shiny hair. He took the tray from her and sighed. She'd barely touched the soup.

Dora opened the front door to the young midwife, who smiled and introduced herself as Nurse Dawson. The midwife removed her snowy boots and left them on the mat, and followed Dora down the hall into the warm sitting room, carrying a large black bag in with her.

'Would you like a hot drink?' Dora offered.

'I'd love one, thank you. It looks lovely in here.' She took off her coat and put it over a chair arm. 'May I sit down?'

'Please do.' Dora gestured to the sofa and hurried out to the kitchen, bringing back a tray with two cups of tea and a plate with one of her mam's cheese scones.

'Oh, what a treat,' Nurse Dawson said. 'Did *you* bake it?'

Dora shook her head. 'My mam did.'

They sat in companionable silence while the midwife finished her snack. Dora cleared the tray away as Nurse Dawson opened her bag and took out a large buff envelope.

'Doctor Owens told me you've suffered bad bouts of all-day sickness for quite some time now,' she said, removing a sheaf of papers. 'And that you've opted to stop taking the sedatives he prescribed.'

Dora nodded. 'I feel less fuzzy-headed now I've stopped, but I can't win. I'm queasy from the minute I get up to the minute I go to bed.' She didn't know which was the easiest to deal with, sickness or fuzziness. She was desperate to get back to work once the weather started to improve, but feeling as she did right now, she knew she'd never be able to cope with the journey, never mind anything else.

Nurse Dawson smiled sympathetically. 'Yes, it's a difficult one. Hopefully the sickness will stop of its own accord, although there have been cases where it carries on until the end of the pregnancy. We just need to keep an eye on you and make sure your body is getting enough fluid. Plenty of boiled water and soups, and perhaps some jelly if you feel like something sweet now and again. If you fancy a biscuit with a cuppa, try ginger snaps. Ginger's good for settling sickness. But do keep trying to eat, little and often.'

Dora chewed her lip anxiously. 'I just wondered, the sickness doesn't mean there's anything wrong with my baby, does it? It's not a sign of a problem, or anything? It's just that a girl I used to work with had a baby born with a hole in his back. She was sick a lot like me.'

'No, love. I think this is just your hormones. Believe me, I understand your worries, but with a bit of luck, one day you'll get up and it will be gone. Now I'm going to take some details and then we'll discuss your antenatal care and where you've decided you'd like to give birth. I expect you've talked that over with your husband already?'

Dora shrugged. She and Joe hadn't actually talked about the birth at all. She'd just not felt in the mood. 'My mam did say that if I have it at home, she'd be here with me.'

'It's up to you, of course. You can have baby here, and I'll attend the delivery, or we can make arrangements for you to go into our own maternity home. Can I take a quick look around while I'm here? I've delivered a few babies on this estate so I'm quite used to the layout of the bungalows, but I need to put it on my notes that I've actually looked.'

'Of course.' Dora led the way into the main bedroom and the bathroom and the midwife nodded her approval. The door to the sewing room stood open and Nurse Dawson pointed towards the room. 'And will that be baby's room eventually?'

Dora chewed her lip. 'It will be, in time. It's currently a work-room, or it was. I just haven't felt up to doing anything since New Year.' She fought to hold back the tears but they ran down her cheeks as she showed the midwife inside the room. She found herself crying at the least little thing lately. 'It was to be the start of a new future for me and my best friend.' She told Nurse Dawson of her and Joanie's plans.

The midwife nodded. 'And does Joanie still wish to carry on with the business?'

Dora half-smiled through her tears. 'Oh yes, she does. We've got her wedding dress to make soon. But she also knows how horrible I've been feeling lately.'

'Well why don't you give it a try on a day when you're feeling a bit better? Sometimes it can be mind over matter with things. If you're occupied it takes your mind off feeling rotten. It will keep you busy. You can't go far in this awful weather, so make something for yourself, or for the baby. Don't do too much to start with and then you'll feel ready for tackling your friend's wedding dress.'

'I might do that. I felt dizzy sitting at the machine last time I tried. I'm really hoping to go back to work at the factory for a few months before the baby arrives, but they won't let me use a machine while I'm feeling dizzy.'

'In time, my dear, in time.'

Back in the lounge Nurse Dawson finished writing up her notes, checked Dora's blood pressure, which she announced was normal, and packed everything back in her bag. 'If you decide on a home birth I'll fetch the delivery pack round in a few weeks' time. Hopefully this weather won't last for much longer, although I heard it's been forecast until March.' She shook her head. 'That makes for a very long winter.'

'It does, and it's difficult for visitors to get here. The buses have stopped running and it's hard for the likes of my mam to walk on the snow. I'd be frightened of her falling and breaking something. I feel a bit cut off. We're supposed to be having a phone put in soon. My husband's arranging it.'

'That'll be handy for when baby's on the way,' Nurse Dawson said.

Dora said goodbye and saw her out. She thought about what the midwife had said and knew she was right: she needed to distract herself. Dora went back into the sewing room and sat on the chair in front of her treadle machine. Making something for the baby would be a nice start. For the first time in weeks she felt a buzz of enthusiasm. Joanie would be glad to hear that as she wanted them to start working on her wedding dress. Hopefully she'd come over this week with Frank if the roads weren't too bad, and with a bit of luck she'd have possession of the silky material Frank was supposed to be getting for the dress lining. She'd already got some white Guipure lace that was similar to her own wedding dress.

Chapter Thirteen

The bad winter dragged on and once the snow started to melt, floods occurred in parts of the country that had already suffered when cut off by snow drifts. News bulletins reported that it was the coldest winter the UK had suffered for *three* centuries. Herds of animals froze out in the fields and starved to death creating another meat shortage. There had been power disruptions to homes and Dora and Joe had sat at night with candles burning several times. The fridge had defrosted, each time leaking water all over the kitchen floor and Dora had struggled on her hands and knees to mop it up. When the power *was* on, radio programmes were limited; some magazine publishers were ordered not to print for a few weeks and newspapers were cut in size. Towards the end of February there was further fear of food shortages as vegetables were frozen into the ground. Mid-March brought the worst of the widespread flooding and again the country came to a standstill, with roads and railways affected and many homes and businesses damaged by the floods.

By the beginning of April the weather had improved and Dora's sickness had stopped completely, just as the midwife had told her it would. She felt almost human again and anxious to get back to work. Joanie met her off the bus the first day and they walked into Palmer's together. Her workmates greeted her warmly and Jack Carter asked if she was sure she felt up to it.

'I'm fine, Jack,' she said, smiling. 'I know I won't be here for long, but it's good to be back.' She'd be finishing in May, so she only had a few weeks to go anyway and it was nice to have the company again. She'd spent some of her time at home working on Joanie's wedding dress, and it was looking lovely.

Dora's bump had grown so big while she'd been off ill that she felt like an elephant and found it awkward to balance on her factory seat and reach across to her machine. Mam had joked that there must be more than one in there but the midwife had just smiled and shaken her head. She said it was probably because Dora's appetite had come back and she was eating for two again, making up for all the weeks on her liquid diet.

She and Joanie had tackled a couple of simple skirt orders last week, but the tiredness was overwhelming at night and Joe had put his foot down about her doing too much. There was no question of her coming back to Palmer's after the birth, as speculation was that they would definitely be closed by the end of September. The new rep had only managed to secure two shirt orders and had been fired within weeks. George Kane had been reported as saying he was a waste of good money to employ and they would have got those orders in anyway. It was dresses and other ladies' fashion contracts he'd been after, not more shirts. But time and money were running out and although no firm date had been set for closure, they all knew it was looming. Dora hung onto Joanie's arm as she was led blindfolded into Palmer's canteen. It was the afternoon tea break and Jack had agreed they could all have an extra fifteen minutes today as it was Friday afternoon and Dora's final day at work before she finished for the birth of her baby.

'Are you ready?' Joanie whipped off her blindfold as a cheer went up. The small workforce was gathered in the canteen. Someone yelled 'Speech!' 'Give her a minute,' Joanie yelled back, laughing. She led Dora to a table set out with plates of Spam sandwiches and little iced buns, courtesy of Mavis. The table next to it was decorated with bunting left over from the end-of-war parties, and piled high with gaily wrapped parcels.

Mavis bustled over with the tea trolley and handed out mugs of her welcome brew.

'All the very best, chuck.' She planted a kiss on Dora's cheek. 'Just make sure you bring that babby in to see us as soon as you can.'

'Oh I will, definitely,' Dora said, smiling. She shook her head as she looked around. All the secrecy and whispering behind her back this week and she'd not had a clue what they were up to. She sat down and the rest of the girls followed suit and tucked into the food.

'Bet you're glad to see this day at last?' Peggy said and blew on her hot tea to cool it.

Dora, her mouth full of sandwich, nodded. She swallowed and took a sip of tea. 'But I'll miss you all. You must come and visit when the baby arrives. Joanie will let you know when it does. And I'll definitely pop in for a visit when I'm over at my mam's house.' She meant what she said, she really would miss her friends at Palmer's, but it would be a relief to work from home again with a new baby to look after as well. Besides, there would be no job to come back to here, and like Joe had said recently, it was up to him as the man of the house to take care of his wife and child. It was what men did. He didn't mind her doing some work at home and she was glad of that as she liked to keep a bit of independence and earn her own money. But it would also be nice to be taken care of by Joe. She felt very lucky as she had the best of both worlds.

Joanie passed her some of the parcels and Dora opened the first one, her eyes filling with tears as she looked at the beautiful knitted matinee jacket and booties in a pale lemon shade, threaded with narrow white ribbons. 'Peggy, these are gorgeous. Did *you* make them?'

Peggy laughed. 'I can't knit for toffee, queen. My mam made them. She really enjoyed doing it as well. Kept her occupied while I'm at work.'

Dora got up and put her arms around Peggy. She gave her a kiss on the cheek. 'Tell her thank you so much. I'll bring the baby to see her, wearing them specially.'

Peggy beamed. 'She'd like that, Dora. Mam loves babbies.'

Dora opened Maude's parcel next, which contained two tiny white flannelette nightdresses, embroidered across the front with cross-stitching in shades of blue and pink. Maude's plump face lit up as Dora exclaimed with delight. The stitching was neat and perfect. 'Beautiful, Maude. And I know you made these because the embroidery is so neat.' Maude always had some embroidery on the go in the old carpet bag she brought in to work. She often stitched on her breaks. 'They're lovely.'

'I thought if I used pink and blue threads they would do for either boy or girl,' Maude said as Dora hugged her and dropped a kiss on her cheek.

The rest of the parcels contained a small teddy bear, a baby rattle and bibs, and some toiletries for Dora's confinement. A soft pink flannel, her favourite Pears' soap and matching talcum powder. Dora felt overwhelmed by the kindness of her co-workers. Money was tight for everyone and the carefully chosen gifts were much appreciated.

'I just want to say a big thank you, to all of you. You're so kind and I'm most grateful. I know I speak for Joe too when I say thank you so much. And I'll miss you all.' She burst into tears and Joanie handed her a handkerchief and gave her a hug.

There were cries of 'We'll miss you too, Dora,' and, 'When you get your own factory you can give us all a job.'

She laughed. 'I'll see what I can do.'

As Dora followed Joanie down the aisle she felt like she was draped in a circus marquee and that everyone was staring at her, but thankfully all eyes were on Joanie as she held on to her proud eldest brother's arm. Frank was standing by the altar with his best man, Joe. A role reversal from their own wedding day. Joanie handed the bouquet of Dora's dad's roses to her. Joanie looked a picture in her calf-length lace gown with a sweetheart neckline, exactly as she'd drawn in a sketch for Dora. A circle of white silk roses topped her corkscrew curls and held her short veil in place.

Dora's dress was also calf length. She couldn't take the risk of tripping over a full-length gown and ending up on her back like a beached whale or overturned tortoise, unable to move. She'd chosen the palest turquoise crêpe fabric, hoping to blend into the background, but still felt ridiculously huge, and had to wear flat white shoes as her feet were swollen and high heels would have crippled her. What a sorry state of affairs, and she'd be forever immortalised in the wedding photos too. Frank and Joanie's future kids would point at her and say there's fat Aunty Dora. She felt a giggle rising and hoped she wouldn't burst out laughing as the vicar conducted the ceremony. Damn, she needed the toilet too and the one in the church was so tiny, she'd be sure to get stuck inside the cubicle. She'd just have to wait until they went outside and nip across to the village hall. She willed her baby to keep still and not play football with her bladder. She focused her attention back on Joanie and Frank and felt moved by the proud look in her brother's eyes as he gazed into Joanie's.

The ceremony over and the register signed, Dora breathed a sigh of relief as the bridal party left the church. She excused herself and hurried across the village green as quickly as she could, into the sanctuary of the toilets in the hall.

'Never again,' she muttered. 'Joe will have to make do with one child.' The indignity of being pregnant was not something she was going to go through again in a hurry. She went back outside, fixed a smile on her face and waddled back across the green in time for the photographs. Joanie looked radiant, her face glowing, and Frank's smile split *his* face in two.

'Stand sideways on,' Mam said in her usual blunt way as Dora took her place beside Joe. 'You won't look as big then.'

'Mam, I will. I'm better facing the front.' Dora plastered on a smile as Joe's hand searched for hers and gave it a reassuring squeeze. She felt relieved. He still loved her, fat or otherwise.

Chapter Fourteen

June 1947

'Twins?' Dora gasped. 'Are you absolutely sure?'

'Quite sure, Mrs Rodgers.' Doctor Owens pushed his glasses back up his nose. He'd been summoned into the Friday morning antenatal clinic session by Nurse Dawson, who had told him she was certain she'd heard two heartbeats and judging by the size of Mrs Rodgers's fundal height measurements, two babies were more likely than one on this occasion.

'There's definitely an extra heartbeat, but because of the way baby two seems to be hiding behind baby one, it's hard to check the position of them both. Maybe at the next clinic they'll have shifted around a bit and we'll be able to feel them better. That's if you don't deliver before the next clinic. But you need to prepare yourself for an extra baby. And once again, may I offer my congratulations.' He said goodbye and left the curtained-off cubicle.

Dora lay back on the bed, her mind in a whirl. How the devil was she going to cope with two babies?

'I think we may need to book you into our maternity home now, Mrs Rodgers,' Nurse Dawson said. 'I know we were all set for a home delivery, but with two you might want to have a think about it, and discuss it with your husband. If you decide to go ahead with a home birth, ring the clinic and I'll bring you another delivery pack so that we're ready. Doctor Owens will be available to us as well. You could pop any day now really.'

'I'll talk to Joe tonight.' Dora pulled herself into a sitting position and slid off the bed, straightening her clothes. 'No wonder

I'm the size of a house.' She began to giggle. 'Wait till I tell Joanie. We'll have a baby each to play with.' She felt, stunned, terrified and thrilled in equal measures.

Nurse Dawson smiled. 'I'm sure she'll be delighted with your good news.'

'Oh she will, definitely. We always shared our dollies. Do you think this is the reason I felt so sick all the time?'

'Quite possibly. A double dose of hormones. Just take it easy. Would you take your notes through to reception for me, please?' Nurse Dawson handed over the file and Dora went on her way, her mind whirling. Her mam had accompanied her on the clinic visit and she was seated in the waiting area, chatting to a woman Dora recognised. The woman had a reputation for being a bit of a gossip in Knowsley village.

'I'm ready, Mam, just got to hand these in.' She indicated the file as her mam got to her feet.

'Everything okay, love? You look a bit anxious.' Mam followed her to reception.

'Tell you when we get back to my place,' Dora whispered. The last thing she needed was her business bandied around the village before she got the chance to tell Joe. He'd be reeling with shock when he heard the news. Being an only child himself, he'd always hinted at wanting a few kids. He was certainly off to a flying start now.

She linked Mam's arm as they made their way to the bus stop and they were soon trundling towards the prefab estate, where the buses now had a permanent stop at the top of their road. It was much better than when they first moved here. It was less distance for her mam to walk with her bad knees and more convenient for Dora as she struggled with her huge baby bump.

Back at the bungalow Mam told her to sit down while she brewed them a cuppa. 'So come on, what did you want to tell me?' she called as she filled the kettle.

Dora began to laugh and she couldn't stop. She giggled until hysterical tears spilled down her cheeks. Her mam brought two cups of tea through and stared at her daughter as though she'd gone quite mad.

'Has Dad got any wood left over from making the cradle and highchair?' Dora asked, still grinning like a madwoman.

'Probably. He has all sorts in that shed of his. I never go in there, more than my life's worth to go rooting around in his hidey hole. Why do you ask, love?'

'Because we're going to need one more of each,' Dora spluttered, tears still running down her cheeks. 'You were right about there being more than one in there, Mam. I'm having twins!'

Dora didn't really feel hungry, so she sat at the table with a cuppa and let Joe eat his sausage and mash while she made small talk about her day and how nice the weather had been. Bit too warm for her, but she wasn't complaining after the awful winter they'd had. He let her waffle on while he finished his meal, finally interrupting her when she paused to take a breath.

'Dora, slow down, I can't get a word in with you tonight,' he said, laughing. 'I've been trying to ask you how you went on at the clinic today. Is everything okay?'

She adopted a solemn expression and told him to go and sit on the sofa. He got up, frowning, and did as she asked. She sat beside him and took his hand.

'Shit, Dora, what is it? You've been acting a bit odd since I got home. I knew something wasn't right. Is it the baby, is something wrong with it? Was all that sickness an indication?'

She shook her head and started to laugh. He looked so worried. 'Nothing wrong at all, as far as I know. They've *both* got a strong heartbeat, but one likes to play hide and seek behind the other.'

He stared at her and then said, 'Did you say both?'

'I did. We're having twins, Joe.'

He was silent for a few seconds until it sank in. She saw shock, and then delight, cross his face. He shook his head and burst out laughing.

'Twins?'

'Yep.'

'Twins?'

'Two babies, Joe.'

'I don't believe it.' He pulled her into his arms and kissed her. 'Are you okay with this? I mean, you always wanted a few years between each kiddie.'

'Well, that was my original plan. But there's not a lot I can do about it now, is there? I'm fine, Joe. Quite excited in fact. And it explains why I look like I'm carrying an elephant around. I haven't phoned your mum yet. I thought you should tell her.'

'I will. I bet you can't wait to tell Joanie.'

'I know. She'll be that surprised. I've warned Mam not to say anything, but she'll tell Joanie and Frank to come over after tea. I can't wait to see her face.'

'We need to choose another name now,' Joe said. 'We'll still stick with Carol because I like that and it reminds me of Christmas and when we found out you were pregnant.'

Dora nodded. 'I like Carol too. Maybe call another girl after Joanie?'

'Carol and Joanie. Sounds good. And if they're boys?'

'Well we said David, didn't we? And what about James after my dad? Not that anyone calls him that. I've only ever known him as Jim.'

'Sounds fine to me, Dave and Jimmy. Good lads' names.'

'And if they're one of each, then we'll go with the first names we chose, Carol and David,' Dora said.

Joe held her close and dropped a kiss on her lips. 'Well that's the easy bit sorted.'

Dora sighed and patted her huge baby bump. 'Yep. Now I've just got to carry them around for another three weeks. I was asked today if I wanted to go into the maternity home for the birth, or have them here. Mam will be with me if I stay at home, and the midwife and doctor of course. What do you think?'

He stroked his chin and looked thoughtful. 'If you feel you'll be more comfortable here, then that's fine by me. I don't mind, just as long as there's no risk to you or the babies.'

'I think I'd like to have them at home. And maybe they'll let Joanie be here too.' She paused as the doorbell rang. 'That'll be the newlyweds. Go and let them in, Joe. And try and keep your face straight until I tell them. You look like the cat that got the cream with that big grin.'

Joe ushered in the visitors and took their coats through to the spare room.

'Have a seat, you two.' Dora gestured to the chairs. 'Joe will brew up in a minute. I don't think I could get up off the sofa if I tried.' She laughed and held on to her bump as it heaved from side to side with the babies wriggling around.

'How did you go on at the antenatal clinic?' Joanie asked, sitting on the floor and leaning against Frank's legs as he reclined in a chair.

'Okay, I suppose,' Dora began as Joe rejoined her on the sofa and took her hand in his.

Joanie looked at the pair and frowned. 'Dora, is something wrong? Joe looks dead serious.'

'No, not really,' Dora began and then started laughing as her brother leant forward, looking worried. 'I'll put you out of your misery. You're going to be aunty and uncle to not just one, but *two* little blighters very soon.'

Joanie let out a yell and jumped to her feet. 'Twins! Oh my God. No wonder you're so huge.' She jumped up and down and heaved Dora to her feet with an extra push from Joe. 'I can't even get my arms around you properly. Oh, I'm so excited and thrilled for you.'

Frank got up and hugged his sister, his blue eyes moist, and he shook Joe by the hand. 'Well, well, congratulations. This calls for a celebration. Have you anything in, mate?' he directed at Joe.

'There's a drop of whisky and sherry left over from Christmas in the kitchen cupboard,' Joe said. 'Dora, are you joining us?'

'Not for me, love. I get awful heartburn with sherry at the minute,' she said, sitting back down. 'I'll have a cuppa when you lot have drunk us dry.'

Joe and Frank went into the kitchen and Joanie flopped down beside Dora on the sofa and shook her head. 'I just can't take it in. I bet you're still in shock, too.'

'Just a bit.' Dora laughed. 'We chose some names before you two arrived. Carol and Joanie, or David and James.'

Joanie nodded. 'I love Carol, but don't inflict *my* name on the poor little thing. Give her something more modern. Why not Joanna? It's similar but much nicer.'

Dora frowned. 'Do you prefer that? You can choose, Aunty Joanie.'

'Oh, thank you for the honour.' Joanie smiled happily. 'Then I choose Joanna. It's really modern. Joanie's a bit old-fashioned now.'

'Joanna it is then,' Dora announced as Joe and Frank carried in the drinks and a mug of tea for her. 'Slight change of a girl's name,' she told Joe. She held up her mug and proposed a toast. 'Here's to Carol and Joanna, or David and James.'

Ivy Bennett lifted the frying pans onto the large gas stove and dropped a lump of dripping into each. She swirled the greasy dollops around to coat the pans and pricked a mountain of sausages with a fork before placing them into one of the pans of hot smoking fat. In no time she had eggs frying in the other pan and proceeded to slice a loaf of bread while keeping an eye on the food. There was no bacon today, although she wasn't complaining as the sausages looked a bit meatier than the last lot the butcher had delivered; a sure sign that things were looking up on the meat ration front. She fished the eggs out of the pan, slid them onto a large enamel plate and popped it onto the rack above the stove to keep warm.

The Sunday nightshift would be down for their breakfasts soon. She liked to have everything ready for the hungry men who would wolf down their food and then head off home for a well-deserved sleep. As soon as they left, the early Monday shift arrived, many of them wanting a breakfast too; they usually allowed themselves ten minutes to eat and washed it down with a mug of hot, sweet tea. The men didn't have the luxury of time to waste, so having their food ready and waiting was Ivy's daily mission. She looked pointedly at the clock on the wall above the stove as her assistant Flo hurried in, same apology as always: the tram was late again.

'I can't understand why yours is always late and mine's always on time,' Ivy said. 'Try getting the earlier one. I need you here on the dot of seven thirty tomorrow.'

Flo hurriedly took off her jacket, slipped on her white overall and topped it with a navy and white checked pinny, same as Ivy's. She pushed her untidy mop of hair under a matching turban.

Ivy sniffed and turned her attention back to the sausages. 'Get that bread under the grill for me and butter it when it's done. They'll be down in less than five minutes.' She turned the heat off under the pans, lifted the sausages onto dishes and transferred everything over to the warmers. 'Don't let that toast burn, I've only one small loaf left until the delivery arrives.'

She hoped Joe Rodgers would be in for breakfast. Although if he started going on again about the twins that he and his wife were expecting, she'd go mad. He talked non-stop to anyone who would listen about how wonderful Dora was. How the baby she was carrying had turned out to be not just one but two.

Dora had everything and it made Ivy sick. There'd been no doting parents to look after *her* when she'd been widowed and miscarried her baby during the war. No older brother who'd walk over hot coals for her either, and she had no close friends to turn to. No one from the ROF knew her past history, and that's how she liked to keep it. She couldn't handle sympathy and had built a hard shell around herself. By working hard she could switch off her emotions. The ROF canteen had become her second home and her world.

Dora Rodgers didn't know how lucky she was, or how easy her life was either, Ivy thought. Her own life consisted of living in a tiny rented flat at the top of an old Victorian house, with the owner's elderly cat for company. She wasn't short of male admirers, but sadly they were in the main married men.

It was Joe Rodgers she'd had her eye on from the first time he'd walked into her canteen early last year. She'd always been attracted to him, even though he gave her no real encouragement. He was polite and friendly, but he was like that with everyone. She followed his band everywhere; went to as many of the dances that she could get to, dragging Flo along as she had no one else to take, and she was someone to partner on the floor with.

Flo had buttered the toast and was stacking plates ready for the onslaught. Ivy grabbed one of the plates, put two sausages on it and surreptitiously slid it to one end of the serving area. 'One sausage, one egg and one slice of toast today,' she instructed as the doors swung open and the nightshift hurried in.

Once served, the men took to the tables and Flo pushed the tea trolley around while Ivy got more plates out ready for the day shift. The two sausages were still hidden away and she fried more eggs and sliced her last loaf, ready for toast. Her nerves were getting the better of her now that it was nearly time for Joe to dash in for his hurried breakfast. He'd been coming in for his dinner lately as well, after a spell of bringing sarnies from home. Likely as not Dora had got fed up of fussing around him like most wives seemed to do after a few months of marriage. He'd be even more neglected when she had two babies to care for. That's when Ivy planned to step up her campaign of making sure he was properly fed while he was at work.

Flo brought the tea trolley back laden with dirty pots and cutlery and started to fill the sink with hot water and soap suds.

The night workers called their goodbyes as the day shift arrived. Ivy's heart sank when she couldn't see Joe amongst them. She'd just about given up hope when he dashed in and hurried straight across to the counter, his brown hair flopping into his eyes.

'I bet you've nothing left,' he gasped as Ivy produced a plate with two sausages and two slices of toast and a fried egg.

'I made sure I saved you something.'

'Oh, Ivy, you're an absolute doll, do you know that?' Joe said with a broad grin, and handed her some money. 'Bloody motorbike broke down. I had to run for the bus and then the connecting tram was late. Something I could do without now Dora's so close to dropping the babies. Thank you.' He hurried away with his meal and Flo took him a mug of tea over to the table where his mates were just finishing eating.

Ivy preened behind the counter. He'd called her a doll. What a nice compliment. She watched as the other men left the canteen. Joe was sitting alone now, wolfing down his breakfast in-between slurps of hot tea. She poured herself a mug of tea while Flo started washing up behind the screens at the back of the kitchen area.

'Mind if I sit here for my break?' Ivy said, sidling over to Joe's table.

Chapter Fifteen

Dora finished the toast and tea Joe had left her and heaved herself out of bed. She drew back the curtains and opened the window. It was another lovely, sunny day with blue skies and just the occasional fluffy white cloud. Her dad had planted seeds in the borders at the front in the spring and they were now a colourful mass of assorted flowers. Sweet williams and pinks nodded their heads alongside marigolds and night-scented stock. The lawn looked neat and trim and she pictured how it would look in a very short time with the twin pram that Joe's mother had bought them standing in the middle, her two sleeping babies inside.

Little Freddie Parker was riding up and down the pavement and Dolly waved as she pushed Alice in her trolley.

'Do you need owt from the shops, Dora?' Dolly called.

'No thanks, Dolly. Mam will be here soon and she was getting some shopping in for us.'

'Okay, if you need me, I'll be back in a bit.'

Dora had a quick strip-wash; she couldn't manage the bath when she was alone in the house in case she got stuck. In the bedroom she gazed at the dress she'd laid out on the bed and shook her head. Yet another huge tent, this time navy and white spotted, but it would have to do. It wasn't for much longer anyway and then she could cut them all up and make herself some nice summer dresses and skirts. No point in wasting good material. She was sick of wearing giant size clothes and huge knickers that looked like parachutes. God knows what Joe thought of her appearance at the moment, although he was nothing but loving and kind. She slipped the dress on over her head and checked her appearance in the mirror. She looked pale with shadows under her eyes, but no wonder: she'd hardly slept a wink for the last week. The babies had quietened down a little in the last day or so, but prior to that they'd been on the move night and day. The midwife had called in yesterday to check her over, and everything had been okay. It could be any day now she'd said, and Dora was ready and waiting.

She waddled into the sewing room, now taken over by baby paraphernalia. Her dad and Frank had made another cradle on Friday, painted it Saturday and brought it round last night. She could still smell the fresh paint. Joanie had made two pretty patchwork coverlets and matching pillowcases for the cradles. The cupboards and drawers that had held her sewing equipment were stocked with neatly folded nappies, sheets and blankets, tiny vests and nighties. Her mam had brought a wicker basket round that she'd lined in yellow and white gingham and the members of her WI group from the village hall had filled with useful items: Johnson's baby powder and soap, nappy pins, Fuller's Earth Cream and fluffy white flannels and matching towels. Joe's mother had kept the twin pram up at her house for now. It was standing covered with a sheet in the morning room. Mam had said it was bad luck to bring a pram into the house until the babies had arrived. Dora was certain it was an old wives' tale, but she was taking no chances.

She pottered into the kitchen and swung the back door open to let some air in. The bungalow felt stifling as she drew the sitting room curtains back and opened the window in there. She switched on the radio: Bing Crosby was singing 'Swinging on a Star' and she joined in. She really missed going out with Joe at the weekends and dancing to his band. As the announcer read out the next request for 'Five Minutes More' by Frank Sinatra, Dora sank down onto the sofa and put her swollen feet up on the coffee table. Her mam had offered to babysit occasionally once the babies were old enough and Joe said he'd get a single bed for the spare room, so that she could stay over.

She hated not being with him and was sure that Ivy woman would be making the most of her being out of action. Joe had been eating in the canteen since she'd been unable to get up early and make his sarnies. He had laughed at her when she'd had a grumble last week. Said she was imagining things that were never going to happen. And that yes, Ivy was always in the canteen when he went in for food, as she was in charge, but there was nothing he could do about that and she mustn't get worked up about it. She knew it was those hormone things at work again, making her feel jealous, but she couldn't help it.

The babies did their usual wriggle just as she'd got herself comfy, dancing on her bladder and getting their feet caught in her ribs. Christ, she needed a wee *again.* She banged her mug down onto the table, slopping tea onto last night's *Echo,* and heaved herself to her feet. She lumbered to the bathroom and let out a yelp as warm liquid trickled down her legs and pooled by her bare feet on the lino floor. 'Damn it, now you've made me wet myself, you little buggers.' She yanked off her soggy underwear and filled the sink with water for another wash. But the liquid continued to trickle and then a tightening sensation around her middle, followed by a breath-taking abdominal pain, made her call out in fright. She hadn't wet herself after all; the liquid was her waters breaking. Oh God and her mam hadn't arrived yet. Dora hurriedly dried her legs and bent to wipe the floor with the towel, but she couldn't reach and another pain shot through her. She caught hold of the sink to steady herself. If she moved there'd be a trail of water over the carpets, but she couldn't stay in the bathroom: she needed to get to the phone and then onto her bed.

She grabbed another hand towel off the rail, folded it and held it between her legs while she shuffled to the hall. The numbers for the midwife, Joe's works and one of her mam's neighbours were written on a pad on the small telephone table and she called the midwife first. She was assured that someone would be with her as soon as possible and to make sure they were able to obtain access to the house. Dora made sure the front door was already unlocked, then called the number for Joe. The ROF workforce had a telephone in a small alcove in the canteen, and was allowed to take personal calls for emergencies only. The message was passed to the worker, who was expected to use their discretion about returning the call. Dora held onto the doorframe and tried to cross her legs to stop another wave of pain from taking her breath away. The call was answered by a woman but with music playing in the canteen background she didn't recognise the voice.

'This is Dora Rodgers,' she gasped. 'Can you get a message to my husband Joe Rodgers on the factory floor, please? Tell him I've gone into labour. Thank you.' There was a sharp intake of breath from the person on the end of the line, but before Dora could say anything more the phone went dead.

She hung up, hoping the message would be passed on, and made her way into the bedroom where everything was ready and waiting. The delivery packs were on top of the chest of drawers alongside several old towels that her mam had boiled, so they were sterilised. They would be disposed of after the birth. A plastic sheet was already on the bed, under the cotton sheet, to protect the mattress, just in case her waters broke during the night. There was nothing to do now other than wait for the midwife, her mam and Joe. Not that he'd be much use, and as her mam had said, birthing wasn't a man's place, but she just needed to know that he was close by and could hold her in his arms when it was all over. She folded back the green candlewick bedspread and blankets, spread a couple of the old towels on top of the sheet and hoisted herself up onto the bed to wait.

* * *

Ivy slammed down the phone, took a deep breath and went back to making a large pan of custard. That's one message she wasn't passing on to anyone. If Joe went dashing off now he'd miss the dinner he was looking forward to. Dora could lump it. She didn't need him there; she'd have her mother and the midwife and probably a doctor too, with it being twins. Joe would only get in the way. Better he stayed here for the time being.

Flo came back into the kitchen and started to sort out the cutlery and plates.

'Right. Get ready for the onslaught,' Ivy said as the bell signalled the first dinnertime shift. Joe was usually amongst the second lot of workers at one o'clock. She'd make sure he got two dumplings to keep him going. The doors swung open and the hungry workers surged towards the counter, picking up trays from the end to carry their hot plates to the tables.

'A good scoop of stew and one dumpling each,' Ivy called to Flo, who was ladling the stew onto plates.

The hungry workforce tucked in. The time flew by as it always did on the dinnertime shift and the next lot of workers came hurrying in, Joe one of the last, as usual.

His face lit up as Ivy passed him his laden plate and she watched as he carried it back to the table and joined his workmates. She heard them ribbing him about the double dumplings, threatening to tell his missus. He didn't rise to the bait, just got stuck in. His neighbour, Eric, seated opposite him, lit a cigarette and asked him how Dora was doing.

'She's weary, mate. Can hardly move, poor love. Still, she could start any day now. I'll try and ring her before I go back upstairs if the phone's free. Otherwise it'll have to wait until the afternoon break. Her mam was coming over again today to look after her, and your Dolly always knocks on to see if she needs anything. Still can't believe we're having two.'

'Aye, I'll bet,' Eric said with a grin. 'You'll enjoy them.'

Ivy was keeping one ear on Joe and Eric's conversation while she cleared the table behind them. Joe had finished his stew and she fetched his pudding over.

'Bloody hell, *we* have to queue up and get our own,' another pal shouted from the top of the table. 'Stop mollycoddling him, Ivy. It's his missus that's carrying the babbies, not him.'

Ivy could feel her cheeks warming. Was she making her favouritism a bit too obvious? 'I could see he'd finished his stew and I was going to the counter anyway,' she blustered. 'If you lot were a bit more polite to me you might get treated with a bit of respect, too.' She swung the trolley round with such force it hit Eric's chair leg and he dropped his ciggie on the table. 'Oops, hit a nerve, have they?' he teased as Ivy flounced away.

She busied herself behind the counter and glanced across at Joe, who was shovelling his pudding away like he was starving. When he'd finished he got to his feet and carried his empty dish over.

'To save your lovely legs,' he said. 'Thank you, that was delicious. Ignore that lot. I'm sorry if they embarrassed you. They don't mean any harm.'

She half-smiled and took his dish. Lovely legs, eh? 'See you later at tea break,' she said as he nodded and went back to join his mates, who were getting ready to go back upstairs to the factory floor.

Chapter Sixteen

Dora cried out in agony as the midwife knocked on the front door, pushed it open and called out that she was here.

'I'm in the bedroom,' Dora shouted. 'Oh thank goodness you're here. I was getting really frightened.'

'Oh, you're on your own.' Nurse Dawson hurried to her side and took charge. 'Where's your mother?'

'She's not here yet, and I've called for Joe. His bike broke down earlier, so he'll have to get the bus and tram home. He shouldn't be too long now, though.' Dora took another deep breath and let out a yell.

'I'm just going to get unpacked and make sure we've got everything we need. Doctor Owens will be here later.'

As Nurse Dawson laid out the contents of the delivery packs the front door opened again and Dora's mam called out that it was only her. 'Is the midwife here, chuck? There's a bicycle near the front door.'

'We're in the bedroom, Mrs Evans. Dora's gone into labour, but she's doing very well. I need some boiled water, so if you want to get the kettle on the go, I'll examine her and see how we're doing.'

'Oh my lord, I'm sorry I'm late, today of all days,' Mam said. 'Have you let Joe know?'

Dora nodded. 'Ages ago,' she grunted as a spasm of pain hit her. She lay back on the pillows and grimaced as the midwife wiped her face with a cool flannel and then listened to the babies' heartbeats with the ear trumpet pressed close to Dora's tummy.

'Is everything okay?' Dora asked anxiously. 'I can't feel them moving very much at all now.'

'Movement usually slows down in labour. Everything is fine, both heartbeats are loud and clear, that's what I like to hear,' the midwife reassured her. 'Try and relax a little in-between your contractions. Take some deep breaths. Have you thought of any names for the babies?'

Dora nodded. 'They're written on the pad on the bedside table. In order as they come out. But if it's one of each, it's the first names. Owwweee,' she gasped. She'd never felt such pain. Surely that couldn't be right? But the midwife didn't seem unduly worried. She closed her eyes and tried to relax and do the deep breathing she'd been told about at the antenatal clinic. It was supposed to help, though God knew how. She groaned. 'I wish Joe was here. I need to know he's close by.'

'He won't be long now,' the midwife said, patting her hand reassuringly.

At three o'clock Joe went into the canteen for his afternoon tea break, hoping to get a chance to use the phone to call Dora. It hadn't been free at dinnertime, but no news was good news and there'd been no messages brought up to him. He looked across to see Eric waving frantically and holding the phone out.

'What's up?' he called hurrying over.

'It's my missus, you'd best get home. Dora's been in labour since this morning, apparently. Dolly popped in and Dora's mam was worried because you'd not shown up yet. I was just coming upstairs to get you.'

'I'd no idea,' Joe said, snatching the phone. 'Dolly, tell them I'll be with them as soon as I can. I'll get a taxi. Hang the expense.'

He handed the phone to Eric, who told him Dora had rung ages ago and spoken to a woman.

'No one gave me the message. Bet it was that dozy bloody Flo.' He yelled across to where Flo was pouring tea and Ivy was slicing seed cake. 'Who took a call from my wife this morning?'

Both looked up and Ivy shrugged and carried on slicing cake. Flo shook her head. 'Not me, Joe. It's not rung all day as far as I know.'

'Really? Well that's odd.'

Eric called across that he'd got a number from Dolly and had booked him a taxi for as soon as possible. 'Thanks, mate,' Joe called back. 'Dolly said Dora spoke to a woman,' he told Ivy and Flo. 'No one gave me the message. She's in labour and needs me.' He hurried away and out of the canteen to collect his things from upstairs and to wait in the foyer for his taxi.

He was home within fifteen minutes and dashed indoors to be met by his mother-in-law wringing her hands in the hall-way as his wife screamed in pain in their bedroom. He flung his working things onto the hall floor and hurried to wash his hands at the kitchen sink. Before he could say anything a baby's cry rent the air and Dora's mam burst into tears and flung her arms around him.

'Oh, thank the lord for that,' she cried. 'Doctor's in with her now. She's having a hard time, Joe. I really wish she was in the maternity home with all its facilities.'

'I didn't get the message,' Joe said, tears running down his cheeks. 'I'd have been here hours ago if I'd known.'

'You're here now, that's all that matters. They sent me out while they delivered the baby. I'll pop in and see what it is. It's got a good pair of lungs anyway. She's been crying for Joanie but the midwife said she couldn't go in with her, so there was no point in getting her back from work.'

Joe took a deep breath and leant against the sink unit, his heart beating overtime. He should have been here. That blasted Ivy, he bet it was her. Dora was always saying the woman was jeal-ous and he'd laughed her concerns away. But surely she wouldn't be so cruel? Nobody would at a time like this. He held his breath as the bedroom door opened and Dora's mam came out holding a little bundle wrapped in a white sheet.

'Go and sit on the sofa and I'll introduce you to your daughter,' she said, tears tumbling down her lined cheeks.

Joe did as he was told and the little bundle was placed into his arms and then Dora's mam dashed back into the bedroom and closed the door.

He sat silently as the light blue eyes peered at him unblinkingly, and the wrinkled brow creased further in a slight frown. Her hair was brown, like his, but her eye colour was much lighter than Dora's bright blue so he guessed that would change later and maybe his firstborn would have hazel eyes like his own. 'Hello, little lady,' he said softly and stroked her cheek with his index finger. 'I'm your daddy. I guess you must be Carol.' Joe felt a rush of love for the tiny baby in his arms and prayed that the next one wouldn't take too long to deliver as Dora was screaming at the top of her voice again. It was a shame they wouldn't allow Joanie to be here with her. This was a time when his wife really needed the support of her best friend. Tears filled his eyes: he'd never felt so full of emotion in his life: fear, pride, love, anxiety, all coursed through his veins and he sent up a prayer to God to let it all be over soon.

His daughter had closed her eyes and he cuddled her close, feeling a bond with her already. As she slept in his arms he promised to protect her and love her always. Dora's mam joined him, once more banished from the bedroom as the doctor and Nurse Dawson prepared to help baby number two into the world.

'As soon as the next one's out she wants to see you,' she said. 'They're going to use forceps because the poor little bugger's got itself stuck. Don't worry,' she added as a look of panic flashed across Joe's face. 'It does happen with twins when there's not been the space for the pair to get into the right position for birthing. Now little madam here is out, the other one has moved down, but it needs a bit of extra help.'

Joe nodded, lost for words as Dora cursed and swore like he'd never heard her swear before.

'She's a bonny little thing, isn't she?' Dora's mam said, stroking the top of her granddaughter's downy head. 'I've made a cottage pie for your tea, it'll just need heating through, and the washing's on the line, so don't forget to fetch it indoors and put it on the clothes rack later.'

Joe nodded, wondering how the heck his mother-in-law could think straight and hold such a normal conversation when all this was going on around them. He handed the baby to her granny and got up to pace the floor. His head swimming, he felt like he might pass out at any minute. 'Oh God, I feel sick,' he gasped and dashed to the toilet, where he dropped to his knees and threw up his dinner in the pan. He pulled the chain and sat on the side of the bath, taking deep breaths, and then washed his face and brushed his teeth. Back in the hall he could hear Dora cursing him to kingdom come and that she was never having any more kids, and then one final heart-rending scream followed by the reedy wail of another baby. Jesus. His legs gave way and he broke down and cried like he'd never cried before. Dora's mam came into the hall holding baby number one and told him to go back into the sitting room while she went in to see Dora. She handed the baby to him and pushed him gently towards the door.

He sat back down on the sofa and held the baby to his shoulder, patting her back as she made little snuffling sounds and sighs.

It seemed a while before Dora's mam returned, looking weary. He sat forward, cold fingers of fear running down his spine. 'What's wrong?' He realised it had gone quiet now and there was no baby crying.

'They're just sorting Dora out. She's torn a bit and Doctor Owens is stitching her up. Baby's a bit tired and the midwife's washing her. She'll bring her through when she's got her dressed.'

'She? So it's another girl?'

'Identical to that one, just a bit smaller.' Dora's mam smiled.

'And is Dora okay?' He wished they'd let him see her. She'd have been worrying why he hadn't come home after she'd called. He hated to think of her in pain and needing him close by and he wasn't there

'She'll be fine, love. I'll stay over tonight and then I'm on hand for tomorrow when you go off to work.'

'I'm not going to work,' Joe said. 'I'd arranged to have my holidays as and when the babies arrived, and the ROF's been great in sorting that out for me. I need to pop in for my wages on Thursday, but I'm off for two weeks now.'

'That's good, love. But I'll still stay here tonight, just in case. Dolly said she's got a camp bed we can borrow. You can go and get it later and tell her your news at the same time.'

Dora gritted her teeth as Doctor Owens inserted the last stitch down below. He'd put something on her tear to numb it, but she could still feel the needle going into her flesh. She couldn't believe the agony she'd suffered.

'All done, Mrs Rodgers.' Doctor Owens dropped the needle into the kidney dish on the bedside table. 'I'll be in to see you tomorrow morning. Nurse Dawson will stay to help you establish breastfeeding, and she'll also pop back this evening. If there are any problems at all during the night, you only need to call us. Well done, and congratulations. You have two beautiful little girls.'

Dora smiled wearily as he left the room.

'I'm going to take baby through to your mam, Dora,' Nurse Dawson said. 'Then I'll come back and get you freshened up and ready to see your husband.'

Dora looked up as Joe came into the room and lay down on the bed beside her. He kissed her and stroked the hair from her eyes. 'I'm so tired,' she whispered. 'I could sleep for a week.'

'I bet you could. I'm so proud of you.'

She smiled, feeling sore but blissfully happy. It had been a nightmare of an afternoon, and not one she'd like to repeat in a hurry. But they now had two beautiful identical daughters, so it had all been worth it. Carol weighed slightly more at six pounds five ounces while Joanna was six pounds two. They were good weights, according to Nurse Dawson; combined it was no wonder Dora could hardly move during the last few weeks. Her mam had phoned Mr Jones and he'd gone to bring Dora's delighted dad and Frank to the phone. Frank and an over-excited Joanie, her arms full of parcels, had popped in earlier, but only for half an hour as Mam said it was quite long enough for the first night.

Joanie cuddled both of her nieces while Dora unwrapped matching white knitted matinee jackets and two white crochet shawls with lemon edging. 'These are gorgeous,' she said, examining the delicate web-like crochet. 'Your mam is so clever.'

'She is,' Joanie said. 'Nice that they're both girls with those shawls being so dainty.' Her eyes filled with tears as she gazed at her nieces' little faces. 'They're so beautiful. I can't really tell them apart. That's going to be a hard one as they get bigger. You'll have to use different colour hair ribbons so we don't get confused. Oh, I'm going to spoil you two something rotten,' she promised.

Dora laughed. 'Joanna's a little smaller, but not enough to make much difference. So are you and Frank up for being godparents then? When we get around to sorting things out, that is.'

Frank's face lit up and he nodded. 'I'd be very proud. It would be an honour.'

Joanie smiled. 'Indeed it would. Are you going to have a little cuddle, Uncle Frank?'

He looked nervously at Dora, who nodded encouragement. 'Go on, they won't bite you. Take one at a time.'

Dora's eyes filled as she looked at the tender way her brother stroked Carol's rounded cheek. He looked across and his own eyes were moist. 'She's beautiful, our Dora. They both are. Can't wait until they're old enough to take on the park and push them on the swings.'

Joe laughed. 'We've a few sleepless nights to go before then, mate.'

'What did your mother say, Joe?' Joanie asked, rocking little Joanna who had started to stir and snuffle.

'Oh you know, she was her usual reserved self, but there was a hint of excitement in her voice and she's coming over in a taxi on Saturday afternoon to see us all.'

Mam popped her head around the bedroom door. 'Right, I'll make a nice pot of tea and then you two can go home,' she directed at Frank and Joanie. 'Our Dora needs some rest. You can come again tomorrow after work.'

Both babies looked like their father, Dora thought, as she cuddled Carol to sleep while Joe had a wash and shave. Joanna lay on the bed beside her, cocooned in a sheet, just her tiny round face showing, dark lashes sweeping her cheeks. They had Joe's brown hair colour and matching dimples in their chins. Although their eyes were light blue at the moment, she expected they'd change to hazel eventually. She lay the now sleeping Carol beside her sister, imagining the family fun they'd have as the girls grew. Birthdays, Christmases and days at the beach in New Brighton. Their first day at school. So much to look forward to; so many things to show them. She couldn't wait to make pretty identical dresses for them and push them out in the twin pram.

Joe popped his head around the door, disturbing her reverie. 'Just popping to Dolly's to get the camp bed for your mam to sleep on.'

She nodded. 'I'm planning outings for the future,' she said. 'We'll have such fun with them. Double trouble.' She laughed as a big smile lit up his face.

* * *

Dolly was agog with excitement and bursting with gossip as she let Joe in. She congratulated him with a hug and a sloppy kiss on the cheek and Eric shook his hand and slapped him on the back.

'Come on through into the sitting room,' Dolly said. 'The bed's all ready for you to take. Have you enough spare blankets?'

'Yes, thanks, that's taken care of. I intend to get a single bed for the spare room, just haven't got around to it yet and Dora's mam insists on staying tonight.'

'Is Dora okay?' Dolly asked.

'She is now. She had a right rough time though. Sounded horrendous. Little Joanna was stuck. Doctor yanked her out with forceps and Dora had to have stitches. She doesn't want any more babies, she's made that quite clear.'

'Oh we all say that, and threaten to kill our husbands as well, but we soon forget it,' Dolly said, laughing.

'I'm not so sure Dora will. But we'll see.'

'Fancy that Ivy woman not passing on Dora's message this morning. That was a wicked thing to do.' Dolly pursed her lips. 'She needs locking up, that one.'

'Dolly,' Eric said, shaking his head. 'We don't know for sure that it was Ivy who took the message. I told you in confidence. You can't go accusing without proof. I'm sure Joe will sort it out when he's back at work.'

'I'll have a word when I go in to get my wages on Thursday,' Joe said. 'Right, I'd best get back and sort out this bed. Thanks very much for the loan of it.'

As he strolled back to his bungalow the midwife was arriving for her final call. He let her in, put the bed in the hall and then stood outside and lit a cigarette. He stared up at the clear night sky, peppered with bright stars, and wondered which one was his dad. When he was a little boy his late granny had told him that stars were people who had gone to heaven and were keeping an eye on all their loved ones. It was a nice thought to hang on to. He wondered if it was true what Dolly had said, that it *was* Ivy who hadn't passed on Dora's message. Why would she do that? She'd always been nice to him, giving him extra food and always pleasant and smiling. It didn't make sense and must be a mistake. He'd be certain to talk to her when he saw her next, and get to the bottom of it all.

Chapter Seventeen

Dora winded Carol, and leant over the side of the bed to put her contented daughter back in the cradle. Joe slept soundly beside her; he hadn't even stirred when Carol whimpered and there seemed no point in disturbing him; feeding them was something only she could do. She leant to pick up Joanna; she wasn't awake, but if she fed her now, it would mean she could have a few hours' sleep before they awoke for the early morning feed. The midwife had told her to try to keep their feeding times as close together as she possibly could, otherwise she'd be at it all day and night as well. Joanna would soon stir once she'd persuaded her to latch onto the breast. She tickled her under the chin and blew gently into her face but there was no response from the baby. Dora frowned and pushed the tip of her finger into her mouth to encourage her to suck, and then tried to get her to take a nipple, but Joanna was very still, her arms flopping limply by her sides. Dora realised how cold she felt to the touch and her stomach turned over.

'Joe,' she screamed and shook him by the shoulder.

He awoke with a jump and sat up, blinking in the bright light of the bedside lamp. 'What's wrong?'

'Joanna won't feed and she's all floppy,' she cried.

Joe looked at the tiny baby lying against Dora's breast. He took her in his arms, flicking at her feet as the midwife had done earlier in an attempt to get Joanna to feed.

Dora looked on in horror as he blew into her mouth, trying to rouse her to take a breath on her own, but she lay limply in his arms.

'Try again, Joe, please,' Dora begged him.

'Come on, little one, breathe,' he cried, his frantic eyes meeting hers. 'I need to call the doctor and wake your mam. No, you're not allowed out of bed,' he said as Dora made to get up. 'Try and feed her again. Maybe she's just in a deep sleep or something.' He handed the baby back to Dora, whose tears dripped onto the tiny face. Joanna didn't even flinch. As Joe shot out of the room Dora knew in her heart of hearts their little daughter was lost to them. She howled heartbrokenly as Joe came back followed by her mam.

'There's an ambulance on its way,' he said, shrugging helplessly. 'Doctor Owens will meet us at the hospital.'

Dora silently handed Joanna to Joe and turned to her mam, who enveloped her in her arms while she sobbed on her shoulder. 'Why, Mam? Why? She was fine earlier.' She missed the look of despair that passed between Mam and Joe as her mam rocked her back and forth like she was a child while Joe went to answer the door and let in the ambulance attendants.

One of them saw to Dora as the other checked Joanna and then, wrapping her tightly in a sheet, he rushed out to the ambulance with her.

'We're taking you to hospital,' Dora's attendant told her. 'Your doctor is meeting us there. Mr Rodgers, you can accompany your wife.'

Still crying, her heart breaking, Dora allowed them to tuck her up on a stretcher and carry her outside while Joe followed, leaving her mam behind to look after Carol. In the ambulance one of the attendants worked on Joanna, trying to revive her, but Dora knew the resuscitation attempt was in vain.

At the hospital they were greeted by Doctor Owens who instructed a nurse to take Joanna. Dora cried out for Joe as she was rushed into a cubicle while Doctor Owens spoke to the ambulance attendants. The nurse beckoned Joe to come to Dora's side.

She swished the curtains closed and left them alone. Joe reached for Dora's hand as she sobbed inconsolably.

He chewed his lip as tears ran down his cheeks.

Doctor Owens appeared with a nurse and explained to them that there was nothing they could do for Joanna.

Joe held her in his arms as Dora screamed for her baby, begging Doctor Owens to check again. The last thing she remembered was the doctor telling her that he was going to give her something to help her sleep.

Joe sat beside Dora's mam as she bottle-fed Carol, who was sucking enthusiastically at the teat, her eyes closed in ecstasy. At Doctor Owens' request, Nurse Dawson had turned up last night with powdered baby milk, feeding bottles and teats. She'd shown Dora's mam what to do and how often to feed Carol. Joe had just come back from sitting all night with Dora, who had been transferred to a small private side ward that nursed newly bereaved mothers, and she was still under sedation. Doctor Owens had told Joe to keep baby Carol at home if Dora's mam could look after her. Mam was more than happy to do whatever she could and Nurse Dawson had promised to pop in again today on her rounds.

'Thanks so much for being here. I don't know what I'd do without you. I can't believe this is happening to us.' Tears trickled down Joe's cheeks and he dashed them away with the back of his hand. 'Why?'

Dora's mam winded Carol and laid her in the little white cradle, tucking a sheet around her. 'I don't know, Joe. It's so unfair. I feel numb. I can't believe what's happened either. But I have to keep going for this little one while you look after my Dora for me. She'll be heartbroken. She can't look after Carol while she's under sedation and she certainly won't be able to breastfeed her any more. They'll keep her in there for a while so she gets some rest. She should have had the babies in hospital. Birthing twins is always a risk at home.'

Joe shook his head. 'I asked the nurses and they said it could have happened in there or here. There are no guarantees. There'll be a post-mortem. Our poor little girl. We didn't even have time to get her christened.'

'We need to let Dora's dad and Frank and Joanie know and your mother. I can do it if it will help. But we can leave it for a couple of hours; it's too early to be waking folk up just yet.' She stopped as there came a quiet knock on the front door. Joe went to answer it and let in a white-faced Dolly in her dressing gown and slippers, her red hair standing out around her head like a wonky halo.

'We saw the ambulance last night,' she began. 'But we didn't want to bother you, and then I spotted you getting out of a taxi a few minutes ago, Joe. What's happened? Is Dora okay?'

Joe invited her to sit down while Dora's mam went to put the kettle on. Joe told Dolly the news and her hand flew to her mouth as tears filled her eyes.

'Oh my God,' she wailed. 'Poor little girl, and poor, poor Dora. Oh and you too, Joe. You were that thrilled to bits last night. I'm so sorry, I really am.'

Joe shook his head. 'It's not really sunk in yet.'

Dolly looked down at Carol lying contentedly in her cradle near the sofa. 'Bless her, the little love. You must let me know if you need any help at all over the next few weeks. I can take my kids to my mam's any time, so please don't hesitate to ask.'

'Thank you, chuck,' Mam said, handing Dolly a mug of hot sweet tea. 'I've put extra sugar in it for you.'

Dora slowly opened her eyes and looked around in a confused state. Her head felt strange and she didn't recognise her surroundings. The walls were half glass and the narrow bed definitely wasn't hers and Joe's. She licked her dry lips and called out for him, but there was no answer. Why wasn't he with her? The door opened and a young girl, wearing the pale blue dress and starched white apron and cap of a student nurse, popped her head around, a bright smile on her face.

'Hello, Mrs Rodgers. How are you feeling now?' She walked over to the bed and helped Dora sit up, adjusting the backrest and pillows. 'Can I get you some tea and toast?'

'What happened? Why am I here?' A feeling of panic overwhelmed Dora as she realised she was in a hospital room. She was conscious of stillness about her body and dropped her hands down onto her empty stomach. She glanced wildly around. 'My babies! Where are my babies?' She must have given birth, but she had no recollection of it.

'I'll just get Sister,' the young nurse said and hurried away. She was back in seconds accompanied by an older woman wearing the navy uniform of a senior nurse, who introduced herself as Sister Smith and took a seat beside the bed and held Dora's hand.

'Where are my babies?' Dora demanded again, feeling terrified by the sympathetic look in the older woman's eyes. 'What have you done with them? Where's Joe? Where's my husband?'

'Dora, listen to me,' Sister Smith began quietly. 'You had your babies yesterday, but sadly one of them passed away. Your other little girl is at home with your husband and your mother. She's being well looked after. Your husband will be in later to see you.' Her words were drowned out by hysterical screams and she asked the young nurse to fetch a doctor immediately while she held Dora in her arms. Dora clutched at her stomach and, in-between sobs, tried to explain that she needed the toilet as the nurse came back.

A bedpan was brought to the room and the young nurse helped her to sit on it while Sister Smith left to get her notes in readiness for the doctor arriving.

Dora was aware of an acute abdominal pain and a sudden rush that wasn't urine. She cried out as blood flooded into the bedpan beneath her. The nurse helped her to lie back and removed the pan as Sister Smith rushed back into the room with a white-coated doctor.

'Haemorrhage,' the doctor exclaimed and instructed that his patient be prepared immediately for theatre. 'I'll sedate her first.'

Dora was feeling terrified and confused. The jab of a needle in her upper arm was the last thing she was conscious of before slipping into oblivion.

Joe left the wages office feeling a bit better about asking for extra time off. They'd given him six weeks in total, with pay. Two weeks' holiday and four weeks' compassionate leave. The girls in the office had also had a whip round and had given him a parcel for Carol and a large bunch of flowers for Dora. He felt relieved at the extra time off as her mam was looking so tired and he needed to be there for her. Dora was still under sedation in hospital and an emergency operation she'd had yesterday had taken its toll. All in all his young wife was in a bad way and she'd need a lot of looking after when they allowed her home. He checked his watch; the lads would be coming down for their morning break, so he made his way to the canteen. He knew he had to speak to Ivy, if only to put a stop to the rumours. If she hadn't taken the call then she must be feeling really upset by all the accusations that Dolly had been quick to report on.

He strolled into the canteen. Ivy looked up and he saw a flush creep up her neck. She quickly looked away and said something to Flo.

'Ivy, can I speak to you, please?' he began. 'In private, if you don't mind.' Flo's slack jaw had dropped even further as he spoke, her curious eyes wide in her narrow face.

'Bring us two mugs of tea, Flo,' Ivy ordered and led Joe across to the far side of the room. She sat down at a table and gestured for Joe to take a seat.

Joe sat down and offered her a cigarette. She declined so he lit one for himself and sat back, staring at her through the cloud of smoke he exhaled. Flo bustled across with the mugs of tea and Ivy dismissed her with a flap of her hand, instructing her to take over for five minutes at the counter when the workers came in.

'I'm very sorry to hear about your daughter and wife,' she began, 'but I'm not happy about the rumours that are going around. *I'm* not the cause of your baby's death.' Her lips quivered as she continued. 'If the phone *did* ring out we didn't hear it. I think your wife must have dialled the wrong number.' She folded her arms, a mutinous expression on her face. 'I'd like you to make sure that people are told the truth. I love my job here, but I'll be forced to leave if I get one more unpleasant remark from the workers.'

Joe stubbed out his ciggie and took a sip of tea. 'I'll speak to them when they come down. All I can do is apologise. Maybe Dora was in a lot of pain when she dialled and got confused - like you say, she probably called the wrong number and spoke to God knows who, who hung up on her. We'll never know, will we? She's not well enough to be questioned about it. I think we should just put it to rest and move on. I'm off work now for six weeks on compassionate leave, so hopefully things will settle down for you.'

He frowned as Ivy reached out and patted his hand, a sympathetic look in her eyes. 'I've been there, Joe,' she whispered. 'Lost a baby, I mean, lost my husband too, the same year. It's a painful time. But that's between me and you and I don't want to talk about it, nor do I want you to repeat to anyone what I've just told you. I trust you to keep it to yourself.' She got to her feet and placed a hand on his shoulder. 'I need to get back to work now. I hope Dora recovers and that your remaining daughter continues to thrive. You know where I am if you ever need someone to talk to.'

She walked away, leaving Joe staring thoughtfully after her. After that little admission about the lost hubby and baby, if it were true, he'd feel a right heel bringing up the phone call subject again. The doors swung open and he spotted Eric and a couple of others he worked alongside. Best to go and set things right and get the rumour quashed once and for all, before he dashed back home to check on Carol and his mother-in-law and then go and spend the afternoon sitting beside Dora's bed. Good job he'd managed to get his bike fixed and it hadn't cost too much. At least now he wasn't dependent on the vagaries of the trams and buses.

Dora held onto Joe's hand as the doctor came into the room. He'd come to collect her from the hospital to take her home. Two weeks she'd been in here and it felt like a lifetime. She'd felt lost without her babies and lay awake most nights, reliving the awful moment she'd realised Joanna wasn't breathing. She wondered if the feeling would ever go away. Visits from her mam and Joanie had helped, but the tears were never far away and the more they sympathised the worse she felt. But at last she was being allowed to get up and go home. She still didn't feel right. Her head was fuzzy and she felt weak and tired from lack of sleep. Following the emergency D&C operation she'd been given blood transfusions and kept in bed the whole time she'd been here. She was desperate to get in the bath and to wash her hair, but most of all she wanted to see her surviving baby. Joe had brought her daily updates on how Carol was doing and Dora was happy that she seemed to be thriving, but it wasn't the same as spending time with her.

'We have the results of the post-mortem on your daughter, Joanna,' the doctor began. He referred to the file in his hand. 'We could find no obvious causes of death. We detected no heart, brain or lung defects. Apart from mild bruising to the head and face, which is quite usual following a forceps delivery, there was nothing at all that contributed to her death. The death certificate shows natural causes. Please accept my sincere condolences. It's never easy to lose a child, but to lose a newborn is a particular tragedy. We are now able to release her body so that you can arrange a funeral.'

He handed over a white envelope to Joe and bade them good afternoon.

'So that's it,' Dora said, tears running down her cheeks as Joe showed her the death certificate. 'Now we have to go and pick up the pieces like Joanna never existed.'

'Shh, love.' Joe held her as she sobbed. 'We'll get through this. We need to be strong for each other and for Carol too.'

She nodded as he wiped her eyes with his hanky. 'Let's go home, Joe. I want to get out of this place and see my baby.'

Joe's mother had managed to swap the twin pram for a single pram without any problem and Dora's dad had removed the second cradle from the spare room. Fingers crossed there was nothing to set Dora back once he got her home, Joe thought. She'd seemed better during his last few visits: very quiet, but the doctor agreed that being in her own home and learning to bond with her baby were the best things to put her fully on the road to recovery. All he could do was bring her back to where she belonged and keep his fingers crossed.

Dora's dad's parents were buried in a family plot in St Mary's church yard in Knowsley, and Dora had agreed that that was where Joanna's resting place should be, alongside her great-grand-parents. Giving her a nice send-off was the last thing they could do for their beautiful little lost daughter.

As they pulled up outside the bungalow Dora leant back in the pas-senger seat of the car Joe had borrowed to bring her home. She just wanted to get inside before anyone saw her. She couldn't face the looks of pity she knew would be cast in her direction. She felt sick as Joe helped her out and escorted her to the front door, which her mam had thrown open, a welcoming smile on her face. Her stomach plummeted as Dolly called out and came running towards them.

'Joe,' she whispered, gripping his hand tightly.

'It's okay, I'll ward her off. Go inside with your mam.'

Mam took her coat as Dora went into the sitting room and sank down onto the sofa. Her legs felt shaky, as though she'd lost all the strength in them, no doubt through lying in bed for all that time.

She held her breath and looked around the tidy room, but could see no sign of the little white cradle. 'Where's Carol?' she asked as her mam sat down beside her and took her hand.

'Having a little nap in the spare room. It's where I've been sleeping so she's been in with me. She'll be awake shortly, starving as usual. It's good to have you home, my love. Now sit there with your feet up while I go and put the kettle on.'

Dora looked up as Joe appeared in the doorway, shaking his head. 'Bloody hell, that woman can yap for England.'

'She means well. But I couldn't face her, not today anyway.'

She sighed as he came to sit beside her and put his arm around her shoulders. He dropped a kiss on her lips. 'It's good to be home,' she said, relaxing against him. She wondered how it would feel to have her baby in her arms again after so many days away. In her head, which still felt a bit fuzzy, it was almost as though she hadn't really given birth and the last couple of weeks were just a bad dream. She'd had no time to get used to being a mother, less than twenty-four hours, before being rushed away. Even though the staff at the hospital had assured her otherwise, deep down she was worried that it had been her fault Joanna had died. Much as she'd been looking forward to seeing her little Carol, now it was about to happen she was glad of this chance to catch her breath before holding her again.

Chapter Eighteen

September 1947

'Dora, Dora, come on, chuck, you're miles away.' Dora looked up from her seat on the sofa at her mam standing in front of her with Carol, fresh from her morning bath, in her arms. Mam wrapped the squirming baby in a towel and held her out to Dora. 'Just dry and powder her while I go and make a bottle.'

Dora took the wriggling child onto her knee and stared at her. Carol looked at her mother. Her eyes, now turned hazel, like Joe's, stared unblinkingly. Dora rubbed her gently with the towel and sprinkled Johnson's baby powder over the little body that was filling out nicely, patting the fine powder into crevices and folds and in-between her tiny toes. Carol smiled and cooed as Dora stared back at her.

'Isn't she gorgeous?' said Mam.

Dora bit her lip. This was so hard. She'd hardly seen her daughter for the first few weeks of her life, but instead of being overjoyed at finally being with her, it felt like the baby belonged to someone else. She should be gushing, she should be overjoyed. Shouldn't she? Her mam and Joanie were great with Carol, and Joe was besotted with her, but Dora looked at Carol and felt nothing. No, in fact, she *did* feel something - she wanted to scream. There should be two babies in her arms, another little girl smiling back. How could she be happy when she'd lost her daughter? She'd been robbed. Dora's heart had broken on the day she lost Joanna.

She lay Carol down in her cradle and balled her fists, trying not to cry. Why did people assume she could just carry on as though nothing had happened? She was trying so hard to love Carol and she had to admit that the baby was a pretty little thing with a lovely smile, but she just couldn't look at her without thinking of Joanna.

As if reading her mind, Mam took Dora's hand in hers. 'It's not going to be easy, love. You'll never get over Joanna's death, but you have to stay strong for Carol, you have to fight it. I'll go and make her feed while you have five minutes' peace with her.'

After her mam had left the room Dora tentatively bent and took Carol's finger, but couldn't bring herself to look at her. was so soft, so tiny, so fragile and innocent. How could she not adore her? The doctors at the hospital told her that sometimes depression set in following birth, bringing these unusual feelings for a child. And that in time those feelings would go. She hoped that the love she had felt during her pregnancy would come back, but for now she felt so lost and lonely.

She thought back to Saturday and the argument she'd had with Joe when he told her he would be going out later as he was playing with the band again. He'd played for the last couple of Saturdays but her mam had been here. All she could think about was how different things were between them now, how detached they were from each other. Even when he was around she felt so very lonely.

'I can't cope if you go out,' she'd cried. 'I need somebody to be with me. Mam's at home this weekend.'

He'd taken her hand in his. 'Dora, listen to me. We need the money. I have to work tonight. I've arranged for Joanie and Frank to come over for a couple of hours. Carol will sleep for most of the time anyway. I'm really trying, Dora, but you've also got to try, so we can get back to normal.'

She had pulled away from him and hurried into their bedroom, but he didn't follow her. She knew she'd shut him out since coming home from the hospital, but couldn't help it. She wished with all her heart that she *could* get back to normal, whatever that was.

Dora had felt like a nervous wreck until Frank and Joanie arrived, even though she'd only been alone for an hour and Carol had been asleep. She'd looked over once or twice at Carol's cradle, but had felt terrified. It was like a huge weight had been lifted from her when Joanie took over as soon as they'd arrived.

It was just as bad when they tried to get out of the house. Yesterday she and Joe had taken the baby out for a walk, but it was he who had pushed the pram and chatted to people who stopped to ask how they were all doing. Dora had felt uncomfortable and kept a few paces behind him. She avoided speaking to anyone in case they looked at her with sympathy. She felt worried that there seemed to be an ever-widening gulf between her and Joe.

Joe had bought the single bed for the spare room and had slept in it each night since she'd been discharged from hospital. She couldn't stand to share a bed with him. No one knew he slept alone; he made sure the bed was tidy before he left for work and her mam arrived. Dora knew that looking after her all week was getting too much for her mam and that she couldn't rely on her for ever.

Carol started to wail as Mam came back into the room holding a bottle out to her, ready for feeding time. Dora dutifully took the bottle. She could do it, surely she could pick up and feed her daughter by herself? But as soon as she looked at Carol crying in her cradle, it was as if all the energy drained out of her body and she collapsed back onto her chair again.

'I can't do it, Mam. I'm rubbish at being a mother.' She burst into tears, which only made Carol cry even louder. Dora couldn't take it. She closed her eyes and tried to block out the noise. All she could think of was her peaceful little Joanna.

'I just don't know what to do with her,' Mary Evans said to Jim, Frank and Joanie over their liver and onions at tea time. 'It's like she's got a mental block where young Carol's concerned. And she's pushing poor Joe out too. He's sleeping in the new single bed at night. She doesn't know I know that, but I'm not daft. He has the cradle in there with him, so he must be seeing to that baby in the night as well as working as much overtime as he can again, and playing in the band at the weekend. He's going to make himself poorly at this rate, then God knows what they'll do if he can't work. But I'll tell you, that marriage is heading for a breakdown unless our Dora bucks her ideas up a bit. I know she's suffered an awful loss, but we all have to carry on regardless. I'm fair worn out and I can't keep running about after her like I do. My knees are crippling me these days.'

Joanie chewed her lip and Frank shook his head. 'It's hard when you lose someone you love. But life's got to go on. I've been having a good think about what we can do to help her, to make her feel herself again. Maybe she should slowly start sewing again and eventually you and Dora should think about starting up the sewing business again, Joanie?'

'Well that's a good idea, Frank, but our Dora barely has the energy to stand up at the moment,' Mam said. 'But Joe and Dora need to get back on track too and our Dora really needs to start showing that little girl some love, otherwise I don't know what will happen.'

Jim lit a cigarette and coughed out a cloud of smoke and Mary gave him a look of disapproval. 'And *you* need to pack that in as well. Your chest is whistling and crackling more than ever lately and it's not even bad weather and thick fogs.' She got up to clear the dishes, clattering them into the sink. Jim's wheezy chest bothered her more than she let on. He was always bad when the thick

Mersey mists rolled in off the river, but that was in the winter and they'd just had a lovely warm and dry summer after that awful cold winter, so he shouldn't be too chesty right now.

'I've got a few days off next week,' Jim said, ignoring his wife's moaning. 'I was thinking about popping over to our Dora's to do a bit of work. I bet the gardens are full of weeds and I can get the borders ready for planting some bulbs now it's coming up close to the back end. Weather forecast is decent so I'll try and persuade her to give me a hand. You have a break, love. She's got to start pulling her weight a bit more. She's not the only woman to lose a babby, and others that do just have to get on with it. I can keep my eye on her, but I'm not offering to do any baby minding so she'll have to do it herself. Perhaps we've all mollycoddled her too much and now she simply doesn't know how to do things for herself or for Carol.'

Frank lay back on the bed, his hands behind his head, thinking about what Mam had said over tea. Joanie was downstairs in the kitchen having a strip-wash and he had an idea to share with her when she came up to join him. His sister was struggling, that much was certain. To lose her little daughter was an awful lot to cope with. It was hard knowing what to do to help her, but getting back to sewing again was a good start. And Joanie had two more months of work left at Palmer's before it closed down for good, so now was an ideal time to put his plan into action.

The bedroom door opened and Joanie slipped into the room, a big smile on her face as she put her toiletries away in a drawer and bounced down beside him on the big double bed they'd bought on the never-never, from Epstein's furniture shop in town. The curtain partition that had divided the room when he shared it with Dora had been removed and the room was spacious now it was opened up. Joanie had made curtains and a matching bedspread from some old curtains that one of Mam's WI ladies had given her. He pulled Joanie into his arms and whispered his plan to her. She beamed and nodded.

'Yes, that's perfect. Just what Dora needs. And me, for that matter. Do it, Frank. Do it as soon as you can.'

He smiled. A trip to Lewis's department store tomorrow was a must.

Dora opened the door to her brother Frank. He'd rung her earlier to say he was calling in on his way home from work, and she was pleased to see him. 'Come on in. It's good to see you. I'll make you a coffee.'

'Oh, hang on, I just need to get something out of the car,' he said. 'Leave the door open for me.'

Dora nodded and went back inside where Carol lay on the rug, cooing and blowing raspberries. She sat down on the sofa as Frank hurried back into the room carrying a cardboard box. Dora frowned as he gestured towards it.

'All yours, *and* it's portable so it can be used on the dining table in here.'

Dora bit her lip as she stared at the illustration on the side of the box. A sewing machine; a Singer electric machine, at that. How she and Joanie had always craved one. Her eyes filled. 'I don't know what to say. Thank you so much.' She threw her arms around her brother and hugged him, feeling thrilled but apprehensive at the same time. Since the birth of her babies, she hadn't been near her old machine, or done any hand-sewing for that matter. She knew she should and Joanie had been more than patient with her. She'd mentioned that Palmer's was closing in a couple of months and she would need to look for another job. She couldn't let her down.

Carol needed new clothes too. She'd outgrown all her first size things and Joanie had made her a couple of print dresses at work during her dinner breaks. But mainly she wore second-hand dresses passed down from Dolly's little daughter, Alice. They were adequate but faded from many washes and Dora knew she should get cracking, but her heart wasn't in it. As though reading her mind, Frank handed her a small bag that had been looped over his arm.

'Some bits of material to get you started,' he said. 'Might be enough in them fents to make a little frock or two for Carol. Joanie will come round and give you a hand this weekend.'

It was the push she needed. She and Joanie working together again, just like old times. She peeped inside the bag and tears came to her eyes as she saw the pretty prints and ginghams and broderie anglaise pieces. Enough in there for at least half a dozen little summer dresses while they still had nice weather for Carol to get some wear from them. 'Thank you; this is just what I need. I'll make a start tomorrow.'

Frank got down on his knees and tickled his niece's tummy. 'Hear that, gel? Mammy's gonna make you some pretty clothes.'

Seeing her daughter waving her hands at Frank brought the first smile to Dora's face in a long time. 'She really likes you.'

'Well I really like her,' he said, laughing as Carol blew a huge raspberry at him and giggled. 'She's gorgeous, aren't you, our kid? Right, I best get going.'

She really was, and yet why had Dora struggled to see or feel this before? But the thought of Frank leaving still unsettled her. He made her feel like herself again. 'Um, will you show me how to set up the machine before you go? I might try and do a bit tonight. Joe's got his Friday band rehearsal, so it will be something to do once he's settled Carol down.'

Frank frowned. 'Is Joe still doing everything for Carol at night? Maybe it's time you gave it a go? She looks an easy little thing to sort out.'

Dora chewed her lip. 'I'm terrified of hurting her, or her drowning in the bath, or something.' Her lips trembled. 'What if I do something wrong and lose her too?'

Frank put down his mug and took her in his arms. 'Is that what this is all about? You're worried that it was your fault you lost Joanna?'

'Yes,' Dora nodded tearfully. 'She struggled to come into the world, and when she did she died because I couldn't get her to feed that night, so it must have been my fault. All those sedatives I took for the sickness might have damaged her. We'll never know. But it's better if Mam and Joe do everything for Carol and then she stays safe.'

'Oh Dora, none of it was your fault. These things happen, love. And your Carol needs her mammy, look at her staring at you.' He picked the baby up, gave her a cuddle and handed her to Dora. 'Your turn now,' he said as the front door opened and Joe came in.

Dora saw the look of surprise on her husband's tired face as he watched her cuddling their daughter. 'Hiya, Joe. Look what our Frank's bought me,' she said, pointing to the machine. 'And there's material to make some dresses for Carol.'

Frank got to his feet and picked up the box as Joe's delighted smile lit up his face. 'Right, let's have a go at getting this up and running and then I'll love you and leave you. Oh, and before I forget, Dad's coming over on Monday and Tuesday to do some gardening. Mam's having a bit of a rest so you'll have to manage on your own.'

Dora sat at the table, reading the instructions that had been inside the box. The machine was all threaded up and ready to go. She'd found some old scraps of white fabric in the sewing room cupboard to do a few lines of practice stitching on while she got the hang of her new toy. It had been a good feeling to actually root through all her sewing things again, finding clothes patterns she'd forgotten all about. She'd put a couple of dress patterns on one side for when she had time to make a few new things for herself. She took a deep breath and set to, the machine purring along, so quiet and smooth after the old rickety treadle. She felt a little thrill run through her. It was a dream to use and similar in speed to the industrial machines at Palmer's. She knew Joanie would be over the moon when she saw it. She couldn't wait to start making a little sundress for Carol.

Before Joe left she'd joined him and Carol in the bathroom. They'd bathed her together and it had been lovely to see her chubby legs kicking and to hear her squealing with delight when they splashed her with water. Joe had reached for her hand and squeezed it gently but Dora had pulled her hand away, unsure of how to react to him.

'You dry her,' Joe said, handing their squirming daughter over, wrapped in a towel. 'I'll go and mix her feed.'

Carol wriggled on the bed as Dora dried her and fastened her nappy as she'd seen her mam and Joe do so many times. 'There, little lady, that wasn't so bad, was it?' she said and tickled Carol's tummy as she pulled rubber pants on over the nappy. She felt ashamed that she'd not managed it before. Their baby was three months old and it had taken her all that time. She slipped one of the little white embroidered nightdresses that Maude had made over Carol's head and fastened the ties, aware of Carol staring at her as though wondering who the heck she was. 'Don't you look lovely in Aunty Maude's pretty nightie?' She picked up her daughter and gave her a cuddle, feeling more confidence in her ability to handle Carol than she'd felt before.

As she sat down on the sofa Joe brought the bottle through and Dora fed Carol while he got himself ready to go out. Carol fell asleep quickly and Dora put her in the cradle next to Joe's single bed.

Chapter Nineteen

Joe let himself into the house and cocked an ear. All was quiet. He popped his head around his bedroom door and smiled. The cradle wasn't there. Dora's bedroom door was slightly ajar and he could hear the familiar snuffling of his daughter. He pushed the door open wider: Dora was fast asleep and Carol was too. The cradle was positioned by the bed on Dora's side. That was a good sign; a welcome breakthrough.

He pulled the door closed and made his way to the kitchen for a glass of water. Over the back of the sofa lay two tiny half-finished dresses; one in pink and white gingham, and the other in a pale lemon fabric with dainty white flowers. He felt a rush of emotion and blinked away the sudden tears. Thank God for Frank and his brainwave of buying Dora a new machine. Bit by bit his wife was coming back to him. He couldn't wait for the day when she'd allow him to get close again and make love to her.

Living like a monk was so frustrating that even Ivy had begun to look attractive and she'd more than made it obvious that she was available. It was his own fault. He'd confided in her during his low days when he felt like he couldn't go on. He should never have let it slip that he was in the spare room with the baby. Dora would go mad if she ever found out that he'd told Ivy and he wasn't sure he could trust the woman to keep her gob shut. He needed to keep her on his side and had bought her and dopey Flo the odd drink. He'd also had a couple of dances with Ivy. Dora must never find out about that either. She'd go crackers.

His workmates weren't really the type he could confide any delicate issues in. There was only Ivy who, probably because of her own sad losses, seemed to understand how down he was feeling.

But tonight when he'd danced with her she'd been a bit too clingy, holding on to him like she owned him. He'd had nowhere to avert his eyes other than down the front of her blouse, which was open enough to display the creamy flesh of her ample breasts. The sight made him feel hot under the collar. He'd pulled away from her close embrace before she realised he was becoming aroused, and bent to peck her on the cheek to thank her for the dance. She'd grabbed his face and dropped a smacker on his lips.

He'd mumbled an excuse about needing the carsey and dashed away, leaving her standing in the middle of the floor with an unfathomable look on her face. He'd avoided her eyes after that and then he was back on stage for the rest of the night. By the time the band had packed away, Ivy and Flo had left the club and he'd breathed a sigh of relief and accepted a lift home from drummer Johnnie in his van. He really should keep his distance from Ivy. On Monday he'd make a start by having breakfast at home and taking sarnies for his dinner again, limiting canteen time to tea breaks only.

Joanie whizzed around the hem of the little gingham dress, snipped the thread and held it aloft. 'How smashing is that? It took seconds.'

'Looks lovely,' Dora said, handing her another dress in a floral print. 'This is good; us working together as a team again.'

It was Saturday afternoon, the lads were at a football match and Dora had put Carol in her little cradle and she was sleeping soundly.

'Yes,' Joanie said, grinning. 'It does feel good. Are you ready for us to start advertising again? If you are I'll put a couple of postcards up in newspaper shop windows next week.'

Dora smiled. 'I think so. And if we advertise now, we'll be in time for the Christmas parties and stuff. When do you finish at Palmer's?'

'End of October,' Joanie replied. 'And it can't come quick enough. We're working on the final order. We'll be doing this at the right time. And with two machines we should be able to get loads done, especially when I finish work. Are you bringing Carol in next week to see the girls and say goodbye? They ask about you all the time. They'll be glad to see you, and Carol too.' Joanie finished the hem of the second dress and handed it to Dora.

'Yes, I will do,' Dora said. 'I've got to try and get out a bit more on my own.'

'That'll be lovely.' Joanie jumped to her feet. 'I've got something to tell you.' She chewed her lip and hoped what she was about to say wouldn't upset Dora too much, but she just had to tell her.

'What's up?' Dora frowned. 'Have you found somewhere to live? Oh I hope you're not going too far from here.'

'No, it's not that, although we'll need to soon. I'm, er, pregnant, Dora. I just found out yesterday afternoon.'

'Oh my God!' Dora exclaimed. 'Oh, Joanie, that's wonderful news.' She flung her arms around her and the pair laughed and cried at the same time. 'What does our Frank say? No wonder he looked a bit smug when he left here.'

'He's thrilled to bits. We haven't told anyone yet. I wanted you and Joe to be the first to know. So there'll be another baby to look after between us when we work now.' Joanie stopped as Dora's lips trembled. 'Oh, God, I'm so sorry, Dora, it came out without thinking.'

'No, no, it's okay,' Dora cried. 'Please don't get upset. I'm fine, really. It's just that sometimes, well, you know...'

'I do.' Joanie gave her a hug. 'It's early days. But I'm here for you and we're going to make a success of our business. We'll be good together, me and you and our little ones.'

Dora felt her spirits lifting as Joe took her hand. They'd borrowed Frank's car and Dolly had lent them Alice's trolley for Carol to lie in and they'd driven over to Sefton Park for a Sunday afternoon picnic. The weather was glorious with not a cloud in the bright blue sky. The park was packed with families and the queue for the boating lake stretched right around the water's edge. She'd got up early when Carol woke at six. She'd given the baby her breakfast of Farley's rusk and milk with no problem, and by the time Joe woke up she'd got a line of nappies hanging out and was busy cooking him bacon and eggs. Carol was sleeping in her pram on the lawn in the front garden. Dora felt proud of her achievements.

Her daughter looked so pretty in the pink and white gingham and a white sunbonnet that Joanie had bought her, with the white frilly sun canopy above her head. She was attracting admiring glances from other mothers with babies. Joe pushed the trolley over to a lawned area and parked up beneath a tree that cast a dappled shade on the ground. He'd brought a box Brownie camera out with him that had belonged to his late father and he took a few photographs of Dora and Carol. Dora took some of him with Carol, and then a passer-by offered to take a photo of the three of them.

As Dora unpacked their picnic and a flask she felt a great weight had lifted from her shoulders. It was lovely to be out in the sunshine as a family. She actually felt free from the depression at last and could see herself looking forward to life again. Carol had fallen asleep and Joe unfastened the trolley reins, lifted her out and lay her down on the picnic rug in the shade.

Dora unwrapped the greaseproof-wrapped cheese and tomato sarnies and poured them a coffee from the flask.

'This is smashing,' Joe said. 'To be out with my little family, it's all I've wanted for weeks. I'm so glad you're feeling better, love. But take it slowly, and if on the odd day you don't feel right, or you're not coping, you must tell me.'

Dora nodded and took a sip of coffee. 'I feel so much better. It's like someone's lifted a veil from my eyes and switched the lights back on. Now Joanie and I have made the decision to start the business again I couldn't be happier. And hearing her and Frank's good news yesterday has made me realise that life has to go on. We'll never forget Joanna, but we should be thankful we still have Carol. Her new dress has had a lot of admiring glances today. Children's clothes are something we might start with and gradually build up to ladies' when we're up and running.'

Joe smiled at her enthusiasm. 'I'm proud of you, love, but like I say, take it a day at a time.'

Dora looked through the window as her dad stood up and put his hands to his back. He looked tired. She banged on the glass. 'Are you ready for a bit of dinner, Dad?'

He waved and put down his secateurs. 'Be in shortly.'

Dora went back into the kitchen where Carol was propped in the high chair, a cushion wedged in behind her back and a blanket folded under her bottom to give her height. At three months old she was still a bit too small for the chair really, but Dora had discovered that Carol was happier if she could see her as she got on with chores, rather than lying in the pram or cradle. Dolly had bought her a rattle and Carol loved the bright colours and the noise as she pushed it around the tray of her chair. Dora's friend Agnes was coming over this afternoon. She'd got a rare day off from her typing job at a solicitor's in the city, and it would give them a chance to catch up with all the gossip. Agnes had confided that she had some good news to share. Dora was looking forward to seeing her again as, what with one thing after another, she'd seen little of her friend since her and Joe's wedding day last year.

The front door opened and her dad came in. He went to the bathroom to wash his hands and Dora heard him coughing and spluttering and then spitting. She bit her lip as she heard him pull the toilet chain. That cough was getting worse. She wished he'd go to the doctor's. He'd laughed when she'd nagged him about it yesterday and told her she was as bad as her mam and to stop fussing over nothing. He strolled into the kitchen and picked up the mug of tea Dora pointed at. He smiled at Carol, who gave him a gummy grin back.

'She's a little smasher,' he said, tickling her under the chin. 'What have we got in the sarnies today, chuck?'

'Hard boiled eggs and salad, as you well know.' Dora laughed. 'Thanks, Dad, for bringing the food I mean. Mam's bread, eggs, and the salad from your garden. That's mine and Joe's tea sorted as well.'

'Aye well, there's always more than we can eat before it goes off, and I reckon your mam always thinks she's baking for an army.'

They sat at the little table in the sitting room and enjoyed their dinner, with Carol chomping and sucking on a buttered corner cut from the end of the loaf. Her mam had told Dora it helped when they were cutting teeth to have something hard to chew on. Carol was always dribbling and although she seemed a bit young to be teething, Mam said they could start at any age and that Frank had cut his first tooth at three months.

She'd also warned about the need to watch that Carol didn't choke on a stray piece of bread that may break off. Dora felt paranoid about that bit of advice and kept a close eye on her daughter. When the baby gagged Dora flew from her seat, took the crust away and scooped the piece of soggy bread from her mouth. Carol arched her back and screamed until her little face went purple. Dora dipped her finger in some connie-onnie and put it in her mouth.

'By heck, she's got a temper, that one,' Dad said, laughing as his granddaughter calmed down and clamped her gums around Dora's finger, sucking hard. 'You'll have to watch her.'

'Little madam,' Dora said, laughing. 'Never heard her scream like that before. Mind you, no one has ever taken anything off her. She'll learn.'

'Right, I'll get back to them borders. They look a lot better than they did.'

'I'll put her down for a nap and come and help you until Agnes arrives.'

Dora took Carol into the bedroom, changed her nappy and settled her in the cradle. It was getting a bit small for her now and she would need a cot soon. Maybe she and Joe could go and look for one in town on Saturday. She hadn't been into Liverpool centre for months. She'd ask Mam if they could leave the baby with her and then they wouldn't have to carry her everywhere. Hard to get the pram on the tram and bus. She thought about how Dolly usually went out shopping on a Saturday with Alice in the trolley, so they couldn't borrow it. That was another thing they needed to buy, then they could get out a bit more. She and Joe could make a day of it and have some dinner in the Kardomah coffee bar. The band was playing that night, but they'd be back before Joe needed to go out. Dare she ask Mam if Carol could stay over and then she could go out with Joe? They needed some time together and it would be something nice to look forward to. She felt ready for a good night out with her husband. And maybe Agnes and Alan would join them.

Dora watched her dad as he prepared the soil for the bulbs he'd told her he would plant at the end of the month when he next had a couple of days off work. The daffodils would bloom in the spring, and snowdrops and crocuses along with them. He'd cleared all the weeds and removed the now dead remains of early summer flowers. There was still a bit of colour left, with the chrysanthemums and Michaelmas daisies and some late roses. She lifted the last of the dead plants from the lawn where they'd been thrown and chucked them into the wheelbarrow. She'd enjoyed spending the last couple of days with her dad; they should do it more often. She was worried about him though. While she'd been knelt beside him she could hear the rattle in his chest and his colour wasn't the best it could be either. He'd always had a golden tan from spending long days working outdoors, but now he looked pale by comparison.

He slowly got to his feet and took a couple of deep breaths. 'I'll go and pay a visit and then I'll get off home to your mam.' He trundled the wheelbarrow around to the back garden and Dora followed him.

'Do you want another cuppa before you go?'

'No thanks, chuck.' He pushed his bike around to the front and leant it against the chain link fencing as Dolly strolled by with the kids and stopped to admire the neat and tidy garden.

'He's done a good job. You can come and do mine next, Jim. Fancy a brew?' she aimed at Dora.

'Er, not at the moment, thanks, Dolly,' Dora replied. 'I'm going to see to Carol in a minute then I want to get the tea on for Joe.' She hoped her cheeks weren't giving away her lie by pinking up, because their egg salad tea was in the fridge, ready and waiting, and Carol was still flat out or she'd be screaming for England by now. Agnes would be here in about ten minutes and Dora had a feeling she would keep her news to herself if Dolly were around: besides, she had something she wanted to discuss with Agnes and it was private. The last person she'd divulge anything like that to was Dolly, good neighbour though she was.

Her dad dashed inside and she followed him, waving a firm goodbye to Dolly. He was coughing his guts up again. Dora waited in the kitchen until he'd finished in the bathroom, then handed him a glass of water. 'Promise you'll go to the doctor's,

Dad, please. You need to get yourself right. You've got another grandchild on the way and they'll both want a grandpa that's fit to play with them.'

'Aye, I know. And me and your mam are right chuffed about it too. But I've no time for all that doctor stuff and nonsense,' he said, swigging a mouthful of water and handing the glass back to her. 'I'm back at work tomorrow. Your mam will boil me some onions tonight. Best thing for a bad chest, onion water. It'll cure anything. Right, I'm off.'

Dora shook her head after his departing back. She followed him outside and gave him a hug. 'You're a stubborn old bugger. But I love you.'

He laughed and ruffled her hair. 'Aye, and I love you too, my little queen. I'll be seeing you soon.' He lifted his leg over the crossbar of his bike and rode away, waving as he turned the corner and out of sight.

Dora went back indoors and peeped into the bedroom. Carol was still asleep, flat on her back, sheet kicked off, one hand flung above her head and her fine brown hair sticking to her head with sweat. It was still so warm, even with all the windows open right through the bungalow. Her dad said he'd heard they were due to have an Indian summer in the next few weeks. She'd believe it when she saw it, but after the awful winter it was no more than they deserved.

Chapter Twenty

Agnes perched on the edge of the chair, her red hair pinned up in a neat chignon. Her pale green summer dress, with a sweetheart neckline and slightly flared knee-length skirt, suited her tall, slim figure perfectly. Dora loved the style and thought she might have a go at making something similar for herself. She smiled as she saw excitement dancing in her friend's green eyes.

'So, come on,' she said, handing Agnes a mug. 'You're bursting to tell me something, I can see it in your face.'

Agnes smiled and took a sip of tea. She put the mug down on the coffee table and laced her hands around her knees. 'Alan's asked me to marry him. And I said yes.'

With a yell, Dora leapt to her feet at the same time as Agnes, and the pair did a happy jig around the sitting room, laughing and giggling like schoolgirls. Carol, propped in a corner of the sofa with the cushions, let out an excited squeal.

'That is the best news,' Dora said. 'Something else to really look forward to. I'm so happy for you.'

Agnes smiled. 'Something else? Why, what else has happened?'

'Joanie and Frank are having a baby.'

'Oh, that's wonderful news. When?'

'She's three months now, she's due in March.'

'Oh, I bet she's thrilled to bits, *and* Frank.'

'They are. I'm so happy for them.'

'Well, I was going to ask you if you'd have the time to make my wedding dress, but I can see you'll both have your hands full.'

'When's the wedding?'

'Next July. Gives us a bit more time to get some savings behind us. Alan wants to buy a house. There are some nice new semis around the corner from my mam on the avenues. He's got his eye on those. Mam rents our terraced on Fourth Avenue, as you know, and it'll be handy to live near her. It's close to the shops and stuff too. She'd get lonely if I moved away like my sister did.'

'She would,' Dora said. Agnes's married sister had moved from Fazakerley to Chester last year and had recently had her first baby. 'Sounds good. And yes, we can make your dress; we've got loads of time and I know Joanie will insist on it when I tell her. We'll really enjoy doing it. In fact, we'll be proud to.'

'Oh, Dora, that's wonderful. Thank you. And I've got one more favour to ask. Would you be my matron of honour? And by then she might be walking, so I'd love Carol to be my little flower-girl.'

'We'd love that, wouldn't we, chuck?' Dora tickled Carol, who smiled and kicked her legs.

'Well that's sorted then.' Agnes picked up Carol and gave her a cuddle. 'I can't wait to have a baby too. I'm so looking forward to being a mam. Are you and Joe thinking of having any more? It would be lovely if we got it right and had one about the same time. You'll have to wait until after my wedding day though. Mam would kill me if it happened before.'

Dora chewed her lip as Agnes sat down with Carol on her knee. 'I said I didn't want any more, and I'm still not sure, but I think I might change my mind now I'm feeling better. The trouble is, me and Joe – well, we haven't done it since Carol was born. I had such an awful time and I've been so frightened of getting pregnant again with losing Joanna that I pushed him out and now I think he's gone off me.'

'Give over; Joe thinks the world of you. You know he does. You've had a horrible time and it's bound to put a strain on things.'

'Yes, it has, but he's sleeping in the spare room, and Carol was in with him until recently.' Dora could feel her eyes filling and tears ran down her cheeks. She wiped them away with the back of her hand. 'It seemed the best thing at the time as I couldn't cope with either of them, and I felt so fat and ugly that I couldn't see how he'd ever want me again, but now, well, I'd really like him to come back to me.'

'You were never fat and ugly. Just extremely pregnant. And he will come back to you. You need to let him know that you're ready to have him share your bed again. Joe's a good man and he won't want to feel he's pushing you into anything. It needs to be in your time, Dora. You'll find a way of letting him know.'

Dora nodded. 'I haven't spoken about this to anyone, not even Joanie. She might say something to Frank and if he says anything to Joe, he'd be mortified if people knew we were in separate beds. But I had to confide in someone. I hope you don't mind.'

'Not at all. I'm always here if you need me.'

Dora smiled. 'Thank you. I'm going to ask Mam if she'll have Carol to stay over on Saturday while we have a day out, and then I can go out with him at night. The band's playing at Litherland Town Hall. It's a big dance and a good excuse to get all dressed up. Do you fancy coming with Alan?'

'Oh yes, I'd love to and I'm sure Alan will. Ring me at my mam's with the time and what have you. We can pick you up in Alan's car.'

'That'll be lovely. Frank and Joanie are out with friends on Saturday, so it'll just be the four of us.'

Ivy sat with her hands wrapped around a mug of tea and watched the canteen doors open for the afternoon break. Joe hadn't been in for his breakfast or dinner for three days running. He didn't even come in for a break in the morning. She'd seen him sat on the wall outside with a cup from the top of a flask. He'd brought his drinks from home. He'd dashed in yesterday afternoon, grabbed a mug of tea from Flo, dropped a threepenny bit on the trolley and dashed back out again. Today she was determined to corner him.

He'd kissed her on Saturday, full on the lips, and it had left her feeling breathless. Surely *he'd* felt something too, even though he'd pushed her away afterwards and avoided her for the rest of the night. She caught her breath as he walked in alongside Eric and picked up a mug. He ignored her and sat down at the same table as Eric and some of the other workers, his back to her. What was his game? He'd seemed keen enough when he'd danced with her, eyes staring down the top of her blouse, and he needn't think she wasn't aware he'd been aroused either. She wasn't that naïve. Surely a response like that proved he cared? She got to her feet, walked across to where he was seated and put her hand firmly on his shoulder. He jumped at the contact and slopped his tea onto the table.

'You avoiding me, Joe? Anyone would think I'd done something to offend you.'

Joe turned to face her, his cheeks going red and the curious stares of his workmates burning into his back. 'Er, no, of course not. I brought sarnies from home this week. We're trying to save a bit of money to get the baby a new cot.'

Ivy frowned. It sounded a reasonable enough excuse. A lot of the men brought food from home when times were hard. She wasn't going to embarrass him in front of his workmates. She just wanted a reason as to why he hadn't been in to see her.

'Oh well, I'll catch up with you at the dance on Saturday then, won't I?' She walked away in as dignified a manner as she could muster. A man who confided in her in the way Joe had done wasn't going to treat her badly. Not when she knew his personal secrets, anyway.

Joe stared after Ivy's retreating back, beads of sweat breaking on his brow. Bloody hell. Dora had told him last night that she wanted to go to the dance on Saturday if her mam would have Carol and that she'd invited Agnes and Alan along, who would give them a lift. She'd been so excited and bursting with the good news as soon as he'd got through the door and he'd been delighted to see her so happy. It hadn't even entered his head that Ivy would be going to Litherland to see the band. It was a bit too far from the area where she usually went out, a good fifteen miles. It would cost her an arm and a leg in a taxi. Hopefully he could put her off. 'Er, Ivy,' he called. 'We're not local this weekend. Bit of a long way without a car.'

She turned and smiled. 'We'll get buses there and a taxi home. Don't worry. We've never missed a dance yet. We won't let you down.'

Shit. Ah well, all he could do was keep her and Dora apart and hope for the best.

Dora finished hand-stitching the hem of her new dress and shook it out. She held it against her. Perfect. It was the same style as Agnes's pale green dress, with a sweetheart neckline and gently flared skirt that finished just above her knee. The soft blue flowers on the navy background brought out the blue of her eyes. Tomorrow she was hoping to find a pair of navy court shoes in TJ Hughes at a bargain price. Her mam had offered to have Carol until Sunday afternoon when Dora and Joe could join them all for Sunday dinner. Dora was thrilled at the prospect of having Joe all to herself for nearly two whole days. It would feel like they were a courting couple again. Frank was coming over early tomorrow morning with Joanie to pick Carol up, along with the cradle and high chair and all the other baby paraphernalia they'd need. She'd packed more stuff for the baby than she and Joe had taken on their honeymoon between them.

Joe was collecting fish and chips on his way home from work so she put the plates in the oven to warm. Carol was bathed, fed and tucked up for the night; well, at least until she woke for her last feed around eleven. Dora sat down on the sofa with a pad and pencil and started to sketch a few ideas for Agnes's wedding dress and her own matron of honour outfit.

Dora and Agnes ran up the steps to the red-painted front door of Litherland Town Hall with Joe, while Alan found a parking space round the side. They waited until he joined them and hurried inside. The doorman stopped them and asked for their tickets but Joe held up his saxophone case and said, 'We're with the band, mate.' They were waved on and the girls made their way to the cloakroom to hang up their jackets, touch up their lippy and mess with their hair.

Dora felt a thrill of excitement as she thought of dancing with Joe and spending hours with him. He hadn't said anything yet, but she knew from the looks he'd given her as she'd walked into the sitting room ready to go that he was hoping she'd ask him to come back to their bed tonight. And she planned to do just that. She'd felt him tremble as he'd held her in his arms just before Alan had tooted that they were outside.

When she and Agnes went into the ballroom and looked for the boys, Alan had drinks ready and waiting on the table and Joe was on stage with the band at the top of the room, doing a quick warm-up session. Dora looked around. She'd never been here before and admired the traditional, classy decor and soft lighting. The wooden dance floor looked freshly varnished and inviting with tables and chairs placed around the perimeter. Couples started to arrive and the large room quickly filled. The band leader had agreed to play a selection of records in-between the band spots and the popular Glenn Miller songs had people getting up to dance already.

Dora sipped her gin and tonic and looked to see if she recognised anyone. It was a bit of a drive from Kirkby, so it would be unlikely. Joe had told her the dances here attracted mainly locals and people from nearby Bootle and Crosby and as they were quite popular, it was hard to get tickets.

Ivy bundled Flo off the bus, pulling her along towards Litherland Town Hall. She was fuming because Flo had told her at the last minute that she didn't want to go to the dance. But Ivy was having none of it and ordered her to get ready. Now she wished she'd come on her own; Flo's greasy hair was sticking to her head from lack of washing and being tucked under a turban all day while she'd cleaned the house. She'd done her best to help Flo titivate it with lacquer and curlers but to no avail. The crème puff and lippy she'd hurriedly slapped on were patchy and smudged and Ivy had raised her eyes to the ceiling when Flo had presented herself as ready to go five minutes before the bus was due. She said her best dress needed a wash: the one she had on was dipping at the hemline, and her cardigan was done up on the wrong buttons. Ivy bit her tongue, handed Flo her coat and they'd travelled on the bus in silence.

The one thing keeping Ivy going was the thought of seeing Joe again. She hoped he'd be more relaxed than he'd been that week. It would be unlikely there'd be anyone there from work and he'd have had a drink or two by the time they arrived and would probably be in an amiable mood. She'd get another close dance and a kiss tonight if it killed her.

There was a bit of hassle with the doorman, who demanded their tickets.

'I thought it was pay on the door, like most dances,' Ivy said, pulling herself up to her full five-foot-three and thrusting her ample bosom in his direction.

'Sorry, miss, tickets only here, always has been,' he said averting his gaze, his cheeks turning pink.

The man had a look of Hitler with his shifty eyes and tooth-brush moustache, and he clicked his heels together in a way that irritated Ivy. He was uniformed and he obviously felt it gave him the edge over the usual social club doormen who just wore smart suits.

'Now, see here,' Ivy whispered and drew him to one side. 'That's my sister.' She inclined her head towards Flo. 'You can see she's *not quite right*, can't you? And we've come a long way on the bus tonight. She'll be so disappointed if I have to take her home without seeing the band play and having a little dance. It keeps her happy, you see.'

The man looked at Flo, who was staring at her surroundings, her slack jaw droopier than ever tonight. She did indeed look *not quite right*. He nodded. 'Go on then, miss. That's one and six for you and you can take *her* in for free.'

Ivy smiled, paid up, thanked him and beckoned to Flo to follow her. Flo's scruffy appearance had paid off nicely and stood them the price of a drink each. They gave their coats to the cloakroom attendant and Ivy led the way into the ballroom, Flo following meekly on her heels. The band was already up on stage and waiting to start the first set of songs. Ivy could see Joe standing with his back to her, talking to the drummer, who was perched on his stool. She hurried across to a table at the back of the room so that she wasn't in full view of Joe. She didn't want to put him off his stride just yet. Flo plonked herself down on a chair and Ivy dashed to the bar and got two small schooners of sherry. Joe always got them a large one, but in view of the fact they needed taxi fare to get home, as the buses would have stopped running by the time the dance finished, she was watching her pennies.

There was a table near to the stage and it only had one fella sitting at it. Maybe he'd shift himself soon enough and then she'd move Flo over there. The lights went down and the MC announced the name of the band. A round of applause and a cheer went up and the band started up with their usual opener of 'Chattanooga Choo Choo'. Ivy saw the doors fly open and two smartly dressed young women hurry to sit in the spare seats at the front table. As the blonde picked up a glass and turned to the stage she saw Joe raise his hand and the woman smiled and did a little wave back. As she flicked her long wavy hair over her shoulders Ivy realised the woman was Dora, Joe's wife. Her stomach plummeted as she saw how pretty and slender Dora looked and the adoration in her eyes as she watched her husband playing his heart out. As Joe paused after his solo Ivy saw that same look in *his* eyes as he waved again to his wife. An overwhelming feeling of jealousy swept over her. They'd obviously got over their problems and he didn't need her to confide in any more. That was one pair who wouldn't be sleeping in separate beds tonight.

Chapter Twenty-One

Joe swept Dora into his arms and dropped a kiss on her lips as they danced to Nat King Cole's 'Embraceable You'. He hadn't seen her look this happy for months. 'I love you so much,' he whispered. 'It's been a wonderful day.' He hoped it was going to be a wonderful night when they got home. But that was up to Dora. They would go forward at her pace. They'd come this far and he wasn't about to break that new-found closeness now.

'I love you too.' She smiled and lay her head on his chest as his hands moved slowly up and down her spine. He held her tight and to Joe it felt like they were the only couple on the dance floor. 'New beginnings,' he said.

'That's what Joanie said.' She smiled as he led her back to her seat.

'I'm nipping to the gents, then I'll get us a refill,' Joe said. 'Same again?'

He hurried out of the ballroom, oblivious to the fact that someone was watching his every move and had followed him into the corridor. He dashed into the gents and was out within minutes. As he rounded a corner he walked straight into Ivy, who had her arms folded under her ample bosom, a furious expression on her round face.

'Ivy! What are you doing here?'

'I told you I was coming. But I see you've brought your wife.'

'Well, yes. She's feeling much better now and wanted to come with me. She *does* have a right, you know?'

'And so do I.'

Joe stepped back as Ivy was practically shoving her face into his. 'Of course you do. Everyone who pays for a ticket has a right to be here.'

'I didn't mean that, Joe, and well you know it.'

Joe shook his head. 'You've lost me, I'm afraid.'

'You kissed me last week, made me think there was something between us.'

Joe held up his hands. Shit, this was all he needed. 'No, Ivy, you've got that wrong. *You* kissed me. I pushed you away, remember? I only ever pecked your cheek to thank you for the dance.'

Ivy folded her arms. 'All those things you told me about your unhappy marriage. I don't think Dora will like it that I know all your secrets, do you?'

Joe frowned. 'What's all this about? I never told you that I was *unhappy*. I took you into my confidence when I lost my daughter, and my wife was very ill. I needed someone understanding to talk to. I thought that someone might be you after what you told me about your own losses. I didn't realise you'd take it all out of context, read something into it.' He pushed her away. 'Don't try and cause trouble for me. You'll be sorry if you do, *really* sorry, and I mean that. I've given you the benefit of the doubt. But I can easily get to the bottom of that phone call Dora made when she was in labour. The exchange will confirm whether a call was logged from my home number to the canteen number on that date.'

As he stormed off back into the ballroom Ivy realised what a fool she'd nearly made of herself in her jealous rage. She shouldn't have come here tonight. It was true, Joe hadn't kissed her; *she'd* kissed him, clinging to him when he'd tried to break free. But in her thoughts it was easy to turn around her memory of that kiss and make it out to be more than it was. She'd never win back his friendship now. He wouldn't confide in her again. Why would he even look twice at her when he'd got Dora in tow? And if he did get to the bottom of that phone call then she'd be ostracised by everyone at the ROF again and her life would be hell. She hurried into the ladies feeling sick.

Back in the ballroom Flo was staring into her empty glass. Ivy handed her coat over. 'We're leaving.'

'Why? You haven't had a dance with Joe yet and we've only had one drink.'

Ivy inclined her head to the front of the stage area. 'He's with his wife,' she whispered.

'Oh my God, does she know?'

'Know what?' Ivy grabbed her handbag from the back of the chair.

'About you and him.'

'There's nothing to know.' Ivy wished now that she'd kept her mouth shut and not told Flo the richly embellished tales that she had done. Too late now: she just needed to get her out of the building and on that bus home. She'd got a lot of making-up and apologising to do next week when they were back at work. If Joe realised that she'd gone home without any hassle tonight, he might even thank her. It would be a start. And then she would reassure him that she had no intention of causing him any trouble with his wife. And she didn't - not yet, anyway. She'd get him on side again, keep in the background for a while, and see how things went. But she'd also make sure that Joe understood the implications of *what* he'd confided in her. That she could, if she so chose to, quite easily blow his marriage apart.

Dora sat on the sofa with her hands wrapped around a mug of tea. It was still early but she'd woken with the birds, expecting Carol to be whimpering in her cradle by the side of the bed. As she'd lain sleepily in the half-light she'd become aware of a soft rhythmic sound beside her and for a few seconds had been unable to place the noise. Then it had come back to her Carol wasn't there, but Joe was, flat on his back and fast asleep. She smiled and slid quietly out of bed so as not to disturb him. It had been a late night. The band worked hard and performed three encores. Alan had brought them back home and he and Agnes had gone on their way, turning down Joe's offer of a nightcap as they too were tired.

Both more than merry with the drinks they'd consumed, Joe had helped Dora up the garden path and then lifted her into his arms and carried her over the threshold. They'd collapsed in a heap on the hall floor, laughing until their sides ached.

When Dora asked him why he'd carried her, he said it was what he should have done when they'd moved in, and as this was a new beginning, he'd decided to do it tonight. She smiled now, remembering how they'd tumbled onto the bed, removing each other's clothes and swearing they'd never spend a night in separate beds again. Their lovemaking had been loving and passionate, but Joe had taken the time not to rush her and Dora had been grateful for that. It was like they'd never been apart.

'Dora,' Joe called. 'Where are you?'

She popped her head around the door. 'I'm here.'

'Come back to bed. We've got a lot of lost time to make up.'

'We need to get ready to go to Mam's.'

'It's only half-eight. We've got hours yet.'

Dora smiled, undid the belt of her silky dressing gown and let it fall slowly to the floor, loving the way his eyes lit up as he stared at her naked body with love and hunger in his eyes.

Dora frowned as her dad hurriedly pushed a handkerchief into the pocket of his old gardening trousers. He'd come round to help with the garden again and was planting bulbs in the freshly prepared flower borders. Through the open window she'd heard him coughing quite badly and had stuck her head out to ask if he wanted a drink of water. Even from a distance she could see that the handkerchief was covered in blood and she dashed outside.

'Dad, how long has this been going on?'

He wiped his hand across his mouth, looking sheepish. She could hear his chest wheezing and rushed back inside to get a chair. She sat him down near the front door and undid the top buttons of his flannel shirt while he caught his breath. He grabbed her hand.

'Don't tell your mam, chuck, please. I don't want to worry her. It's only been a day or two. It'll clear soon. I've been coughing that hard I've maybe popped a blood vessel in my throat or summat.'

He looked so worried that Dora put her arm around his shoulders and assured him she'd keep it to herself. 'But on one condition, Dad. You go to the doctor's tomorrow morning before you come here. Otherwise I'm telling Mam. Now I'm going to put Carol in the pram and I'll walk to the chemist's and get some linctus for you to take. See if it soothes it, never mind Mam's boiled onion rubbish. That's obviously not working.'

'There's no need to do that, I'll be fine.' He took a sip of water and smiled. 'See, right as rain.'

'No, you're not and I'm not arguing with you.' Dora went back inside, shaking her head. She fastened Carol into the pram and manoeuvred it out of the front door. She was halfway down Belle Vale Road before it dawned on her that this was the first time she'd been out on her own with Carol in the pram since her birth. She took a deep breath, muttered 'New beginnings' and carried on her way before she lost her nerve and turned back.

She parked Carol outside West's chemist's and nodded hello to a neighbour she vaguely recognised as living in the prefabs, who followed her into the dark little shop. Dora loved the smell in here, aniseed, liquorice, and surgical spirits vying for space with the scent of lavender, mint and coal-tar soap. She asked for a product she saw advertised on a poster on the wall behind the counter: a bottle of Stoddard's glycerine, lemon and ipecac linctus. She remembered her mam dosing her and Frank with it one winter during the war when they'd both developed stubborn chesty coughs that just wouldn't go away. Mam had blamed the thick Mersey mists and bloody Hitler and his bombs. Dad's bad chest was no doubt due to the fires he'd helped put out during the Blitz and all the nasty stuff he'd breathed in while doing that. The damage was done, but making sure he got some help now instead of ignoring it was vital.

'That'll be sixpence, please, love.' The white-coated assistant handed her a paper bag with the bottle inside.

'Thank you. I don't suppose you've got any Uncle Luke's chest and throat sweets?' Dora asked. Even cough sweets had been hit by rationing, but her dad liked those and they'd help soothe his throat.

The assistant rooted under the counter and produced a half-full jar. 'I can let you have two ounces,' she said. 'Are they for you?'

'My dad. He's got a shocking cough and it won't go away.'

'Poor fella, I'll slip an extra couple in for him. Twopence to you, love.' She twisted the corners of the little white paper bag and handed it to Dora.

'You could try rubbing his chest with goose grease,' the neighbour who'd followed Dora into the shop chipped in. 'Always helps my 'Arry's chest when he starts coughing his guts up. Mind you, it gets all over the sheets and it's a right job on washing day to get rid of it. I have to boil them three times before the grease comes out. You could try it on a poultice to save the mess, I suppose,' she added as an afterthought.

Dora smiled and thanked her neighbour for the tip. She didn't think Mam would take too kindly to washing greasy sheets; and how on earth could fat taken from cooking a goose help a bad chest? She dropped the cough sweets and linctus into her shopping bag and thanked the assistant.

'Hope your dad gets better soon,' the shop assistant said as Dora waved her goodbyes.

Outside she gripped the pram handle and took a deep breath. It had taken some effort to get this far and as she was here she might as well do a bit more shopping. She walked to the haberdasher's and bought a spool of white thread, and some pink wool to knit a new cardigan for Carol for when the cooler autumn days began to set in. In the bakery she treated herself and her dad to meat and potato pies, fresh from the oven, and a vanilla cut each. Carol started to grizzle and chew on her fingers. Dora popped her dummy in her mouth and she sucked hard and then spat it out with a look of disgust.

Dora laughed as the cross little face screwed up in readiness for a screaming session. 'Soon be home, madam. Anyone would think I starved you.' She set off at a brisk pace, happy that she'd made a bit more headway today with getting her independence back.

Dora lit the oven and popped the pies on a plate to keep warm while she fed Carol, and then she and Dad could enjoy their dinner in peace. She placed the vanilla cuts in the fridge. Her dad had always enjoyed them before the war so it would be a nice surprise for him. It was lovely to look after him; she missed being at home with her family and seeing her parents and brother each day. But this was home now and she and Joe were getting back to normal and she loved being a mammy to Carol. She mixed Carol's feed and sat with her on the sofa while she fed her. It was such a pity she'd missed out on breastfeeding her and the closeness that it was supposed to bring. Carol's cheeks were pink with the effort of sucking and her eyes rolled in ecstasy. She'd be asleep before much longer. Good - this afternoon Dora planned on doing a few more wedding dress sketches for the next time Agnes popped over. To-morrow morning, if she felt okay, she might tackle another step towards regaining her independence and get the bus with Carol to visit Palmer's to see Joanie and her old workmates.

Dora smiled as her dad tucked into his pie. The gravy ran down his bristly chin and he wiped it with his fingers.

'These are good,' he said. 'Best I've had in a long time. More meat in 'em as well. Been potato and meat pies for long enough. Now we're getting back to the real thing. Meat and potato, just as it used to be.'

Dora cleared their plates away and poured two mugs of tea. She brought the vanilla cuts through and her dad's eyes lit up.

'You're spoiling me, queen.'

'No, *you're* spoiling *me* by doing our garden.'

He laughed. 'If I can't spoil my little girl now and then it's a poor show.' He took a bite of his vanilla cut and smiled.

Dora swallowed the lump that had risen in her throat and took a sip of tea. Her dad looked at her like Joe always looked at Carol. Looks of adoration. It was lovely to spend this precious time with him.

'Right, open wide,' Dora ordered in a no-nonsense voice.

'That feels a bit better,' her dad said as she spooned the cough mixture down him. He patted his chest. 'Nice and warming. And I'll suck on an Uncle Luke's while I'm outside. I'll be right as rain in a day or two, I tell you. And those pies really were lovely. And you spoiled me with that vanilla cut. It's ages since I had one.'

'But you will go to the doctor's tomorrow morning, won't you?' Dora knew he was only changing the subject in the hope she'd forget about the cough. 'You promised me, Dad. I'll tell Mam about that blood if you don't.' She didn't like to threaten him, but if it was the only way to get him to agree, then it would have to do.

'Bloody hell, stop nagging, gel. Yes, I promise.'

'Good. Do you want another cuppa before you go back outside?'

'No ta. I'll get on and have one later.'

Dora sighed and watched as he limped back outside. She meant what she said though; if he didn't go tomorrow then she'd get Mam on to him and Joanie and Frank too if necessary. Her dad meant the world to her and it terrified her that something might be seriously wrong with him.

Chapter Twenty-Two

'Peggy's turn now,' Dora said, removing her wriggling daughter from Maude's arms and handing her over to Peggy, whose smile lit up her face as she gazed at the little girl. 'Eat your dinner now, Maude, before it gets too cold to enjoy it.'

Maude's fried egg and chips were congealing on the plate in a pool of dripping, but she tucked hungrily into them as Peggy tickled Carol under the chin, trying to coax a smile from the baby, who frowned at the unfamiliar face gazing down at her.

'I'll go and ask Mavis to heat Carol's bottle.' Dora smiled as the two girls cooed over Carol, who was decidedly grumpy today. Hopefully she'd be quieter when she'd had her milk. She'd grizzled all the way over on the bus, chomping on her fingers like she was starving.

Mavis greeted her warmly at the counter and stood the bottle in a jug of hot water. 'As soon as I've finished up here I'm coming over for *my* cuddle too,' she said. 'She's a bonny little thing, isn't she?'

'She is,' Dora agreed.

Mavis tested the milk on her wrist and wrapped the bottle in a tea towel, handing it over to Dora, who thanked her and went back to the table near the window, where Peggy was now holding Carol up so that Len, one of the only remaining packers, could pull faces at her through the glass. Carol was smiling and she blew a raspberry at Len, who blew one back. Carol squealed and flapped her arms up and down.

Peggy laughed. 'Can I give her the bottle please? Let you have your cuppa in peace and a catch-up with Joanie. She's been trying to tell you summat since you came in, but we haven't given her the chance to open her gob yet!'

Dora handed the bottle over and tied a bib under Carol's dribbly chin. 'Wind her halfway, but be prepared for her to kick off as soon as you remove the bottle from her mouth,' she warned. She sat down again and turned to Joanie, breathing a sigh of relief as Peggy, with Maude practically glued to her elbow, fed Carol. 'Phew. Peace at last.'

Joanie smiled. 'Are you trying to say my niece is hard work?'

'She is, just a bit.' Dora laughed. 'Let's hope yours is a little angel.' She took a welcome swig of tea. 'Ah, that's nice. No one makes a brew as good as Mavis.'

'Dead right,' Joanie said. 'Anyway, one of Frank's mates' girls, who we were out with on Saturday night, has been looking for someone to make three bridesmaids' dresses. I told her to look no further. I completely forgot to tell you on Sunday when you came for dinner and to pick Carol up. It was that noisy, with everyone talking at once and neighbours popping in to see the baby. The dresses are for her young nieces, and she's already got the fabric and trimmings. She's also done a simple sketch and we should be able to tackle them, no problem.'

'Oh, that's great. When does she need them for?'

'Early November. We've got a few weeks.' Joanie lowered her voice. 'The fabric's dark pink satin, so I can do the seam edges here. And by the way, Jack told me this morning that George Kane said no to us having an over-locker. Apparently there's a party interested in buying the fittings but not the factory and fixtures. I suppose he's got to get his money where he can.'

'Miserable bugger,' Dora said. 'Bet he won't get much more than we could offer him. Ah well, we've got the zigzag stitch option on the new Singer.' She glanced around the almost empty canteen. It felt echoey. 'I see he's got rid of most of the furniture from in here.'

Joanie nodded. 'There are hardly any of us left. No point in keeping the tables and chairs when there's no one to sit on them.

A big van came and took them away last week. God knows where they've gone.'

Mavis bustled across and sat down with a cuppa while she waited for Carol to finish her bottle. 'I see she's wearing that nice little coat that Peggy's mam made.'

'She is. I'm sorry I didn't get to see your mam, Peggy, but well, you know... I wasn't very well for a while, as Joanie told you.'

'We know, queen, and we were all very upset for youse,' Peggy said, nodding her head. 'But this little smasher will keep you busy, I'll bet.' She prised Carol away from the teat and sat her forward. Carol arched her back and screamed, belching at the same time. 'Blimey, she's got some lungs on her, little madam.' The bell signalling the end of dinner break sounded and Peggy handed Carol back to Dora.

Dora plugged the teat back in quickly as Peggy and Maude dropped kisses on her cheek.

'It's been nice to see you. Keep in touch.' Peggy linked her arm through Maude's as they left the canteen.

'I will,' Dora called after them. 'Good luck looking for new jobs. You must come round for a cuppa if you're at a loose end any time.'

Joanie got to her feet. She looked pale and Dora stroked her arm. 'Not long now and then you can take it a bit easier. You feeling a bit washed out?'

'Very tired,' Joanie replied. 'And weeing for England.'

'Tell me about it.' Dora laughed. 'I was never off the carsey.'

'Well every time I want to go, your dad's in there,' Joanie said, rolling her eyes. 'Me and Frank need to find our own place.'

'You do, in time. By the way, did Dad mention going to the doctor's this morning?'

'Not to me, he didn't. Are you worried about his cough? Your mam has been nagging him for weeks now. But he's so stubborn.'

Dora nodded. 'Can I give Carol to you for the last of her feed, Mavis? I just want a quiet word with Joanie.'

'Course you can. Come here, my little love.' Mavis held her arms out and Carol nestled into them and sucked contentedly on the teat.

Dora followed Joanie out of the canteen and up the stairs to the first floor. 'Might as well as say hello to Jack while I'm here. But yes, Dad's cough is really bad. Don't say anything to him or Mam yet or Frank either for now, but he coughed up loads of blood yesterday. It was in his hanky.'

Joanie sighed. 'I've seen him do it too, when he thinks no one is watching. He shouted at your mam recently about the doctor costing too much money and he'd wait until the new National Health Service starts next year, then it'll be free.'

'But he pays into that policy Mam took out. We all do, so we never have to worry about going to the doctor's. Good job we had it with what happened to me and the twins. The new service doesn't start until next July and he can't wait that long. Right, he should be at mine doing the garden when I get back. If he hasn't been to the doctor's I'm telling Mam. It's for his own good.'

Jack Carter waved at Dora as she and Joanie went onto the factory floor.

'How's it going, chuck?' He gave her a hug. 'Not brought the baby up to see me?'

'She's in the canteen with Mavis. Nip down and see her. I'm just saying a quick bye to everyone and then we're going home.'

'Will do.'

Jack left the floor and Dora looked around. It made her feel sad to see how depleted and downcast the staff were. Half a dozen left, if that, including Jack. It should be so different and busy up here. They'd all survived the war; the factory was still standing and the staff well-trained. Such a wicked waste of skills. She hoped

George Kane lost everything for what he'd put his loyal workforce through while still enjoying his lavish lifestyle. His father-in-law would be spinning in his grave right now.

Dora said her goodbyes and Joanie promised to come over on Friday night when she'd picked up the fabric from their new customer. Downstairs Dora reclaimed her daughter, who was now on Jack's lap, cooing and making eyes at him, tummy full and quite contented. Hopefully she'd fall asleep on the bus and then Dora could have a bit of time with her dad before he went home.

On Saturday afternoon, three excited bridesmaids played with Carol on the rug while Dora and Joanie got their dresses ready for the first fitting. Their mum had thoughtfully provided measurements along with the fabric that Joanie had brought round in the week. Dora had designed and cut out the dresses and she and Joanie had tacked the pieces together over a couple of evenings.

'Okay,' Dora called over the giggling and the shrieks from Carol as she joined in with their laughter, 'let's have Alice in the fitting room first.'

Ten-year-old Alice followed Dora and Joanie into the second bedroom, an important smile on her face. As chief bridesmaid, she had the responsibility of holding the bouquet for her aunt during the ceremony.

'Just slip your dress off, sweetheart,' Joanie said and undid the back zip for her.

Alice did as she was told and stood self-consciously in her vest and knickers with her arms in the air while Joanie slid the new dress over her head and shoulders. She gasped as it slid down to her feet.

'Oh, it's luverley,' she said as Joanie pinned the back together.

'Yes, you look beautiful and the colour really suits you,' Dora said. The dark pink gave a bloom to the little girl's pale cheeks, and made her glossy dark hair and brown eyes shine. 'I'll just call your mummy in.'

Alice's mum, Mags, came in and smiled at her daughter. 'What a picture,' she said proudly as Alice twirled around, lifting the long skirt. 'Be careful, love. It's got to be stitched together yet and you'll be popping the temporary seams.'

'Okay,' Dora said. 'I think we're fine there with that one. Let Joanie help you to take it off and then we'll have May and Molly in for their fittings.'

'God help you,' Mags said with a grin. 'They're the biggest pair of fidgets in town. Do one at a time, or they'll egg each other on with the giggles.' She waited until Alice had dressed herself, then took her back into the sitting room to play with Carol, while Dora and Joanie tackled the five-and six-year-olds.

Seeing the visitors out, Dora closed the door after them and smiled. The two youngest girls were similar in age, just as her and Joanie's babies would be. She had convinced herself that Joanie was expecting a girl, although she'd no idea why. Their two would play together just like she and Joanie had done as little girls, and would grow up to be the best of friends. It gave her a warm glow of satisfaction.

Joanie had the kettle on when Dora went into the kitchen. 'Those little ones were a pair of pickles, weren't they?' she said. 'Such happy little girls and all three were lovely with it.' She rubbed her tummy. 'I can't wait for mine. Wonder what it'll be?'

They took their cuppas through to the sitting room and sat down on the sofa. Carol studied them from her position on the rag rug. She raised her legs in the air and flung herself sideways, perfecting a roll onto her tummy that she'd been trying all week.

'Oh my God, she's done it,' Joanie cried. 'Clever girl.'

Dora laughed until tears rolled down her cheeks, for her daughter looked so shocked she didn't know whether to laugh or cry as her lip pouted. 'She wasn't expecting that.' She put down her cup and scooped Carol up. 'Next thing she'll be crawling and then we'll know we've got her, won't we, missy?' She tickled Carol, who giggled and hiccupped. 'Wait until Daddy sees what you can do.'

'Are you going with Joe to the club tonight?' Joanie asked, dunking her ginger snap in her tea.

'No, I'm going to get on with the dress bodices once Carol goes to sleep. Are you?'

'Might do. It's Fazakerley Legion, isn't it?'

'Yeah, Agnes and Alan are going, it's only down the road for them.'

'Might join them then,' Joanie said.

'I didn't like to mither Mam to have Carol with Dad not being too good. I'm glad he went to the doctor's though. Once he's had that X-ray we might get to the bottom of things.' Her dad had done as he was told and Dora's mam had accompanied him to see the doctor. He'd been prescribed linctus and arrangements were being made for him to see a specialist after the X-ray results were in.

Joanie nodded. 'I'll come over in the week and help you with the sewing and then next week I'll try and get to the over-locker upstairs. Should be easy enough as people are all distracted at the moment with things winding down. Can't believe I've only got two weeks left to work there and then Palmer's will be no more. Sad really. Stupid, bloody Kane!'

Joanie hid the bag with the bridesmaids' dresses under her machine bench and picked up a shirt collar. The box was almost empty and tomorrow was the final day in work. The workforce was quiet and Jack Carter nowhere to be seen. Peggy said he was in a meeting with Mr Kane. There was no heating on in the building as the janitor had left last week. The boiler had remained unlit for days and although it wasn't freezing for late October, the temperature had dropped considerably now the nights were darker. The forecasted Indian summer had been short-lived. Mavis had complained about having to boil water for pot washing, telling anyone who would listen that it was hard work and she was cooking no hot dinners this week. It was sandwiches only.

The day wore on, with Jack keeping out of the way. Joanie was anxious to get on and do the bridesmaids' dresses but it would be sod's law that if she sneaked upstairs now both Jack *and* George Kane would put in an appearance, and they might dock her wages. As tomorrow's money was the last she'd be paid from here, she didn't want to risk them finding any excuse to hold some back. The remaining staff had been promised a week's holiday pay along with their wages as no one had dared to take a holiday this year for fear of coming back to no job. As soon as the leaving bell went she would be upstairs faster than a rat up a drain pipe. It wouldn't take her long. The dresses were small, with only the side seams to over-lock as Dora had neatened the back ones by hand when she'd inserted the zips. She'd be in and out while Jack had his fag and a brew as he waited for Mavis to close down the canteen before his last lights check. Frank was coming to pick her up and then they were going straight to Joe and Dora's for tea. Her sister-in-law had promised lamb Scouse. Joanie's tummy rumbled with anticipation.

Jack Carter saw Mavis off the premises and locked up the canteen. He went into the office, shut the door and poured himself a tumbler of whisky from Gerald Kane's silver hip flask that the boss kept in his desk. He lit a cigar from the silver case, using Kane's fancy engraved lighter. He blew a cloud of smoke into the air above his head and took a large swig from the tumbler. Serve Kane right if he polished the lot off. Bloody coward, pissing off to London earlier with his missus and leaving Jack behind with all the shit to deal with. Seeing his workers off home tonight, who all thought they were coming in for their last pay packets tomorrow, with the addition of the promised holiday pay that they'd never see, made him feel guilty beyond belief. He just hoped they would find new jobs in the not too distant future. Peggy looked after her old mam and her wage was the only one going into that household, and the same with Maude, whose mam relied on her daughter's wages just to exist.

At least Joanie would be making a bit of money alongside Dora and he really wished he could give them a bloody overlocker, because with what he was going to do next, there'd be no machines being sold at auction. If only there was a way he could help them all, but there wasn't and that's why he'd agreed to Kane's harebrained idea. At least Jack could now see his family and his demanding wife right for a few weeks while he looked for another job, and that was better than nothing, he supposed. He finished the cigar, stubbed the end out in the fancy marble ashtray and reluctantly got to his feet. Then, as an afterthought, he emptied the ashtray onto the floor and shoved it into his overall pocket. It would do nicely at home on the sideboard, better than the old chipped saucer he used now. He also grabbed hold of the silver hip flask, cigar case and lighter. Kane would have no need of them any more and he might get a few bob for them down at the pawnshop.

His overcoat was on the back of Kane's chair and Jack took four cans of lighter fuel and a box of matches from the coat's deep pockets. He felt sick with nerves as he lifted boxes of off-cut rags that he'd gathered together earlier up onto the desk. Working quickly, he doused the rags in fuel and placed them near the four corners of the factory floor. He piled bales of fabric next to each box, and scattered the shirts that the girls had been working on across the floor. He put on his coat, making sure he had the factory keys in his pocket, and sprinkled the remaining lighter fuel over the shirts and fabric bales. He threw a lit match into one box. It ignited immediately and quickly spread to the wooden floor. Patches of machine oil, soaked into the floorboards, added further fuel to the fire. As the flames took hold they practically danced across to the opposite corner and with a whoosh the other box of rags caught easily.

Jack chucked a lit match into the nearest box by the door and dashed out of the room, closing the door behind him. He stopped for a brief second when he thought he heard a noise, but decided it would be pigeons on the upstairs floor. They often came inside through a broken window, making a racket with their billing and cooing, and were probably sheltering from the cold. Well, there was no way he was shooing them out now and pigeon shit on fabric bales that would never be used was not his problem. He ran lightly down the stairs and hurried outside, locking the big double front doors.

His motorbike was standing by the wall. With legs that felt like jelly and his stomach churning, he kick-started the bike to life and roared off down the lane towards his home, without so much as a backward glance at his place of work. It was only as he pulled onto the road leading to his house that he realised he'd left the empty lighter fuel cans standing on one of the machines. Well, it was too late now, he wasn't turning back. Hopefully they'd be destroyed beyond recognition in the inferno he was certain would now be well underway.

During their recent meeting, Kane had told Jack that when the girls came in to work today they'd be feeling despondent as it was their next to last day, and may be careless about dropping cigarette ends. It would be easy to blame a fire on a worker having a sneaky ciggie on the factory floor. Kane had promised him money if he agreed to start the fire; he'd received the equivalent of six weeks' wages already, with promise of more when the insurance company paid out on the subsequent claim for the damaged building and fixtures. All the paperwork showing the business was in dire straits would go up in flames, and Mr Kane had assured him that his accountant, who was also an acquaintance at the golf club, would be easily persuaded with a back-hander to keep quiet if necessary. When Jack voiced his worries that the girls might speak up if questioned, Mr Kane told him it was unlikely they'd even be asked. With money from the claim it might be possible to start another business, he'd said, with new jobs for all. Once that rumour reached their ears they'd be unlikely to jeopardise the possibility, even though Jack knew it would never happen. Kane just wanted out of this mess. Jack wasn't in a position financially to think twice about Kane's offer. With four kids to keep, and a wife who didn't know the meaning of getting off her fat arse to work, his wages were all that had kept the wolf and the tally-man from the door.

Joanie snipped the final thread and shook out the dress. It hadn't taken too long to do all three. She'd had a bit of a delay when the cotton got tangled under the foot of the machine and she'd had to cut and pull out all the knots from below the shuttle area. Jack would still be around and there would be lights on as she made a dash back to the floor below. It was getting really dark now and hard to see what she was doing. She switched off the power to the over-locker, carefully folded the dresses and put them back in the bag. The door was shut but she could see from the glow through the dirty glass panels that a light was on outside on the landing, which meant Jack was on the premises. She pulled on her coat, picked up her handbag and the dress bag and hurried out of the room. A wall of smoke hit her as she ran down the first few stairs and she could hear the crackle and popping of fire that sounded like wood burning in a stove. She realised with horror that the glow she had seen wasn't a light, but was coming from a fire on the floor below, and the flames were now licking up the wooden staircase. The heat was immense.

She sank back against the wall, choking on the smoke and feeling more frightened than she'd ever felt in her life. Where was Jack Carter? She yelled his name, and then ran back up the stairs to the top, looking down at the grounds below through the window. She could see by the pale moonlight where Jack usually parked his motorbike by the wall, but he must have left, because the bike had gone. That meant the doors would be locked and she was trapped alone in the burning building. She was gasping for breath now and ran back into the workroom, slamming the door closed behind her.

The smoke had followed her. Although it wasn't as dense in here, she could still taste it and it caught the back of her throat. She ran to the window, picked up a metal box and hurled it at the glass. The window shattered and the cold night air rushed in. She broke each of the four large windows in turn and screamed for help at the top of her voice, but there wasn't a soul in sight. Shivering and terrified, Joanie slid to the floor and wept. Frank would be here soon, she told herself; he'd see what was happening and call the fire brigade. She could hear roaring now and the crash and explosion of glass as the flames shattered the windows on the floor below.

Had the other girls got out safely? She huddled into a tight ball and stuffed her fists into her mouth, trying not to breathe in the acrid fumes. She'd never felt so frightened, even in the war when the bombs were dropping on Liverpool during the Blitz. Somehow she'd known they'd all be fine in the little Anderson shelter down at the bottom of the garden.

She thought about her mam and all her brothers, but most of all she thought about Frank. He'd be here soon, she thought again; he'd rescue her. The smoke was stinging her eyes now and as she looked across the room she could see the flames licking the wooden frame of the doors: then the glass panels made a loud cracking sound as they broke and the flames leapt in, hot and fierce. She gently rubbed her tummy and thought of her precious baby growing in there and hoped that inhaling smoke wouldn't do it any lasting damage.

Bales of fabric piled up near the door caught fire and all around her the floorboards were hot and fingers of smoke crept up through the gaps from the floor below. Joanie pulled herself to her feet and pressed as close to the window frame as she could, trying to take deep breaths, but nothing entered her lungs except the smoke. As she stared at the road she saw a bright light coming towards the factory and it turned in at the gates. Frank, on his motorbike? It had to be. Thank goodness for that, he'd come to rescue her. 'Daddy's come to take us home,' she whispered to her unborn child. She tried to take in a lungful of air to call Frank's name as the bike engine stopped. But her legs gave way and she collapsed onto her knees as the flames and thick, choking smoke enveloped her and robbed her of her last breath.

Frank dismounted his motorbike and looked up at the factory building in disbelief. Flames leapt from each broken window and smoke was billowing from the roof in places. He'd spotted the thick smoke as he'd roared up the lane and an inner fear told him it was coming from Palmer's. There was no sign of the fire brigade - or anyone for that matter. Jesus, what if Joanie was still in there? He couldn't see her anywhere on the lane or near the bus shelter.

On shaking legs he ran to the phone box down the lane and dialled 999. 'There's a fire at Palmer's factory on Old Mill Lane,' he yelled at the telephonist.

'Just putting you through, caller,' she said. Someone from the fire brigade answered his call. He gasped out his tale and said that his wife might be in the building. He was told an ambulance, the fire brigade and police were on their way. He dashed back to the factory and hammered on the door; he tried the handle, but it was locked. Thankfully it looked like everyone had left early and he relaxed slightly, wondering what he should do while he waited.

A man walking his dog shouted from the lane. 'You all right, mate? Have you phoned for help?' He walked across to Frank. 'Is everybody out?'

'I think so. The doors are locked. There are no bikes or cars on the car park. I've come to meet my wife, but she must have finished early and caught the bus. I bet she's at my sister's place now, cursing me for missing her.'

The man nodded and pulled his dog back towards the lane as the clanging bells of a fire engine sounded in the distance.

By the time the man came back with half a dozen of his neighbours, the firemen were uncoiling hoses from two red machines and an ambulance had parked by the factory wall. A police car screeched to a halt and two uniformed officers jumped out. Frank ran over to them and shook his head. 'I think it's empty,' he said. 'I thought my wife might be in there, but the front door was locked when I tried it.'

'So the factory has been open today?' the first officer asked.

Frank nodded. 'Yeah. They close down tomorrow for good. They must have finished early. I've come to pick my wife up, saw the place was ablaze and rang 999.'

'And you're absolutely certain no one is in there?' As the officer spoke a loud cracking and roaring above them saw part of the roof give way and flames leaping skywards. 'Bloody hell! They wouldn't stand a chance in that,' he muttered. 'We need to get all the people that have come to gawp back behind the wall while the fire brigade try to bring this under control. If that's your bike, sir, can you move it to a place of safety?' He shepherded the gathering crowd out of the grounds as the fire blazed out of control and the firemen fought a losing battle.

'I'm going to ride to my sister's to make sure my wife is safe,' Frank told the officer. 'It's only a short distance away.' He could ring, but he might see Joanie walking along the lane. It was possible he'd missed her on his way here.

'Thank you, sir. Would you mind coming back and letting us know she's okay, and then we can be certain the building is definitely empty.'

'Be back as soon as I can,' Frank said and set off to Dora's place.

Dora looked up as she heard the motorbike pull up outside. 'They're here, Joe. Good, I'm starving. Looking forward to a big bowl of Scouse.' She got up to open the door, but only Frank dashed in, looking dishevelled and frantic.

'Is Joanie here with you?' he asked, a catch in his voice.

'No, I thought you were meeting her from work. Wasn't she waiting for you as planned? Maybe she got the bus to Mam's to get changed.'

'She's not at Mam's; I called in quick on my way here.'

Dora frowned. Frank looked like he was about to collapse and she grabbed his arm and sat him on the sofa. 'Well where is she then?' Frank's face was white: all his colour had drained away. 'Frank, what is it? What's happened?'

'The bloody factory's on fire. It's an absolute inferno,' he cried. 'Oh my God, Joanie must still be in there. The door was locked, I tried the handle. If she's not in there, *where* the hell is she?'

Dora clapped her hand to her mouth. 'No, she can't be in there. She should have been out long before Jack Carter locked up. She must have stopped off somewhere and you just missed her.'

'Well where? Tell me where to look?' Frank got to his feet, tearing at his hair in an agitated way.

Joe grabbed his jacket and bike keys. 'Come on; get on the back of my bike. We'll go to the factory and you can look out for her on the way.' He bundled Frank outside as Dora stood and watched them pull away.

'Be careful,' she called after them. She closed the door and stood at the front room window, staring out at the cold dark night. There had to be somewhere Joanie might have gone on her way home, but she couldn't think where. She sat down on the sofa, praying that Joe and Frank would come across her friend happily strolling along the road. She couldn't believe that Jack Carter would lock up and go with Joanie unaware that she'd been left behind. There was a phone in Mr Kane's office, but the door was usually locked before the main doors. Joanie would have been unable to summon help if she'd been accidentally locked in. 'It's an absolute inferno,' Frank had said. She felt sick. What if Joanie was trapped on the top floor? Loud sobs burst from her and tears rolled down her cheeks. She couldn't be. It didn't bear thinking about.

Chapter Twenty-Three

Joe pulled up on the lane by the factory wall and he and Frank ran towards the police officers, who were trying to keep people back. Frank grabbed the arm of the officer he'd spoken to earlier.

'My wife's not at my sister's,' he cried. 'She must be still in there.'

The officer ran towards the fire fighters who were struggling to contain the blaze. He yelled at one of them and pointed to Frank. Frank saw the fireman shake his head and speak to another man who was directing the hose, but to no avail; the fire burned fiercely, out of control. More engines screamed up the lane and swung into the factory yard. Hoses were unfurled, extension ladders on top of the vehicles were unfolded and the firemen climbed up and aimed gallons of water at the top of the building. The officer came back to Frank and Joe.

'I'm sorry, sir, but there's no way in until the fire is under control. It's too dangerous. An officer has gone to get the foreman.'

'No,' Frank screamed. 'Please try and get her out. Joanie! My Joanie. She's pregnant. You have to get her out, please.' He dropped to his knees, sobbing uncontrollably and calling her name, as the officer shook his head at Joe and mouthed 'I'm so sorry.'

Joe dropped down beside Frank. He took him in his arms and held him while Frank sobbed heartbrokenly against his shoulder. Joe swallowed hard and fought to control his own tears. There was no way Joanie could possibly still be alive in that inferno. Another police car pulled into the yard and a man Joe recognised as Jack Carter got out alongside two other officers.

He ran across the yard and pulled on Jack's arm. Jack turned and frowned, but then recognised him as Dora's husband.

'Joe? What are you doing here? Dora hasn't been in today to see us.'

'I know. She and the baby are safely at home.' He pointed at what remained of the factory. 'But Joanie's still in there.'

Jack's face drained of colour. 'She can't be. There was no one on the premises when I locked up. They all left a good half an hour before me.'

'Everyone except Joanie,' Joe said. 'She stayed behind to use an over-locker for a private job. She was presumably on the top floor when you locked up.'

'Sir, did you check the whole of the building before you locked up, including the top floor?' one of the accompanying officers asked.

Jack shook his head; sweat beaded on his top lip. 'There was no need to check the top floor. We'd only used the first floor and canteen today, and the boss's office for a bit of paperwork. Everything was ship-shape when I turned all the lights off and locked up. I'd have seen lights on in the stairwell if someone had been upstairs. It was dark - if Joanie *was* up there she'd have put a light on. And there were definitely no lights on. She's not in there, I'm telling you.' He nodded towards the factory as the front doors caved in. 'Well, you'll not need the keys now, officer.'

Joe raised his hands in agitation. 'This is wasting time. There's nowhere Joanie can be other than in there.' As he spoke the rest of the roof caved in, sending sparks flying up into the night sky. He was aware of howling and turned to look at Frank. The officer summoned one of the ambulance attendants over and Frank was helped to his feet and taken to sit on the back steps of the open ambulance. Joe followed, along with a police officer. A neighbour from the nearby cottages was handing out hot sweet tea and she gave two cups to Joe, telling him she'd put a drop of brandy in them both. Joe thanked her and placed a cup in Frank's trembling hands.

'As soon as they can they'll enter the building and search for your wife,' the officer told Frank, 'but at the moment it's not possible.'

Joe looked across to where Jack Carter was standing with another officer. The man's face was a white mask of horror, his mouth a wide O, as parts of the sandstone walls that had stood for decades fell inwards. Joe walked across and pulled Jack round to face him. 'If Joanie *is* in there, we'll want answers. A fire like this doesn't start from nowhere. You *must* have seen something.'

'I'm telling you I didn't,' Jack protested. 'I did my usual checks, turned off the lights and locked up. You can bet your life one of the workers chucked a fag end down without making sure it was out properly. They've been told not to smoke on the factory floor hundreds of times with all that fabric lying around. I might as well talk to a bloody brick wall.'

Joe raised a cynical eyebrow. 'But no one knows how or where it started until they can get in there to look. So why would *you* think it was one of the workers chucking a fag end away on the factory floor?'

'I, er, I don't, I didn't mean that,' Jack blustered, his face regaining a bit of colour, his cheeks flushing red. 'I'm just making assumptions.'

Joe shrugged and stared at the man, who turned his eyes away from Joe's steely gaze. 'So where's your boss tonight? Why isn't Kane here?'

'That's none of your business.'

'It's my bloody business if my sister-in-law is trapped in his blazing factory,' Joe yelled, clenching his fists.

'Sir, let's try and keep things civilised and remember that a lady is still unaccounted for,' one of the officers said. 'This isn't the time for arguing. Rest assured we'll get to the bottom of what's happened here tonight and we'll be questioning Mr Kane on his return from London.'

'London?' Joe exploded. 'He can afford to go swanning off to fucking London while his workers get laid off? I'll swing for that arsehole if our Joanie *is* in there, so help me God, I will,' he yelled as the officer took his arm and led him back to Frank. 'Something's not right here, officer,' he went on. 'A fire like that doesn't get going with just a fag end. It would take a while, and he'd have seen smouldering or summat as he was leaving, smelt the smoke, or seen the flames, like.'

'Leave it to us, sir. You're very upset and I think it best if we take you both home now - there's nothing you can do here and the young gentleman looks as though he's all in. If you leave your address with me we'll be around as soon as we have any news on his wife. One of our officers will bring your bike home later.'

Joe nodded and pulled Frank to his feet. They were taken to a waiting police car and helped inside. The vehicle pulled away as Joe took a last look at the burning remains of Palmer's factory. He said a silent prayer for Joanie and slung his arm around Frank as they were driven back to his home and Dora. How was he going to tell her?

Dora heard an engine pull up outside and she felt her blood run cold. She hurried to open the front door. Her heart almost stopped at the sight of the black police car and the two uniformed officers who were helping Frank and Joe from the back seats. They accompanied them indoors and she led them all into the sitting room.

'This is my wife, Dora,' Joe introduced her. 'Come on, love. Let's sit down.' He led her to the sofa and sat down beside her, holding her shaking hand.

'Has Joanie turned up here?' Frank's bloodshot eyes implored her to say yes as he flopped wearily onto one of the armchairs.

She shook her head and her eyes filled with tears. 'Was she not at the factory?' she whispered, knowing the answer already, but not wanting to hear it.

Joe's voice trembled as he said, 'I'm sorry, love. There was no sign of her. They couldn't get in, the fire was too fierce.'

One of the two officers spoke gently. 'Dora, is there anywhere at all you can think of where she might have gone tonight after she left the factory?'

A sob caught in Dora's throat as she replied, 'She was staying behind to do a bit of private work. We have a little dressmaking business on the side, you see, and we needed something finishing. She was going to do the job on the over-locker. Then she was coming here for tea with Frank. But he said she wasn't there, or at our mam's place where her and Frank live.'

The officer blew out his cheeks. 'So there's only one place she could be? Okay, thank you. We're going to leave you now, but we'll be back as soon as we have any news, and as promised, someone will bring your motorbike back later, Mr Rodgers. I suggest you all try and get a bit of rest. It could be a long night.'

Joe saw them out as Dora flung herself at her brother and cried heartbrokenly against his shoulder. Frank cried too, and held her tight.

'I don't believe this,' she sobbed. 'It's a horrible dream, isn't it? I'll wake up tomorrow and it'll all be over.'

Jack Carter stared at the remains of his beloved place of work, tears tumbling down his cheeks, his legs ready to buckle beneath him. He'd tried not to show his emotions, but as the policeman led Dora's husband away to join Joanie's devastated husband, the horror of his actions hit home. That faint noise he'd heard as he stood briefly on the landing before making his escape came back to him. The motor of an over-locking machine. He could hear it now and easily identify it, so why hadn't he recognised it back then and checked before locking up? He should have looked upstairs: he usually did - but no one had been up there during the day so he knew lights wouldn't have been left on and there'd seemed no point in chasing off what he'd thought was a pigeon intruder. He'd just needed to get out, what with the fire already spreading rapidly across the first floor. He couldn't bear to think of that poor pregnant girl trapped on her own with flames raging all around her. She must have been terrified.

'You okay, sir?' A police officer gently touched his arm. 'Would you like to sit down over there?' He pointed to the ambulance and led Jack across the yard.

'Can we find a drink for Mr Carter, please?'

Jack sat down on the back steps of the ambulance that Frank had recently vacated and put his head in his hands. His hurriedly eaten tea would be vomited up if he didn't take a few deep breaths and try to get his scrambled thoughts into some sort of order. Bloody Kane should be here to deal with this, it was *his* mess. Getting rid of the factory was one thing, but he'd ended the life of one of his workers - not intentionally, but that wouldn't count for anything once the scuffers started to investigate. She was a lovely young girl too. Been working for him since leaving school along with Dora. Never a minute's trouble. He looked up as a lady handed him a cup of tea.

'Extra sugar in it,' she announced, patting his shoulder. 'I'm afraid I've run out of brandy.'

He smiled his thanks and sipped the hot, sweet liquid.

The police officer who'd accompanied him to the ambulance spoke. 'We're going to take you home, Mr Carter. You will need to present yourself at the station at ten in the morning to make a statement.'

Jack nodded and finished his tea, resigned to the fact that he'd be facing a prison sentence in the not too distant future - if they didn't hang him for murder. He'd given them the contact details for Kane who would no doubt be after his blood too, for messing up a simple instruction.

He looked again at the remains of Palmer's. The fire seemed to be under some sort of control now and, once safe enough, the men would be entering the building to look for Joanie's body. Would they also find the cans from the lighter fuel, or would they now be a molten mess? Without proof they couldn't pin the fire on him, but he'd been the last person in the building and they'd know that a fire from a discarded fag end wouldn't spread so quickly in such a short space of time without help. Should he just confess and have done with it? He might get a lighter sentence. He shook his head. Why was he thinking like this? He'd killed someone. He deserved everything they threw at him, and so did bloody Kane.

Joe helped Dora to shuffle upright and she sat back against the pillows as Doctor Owens examined her. Joe had insisted on calling him out as she had been crying for hours and he'd had no idea what to do.

Dora was now staring ahead of her, looking completely lost. Joe looked at the doctor in despair.

He beckoned Joe to follow him into the hall. 'I'll give her a very mild sedative and I want you to make sure she gets all the rest she possibly can. I'm sure she'll be fine, given time, but in view of her earlier bout of depression after losing your daughter, I'm taking no chances.' He wrote out a prescription and handed it to Joe. 'Any further problems, just ring the surgery. I'll call and see Dora again in the next couple of days. Please accept my condolences. I've known Joanie since she was a little girl too. That pair have always been inseparable.' He shook Joe by the hand and left the house.

Joe made himself a mug of Camp coffee and a cup of tea for Dora. He took hers through and sat on the edge of the bed while she drank it. She'd cried all night and most of the morning, great shuddering sobs that racked her slender body. Frank had been up all night too, shocked into staring at the ceiling for most of it, mainly silent, but occasionally asking, 'Why?' Joe had no answers. He just felt numb. How could life go on as normal now? What would they do without Joanie? Dora had lost her best friend in the world and Frank had lost the love of his life and his unborn baby. How would any of them begin to pick up the pieces and start again? Dora handed him her empty cup and lay back, closing her eyes. He prayed she'd fall asleep and then he could nip out to the chemist and get her sedatives while Carol was having her morning nap.

He took her cup back into the kitchen and went to answer a knock at the front door. It was Dora's mam and dad. He stepped back to let them in.

'How is she?' Mrs Evans asked, removing her coat and hat and hanging them on the hall pegs.

'Heartbroken,' Joe replied. 'I've just had the doctor out. He's prescribed mild sedatives to keep her calm. I was worried in case she slipped back into that awful depression,' he finished, his eyes filling with tears. 'Did Frank get back okay?' Frank had insisted on riding home at about six in the morning; no amount of persuading would change his mind.

'He's in shock,' Mr Evans said, 'but he won't stay in. He's gone down to Palmer's. He wouldn't let me go with him.'

'I'll make you some tea, and then will you stay with Dora while I go to the chemist for her prescription? Carol's asleep in her cot. Do you think I should go after Frank? See if I can persuade him to come back here.'

'You could try,' Mrs Evans said, sitting herself down on the sofa. 'We just called in to see Joanie's mam and brothers to ask if there's anything we can do to help. They're in a shocking state. There's a young police officer with them. The boys were all in tears. It's a terrible tragedy.' She wiped away the tears that were trickling down her cheeks. 'We've known Joanie since she was a baby. Me and her mam worked together at the hall and had our baby girls almost at the same time. She and Dora were as close as sisters. It's going to take some coming to terms with, for all of us.' She patted the seat next to her and Dora's dad sat down and took her hand.

Joe brought tea through for them both and peeped in at Dora who was sleeping. 'She's out for the count,' he told them. 'I'll be as quick as I can. I'll drop her medicine off here first in case she wakes up and you can give it to her, and then I'll go and look for Frank. If she asks for me, tell her I won't be too long.'

Frank stared at the burnt-out shell of Palmer's. He lit a cigarette and sat down on the perimeter wall, tears rolling unashamedly down his cheeks. The fire brigade were still here and smoke still rose from the ruins as they dampened down flames that insisted on trying to regain a foothold on anything that was left to burn. The police officer on duty, stopping people from going beyond the temporary safety barriers the fire brigade had erected, he recognised from last night. The man nodded and came over to talk to him.

'Are you okay, sir?'

Frank shook his head. 'I'll never be okay again. We've only been married a few months. We were expecting our first baby. She was the love of my life.'

'I'm sorry.' The officer patted his shoulder.

'My sister, her best friend, she's the wife of my pal that was with me yesterday, she's heartbroken. I just don't know what we're going to do.' To his embarrassment he began to sob and couldn't stop. A bus pulled up opposite and two young women jumped off and ran across the road towards him. He looked up through his tears and recognised them as Joanie and Dora's workmates, Peggy and Maude, eyes like saucers in their pale faces.

'So it's true then?' Peggy gasped her hand across her mouth. 'Our neighbour knocked on and told me. Oh my lord, look at the state of the place.' Then she looked at Frank and frowned. ''Ere, aren't you Joanie's 'usband? Dora's brother? What's up? Why are you crying?'

Maude shook Peggy's arm in an attempt to stop her asking any more questions. 'What's wrong, Frank?' she asked gently.

'Joanie was in there,' he sobbed, taking great gulps of air. 'She still is.'

Peggy let out a yell. 'She can't be. She was getting ready to go home as we left. Said she wasn't getting the bus with us 'cos you was picking her up. She told us she was waiting for you near the doors.'

Frank shook his head. 'She was on the top floor, working. The place was well and truly alight when I got here. The fire brigade couldn't get in.'

Peggy sat down beside him and put her arm around his shoulders as Maude burst into tears and asked, 'Is she…?'

'She can't be, I tell you, that's not right,' Peggy cried as Joe's bike pulled up nearby.

'Joe,' she called, 'Joanie can't be in there. Where's your Dora?'

'She's at home. She's in a bad way.'

The police officer nodded at Joe. 'Times like this I feel helpless.'

'You and me both,' Joe said. 'Thanks for taking us home last night and bringing my bike back. I really appreciate it.'

'It's the least we could do.' The officer turned to Peggy. 'I expect you ladies will be out of a job now?'

Peggy sniffed back her tears. 'We was out of a job anyway. Palmer's went bust. It should have been our last day today. And I bet we won't get bloody paid now either. Me mam'll go mad.'

'Last day. Really?' The officer scratched his chin thoughtfully as both Peggy and Maude nodded. He took out his notebook.

'Just in case we need a statement from you, can you give me your addresses, please?'

While he wrote down the girls' addresses, Joe spoke to Frank. 'Your mam and dad are at ours looking after Dora. Will you come back with me?'

Frank gazed straight ahead at the factory shell. 'I want to be here when they find her.'

'Frank, no mate, they won't want you around. It's not a good idea.'

Frank stared at him. 'If it was Dora, what would you do?'

Joe shook his head wearily. 'Probably the same as you.'

'Well then.'

Joe waited with Frank for over two hours, torn between his anxiety to get back to Dora and wanting to offer support to her brother. The firemen were in the building, but so far there seemed to be no evidence of them finding Joanie's body.

'Do you think she got out, but was injured and wandered off over the farmland at the back?' Frank asked tearfully, hope in his voice. 'She might have been lying out there all night and we wouldn't have known.'

Joe sighed and patted his shoulder. 'Someone would have seen her if that was the case. The farmer or one of his hands, maybe. I wish I could say yes, it's a possibility.'

As he spoke a shout went up from somewhere within the burnt-out building and several people rushed forward. One of them waved to the ambulance that was still on standby near the wall and the attendants rushed over with a stretcher.

Frank made to run towards the building but was held back by a couple of police officers as the ambulance crew lifted something onto the stretcher and quickly placed a cover over. They carefully carried their load to the ambulance and closed the doors.

'Was that my Joanie?' Frank yelled as the ambulance left the site, no bells ringing.

Joe took his arm. 'Come on, Frank. Let's go home. I'm sure someone will come and see us later,' he finished, feeling helpless.

'We'll be round in a while, Mr Rodgers,' an officer confirmed. 'If you take Mr Evans home with you, we'll see him there. Leave his bike, we'll bring it.'

Joe dug in Frank's jacket pocket and handed the officer the bike keys. He led Frank away and helped him onto the motorbike, instructing him to hang on tight.

Joe could hardly see for the tears that blinded him on the short ride home. He felt overwhelmed with sadness and hoped that Dora was still sleeping. Her brother's grief would set her off again and he was terrified she'd get into such a state that she'd go back into the depression.

On Monday morning Dora felt like a zombie as she sat next to Joe on the sofa. The two visiting police officers were trying to put together an idea of Joanie's last few hours. The weekend had passed by in a haze of tears and visitors, calling to pay their respects. She'd slept most of the time and cried when she'd been awake; she'd felt mainly out of it as the sedatives did their work. She'd hardly eaten a thing but this morning Joe had made her a slice of toast with her tea and she'd forced it down.

The tears fell again as the awful realisation hit her that her dear sister-in-law had been locked in Palmer's, all alone, with a fire raging and no way out. She must have been terrified. But if the fire had been already burning when Jack Carter left, surely he'd have seen it? She voiced her thoughts to the officer, her voice wobbling as she choked on her tears.

'We'll be making a complete investigation into the cause of the fire,' one of the officers said. 'You've been very helpful, Mrs Rodgers. This isn't an easy time for you and we do appreciate that. Make sure you get plenty of rest. We'll be in touch again soon.'

Chapter Twenty-Four

December 1947

Dora sat Carol in her high chair with a Farley's rusk to chew on and flopped down onto the sofa. She curled her feet up beneath her. Her mind still felt slightly hazy, although she'd stopped taking the sedatives and was trying to pull herself together. Carol and Joe needed her and so did her brother and her parents. A few weeks of being in a fog was quite long enough.

For one thing, in quiet moments of reflection she wanted her head clear to think about Joanie and remember everything she could about her lovely lost friend, their happy times, when they were little girls, playing in the garden with their dollies and sharing their sweets before rations came into force, picking bluebells in the nearby copse on Sugar Lane; playing hopscotch on the flagged pavement outside school, lying on the lawn in the back garden with sugar sarnies for a picnic, and making each other daisy chains. How Joanie had been so thrilled for her when she and Joe had gone on their first date, wanting to know every detail the following day, leaving school together, starting work on their first day at Palmer's, right up to sharing her baby secret.

Seeing the joy on Joanie's face when she'd announced her own baby news. They'd all had a wonderful future to look forward to, and now Joanie's was gone. How was she going to manage without her? There had been times when she didn't feel she could go on and just wanted to close her eyes and never wake up again, but there wasn't a choice. She had to, for everybody's sake.

Even the funeral had seemed surreal. She vaguely remembered being in church and people speaking to her, but the rest had gone by in a blur with hazy recollections of Joe getting her dressed in a black outfit, and helping her in and out of a big black car. Joanie's mam and her four brothers, looking lost.

The police came again after the funeral to tell them that Jack Carter had been charged with arson and involuntary manslaughter. George Kane had been arrested too; something to do with fraud and being an accessory. She couldn't remember all of the conversation as Joe had taken charge again, while she'd been in and out of her own little world. But Jack had presented himself to the police with a full confession, according to Joe. Nothing would bring Joanie back though and life would never be the same for any of them.

The results of her dad's recent X-rays and sputum tests had not been good. Her mam needed Dora's support to get through the next few weeks. Mam had always been there for her, and now it was Dora's turn to give something back. The X-rays showed a large shadow on his left lung and a smaller shadow on the right. The sputum had contained blood. Malignant tumours were the diagnosis. Terminal lung cancer in an advanced state, the specialist called it. It was a lot to take in and most of the information went over Mam and Dad's heads, but Dora understood some of what was said and was glad she'd attended the appointment with them. There was an operation called a lobectomy that could help the larger tumour: it involved part of the lung being removed. And they'd also been told that a new treatment may be offered, depending on how well Dad recovered from the operation. The new treatment, cytotoxic chemotherapy, was still in its early experimental stages but had been successful in slowing down the growth of certain tumours. They'd gone home to digest the news over a cuppa and discuss what her dad wanted to do. Dora thought back to the conversation that had ensued.

'I'm not having it,' he said, banging his mug down on the coffee table and slopping tea over the rim. 'That bloody operation I mean, *or* the treatment. It'll make me ill and I want the last few weeks to be as nice as they can be for us all.'

'But, Dad, it'll slow down the spread of the cancer. That's what the specialist said,' Dora cried. 'It will give you a bit longer with us. Please, Dad, think about it. We need you.'

He shook his head. 'I've done nothing *but* think about it, and the answer's still no. You heard what he said, it's terminal. It won't save my life; we all know it's too late for that now. All it'll do is drag the end out and what's the bloody point in that? I want a nice quiet family Christmas with you all. It's our Carol's first and we should all be together here, not me stuck in hospital and you all having to visit in bad weather. I want everything we've gone through in the last twelve months to be put behind us for a few days and I'm saying no more on the subject.'

Dora and her mam knew better than to argue with him and resigned themselves to the fact it would be the last Christmas they spent with him. Dora planned to make it the best she could for them all. She wasn't looking forward to it, and although they could do with the extra money, Joe had told her he was opting out of working with the band for Christmas and New Year, which hadn't gone down well with the other members as it was their busiest time.

She'd told him to just go ahead and do it, but he wouldn't; he told her his family needed him. She was glad of his support.

All Dora could think about as she half-heartedly wrapped presents and placed them under the little Christmas tree on Christmas Eve, was how last Christmas had been so special with the news of Frank and Joanie's engagement, and then she thought about her little lost daughter Joanna and how she should have been having her first Christmas alongside Carol. It would be the same each year - the memories would always be there; diminishing as time went by, but never quite going away.

Christmas dinner was a subdued affair. No one seemed to be hungry, but they did their best, as Dora had worked hard. Carol had started trying to crawl and kept them all entertained with her antics, rolling over with no effort to get under the tree and pulling at the tinsel and baubles. She rolled over and over until she got to Uncle Frank and looked up at him, beaming. His eyes full of tears, Frank swung her up into his arms and kissed her.

'Thank God we've still got this little one,' he said, his voice husky with emotion. 'Treasure her, you two,' he said to Dora and Joe.

'We will,' Dora said, wiping tears from her eyes.

'Always, mate,' Joe said. 'Always.'

Frank lay in his bed, unable to sleep. He couldn't get Joanie out of his mind. They'd had so short a time together, but it had been precious and he would never forget the girl he'd loved with all his heart. This time last year he'd walked her home with his ring on her finger, both of them thinking they had a lifetime of loving to look forward to. In three months' time he'd have been getting ready for his role as a father. She'd been so excited at the prospect of being a mother. He didn't know how he'd cope when March came around. He'd been hitting the bottle to drown out his sorrows, but it wasn't the answer and such a waste of money. Maybe one day he'd be ready to move on, but tonight he felt nothing other than an overwhelming sadness. They should have cancelled Christmas this year. But his dad had insisted they go ahead, because he knew it would be his last and they couldn't let little Carol's first Christmas Day go by without at least making an effort. Frank was glad it was over. He closed his eyes, willing sleep to come.

* * *

In the second week of January, Dora went on the bus to visit her parents, leaving Carol with Dolly as the weather was cold. Frank had called in last night and told her that Dad had taken to his bed and he and Mam were really worried about him. She let herself in at the front door. All seemed quiet so she opened the sitting room door and went into the kitchen at the back. Mam was seated at the table, hands wrapped around a mug. Her hair fastened up in a blue turban and the faded wrap-over pinny indicated a cleaning day, but Dora couldn't smell the bleach or lavender furniture polish that usually pervaded the air after a cleaning session. Mam's face was tear-stained and her eyes red-rimmed. She looked weary. Dora's heart went out to her.

'Hiya, Mam. Any tea in that pot?' Dora knew any big gestures of sympathy wouldn't go down well. Her mam wasn't one for showing her emotions.

'Help yourself, chuck.'

Dora took a mug off the draining board and picked up the old brown tea pot that had been in the kitchen all her life. The knitted cosy was replaced regularly as and when Mam had spare bits of wool to make a new one. She put a spoonful of sugar in the mug and sat down. 'Having a bad day?'

'It's always a bad day at the moment, love. I just took him a drink up but he's flat out. He's a terrible colour.'

'Has the doctor been this morning?'

Mam looked at the clock above the table. 'He's due any time now. There's not much he can ...' She stopped as a loud bang came from above.

They both shot out of the kitchen and flew upstairs. Dad was lying on the floor and his pyjama bottoms were wet. The bucket that he urinated in was on its side.

'Trying to have a piss,' he wheezed. 'Can't bloody stand up.'

Dora dashed out of the room and ran down the stairs to answer the front door to Doctor Owens. 'Oh thank God. He's fallen,' she gasped and stepped aside as the doctor hurried up the stairs, indicating for Dora to follow him.

Mam had managed to prop Dad up against the bed and wrapped a sheet around him to preserve his dignity while she struggled to remove his wet pyjamas. Doctor Owens helped her and then listened to Dad's chest. He checked his pulse and shook his head. He beckoned Dora onto the tiny landing.

'Run down the road to Mr Jones's house and ask him to call for an ambulance. It's time your father was in hospital.'

Dora dashed out and ran down Sugar Lane as fast as she could. She gasped out her message and Mr Jones ushered her inside while he made the call. Then he accompanied her back down the lane and waited with them until the ambulance arrived. Mam was allowed to travel with Dad and she hurriedly pulled off her pinny and turban and ran a comb through her hair. Dora helped her into a coat and kissed her goodbye.

'I'll get there as soon as I can, Mam,' she said and went back inside to check the kitchen door was locked. Mr Jones had gone to bring his car down and had offered a lift to the hospital. She wished there was a way of getting in touch with Frank at work, but there wasn't. She'd call Joe from a phone once she got there and he could tell Eric to let Dolly know she might be gone some time.

At Fazakerley hospital, pneumonia had been diagnosed on top of the cancer and they were told nothing more could be done other than careful nursing and oxygen from a tank near Dad's bed. Now a mask covered his waxen face and his eyes were closed.

Dora and her mam held a cold hand each and willed him to hang on until the boys arrived. Hopefully Joe would think to go and look for Frank at the docks once he got the message she'd left with one of his workmates. Dad's chest rattled like Dora had never heard it rattle before and he was struggling to take in any air at all. Dora felt numb. Another loved one soon to be taken from her; three in just over a year. What sort of a God did this to people? Her Mam had faith but Dora didn't, not any more. Maybe it was *her* fault because she didn't go to church. But Mam did, and she'd lost the same people as Dora, so how did that work? She willed her dad to hang in a bit longer. Each time he seemed to stop breathing, Dora also held her breath, and then he'd start again with that awful rattling noise.

The door opened just after four and Frank and Joe came in together. The rigid two-to-a-bed visiting rule had been lifted.

'It's just a matter of time now,' Dora told them, choking on her words. 'His breathing is hit and miss, but he's got the oxygen to help.'

'Have you two had anything to drink this afternoon?' Joe asked, putting an arm around her shoulders.

Dora nodded. 'The nurses have been really kind. They brought us tea and biscuits earlier.'

Joe got a chair each for him and Frank and they settled in for a long night.

Her dad passed away just after nine o'clock and Dora felt her heart would break. Joe held her as she wept against his chest. Frank held Mam and the four of them joined hands around the bed and Mam said a little prayer. He looked at peace, all pain gone from his face. Her eyes red-rimmed, Mam smoothed her worn hand across his brow and told him to behave himself up there with the angels, which made them smile.

'I love you, Dad.' Dora dropped a kiss on his forehead and Joe led her from the room. Mam followed with Frank and the kindly ward sister took them to a family room, where tea and sandwiches waited for them on a small table next to a group of comfortable armchairs.

'Just take your time. There's no rush to go. It's been a long day, especially for Mrs Evans and Mrs Rodgers. And I suspect you young men have come straight from work on empty stomachs too. You all need to keep your strength up.' She left them to it and closed the door quietly on her way out.

Although Dora felt her heart had been ripped out, she helped her mam make the arrangements for Dad's funeral and supported Frank the best she could, the memories of Joanie's funeral not even a distant memory. At the end of January, Jim Evans was laid to rest in the same plot as his parents and little granddaughter, and close to Joanie's grave, in the small graveyard at Knowsley Church. People from the village he'd lived and worked in all his life attended the funeral. His work pals from Knowsley Hall turned up to pay their last respects and Joanie's mam and her friend the cook had prepared refreshments for the mourners in the village hall. Dora was grateful and relieved; it was one thing less to worry about. Her mam had been so upset and concerned this last week, because the cottage she'd lived in, since the day she married Jim, came with his job. Frank had spoken to the estate manager, who'd told him not to worry: Jim's part-time job wasn't to be replaced in the gardens due to staffing cutbacks. He'd mentioned that there was a strong possibility of Frank and Mam remaining in the cottage as tenants, paying a nominal rent to be discussed at a later date, which had brought some relief to them all.

Dora sighed as Agnes came over and gave her a hug. The tears she'd held back all morning ran down her cheeks. 'I can't believe he's gone,' she cried.

'I know.' Agnes patted her back. 'When my dad died it hurt like hell. But we're all here for you, and for your mam and Frank too.'

'Thank you.' Dora wiped her eyes. 'He's had a good turnout. I bet he's smiling down now at seeing how well respected he was in the village.'

'Well he was, bless him. Never heard anyone say a bad word about your dad. Listen, I've got tomorrow off work too, so I'll come over and keep you company if you like. Help you with Carol.'

'That would be lovely, Agnes. Joe goes back to work tomorrow and I don't fancy being on my own all day. I hope she's being a good girl for Dolly. She's trying to crawl now. She'll be into everything soon.'

Joe was talking to Frank and Alan, while keeping a close eye on Dora. He'd been worried sick that the shock of losing her dad so close to losing Joanie might send her back down the depression route again, but she'd been an amazing rock, staying strong for them all over the last two weeks, and he felt so proud of her for coping like she had done. He'd had a bit of bad news himself from work, but had said nothing yet. He'd tell Dora when he felt the time was right. The ROF factory at Kirkby was again rumoured to be closing down at the end of the year. The company was apparently losing money, the demand for munitions and small arms no longer as high as during the war. There'd been rumours of closure since before he married Dora, but they'd come to nothing, except the workforce had had less overtime for a while now. He'd need to look for another job if it happened, but for now they still had a wage coming in and there was his paid band work for any extras. They'd manage somehow. But like Dora's dad, their home came with him being employed at the ROF. No one had said anything about losing their homes, and surely it would make sense to let them pay rent to a landlord instead of direct to their employers, rather than evicting them all. Time would tell and he wasn't going to lose sleep worrying about it just yet, or worry Dora with it either.

Chapter Twenty-Five

March 1948

Dora and Agnes sat at the dining table surrounded by the wedding dress sketches Dora had made. Agnes's had been dropping in on a Saturday for the last few weeks and Dora was glad of her company . She missed Joanie dreadfully: the last five months had been lonely without her, and she'd been dreading starting work on Agnes's dress. But she knew deep down that Joanie would have insisted she went ahead and made it. It was a particularly hard month as Joanie's baby would have been due next week.

She was worried about her brother. The death of their dad had hit him hard coming so soon after losing Joanie, and she knew he'd been drinking more than he used to. She voiced her worries about Frank to Joe and Alan, who'd taken Frank under their collective wing, making sure he spent time with them rather than on his own or in the pub.

Liverpool FC were playing at home at Anfield against Huddersfield Town today. An important match, apparently. Dora knew little about football so just took Joe's word for it. But the fact that her brother had arrived earlier and told her the same tale convinced her. It had been good to see him showing a bit of enthusiasm for something that didn't come out of a bottle. There'd been great debate as they'd all left, convinced a win for their team was on the cards.

Carol was having her afternoon nap and Dora and Agnes sipped tea in peace.

'Would you like a slice of Mam's Victoria sponge?' Dora asked, jumping to her feet.

'I'd love one.' Agnes nodded and waved a sketch in the air. 'This is it, this is the one. It's perfect. I love the long bell-shaped sleeves and that square neckline.'

Dora took hold of the drawing and smiled. 'That's the one I thought you'd go for.'

'I'd like a veil too, but nothing fussy. Something similar to what you and Joanie wore would be nice.' Agnes looked at the sketch again. 'Definitely this one. If you work out how much material we need, I'll get Mam to meet me in town on my dinner break one day next week and we'll go and shop. Now are you sure there'll be the time to make it as well as yours and Carol's? I mean, it's March the sixth now and we've only got twenty weeks until the end of July. I really don't want you to feel under pressure with this.'

'We've plenty of time. I'm not taking any other work on at the moment. I couldn't face it. But making your dress is special and Joanie would never forgive me if I let you down. Right, let me get that cake and make a fresh brew before I take your measurements and calculate how much fabric we need.'

Joe, Frank and Alan piled out of Anfield football ground, buzzing with excitement. 'Are we calling for a pint before we go back?' Joe asked. 'Don't want to be home too early or we might interrupt the wedding dress committee meeting.'

'I don't see why not,' Frank said as they followed the crowds into The Albert pub on Walton Breck Road and queued for a pint of ale. They drank standing up; shoulder to shoulder with supporters who were talking about the outcome of the match, in which Liverpool FC had beaten Huddersfield Town by four goals to none, as though they'd all played on the pitch themselves. Backs were patted and pints consumed and a party atmosphere was in full swing when Joe spotted the time on the clock above the bar.

'Shit, we'd best make this our last,' he said. 'Dora's mam's coming for tea and Dora won't be happy if me and Frank get home late.'

Frank nodded. 'We'd never hear the end of it. Thanks, lads, for making me come out with you today. I've enjoyed it. It's done me good.'

Joe swallowed hard, patting Frank's shoulder, and they finished their drinks and made their way to the tram stop.

Joe suggested they call at the outdoor licence when they got off the connecting bus on Childwall Valley Road. 'Let's treat the girls to a bottle of sherry while I can still afford it.'

'Have you not told our Dora about the factory closing yet?' Frank asked.

Joe shook his head as they piled into the small shop that stank like a brewery with the distinctive aroma of hops. 'No point in worrying her unless I have to. Eric's not told his missus yet either. Should have brought a jug and we could have got some more ale.'

'I've a spare bottle here you can have, lads,' Mrs Morris, who ran the outdoor licence, said. 'Want a full jug?' She proceeded to fill up the enamel jug with ale from a tap behind the counter and then rooted out a funnel from a shelf above her head. She poured the ale into the bottle, laughing as it foamed out of the funnel and spilled over her hands. She topped up the jug again, carried on filling the bottle, then fastened the stopper tight. 'Two bob. Enjoy it.'

'Can I have a bottle of sweet sherry as well, please?' Joe dug in his pocket and pulled out a handful of coins. Frank and Alan did likewise. They split the cost between them and made their slightly tipsy way back to the prefab.

Dora put her finger to her lips as the door opened and Joe, Frank and Alan walked into the sitting room. She'd just got Carol settled for the night and the cottage pie was heating in the oven for tea. Her mam and Agnes were in the kitchen, making gravy and cooking vegetables.

'I presume they won?' Dora said as they nodded in unison and held out the bottles like a peace offering. 'You're all staying for tea, so the food will help soak up the alcohol you've no doubt already drunk. Glad to see you thought of us ladies.' She took the drinks into the kitchen.

'What was the score?' she asked coming back into the sitting room and taking their coats to put in the spare bedroom.

'Four nil,' Frank said, beaming. 'It was a cracking game. I reckon our dad was up there spurring them on. He loved his football.'

'He did. We'll raise a toast to him when I've poured the drinks. Right, you three sit at the table and *we'll* manage with trays on our knees.'

Dora handed around their drinks and proposed a toast. 'To Dad, Joanie and our Joanna, look after each other until we meet again.' They all raised their glasses. Mam wiped a tear from the corner of her eye and Frank blinked rapidly.

Dora and Agnes carried the plates through and handed them round. 'Mam's done the cooking, so you'll enjoy it, I'm sure.'

Joe got up to put a record on the new gramophone that Mam had treated them to with a bit of the money Dora's dad had left her. When Dora had protested that she should treat herself to something nice instead, she'd told them there was nothing she needed and she wanted to spoil them as they deserved it after what they'd been through in the last year. Frank had suggested the record player as something they'd both enjoy and get pleasure from, and he and Mam had paid a visit to Epstein's furniture store on Walton Road, where Mr Harry Epstein had demonstrated several modern gramophones, including the one that was now their pride and joy. As the dulcet voice of Nat King Cole filled the little room, they all tucked in to their tea.

'This is a real treat, Mrs Evans,' Alan said. 'I've been suffering Agnes's cooking these last few days. She's learning, but she's not a patch on you yet.' He ducked as Agnes took a swipe at his head.

Mam laughed. 'I'll write you a few recipes out, chuck. Then the poor lad won't starve when you marry him.'

Dora smiled. It was nice to see her mam laughing. She'd enjoyed her afternoon in town with Joanie's mam and had brought back a couple of lengths of pretty cotton print material in pastel shades to make Carol some summer frocks.

Tonight she looked happy in the bosom of her family and the sherry was giving her cheeks a rosy glow. In spite of the last few months being hard for her, Dora felt certain that her mam was going to be okay. And today, out in the front garden, the first of her dad's daffodils had started to flower as if to remind them all that spring was in the air and life must carry on, exactly as he would have wanted it to.

Chapter Twenty-Six

Ivy scanned the queue of people stretching down Longmoor Lane as they waited for tickets outside the Reo picture house. She couldn't see them yet, but she'd overheard Joe telling Eric on Thursday that he was taking Dora to see *Easter Parade* on Saturday night as the band weren't playing, with it being Easter weekend. She'd managed to drag a protesting Flo out with her. As a bus pulled up she ducked behind a couple while she eyed up the passengers who were jumping off the platform. There he was, helping Dora down and hurrying to the back of the queue. She grabbed Flo by the arm and marched her down the road.

'Where are we going? We were nearly at the front. We'll lose our places now,' Flo complained.

'Shh. We'll be fine.' She could see Joe looking in his wallet as Dora spoke to the two women in front of her. Must be someone she knew because they were laughing in a friendly way and had greeted Dora with hugs.

'There's Peggy and Maude,' Dora said as she and Joe took their places in the queue. She called their names and they greeted each other with hugs.

'Nice to see you both,' Dora said. 'Are you looking forward to seeing the film?'

'We are,' Peggy said as the queue surged forward. 'Here's your mate and her fella,' she said as Agnes and Alan came running across the road and joined them. 'We'll catch up with you in the interval.'

Dora greeted their friends as Peggy and Maude made their way inside the Reo.

'I'm so excited about this,' Agnes said, giving Dora a hug.

'Me too. I just love Judy Garland.' As Joe and Alan bought the tickets at the box office, Dora glanced around the foyer. 'Shall we get some sweets?'

Agnes nodded and followed her over to the kiosk in the corner.

'Still not much choice,' Dora said, frowning. 'It's time sweet rationing was over and done with. What about Payne's Poppets, a box between us?'

'That's fine by me.' Agnes smiled as Dora paid for the chocolates and they rejoined Joe and Alan.

As Joe took her arm Dora caught sight of two women in the box office queue. She stiffened. Was that Ivy and her mate from the ROF? What the hell were they doing here? But then again, half the population of Liverpool would be at one picture house or another tonight, all eagerly anticipating the much-advertised film. Maybe Ivy lived over this way. She had no idea as it was something she'd never thought to ask Joe. Before she got a chance to say something to him the foursome were being shown to their seats in the stalls by a uniformed usherette.

As Ivy and Flo quietly took their seats Ivy caught the words 'wedding dress' and 'first fittings next week'. Dora must be making the redhead's dress. So she was back to sewing again. She wondered if she dared ask Dora to make something for *her*. That would mean a few visits to Joe's home. And if she were a paying customer, there wasn't much he could do about it. She'd keep her ears pinned back to see if she heard any more. She had Dora's number because she'd seen it on the card posted in the newsagent's window last year but one, and had made a note of it. The piece of paper was still in her purse.

Joe's party were in the last four seats near the centre aisle and Ivy and Flo were on the row immediately behind. Except it was the redhead and her boyfriend who had the seats directly in front; but it was near enough for Ivy to reach across and tap Joe on the shoulder. That'd give him a shock. She'd bide her time. Maybe in the interval, when no doubt the women would visit the ladies.

As the curtains swung across the screen for the interval and the usherettes made their way to the front of the cinema with laden trays of drinks and ice-cream, Dora and Agnes squeezed out of their seats. Alan went to join the lengthening queue for ice-cream and Joe lit a cigarette. Ivy gave Flo some money and told her to go and queue for two tubs. She took a deep breath and leaned forward, tapping Joe lightly on the shoulder. He turned, a frown on his face.

'Evening, Joe. Fancy seeing *you* here,' she said as a look of shock and then horror crossed his handsome face.

'Ivy,' he spluttered, dropping his cigarette and then jumping to his feet to look for it. He retrieved the ciggie and his composure and sat back down again, his face slightly flushed. 'What the hell are *you* doing here?'

Ivy smiled. 'The same as you of course. It's a good film, isn't it? I've always loved Fred Astaire. It's the dancing you see. That's why I love to come and see you play, even though you ignore me these days.' She did a little pout and watched his face going a darker shade of red.

'I don't do it on purpose. I'm working, or I've got Dora with me.'

'Ah, yes, and how is she? I know she's had a bad time in the last few months.' Ivy was aware of Alan and Flo making their way back to their seats but there was still no sign of Dora and the redhead.

'She's fine, thanks. Just gone to speak to a couple of girls she used to work with at Palmer's. Er, Alan, this is Ivy and Flo. They run the canteen at the ROF.'

'Well, *I* run it,' Ivy said. 'Flo's my assistant. Nice to meet you, Alan.'

'Likewise.' Alan nodded and handed a couple of tubs to Joe. He turned around and looked up the aisle. 'Here're the girls.'

Dora and Agnes took their seats and their ice-cream tubs. Ivy heard him ask how Peggy and Maude were doing.

'Oh they love their new jobs at Tate & Lyle's,' Dora replied. '*And* they're better paid.'

Then Joe nudged Dora and pointed to Ivy, who was still leaning across the back of his seat. 'You remember Ivy, love? From work,' he added.

Dora glared at her. 'Yes, I do. I hope your message-taking has improved.'

'I'm sorry?' Ivy fluttered her eyelashes innocently.

'It was you that didn't give Joe my message when I went into labour.'

'Dora, hush, love,' Joe said. 'Now's not the time for this. It was all sorted out, remember?'

Dora turned her back on Ivy and stabbed the wooden spatula into her ice-cream tub.

Ivy raised an eyebrow at Joe and shook her head. She turned her attention to eating her ice-cream, satisfied that she'd ruffled a few feathers, if nothing else. At least now she was certain that he'd come and say something to her next week when they were in work. It was better than being ignored. She watched as Dora whispered to her friend and the redhead turned around and gave her a filthy stare. Talk about if looks could kill, Ivy thought.

As the second half of the film got underway Ivy had to bear the agony of Joe and Dora cuddling up together to the right, Joe's arm around her shoulders, and the redhead and her boyfriend stealing kisses and whispering sweet-nothings to each other to the left. They could have done that on the sofa at home instead of wasting good money at the pictures. At least Flo was enraptured by the film, and as 'The End' flashed up on screen a loud cheer went up and as one the entire cinema audience rose and left, singing the Easter Bonnet song.

Most of Liverpool was probably right at this minute walking out of cinemas in each suburb singing their heads off, Ivy thought. As they made their way up the aisle a couple whizzed past, dancing as they sang. She wished she could find someone to really belong to and have some fun with. She looked back to see if she could catch a last glimpse of Joe. He was helping Dora on with her coat and then he dropped a kiss on her lips and took her hand. Ivy swore under her breath and dragged Flo out onto the street. It might be all *love's young dream* at the moment, but one day he'd come running when he needed her to confide in again.

'I'm thinking of asking your wife to make me a new frock for my holidays,' Ivy said as Joe joined her with his brew, just as she knew he would. 'Flo would like one as well. We're having a long weekend in New Brighton next month and there's a dance on in the tower ballroom.'

Joe nodded. 'There always is at the weekend. But Dora's busy at the moment. You'll have to ask somebody else.' He took a sip from his mug and tried to change the subject. 'What did you think of the film?'

'We enjoyed it. Er, I don't know of any other dressmaker in the area and Dora has such a good reputation. Maybe if I ring her she might fit us in, or tell me of anyone else she knows that will sort us out.'

Joe shook his head. 'Why would you want Dora to make your frocks, Ivy? Surely her reaction the other night told you that you're not her favourite person.'

'Ah well, I was giving that some thought. This way she'll know that I don't hold any grudges against her for starting that phone-call rumour. It's time we let bygones be bygones, don't you think?'

Joe got to his feet. 'Do what you want. But I think you'll find she'll say no. I sometimes wonder if you ever *do* think. But just remember what I said that night at the Litherland dance. Don't cause me trouble, or you'll regret it.'

Chapter Twenty-Seven

July 1948

Following Agnes's wedding, there was high demand for Dora's dressmaking skills, but she could only take on what she could manage while looking after Carol. Her heart still wasn't really in it; it wasn't the same, working on her own, and she missed Joanie so much that some days the pain was almost physical. But as her mam said, Joanie would want her to carry on and not sit about moping all day. Dora sighed. She was doing her best to keep going. Mam came to help out a couple of days a week and took Carol for walks in the pram while Dora got the cutting out done.

That Ivy had had the cheek to phone her the other week to ask if she'd make her and Flo a new frock each. She'd turned her down, told her she was far too busy and hung up without speaking further. When Joe had come home from work she'd gone absolutely mad with him for giving Ivy their phone number. When she'd finally calmed down and let him get a word in edgeways, he told her he'd done no such thing and maybe Ivy had been given the number from someone Dora had made clothes for, or got it from the postcard that had been in the newsagent's window for ages. He said he'd tackle her about it the next day but Dora told him not to bother. Whether he did or not he didn't say, but Ivy hadn't called again.

Carol's cot had been put back into her and Joe's room again, as she did the machining at night in the second bedroom. By the end of the year the business had built up again to the point where she felt exhausted, and Joe was complaining about having Carol in with them. He'd suggested they book a holiday late summer but Dora told him she was too busy to even think about it.

'Let's get this year out of the way, and Dad's and Joanie's anniversaries, and then I'll have a bit of a break. As soon as next year's holiday vacancies are advertised in the *Echo* we'll book something.'

'When you take a break we're putting Carol back in her own room then,' Joe said. 'Every time I come near you she wakes up, little madam.'

Dora sighed. It was true. Having Carol in with them was putting a bit of a dampener on their love life. It made her feel a bit insecure and she knew she'd have to put a bit of effort in. 'We could do with another bedroom. I wish we could afford to buy a house like Agnes and Alan's.' Dora loved Agnes's posh semi-detached on Second Avenue in Fazakerley. It had bay windows and a separate dining room as well as three bedrooms. Maybe one day.

By the time Easter rolled around again, Dora had agreed on a week in Blackpool at the beginning of June. It was the Whit Week holidays and the weather was usually good at that time of year. Agnes and Alan were going with them and Alan was taking them in his car. The boarding house landlady had agreed to babysit for a small nightly fee. Dora was looking forward to dancing in the Tower Ballroom and maybe seeing a show at the Winter Gardens theatre. She was feeling excited and busy making little sundresses and matching hats for Carol, who was now talking - in her own fashion.

She kept them entertained but had a temper on her if she didn't get her own way. Uncle Frank was the only one who could pacify his niece when she was throwing one of her tantrums. She'd be just two by the time they went away and was forever running off or climbing out of her trolley. Dora made a note on her ever-increasing list of holiday needs to buy some reins. At least then Carol could walk without holding hands, which she hated to do, loving her independence as she toddled along beside them.

'She'll enjoy it on the sands,' Mam said, on an afternoon visit to Dora's home. She produced a little red and blue patterned bucket and spade from her shopping bag. 'I got these from Paddy's at the weekend when I went with Joanie's mam. I ordered a fridge while I was down there too, from Mr Epstein's shop. It's coming on Wednesday. I don't use food up as quickly as I did since your dad died, and I'm chucking such a lot away when it goes off. Our Frank's given me half towards it. I think we'll end up saving a bob or two in the long run. Mr Epstein gave me a bit of a discount. He had his youngest son Brian in helping him at the weekend. Lovely lad; pleasant and polite. Very well spoken. Mr Epstein told me he might be opening a music shop right next door and Brian will be running it for him, along with the oldest boy. That'll be nice, won't it? You and Joe will be able to buy your records from there once it's opened.'

Dora smiled. Her mam's face looked quite lit up when she mentioned the furniture dealer. 'Nice, is he,' she teased, 'your Mr Epstein. Is there a Mrs Epstein?'

Mam realised she was having her leg pulled and laughed good-naturedly. 'As it happens, yes there is, and she's called Queenie. So you can just stop that, our Dora. I'm not looking to replace your dad. He was the best. Anyway, go and get that kettle on. A body could die of thirst waiting for a brew in this place.'

'Shall we have a stroll along the prom?' Joe asked, popping Carol into the trolley and fastening the straps before she tried to clamber out. 'We've got an hour to kill before our evening meal.' The boarding house was on Balmoral Road, the landlady, Mrs Fowler very kind, but guests were not encouraged to go back to their rooms until it was almost meal time. Not that there was much to go back to. Although spotlessly clean, the room that overlooked the back garden, with glimpses through the trees of the pleasure beach, was sparsely furnished, and although adequate, nothing fancy.

'Hee haws,' Carol yelled, as they walked by a row of tired-looking donkeys 'Me go, me go.'

'You can have a ride again tomorrow,' Dora told her and handed her a biscuit in the hope of distracting her, but Carol started to undo the restraining trolley straps, then screamed and chucked her biscuit away.

'Hey, madam, that's enough,' Joe said, taking over the trolley-pushing. He yanked Carol upright as she tried to get under the straps to escape. 'She'll bloody strangle herself one of these days.'

Dora sighed. 'She's a little monkey at times. Mam said they go through an awkward phase at two and I think she's going through hers now. No wonder Agnes and Alan went up to St Anne's today for a change.'

Joe shook his head. The couples were into the third day of their holiday and Carol had proved a handful from day one. 'Hopefully she'll fall asleep after tea tonight. Mrs Fowler said she'd listen out for her if she does and we can have a peaceful drink on the pier.'

Dora waved at Agnes and Alan, who had just jumped off a tram. 'Had a good time?'

'Lovely,' Agnes said and placed a little pink straw coolie hat with a white flower trim onto Carol's head. 'I saw this and thought it was just for you,' she said to the little girl who gave her a wide grin. 'Pretty lady.' She took the reins from Joe, and Carol giggled as Agnes pretended to trot behind her.

Alan smiled at his wife, and Joe slapped him on the back. 'Time you two got cracking, mate. Don't leave it too long.'

As the week progressed Carol settled into a routine of cutting out afternoon naps. Worn out with fresh air, she slept until seven most mornings. With no disturbed nights Dora felt rested and relaxed, and although Carol slept in their bedroom, she didn't stir when they came home from a night out, and the couple resumed their love life with renewed passion.

'That's the trick,' Joe said as he lay contentedly beside Dora. He lit a cigarette and blew smoke rings into the air. 'It's where we've been going wrong.'

'What is?' Dora frowned, her blonde hair fanned across the pillow. 'I wasn't aware we'd been going wrong. I thought that was pretty good just now. I enjoyed it, even if you didn't.'

Joe laughed, a teasing glint in his eyes. 'Of course I enjoyed it. I don't mean the sex, you daft thing. Carol and her afternoon naps; stop her having them and she'll sleep all night.'

Dora grinned and slapped his arm. 'God, I'd never get any peace, not from her *or* from you for that matter. We'll see. She might be different at home. It's the sea air that conks her out here.'

'Last day tomorrow,' Joe said, stubbing out his half cigarette that he'd saved for the morning. 'Dancing in the ballroom tomorrow night to look forward to.' He reached for Dora, who slid back into his arms and kissed him. 'I've really enjoyed this week. Hope we can do it again soon,' he whispered, returning her kisses with fervour.

Chapter Twenty-Eight

September 1949

Dora put the phone down and made a note on her pad that a Miss Florence Braithwaite would be coming for a consultation tomorrow night at seven. She was getting busy with Christmas dress orders already and it was only the third week of September. On top of that, she didn't feel too good, and she had recognised the signs and symptoms almost right away this time. Tomorrow morning she was visiting Doctor Owens for confirmation, but was absolutely certain that she was expecting a Blackpool baby.

Dora had saved all Carol's baby stuff, so at least they wouldn't be starting from scratch this time, but if she had a boy she'd need some new clothes for him. So many thoughts were tumbling through her mind. She was terrified of giving birth again; she was taking no chances and would opt to have the baby in hospital.

No one in the family had been told yet. Joe had suggested they wait until after the doctor had confirmed things. Dora worked out that the new baby was due in March. At least the worst of the winter weather would be out of the way.

Her greatest fear, next to the baby dying, was losing her mind again. What if she did? She'd read articles in magazines about mothers who'd been admitted to mental institutions and never came home. The thought horrified her. Joe and their children would need her and she owed it to them to try and keep herself in check.

Carol was shouting 'Mammy' from the kitchen and Dora braced herself. They could do with a bigger high chair with secure restraints - her daughter had one leg over the back and the other over the tray in an effort to climb out. 'Turn around, Carol, and finish your din-dins. There's a good girl.'

'No, want out,' Carol screamed, her face going red.

Dora lifted her down. It was pointless arguing with her. She wiped her hands and face and Carol toddled off into the sitting room and resumed playing with her building bricks. The phone rang again and Dora hurried to answer it. It was Agnes, on her break at work.

'I've got tomorrow off,' Agnes said. 'Will you be in after dinner?'

'I need to nip out in the morning but should be back about one. Is that okay?'

'Yes, that's smashing. See you tomorrow then.'

'Look forward to it.' She hung up and went back into the sitting room, where Carol had taken a pencil from the coffee table and was busy drawing squiggles on the wall near the chimney breast. Dora sighed: she must remember to put her sketching things out of Carol's reach. She tried to prise the pencil out of her daughter's tight grip, preparing herself for the usual screaming match.

'Naughty girl. Give it to Mammy.'

But Carol kicked and screamed so loud that Dora didn't hear the front door opening and her mam calling hello.

'What's going on in here?'

'Ganny,' Carol sobbed and threw herself at her granny's legs, wiping her eyes and snotty nose on the hem of her skirt.

Mam picked her up and cuddled her and the sobs subsided. 'Oh dear. She's tired, you know. She still needs that afternoon nap.'

'Well she's not having one,' Dora protested. 'If she sleeps now she won't go to bed early and we can't get anything done at night. There's no peace.'

Mam shook her head. 'There's not supposed to be peace when you've got kiddies, chuck. That's what family life's all about. Anyway, Carol, you go and get your Goldilocks book and Granny will read to you.'

Carol toddled off to her room and Dora sighed. 'Mam, I'm so tired. I've got loads of work on and I'm not feeling great at the moment either.'

'Maybe you're doing too much. Do you really need to do as much sewing? Joe's doing a bit of overtime again and he's got his weekend money coming in from the band. Can't you manage without working?'

'Well yes, I suppose we can, but I enjoy it, Mam. It's a bit of independence, having my own money. My customers are really nice and I've got a lot of regulars who recommend me to their friends. There's a new lady coming tomorrow who said her friend told her I was very good. I don't like letting people down.'

'What about trying to get Carol a place in a nursery for a couple of days a week then? There's one in Kirkby that's good.'

Dora chewed her lip. 'Depends how much it costs. And I don't think Joe would like that. We'll have a talk about it later and see. Anyway, let's have a brew now you're here.'

'There are scones in that bag.' Mam pointed to the shopping bag she'd dropped on the floor when Carol had thrown herself at her legs. 'There's a jar of my home-made blackberry jam as well. And there just might be a few dolly mixtures hiding in a corner, if someone promises to be a good girl for their mammy.'

Carol was now sitting on the sofa with an angelic smile on her face and her favourite book clutched in her hands. Butter wouldn't melt, Dora thought as she went into the kitchen. How the hell was she going to cope with two? And, as she knew there was no chance of Joe agreeing to a nursery place as money needed to be saved for when she took a break next year, she wasn't even going to bring the subject up.

Dora had a sense of déjà-vu the following day as she sat in front of Doctor Owens and he confirmed her pregnancy and her due date.

'Can I have this baby in hospital, please?' she asked anxiously.

'Of course, Mrs Rodgers. I would certainly recommend that. Your midwife will pay you a home visit to arrange your antenatal care, but she'll book you into our maternity home for delivery and recuperation. We'll be monitoring you throughout your pregnancy. I'm quite sure you'll have nothing to worry about though.'

'What if it's twins again?' Dora chewed her lip. 'I don't think I could cope.'

'It's highly unlikely. But you mustn't worry. It's something we'll keep a close eye on right from the start.'

Dora nodded. 'Thank you. I'll go and break the news to everyone now.'

Doctor Owens smiled. 'Congratulations once again, Mrs Rodgers.'

Mam had Carol for the afternoon and Frank would bring her home after tea. Dora would tell them both her news then: when she went to the doctor's she'd told Mam a fib that she was meeting up with Agnes in town for a few hours and didn't want to take Carol with her.

Dora rang the canteen phone to speak to Joe. Fortunately it was answered by Eric who told her he'd pass on the message as Joe would be down for his dinner any minute now. The phone rang out within seconds and she snatched up the receiver.

'How did it go?' Joe's anxious voice came down the line.

'Fine, Daddy,' she said, feeling a smile coming on. 'We're expecting number two in March.'

There was silence while he digested her news and then, 'Oh, sweetheart, that's wonderful. And are you okay about it?'

'Yes, I'm fine. We'll talk when you get home, after I've finished with the lady who's coming to be measured up. I'm feeling quite excited now. I can't wait to tell Agnes. She'll be here any minute. And Joe, don't say anything to Eric just yet, otherwise I'll have Dolly under my feet all afternoon. I need to get used to the idea before she passes it around the estate.'

'My lips are sealed. Enjoy your afternoon with Agnes and I'll see you later. I love you, Dora.'

'Love you too,' she replied and hung up, feeling warm inside. She dashed into the kitchen and made a pot of tea and a plate of cheese sandwiches and carried them through to the dining table as the doorbell rang. Praying it wasn't Dolly come for a nosy - Eric was bound to have rung her and told her she'd just called Joe - she dashed to open it. Agnes greeted her with a hug and a bunch of colourful chrysanthemums.

'Oh those are lovely,' she exclaimed. 'Thank you so much. Come on in and I'll put them in water.'

'You okay, Agnes?' Dora asked as they sat on the sofa with a brew. 'You look as though you're bursting with gossip.'

Agnes laughed. 'I am. I've got some really good news to share.'

'So have I,' Dora said with a grin.

'Have you? Go on then, what is it?'

'No, you go first.'

Agnes's smile was lighting up her whole face as she put down her mug. 'I'm pregnant!'

'Oh my goodness, so am I!' Dora exclaimed.

The delighted pair did a little dance around the room and then sat back down on the sofa, laughing and crying at the same time.

After they'd got their breath back they exchanged date details. They were both due the same month. 'I can't believe it,' Agnes said. 'How lovely that we can share this together. Oh, I'm so happy.'

'Me too,' Dora said. 'I'm so glad you're going to go through it with me. I'm a bit scared, I have to admit, but I'm also really excited.'

'We'll both need some new maternity smocks. Will you feel up to making any?'

'I'll do my best. It'll be a while before your own things get too tight, and I'll make us a couple of smock dresses each for Christmas and New Year. I've got a new order coming in tonight and then that's it. With our new dresses now, I'm booked up until Christmas anyway. I'm planning on taking a few months off while I adjust to having two kids. God help me.'

'Is Carol still playing you up?'

Dora pointed to the wall where her daughter had scribbled yesterday. 'Joe said there's some distemper in the shed the same colour, so he'll paint over it when he gets a minute.'

'She might be as different again when the new baby comes along.'

'Maybe. I hope she won't be jealous. It'll take a bit of adjusting for her. But we can live in hope.'

Joe was reading Carol a bedtime story when the doorbell rang. Dora smoothed her hair down and fixed a smile on her face as she swung the door back. Her welcoming smile froze and her jaw dropped as the two women on the path outside greeted her with friendly nods.

'Good evening, Mrs Rodgers.' Ivy Bennett spoke first. 'Miss Braithwaite has come to be measured for a new dress.'

Dora found her voice. 'I'm afraid there must be some mistake. I told you I was too busy ages ago.'

'Well that's not what you told Flo here yesterday, now is it?' Ivy said, the friendly smile leaving her face. 'She's booked in to see you at seven tonight. So I think the mistake must be yours.'

Flo stood in front of Dora where Ivy had pushed her, and Dora could swear from the blank look in the woman's eyes and the way her jaw drooped to one side as she smiled that she wasn't all there, as her mam would say. She pursed her lips. 'You'd better come in then.'

She showed them into the sitting room. 'Please sit down. I'll be with you in a moment.' She hurried out of the room, closing the door behind her. She crept quietly into their bedroom where Joe, on the bed, had his eyes shut with Carol's book flat across his chest. Carol was asleep in her cot. She shook him gently by the shoulder. 'Shh,' she warned as he opened his eyes. 'Bloody Ivy and Flo are in the sitting room. I didn't recognise Flo's name when she booked her appointment. I've no choice now but to see to her, but will you stay in here and I'll get rid as soon as I can.'

Joe sat bolt upright, wide awake now. 'You're pulling my leg?'

'I am *not*,' she whispered. 'I'm fuming. They've duped me into this. But I'm offering no tea and biscuits like I usually do.'

'What if I need a pee?'

'Oh, I don't know, Joe, just cross your legs or something.' Dora dashed back out of the room and closed the door firmly behind her. She put her best businesslike smile on, grabbed her tape measure and sketch pad from the sewing room and went back into the sitting room.

'If you'd just like to remove your jacket, Miss Braithwaite, I'll take some measurements. And I have a pad here with some of the dress designs that I think will suit your figure and shape best.'

'You can call me Flo, if you like.' Flo gave a shy lopsided smile.

'I know the style she wants,' Ivy butted in before Flo could open her mouth further.

'It's not a case of what *you* want, it's what suits Flo best,' Dora said firmly, whisking the tape measure around Flo at strategic points and writing down her measurements. 'People often wear dresses that don't suit and are too tight,' she said, trying not to smile as she thought about Ivy's flab poking out of her red dress when it split a few Christmases ago.

Ivy didn't rise to the bait but just glanced around the neat-as-a-new-pin room, her eyes alighting on Joe and Dora's framed wedding photograph on the mantelpiece next to a photograph of Joanie. 'Joe out tonight, is he?'

Dora shook her head. 'He's busy getting our daughter to sleep.'

Flo smiled and sat back down again with the sketch pad on her knee. 'I like this one, Dora. Do you think it would suit me?'

Dora looked. It was the sweetheart neckline, New Look dress, with the figure-skimming skirt. 'I think it would look lovely, Flo. You can stand to have the skirt a little fuller as you're so slim. And I can put extra darts in the bodice to give more shape up top.'

'What do you think, Ivy? It was your idea to come here, so maybe you can help me choose,' Flo said as Ivy wriggled uncomfortably on the sofa. 'Do you think this one will suit me?'

Dora raised an eyebrow as Ivy's cheeks flushed and her eyes narrowed. 'Caught you,' Dora muttered under her breath. Well, if she had any thoughts about gawping at Joe tonight she was going to be disappointed.

Ivy glanced at the open sketch pad and nodded. 'Anything's better than what you usually wear,' she muttered.

'Right, I'll work out how much fabric you need, Flo. And then you can give it to Joe at work. Save you coming all this way again until I need to see you for a first fitting. And Joe will let you know when that will be.' Dora sat at the table and quickly worked out Flo's fabric requirements and handed her a page from the notebook. 'Keep it safe until you have time to go to the shops. I'll need the fabric within two weeks if you decide to go ahead. Otherwise, I won't be able to fit you in. I'm booked up for Christmas and then will be taking time off early next year for a few months, so I won't be accepting any more orders after this one.'

'Well, thank you for seeing me.' Flo got to her feet and pulled on her jacket. 'I'll get the material at the weekend and give it to Joe on Monday, if that's okay with you.'

Dora nodded and opened the door leading to the hall. 'Thank you for coming. I'll see you soon.' Ivy got to her feet and pushed rudely past, pulling Flo along with her.

'Bye, bye, Mrs Rodgers and thank you,' Flo said as she was practically dragged outside.

Dora closed the front door and leant against it. She took a deep breath and tapped on the bedroom door. 'You can come out now.'

Joe dashed out, shaking his head, and rushed straight into the bathroom. Dora grinned and went to put a light under the pan of blind Scouse she'd made earlier. That had put an end to Ivy's antics. She was no doubt expecting a social evening as their guest, but she'd gone away without as much as a cuppa or a glimpse of Joe. Served her right. Poor Flo had looked so uncomfortable standing at the door and she hadn't had the heart to turn her away. Ah well, one more visit for a fitting - which she'd arrange for a Saturday afternoon to coincide with a football match, when Joe would be out - and then he could take the finished dress in to work before Christmas and collect payment.

She set the table and smiled as he came and stood behind her and slipped his arms around her waist. 'Alone at last,' he murmured into her hair. She turned in the circle of his arms and kissed him. They had so much to look forward to and she couldn't wait to share Agnes's good news with him too.

Chapter Twenty-Nine

March 1950

Weighing in at a healthy seven pounds four ounces, Jacqueline Mary Rodgers came into the world on Sunday 12th March. Her birth had been easy, much to Dora's relief. She hadn't even realised she was in labour, although she'd had twinges all day; they hadn't been significant, and she and Joe had been at the local park with Carol for most of the afternoon. It was only after tea when she went to pay a visit that things started to happen and her waters broke, just like they'd done when the twins were born. She'd panicked and Joe had called for an ambulance, as they'd been instructed to do should labour begin. She'd been in the maternity home since just before seven and her baby had arrived just after half past nine.

Joe took Carol to Mam's and then Frank dropped him off at the maternity home. He'd been allowed in to see them both once Dora and the baby were cleaned up and ready. Dora was relieved that she'd had no forceps or stitches this time and she was keeping her fingers crossed that she would be able to breastfeed her new baby. She smiled at Joe as he looked tenderly at his tiny daughter with wonder in his eyes.

'Isn't she gorgeous?' She smiled proudly, her love for her new daughter overflowing.

'She's beautiful,' he said softly. 'Blonde and blue-eyed, just like her mammy.'

'Well that's one like each of us now. Carol's like you and Jackie's like me.'

'So we're calling her Jackie for short, are we?'

'I think so. Bet Mam will be pleased that we've added Mary as well.'

The door opened and a nurse appeared with a trolley. 'Mr Rodgers, you'll have to go now, I'm afraid. Your wife needs to rest. Visiting times are two until three and seven until eight each day, except weekends and then it's two until four. Children are allowed to visit for a short time, weekend afternoons only.'

Joe nodded. 'Thanks, Nurse. Your mam's keeping hold of Carol for now,' he told Dora. 'I rang Agnes to tell her and she said if she's not in here herself tomorrow, she'll come and see you in the afternoon. She said congratulations and she sends her love. I'll see you tomorrow night. Dolly said she'd look after Carol for me. I'll sort out some holiday leave when I nip into work in the morning. Sleep tight, love, and well done. I'm so proud of you.'

Ivy pursed her lips when she came back from a visit to the ladies to see Joe being patted on the back and congratulated by the workforce on the birth of his new daughter. She fixed a smile on her face and went to shake his hand.

'I'm glad it all went well this time, Joe,' she said, hoping she sounded genuine. 'Give Dora mine and Flo's best wishes.' She walked away, crossing her fingers in her apron pocket. She didn't wish his new daughter any harm, but she hoped that Dora had another mad spell and that Joe would confide in her again. This time she might not get better. Ivy had all the time in the world to wait. She'd put her life on hold for him, so what was a few more years?

She and Flo had paid one further visit to his home for the dress fitting, but he'd been out at a football match. Flo's dress was beautiful and transformed her shape. The burgundy fabric dotted with soft pink flowers suited her. With her hair nicely set and a bit of make-up on, she'd looked passable and had even been asked to dance a couple of times over Christmas. But when she suggested asking Dora to make another dress, Ivy told her not to and reminded Flo that Dora was taking a break. It hadn't taken Ivy long to realise why when Joe proudly announced her pregnancy to all and sundry. So much for that; but it had left her with a tiny seed of hope that Dora might have a relapse following the birth.

'Don't poke the baby, there's a good girl,' Dora said as Carol sat beside her on the bed scowling at her sister who was being breast-fed. Dora had tried to read a story to Carol, but she wasn't paying any attention except to Jackie, so she'd given it up as a bad job.

'My do that?' Carol asked, pointing.

'No, darling, you have your milk in a cup. You're a big girl now.' Joe had had a week's holiday to care for Carol, but had gone back in today. They were waiting for Dora's mam to arrive to help out. Dora had been discharged from the maternity home yesterday afternoon. Jackie had been easy to feed from the word go and she was such a contented baby, far more settled than Carol had ever been. Dora felt very protective towards Jackie and couldn't bear it when anyone else held and cuddled her. She was terrified they'd pass on germs or colds and was forever telling people to wash their hands before they picked her up. The midwife was calling in later and would come each day until Jackie was fourteen days old.

Poor Agnes still hadn't gone into labour and was being admitted to the maternity home today to be induced. She'd told Dora she wasn't looking forward to it as a neighbour had put the fear of God in her, telling her all sorts of tales about things that could go wrong. Cords wrapped around necks and babies getting stuck and having to have limbs amputated. The kindly nurse who'd looked after Dora tried her best to reassure Agnes and told her that inductions were very common and she and her baby would be just fine. Dora wondered how she was getting on; as she would have been in there for at least four hours now. Hopefully there would be a call from Alan later with some good news.

As Jackie stopped sucking Dora cuddled her close. She could sit here all day holding her like this. It was such a nice feeling and she felt sorry that she'd missed the experience with Carol, those precious first weeks when a mother gets to know her newborn. Maybe that was why Carol played her up a lot. At times she seemed closer to Joe and Mam and Frank than she was to Dora herself.

'Only me,' a voice called from the hall.

'Ganny's here, goody!' Carol shot off the bed and Dora breathed a sigh of relief. She could relax now and shut her eyes for a while.

Her mam popped her head around the door, Carol in her arms, looking smug. 'Sorry I'm a bit late. Queue in the butcher's was right outside the door. He'd got lamb chops in and word had got around.' Although rationing was officially over in the main, it was still hard to get a lot of things. 'I got a couple for yours and Joe's tea, and some nice lean mince for tomorrow, and the butcher had just made some potted beef, so I got some of that as well. Do for our dinner today and Joe's sarnies tomorrow.'

'Thanks, Mam. There's some money in the kitchen cupboard in a little toffee tin. Take what we owe you out of that.'

'I will. Now I'll make you a nice cuppa before the midwife comes, and I'll get this little monkey sorted out. Uncle Frank's sent her a colouring book and some crayons, so I'll put a cloth on the table and she can sit on a cushion on a big girl's chair and do a nice picture for Mammy and one for Uncle Frank to say thank you.'

Carol beamed and went off quite happily with Granny. Dora lay back with a sigh of relief and wondered how she was going to cope on days when her mam couldn't be around. She'd had a congratulations letter the other day from Sadie and Stan, her friends from the village, with an invite to pop in for a cuppa any time she was in town. She wondered how they coped with two babies so close together - and Sadie was now expecting a third. That would be three under-fours in a house with no bathroom or inside toilet, and still no sign of the new house or flat they'd been hoping to get by moving from her mother's overcrowded house in Knowsley and into the slum clearance area down near the docks. It didn't bear thinking about, all those germs near a new baby. Even though Dora would like to see more of Sadie, the thought of visiting made her feel sick. Sadie deserved a nice home and a decent length of time in-between having her babies. There was no way Dora ever wanted more. They had a perfect family now. Joe would have to sort things out before she'd let him near her again.

Dora stirred as Joe called her name. She sat up slowly, feeling light-headed. She must have dozed off again after feeding Jackie, who was asleep against her breast. The bungalow was quiet, which meant Carol was also sleeping.

'That was Alan on the phone. Agnes has had a girl. Patricia-Anne. Eight pounds, dead on. Born at ten past seven.' He was reading from a piece of paper and he looked up from it and smiled. 'Thought I'd better write it all down. You know what you women are like for wanting all the details.'

'Oh, thank goodness for that. And are they both okay?'

'They're fine. Not so sure about Alan though, he sounded a bit shell-shocked.' Joe laughed and came to sit on the bed. 'Would you like a drink of something? Your mam said Horlicks is good for you when you're feeding. She showed me how to make it before Frank picked her up. Said she'd see you tomorrow.'

'Thank you, Joe, that would be lovely. I'm so happy for Agnes and Alan. Did he say what colour hair the baby's got?'

'Yeah, red like Agnes's.'

Dora laughed. 'Me and Agnes thought it would have red hair, no matter what it was. I can't wait to see them.'

'Well she's in all week, so why don't you go and visit on Saturday and I'll look after the kids. There's no home game so I won't be going to Anfield.'

A feeling of panic came over her as Dora thought about leaving her baby. 'Oh I'm not sure, Joe. I can't really leave Jackie; she might need feeding while I'm out.' Not only that, what if she picked up germs from the hospital? Saturday was family visiting day. When she'd been moved into a four-bed ward while she was in with Jackie, a woman's husband and five grubby little boys had come to visit. One of them, a skinny little thing with scabby knees and a pronounced squint, had sauntered over to her bed and gawped at her while she was cuddling Jackie. Dora had seen lice running on his scalp and the tell-tale sores of impetigo on his chin. She shuddered at the memory of the fetid smell that had wafted from them all as they passed by her bed on leaving the ward, feeling sorry for the pleasant woman who would be taking her first daughter back to a home that was less than clean. 'I'll wait until they come home,' she muttered.

By the time Jackie was six weeks old Dora felt worn out. Her hands were red and sore from constantly bleaching everything she came into contact with. Joe had complained the bungalow smelled like a hospital ward, because she wiped everything down with Dettol on a daily basis. He'd pushed away his meal last night and said the bacon and eggs tasted odd. When she'd taken a sniff she could smell bleach and threw it in the bin. Joe had settled for a Spam sarnie but she could tell he wasn't happy; he had gone to bed early in a sulk.

The district nurse had been to weigh Jackie and check her progress and had expressed concern when Dora said she wouldn't be bringing the baby to the clinic for regular weight checks as she was worried about her picking up germs that might make her poorly.

'But, Mrs Rodgers, it's important that you bring Jackie so we know she's doing okay,' said Miss Stokes the health visitor. 'We do our best to keep everywhere as germ-free as possible in the clinic, just like you do in your own home, dear.'

'That's what I told her,' Mam said, coming in from the back garden where she'd been hanging nappies on the washing line. 'And a few germs never hurt anyone. You're being too fussy, chuck.'

Dora turned to her mam. 'I'm not. I need to look after her. I couldn't bear to lose another baby, Mam. It must have been something that I did wrong. I'm not taking any chances with Jackie. You don't know what she might pick up where there are crowds of people.'

Mam shook her head. 'Sweetheart, losing Joanna wasn't because of anything you did. It was just one of those things that sometimes happen with birthing babies.'

Miss Sykes nodded her agreement. 'What if we give you a separate appointment for a week or two? Then you can come and be long gone before we get busy.'

'Can't you come here like you've done today?' Dora asked. 'Bring the scales with you again.'

'Let me have a word with Doctor Owens, Mrs Rodgers. I'll come back and see you in a couple of days. Meantime, keep up with the four-hourly feeds and if you feel Jackie isn't getting enough milk from you, then you'll need to top her up with a bottle feed. If you come to the clinic, you can use your milk tokens for the National Dried Milk, and you can get vitamins and orange juice for Carol too. We also need to book you in for your postnatal check-up. It's due this week.'

Dora nodded and sat back on the sofa with Jackie in her arms while Mam showed the health visitor out. When she came back into the sitting room, Dora looked up.

'You think I'm going daft again, don't you, Mam?'

Mam raised an eyebrow. 'I can understand what's behind your obsession for going mad with the cleaning, love, but it's not right. Now listen. Jackie's fast asleep. Carol's playing in the back garden with Dolly's little Alice and you, my girl, are going to get in the bath and have a long soak while we've got some peace. Go on, you'll feel better. And wash your hair while you're about it, you've been scratching again and you'll make your scalp sore if you're not careful. Put Jackie in the cradle and I'll sit with my knitting for a while.'

Dora lay back in the lavender-scented bubbles unable to shake off the feelings of anxiety that were permanently with her. She appreciated all her mam's help and couldn't manage without her, but at times she felt she didn't fully understand her concerns about germs and keeping Jackie safe, and neither did Joe. The only person who would have understood her worries was no longer here. She was missing Joanie more than ever now. Joanie would have known how she felt and she was thankful she had her photograph to talk to. She sighed, dunked her hair under the water and rubbed some soap into her scalp. The clinical smell was horrible, but since leaving the maternity home she couldn't get the thought of picking something up out of her head. She'd overheard her mam and Joe whispering about her the other day while she'd been trying to sleep. It was obvious they thought she was going mad with the depression again, and although they'd not actually said anything to her, she could see it in their faces. They just didn't understand, so there was no point in confiding her worries to them.

While Dora took her bath Mary's thoughts tumbled round in her head. Her daughter was showing signs of not coping again. It had started as soon as she was discharged from the maternity home.

She'd complained of her hair feeling itchy. Mary had checked her scalp several times but had found nothing, even though Dora still scratched her head all the time. Joe had told her of his concerns while Dora was sleeping the other day. The poor man couldn't seem to do right for doing wrong at the moment. She didn't really have an answer but she knew what might buck Dora up a bit - a visit from her pal. She got up from the sofa and found Dora's address book on the hall table by the phone. Agnes picked up right away and promised to pop over tomorrow afternoon. Dora had only seen Agnes and baby Patsy once since her birth. It would be a lovely surprise for her. Mary would make sure she was here nice and early to help her daughter tidy up and then there'd be no excuses that she was too tired for visitors.

She went to the back door, called Carol in and sent Alice back to her mother. While Mary's back was turned for a moment as she watched Alice slip through the gaps in the fencing, Carol ran into the sitting room. Mary called her back, told her off, as shoes weren't allowed on the carpets when they'd been out in the garden, and washed the little girl's grubby hands and face.

'Now go and sit at the table and I'll bring your milk and biscuits through,' she ordered. 'Mammy's in the bath and baby's asleep so we're going to be nice and quiet for a while, aren't we?'

Carol shrugged in that couldn't-care-less way kids had, but did as she was told.

Dora dried herself, sprinkled on talc and brushed her hair. She felt much better for the long soak and her scalp had ceased to feel itchy for the time being. She chose a short-sleeved white cotton dress with buttons down the front for ease of feeding, slipped it on over fresh underwear and dabbed a bit of Poppy perfume behind her ears. Apart from the weight of anxiety, she actually felt almost human again. She thought about what the health visitor had said and that maybe she should accept the appointment offered to go to the clinic early before the other mothers arrived, so she could get away quickly. Once she felt confident that Jackie was not going to get ill and die, it might be easier to cope. Carol was laughing in the sitting room and Mam was singing nursery rhymes to her. Her daughter was marching up and down to 'The Grand Old Duke of York' but paused and scowled as Dora walked into the room.

'Oh, you look better, chuck. Think our Jackie's getting ready for her tea. She's doing a bit of grunting and snuffling, but that might be me waking her up with my singing. I'll make us a nice cuppa.'

Dora bent to pick up her baby as Carol giggled excitedly. 'Worm in there for baby,' she said, pointing at the cradle. Dora let out a scream that had her mam running in from the kitchen, clutching her chest.

'Oh my God. What is it? Is she okay?'

Dora shook her head and pointed. Mam looked down and saw the fat worm wriggling its way towards the baby's head, leaving a trail of soil on the spotless white sheet. She snatched up Jackie and passed her to Dora. 'She's come to no harm, chuck. Go in the bedroom with her. I'll deal with this.' She stripped the cradle of its bedding and fixed Carol with a firm glare. 'Go and sit in your room, young lady.' Carol ran off, for once needing no second telling.

Chapter Thirty

Dora sat with her back against the headboard, feeding Jackie and feeling numb. What if that worm had crawled into her baby's mouth, or tried to get up her nose or down her ears? It didn't bear thinking about.

Mam came into the room with a cup of tea. 'I've put an extra sugar in it. Are you okay, love? You're white as a sheet.'

'Why did she do it, Mam?'

'I've told her off. She's only little, love, not even three yet. She didn't know it was wrong. Kids play with worms all the time and come to no harm. I've put all the bedding through the boiler and it's on the line. I've cleaned the cradle with Dettol, as I know it's what *you* would have done, and I've put fresh bedding on.'

'Thank you, Mam. She's such a little monkey, always doing something naughty.' Dora closed her eyes wearily. 'I know she feels a bit left out, she was the apple of Joe's eye and now she has to share him. Would you mind taking her home with you tonight?'

'Of course, love. She can sleep over and then I'll fetch her back tomorrow afternoon.'

'Thank you, Mam.'

Joe banged on the kitchen window and beckoned for Carol to come inside. She was pushing a doll's pram up and down the garden path in her pyjamas. Dora's mam had filled him in on the worm incident and it had made him smile until he realised what effect it had had on Dora, who had remained in their bedroom since. She refused to budge even to eat her tea. Joe sighed as Carol ignored him.

He felt worried that it seemed to be happening again. He was losing his wife to wherever it was she went in her head after giving birth. He went outside, wrestled Carol away from the pram and carried her kicking and screaming indoors. She was sulking because she wanted to go to stay with Ganny and Uncle Frank as she'd been promised she could, but he'd put his foot down and said she had to stay here otherwise she'd feel more pushed out, if that's what the problem was.

He was in the routine of bathing her and reading her a bedtime story and he felt it was important to carry on doing that. He bounced her onto the bed and removed her slippers.

'Want a story, Daddy,' she demanded.

He started reading her favourite story and before Goldilocks had even sat on baby bear's chair she was out like a light. He crept from the room and closed the door.

Dora was feeding Jackie as Joe came into their room. She half-smiled as he announced that Carol was asleep. 'Good.' She patted the bed beside her and Joe sat down and took her hand.

'I'm worried about you, Dora,' he began.

'I'm fine. Mam told you what that naughty little madam did, I suppose? Joe, if you'd seen the size of that worm. What if it had crawled into Jackie's mouth?' She shuddered.

'I know, love, and she won't do it again. But you need to try and relax a bit. We're not a hospital with strangers bringing in germs. We're your family, we live here and Jackie's a part of you and me. She'll build up her own resistance to germs and stuff in time if you let her. And the doctor told you that breastfeeding is giving her the best start in life that you possibly can. You won't even let *me* cuddle her and that hurts me, you know, that you feel I'm not clean enough to look after my own baby.'

Dora's eyes filled. He was right, but she couldn't help the way she felt. The terror of losing another baby was with her day and night. 'I'm trying to relax but it's not easy. I'm just so scared of anything happening to her, Joe. I couldn't bear to lose her.'

She heard him sigh as he folded his arms around her.

Dora looked up and smiled as her mam showed Agnes in. 'What a lovely surprise. Come and sit down.' She moved up on the sofa and Agnes sat beside her, holding her red-haired Patsy. 'How are you doing?'

'I'm fine. Tired, but she's settling a bit better at night now. How's Jackie doing?'

'Okay.' Dora's arms tightened protectively around her baby as Agnes leant across to take a peek.

The pair swapped baby stories while Dora's mam took Carol out to the shops.

'How are you coping with two to look after?' Agnes asked.

'Well Mam's here most of the time,' Dora said. 'But she said she's cutting down her days for coming over after next week. I'm just going to have to get used to it, I suppose. I can manage Jackie fine. Carol plays me up a bit, but then she always has done.'

'She's just full of beans,' Agnes said, laughing. 'You'll have to take her out to the park and let her run off some of that energy.'

'I suppose so.' Dora could think of nothing worse. All those kids on the swings and slide, full of snotty noses and germs, and Carol catching something nasty and passing it on to the baby.

'Here you go, swap babies,' Agnes said, holding out little Patsy. 'Your Jackie looks so much bigger than the last time I saw her. She must be gaining well. Patsy lost a few ounces in the first couple of weeks, but she's gained it back.'

Dora chewed her lip and didn't respond to the baby swap. Agnes didn't pursue it. Dora didn't really look herself. There seemed to be no enthusiasm in her and she looked a bit bedraggled, her dress stained down the front and her hair unkempt. That wasn't like Dora, who was always so immaculate.

She tried again. 'Are you still breastfeeding? I'm struggling, I've got sore nipples, and it's agony, so I'm topping up with a bottle now.'

Dora raised her eyes away from Jackie's face and shook her head. 'Be careful. You don't know what they put in it.'

'Who?' Agnes frowned.

'Anyone who makes the bottle up for you. Germs and stuff. It's really dangerous.'

'But it's me that makes the bottles.' Agnes shook her head. 'It's perfectly safe, Dora. Everything gets boiled to sterilise it.'

'Well you don't know what comes out of the taps. All those war bombs and poisons in the air from the Germans might have ruined the water in the reservoirs.'

'The government wouldn't allow us to drink it if anything was wrong. There'd be warnings everywhere.'

Dora lowered her eyes again and remained silent. Agnes felt uncomfortable. Something was very wrong with her friend. Dora's mam had gone to the shops now and taken Carol with her so they could have a nice natter and catch up with each other's news. Mary had confided on the phone that she was worried her daughter wasn't well again. She'd explained briefly about the cleaning obsession, and the worm in the cradle episode. Agnes had promised to phone Mary later with her thoughts.

Dora looked up now. 'If I tell you something, will you keep it to yourself?'

'Of course I will. What is, Dora?' Dora's face was a mask of fear; as though she was struggling with something inside that she could hardly bear to admit.

She looked over her shoulder and around the room, and seemed to be checking they were alone. Then her eyes rested on a framed photo of Joanie on the mantelpiece.

'I think Carol's trying to hurt Jackie,' Dora said in a low voice. 'I've spoken to Joanie and she thinks so as well. She says it was her fault Joanna died, for being the bigger twin. She says Carol took all the oxygen before they were born. I can't tell Mam or Joe because they'll just say I'm going mad, but I'm not. Carol is jealous of Jackie and is going to harm her. But me and Joanie will protect her.'

Agnes took a deep breath, unsure of how to deal with this. 'Dora, don't you think you might be just overtired and imagining all that? Let the family help you and catch up on some sleep.'

Dora looked at her with a resigned expression. 'I daren't sleep. I have to watch over Jackie all the time. I'm telling you, Carol's jealous and I need to keep them apart.'

Mary put down the phone and chewed her lip. Agnes had left as soon as Mary got back, with a worried look on her face and a promise to ring later.

Agnes seemed convinced the depression was deeper this time. She confided that Dora had told her she was certain Carol was out to harm the baby and that's why she couldn't bear to let Jackie out of her sight. Then Agnes chilled Mary to the bone when she told her that she was worried Dora might harm Carol if she thought she was a threat to Jackie's safety.

Mary looked in on her daughter who was on the bed, holding Jackie to her breast as usual. She didn't even look up; just sat there with an empty expression in her eyes. Carol was down at Dolly's playing with Alice. She closed the door to Dora's bedroom and went to the phone and left a message at the canteen for Joe to call her as soon as possible. Then she quickly ran down the street to Dolly's and asked if Carol could stay for a while as Dora wasn't well and she was going to get the doctor out.

'Is it her mind again?' Dolly asked in an exaggerated whisper. 'Only I was saying to my Eric only yesterday that Dora doesn't seem right in the 'ead again at the moment.'

'I'm not sure.' Mary dashed back to the bungalow just as the phone started to ring. She snatched up the receiver. It was Joe.

'Come home, please. Jackie's okay, but we need to get help for Dora.' She heard a sharp intake of breath.

'I'm on my way.'

Dora drew her knees up to her chest and hugged them. Jackie lay beside her on the bed. She'd just heard her mam on the phone to Joe, telling him that she was worried about her, saying they needed help. At last they were taking her seriously. Maybe they'd call Doctor Owens, who would know what to do about Carol being a threat to Jackie's safety. Something had to be done before the baby came to any harm. Dora felt helpless, trying to protect her on her own. She cocked an ear. Her mam was talking to someone on the phone again. Hopefully it was the doctor.

Doctor Owens arrived at the same time as Joe turned the corner of Hedgefield Road on his motorbike. Dora's mam was waiting anxiously on the doorstep, wringing her hands. She put her finger to her lips and led them both into the sitting room, closing the door.

'She's in the bedroom with the baby,' she told them and explained her fears and what Agnes had reported to her. 'I feel terrible doing this behind her back, but we can't carry on ignoring it.' Tears rolled down her cheeks and Joe pulled her close.

'You did the right thing, Mam,' he said, a catch in his voice. 'Don't worry. She needs help again, although it breaks my heart to admit it.'

'You stay there, Joe. I don't want to put the fear of God in her when she sees you home from work so early. Doctor can say he's just popped in to see Jackie because she needs weighing, or something. Is that okay with you, Doctor?'

Doctor Owens nodded his head and followed Mary into the hall. She knocked on the bedroom door. 'Dora, chuck, Doctor Owens just wants a little chat with you. I'm letting him in now.'

Mary rejoined Joe in the sitting room. 'Sit down, love, I'll make you a cuppa.'

But Joe followed her into the kitchen, unable to just sit and do nothing. 'So tell me what's happened and why you've brought the doctor in.'

Mary related Agnes's observations and what Dora had confided to her friend. Joe went white and Mary pushed him down onto the stool in the corner.

'Jesus. We need to make sure Carol is safe, never mind Jackie,' he said, his voice filled with disbelief. 'Where *is* Carol, by the way?'

'With Dolly. I'm going to pop down there now you're here. I think they'll take our Dora into hospital, but if they do she'll be pumped full of sedatives or something, like last time, so she won't be able to feed Jackie and it's my guess she won't be allowed to take the baby in with her. God knows how we're going to manage. She'll go hysterical if they try and take Jackie away. I don't want Carol to see that. I'll ask Dolly to keep her for now, and overnight if needs be. Did you know she'd started talking to Joanie's photo?'

Joe nodded. 'Yes, I've heard her. I thought it was helping her, but now I'm not so sure. How will we manage to look after Jackie if Dora has to go away?'

'We'll have to cope between us. Fortunately she sleeps a lot and if they do sedate Dora, we'll have to bottle feed her. Poor little mite.'

* * *

Dora hugged her baby close as she gazed blankly at the doctor. 'Did they tell you? Have you come to help us? Carol wants to harm her. Joanie told me. But I won't let her do it.'

Doctor Owens took her hand. 'I'm here to help you, Dora. I promise you, nothing bad is going to happen to your baby.' He lifted his black bag onto the bed and she stared at it with wild eyes.

'No,' she screamed. 'Move that bag away. It will be covered in germs from all your patients' houses.' She began to cry hysterically. The doctor was in on it too - and she had thought he was someone she could trust. They were all out to harm her baby. It wasn't just Carol, it was all of them.

'I'm just going to give you a little injection that will help your milk to flow better for feeding Jackie. Just try to relax for me,' he said, taking hold of her arm.

Before she could say anything Dora felt a slight pricking sensation in her arm as he injected her with a powerful sedative. She felt her eyes closing and her grip on Jackie loosened.

Doctor Owens removed the baby from her arms and carried her through to Joe and Mary. 'I've given her a strong sedative that will keep her asleep for a while,' he said, handing the baby to her grandmother. 'Now we've two choices here. Dora is suffering from the early stages of a paranoiac nervous condition better known as Puerperal Insanity. She needs careful handling, but I'm not certain that a hospital environment is the right one for her. I *can* admit her, or I can leave her in the care of her family and visit each day to see how she gets along. She'll need regular sedation and someone will have to take over caring for the children.'

Joe nodded. 'How long will she be like this, Doctor? She seems worse than last time.'

'She is, and I can't say how long, Mr Rodgers. It could be months. But I have to warn you, some women never get over this type of depression. If she doesn't show signs of improvement over the next month then I will have no choice but to have her sectioned and the treatment would be quite tough. At the moment it's not a road I want to go down and it would be a last resort. For the time being, I would suggest that she moves in with you, Mrs Evans. Is that something you think you can cope with? She will sleep for most of the day while her mind heals itself. When she's awake she can still have contact with Jackie, but she will need to bottle feed as the sedatives would affect the baby. I think it's better that we don't deny her contact with Jackie, which would happen if we have to hospitalise her.'

Mam sighed and wrung her hands in an agitated fashion. 'I can look after her, that's not a problem; and Jackie too. Our Frank will be there at night to help me. But what about our Carol?'

'I'll sort Carol out,' Joe said, close to tears. 'Dolly will help me with her, I'm sure. Just do whatever is best for Dora and the rest we'll deal with as best we can.'

Doctor Owens nodded. 'I know it's quite disturbing for relatives to see their loved ones in a state like this. All we can do is hope that Dora responds and we can get her back to normal as soon as possible.'

Chapter Thirty-One

July 1950

Dora smiled as her mam handed Jackie to her. It was a beautiful day and the baby had just woken up from sleeping in the pram in Mam's back garden. At four months old Jackie's limbs had filled out to a firm plumpness and her fluffy blonde hair was settling into soft waves. Her bright blue eyes stared trustingly into Dora's and she felt a rush of love for her youngest daughter. Although she still felt anxious about her welfare and safety, she could relax more when there was only herself and Mam around.

'I'll just get her bottle ready, love.'

Dora nodded and sat back on the sofa. She felt a bit fuzzy from the sedatives she took daily, but at least they had a calming effect on her and she was able to cope with caring for Jackie without always feeling that something awful was going to happen. Joe would be here to visit tomorrow with Carol. She missed him and her daughter too, but according to her mam and Frank, who popped around to see Joe after work most nights, they were doing okay with help from Dolly.

Her brother was a rock to Dora. He kept her company when her mam was asleep, and had even given up his bedroom for her and the baby, while he slept on the sitting room sofa or at one of his mates' houses.

The first few weeks had been difficult when Joe visited as Dora had felt it was his fault she was here and no longer able to breast-feed Jackie. When he'd tried to hold her and told her he missed her, she couldn't respond and pushed him away. She knew her condition made her irrational and Joe ignoring her accusations and trying to jolly her along and change the subject only served to irritate her further. Last week she'd asked him to bring Joanie's photo, but her mam had intervened and said not to, which upset her because Mam had told him that her talking to it wasn't good for her recovery. Maybe she'd ask him again tomorrow when her mam's back was turned. She looked up as Mam brought Jackie's bottle in and handed it to her.

'I think we'll take her for a little walk down the lane later in the pram,' Mam announced. 'There's a summer fair on at the village hall. It'll do you good to get out and see a few people.'

Dora felt a rush of panic settle over her. 'Oh, I'm not sure.' She didn't feel ready for talking to anyone other than her close family. And no matter how much she fought it, the thoughts of people looking into the pram and breathing all over her baby made her feel positively queasy. She took a couple of deep breaths and popped the teat into Jackie's eager mouth. 'I'll think about it while I feed her,' she said, knowing full well what her choice would be.

'I'll nip down myself then if you don't feel up to it. I need a breath of fresh air and a bit of company.'

Joe sat down on a park bench and lit a cigarette. Carol ran off towards the swings and a group of little girls she'd spotted, her neat plaits bouncing on her shoulders and the pink coolie hat Agnes had bought her in Blackpool cocked at a rakish angle on her head. She'd turned three two weeks ago and Dolly had kindly thrown her a little birthday party in the garden. Dolly had been a rock and looked after Carol each day while he went to work. Dora's mam had her hands full looking after Dora and Jackie during the week, and he couldn't have coped without either of them.

Tomorrow afternoon was his weekly visit to see Dora. He took Carol with him, although the visits weren't always successful as

Dora still displayed tendencies of suspicion towards Carol when she was anywhere near Jackie. Between them, the family had decided one visit a week was enough for the time being. Dora's mam said Joe had enough to do without running back and fro between the houses; he needed to work and he had Carol to see to at night.

Dora's medication *appeared* to be working in that the frantic cleaning and constant worrying about germs had eased, but it seemed likely that she'd still be receiving treatment for a while longer and would need to remain in her mam's care for some time. The doctor said it may take months before she was back to normal. Her previously sunny nature had diminished, and she rarely smiled now. Joe had no idea how he would cope if and when she did come home.

He'd taken to walking to Belle Vale Park on Saturday mornings. He'd got to know a few faces, mainly mothers and their offspring. Carol had made friends with a couple of little girls who came here regularly. It was a bit of a routine in an otherwise tipped-upside-down life for her and for him too. The kids were not a problem: Jackie was thriving under Dora's mam's watchful eye and Carol loved being with Dolly. It was *he* that was the problem. He felt lonely, miserable and cut off from the fun side of life.

He missed the Dora he'd married, he missed their life together, his football on Saturday afternoons with his pals, and he missed his band and playing at the weekend. But he didn't feel he could ask his mother-in-law to babysit Carol. She had enough to do. Frank came and kept him company on the odd night and they'd have a drink, but if he wasn't looking after Dora while her mam did her WI stuff, he was usually out on the town with his docker mates. Joe envied him his life as a single man at times, although he knew that Frank would give his right arm to have Joanie back and a family, even one with problems.

His own mother was nothing short of useless when it came to childcare and they'd become almost estranged, although she rang up occasionally to enquire how they all were, but never offered him any practical help. The only other person he could rely on was Ivy at work. He'd confided in her again, against his better judgement at first, recalling how she'd mistaken his neediness last time. But she'd kept her distance and just listened when he needed to talk, and besides, he wasn't doing any dances in the clubs so he spent limited time in her company. She'd told him about a new flat she'd moved into near his estate. He'd told her he walked on the park on Saturday mornings and last week she'd turned up with a bag of jelly babies for Carol, who took to her immediately. He wondered if Ivy would do the same today and found himself staring at the entrance from time to time.

Ivy checked her watch as she walked slowly along to the park. She didn't want to appear too eager and get there early. Even if they only spent fifteen minutes together it was better than not see-ing Joe at all. She'd stopped off to get some sweeties for his little girl and had them safely stashed in her handbag. She felt worried about Joe; *he* seemed to be in a bit of a depression, never mind his wife. His life revolved around work, Carol and little else. He'd told her that he needed to keep his job for as long as he could because of the house. If he lost the job through taking time off work, he might lose his home too. It wasn't an easy situation for a man to find himself in and Ivy played the role of caring friend to the best of her ability.

If Joe's marriage was going to be a casualty in all this trouble, then she would make sure he knew where to come should he need to. She she saw him sitting alone on his usual bench near the play area. He looked up and saw her watching him. The smile that lit up his face made her heart sing, but she responded with just a half-smile and a little wave. It wouldn't do to look too eager at the moment. She needed to remember that for Joe right now, she was a confidante and a shoulder to cry on. Also, there would be no embellished tales going back to Flo. She was keeping her mouth firmly shut this time.

Joe braced himself as he walked down Sugar Lane, holding on to Carol's sweaty little hand. To his surprise Dora was sitting on a deckchair in the front garden. Jackie was asleep in her pram under a tree. Dora turned to smile as they came in at the gate and Carol dashed inside calling for Uncle Frank. Dora was wearing one of her summer dresses and her blonde hair looked freshly washed, hanging in soft waves to her shoulders. Although the dress hung off her because she'd lost weight, he recognised it as the navy flower-sprigged one she'd made for the first night she went to a dance with him after being ill last time. The Litherland Town Hall dance. It seemed years ago now, but she'd been so happy that night and they'd made love for hours when they'd got home. He felt tears well and blinked rapidly. Would they ever get back to that stage again? Or would they just have a friendship from now on, where he simply took care of her needs?

He'd been warned by Doctor Owens that further pregnancies were not advisable. The hormonal changes affected Dora's brain and the next time may see her harming both herself and the child. Guaranteeing pregnancy would never happen again was a problem. Dora could have a sterilisation operation, which involved major abdominal surgery and would take weeks of recovery, both in hospital and then when she was discharged. It would mean more work for her mam and he worried about how Mary would cope. Doctor Owens had told Joe that Dora wasn't well enough to make any decisions just yet, but it would be discussed with them both at a later date when he felt the time was right, and was probably the best option open to them as a couple.

Joe didn't care; he just wanted his wife and the mother of his children back to normal. He felt at the end of his tether at times and secretly thanked God for the bit of solace Ivy offered. She'd asked him to bring Carol to tea next Saturday afternoon. Apparently there was a nice garden with a swing that used to belong to her new landlord's grown-up children. He'd been undecided at first and then thought, what the hell. Another Saturday afternoon trying to entertain Carol alone would drive him mad. And no one needed to know. It was just tea, nothing else.

Dora spoke softly and broke his thoughts. 'How are you doing, Joe? Are you coping all right?'

'I'm fine, love. Carol's okay, as you can see. She loves going to Dolly's while I'm at work. I'm just a bit lonely and waiting for the day when you feel ready to come home with me and be a family again.'

Her face clouded. 'I'm not sure when I'll feel ready for that. I'm safer here with my mam and Frank and I know Jackie is safe too now she's away from Carol.' She put her hands up to her breasts. 'The doctor took my milk away. Made me drink something horrible for a few days and it just went.'

Joe nodded. She'd been given Epsom salts. It was heartbreaking to see her so defeated. His lovely wife who was so bright and clever with her hands and her dressmaking skills. And all because of him and his need for her body. He swore he'd take care of her from now on. No matter what it took, he wouldn't put her through this again.

Carol ran shrieking outside with Frank chasing her. He caught her and swung her up in the air. 'Come here, you little monkey,' he said, laughing. 'Joe, how you doing, mate?'

Joe nodded. 'Not bad. Yourself?'

Frank shrugged. 'Getting there. It helps me having our Dora and the little one around.' He lowered his voice. 'When she's well enough and back home with you again, I might look for work abroad for a while. I've got papers stashed away to get a passport. Have to see how it goes here for the next few months.'

Joe sighed. He almost envied Frank his freedom - almost, but not quite. 'Can't say I blame you; a fresh start and all that.'

Frank nodded. 'Not a word to Mam and her,' he mouthed, nodding in Dora's direction. 'Right, monkey, let's get down to the paper shop for some dolly mixtures. See you later.' He grabbed Carol and they set off down the road, Carol shrieking excitedly and swinging from his hand.

'He's good with her.' Joe sat down on the lawn next to Dora's deckchair.

She didn't reply, so he took hold of her hand and caressed it, but she pulled away and glared at him.

'Don't do that.'

'I was only holding your hand, love.'

'I don't want you to.'

Before he could respond, Mam popped her head outside and beckoned him indoors. He got up and followed her.

'How do you think she's doing, Mam?'

Mam shrugged. 'Up and down, love. Some days I feel there's a change for the better and then others we seem back to square one. How are you coping, Joe? You look weary.'

'I'm okay, thanks. Just want things back to normal, whatever that is.' He sighed.

'Well she can't go home yet,' Mam said. 'You'd have to give up work and you can't do that. I wouldn't like to leave her alone with both kiddies. She's smashing with Jackie. Copes very well with her, so I've no worries on that score. But she can't look after Carol as well.'

'Well, all we can do is carry on as we are,' Joe said. 'I think she hates me at the moment. Won't even let me hold her hand. I feel lost, Mam.' He could feel himself welling up and took a deep breath.

She rubbed his arm affectionately. 'We'll soldier on, Joe. Go and sit outside with her again and I'll bring a drink and some sandwiches out for you both.'

Carol ran up and down the lawn, excited to be playing outside, and Ivy's landlord's tubby corgi dog did his best to run after the old tennis ball she threw for him. They'd had a picnic and little cakes, sitting on a blanket under a shady tree on the lawn. Joe relaxed and lit a cigarette as he watched Carol and the dog cavorting around. 'Thanks for doing this, Ivy.'

She smiled. 'You're welcome. Are you going to see Dora tomorrow?'

He nodded. 'Aye, I go every Sunday. It's the only time she gets to see Carol. It's taking a while to get them bonded again.'

'How much longer do you think she'll be like that?'

He shrugged. 'No one seems to know for sure. I'm hoping it won't be too long, and then I can bring her home.' He saw Ivy stiffen beside him. 'But who knows?' He called to Carol. 'Come on, queen, we need to get off home before it rains.'

Carol pulled a face but did as she was told. 'Say thank you to Ivy for having us and for the lovely tea party she made.'

Carol, not generally one for shows of affection, threw her arms around Ivy's neck and gave her a kiss on the cheek.

'Blimey, you're honoured,' Joe said, laughing. 'She's a bit mean with her kisses, that one. Thanks for a lovely afternoon. I've enjoyed the nice change.'

Ivy got to her feet and smoothed the creases out of her skirt. 'It's been lovely to have you here. And I think Roly's enjoyed it as well,' she said as the little corgi sat down and looked a bit sad that his new playmate was going home.

'Can we come again?' Carol asked, dancing from foot to foot. 'Please, Ivy. I just love Roly.'

Ivy smiled. 'I don't see why not. If Daddy says it's okay you can come again next week if you like.'

'Yes, yes, yes!' Carol squealed.

'We'll see, madam,' Joe said. 'Have to see how Mammy is.'

'Now, Carol, do as Daddy says and we'll see,' Ivy said. 'But you have to be a very good girl all week.'

Ivy walked to the gate with them and Joe turned and pecked her on the cheek. His lips brushed her ear as he said thank you again. 'Are you out dancing tonight?'

She shook her head. 'Hopefully next week.'

'I really miss my weekends,' he said wistfully. 'I miss the lads in the band too.'

Ivy looked at him for a long moment. 'I can always babysit for you on a Saturday night while you go out and play with the band. I know you're missing the money as well. Have a think about it and let me know. I can bring a book or some knitting over with me.'

Joe's face brightened. 'We've got a gramophone so you could listen to records as well. I'll think about it. Thank you for offering. See you Monday in work. Save me an extra sausage!'

Ivy took Roly indoors and sent him in to her landlord. She sauntered up to her flat, a happy smile on her face. She'd happily babysit for Joe. Carol was an easy kid to look after. She'd rather go to the dances with him, but if she was at his house he would be coming back to her and they'd sit and chat for a while before she went home. She poured herself a small sweet sherry and took her *Woman's Weekly* magazine with her to sit on the Juliet balcony. Life was certainly looking up. Hopefully Dora would be a while before she was fit to go home.

Joe needed help and she was offering it. If anyone read anything else into that, then it was their problem, not hers or Joe's.

And Carol certainly seemed to like her. Dora had always found the child hard work, from what Joe had told her. Carol would be going to school in another year so would be off his hands for most of the day. She let herself enjoy a little fantasy in which she and Joe were together bringing up Carol, and Dora was happy on her own with Jackie, having realised she didn't either love or need Joe. It was a pleasing thought and she decided it deserved another sherry.

Dolly waved at Joe as he turned the corner of Hedgefield Road. 'Joe, your mother popped by but got tired of waiting. I didn't think you'd be out this long. She left this for you.' She handed him a sealed envelope.

'We've been to Ivy's for tea. She's got a dog,' Carol yelled, dancing up and down with excitement.

Joe felt his cheeks heating when Dolly pursed her lips as he drew close. 'Thanks, Dolly. And thanks for looking after her while I was out.'

'You want to watch that Ivy,' Dolly said, scowling. 'She's trouble with a capital T. Caught her giving my Eric the eye last year.'

'That's my business, Dolly. Ivy's been a good friend to me.' Bloody hell, the whole estate would know by tonight. And he'd *never* seen Ivy giving Eric the eye, or anyone else come to that. He hadn't expected a welcoming committee on arrival home and it had been his plan to sneak inside with Carol and promise her something nice if she didn't tell Aunty Dolly about going to Ivy's for tea. She was easily bribed so he had great faith in her. Too late now. Dolly would give him earache about it. Indoors, he opened the envelope. Inside was a letter and a cheque for £250. His mother explained that she'd sold her house and was moving to Cheadle to be near her sister. He felt bad when he read that she hadn't wanted to mither him as he had enough on his plate. The money was to put towards a car. He sighed. It would certainly make life a bit easier.

Chapter Thirty-Two

Ivy jumped up to answer the phone. It was nine thirty and it might be Joe making sure Carol was okay. He said he'd try to call if there was a phone in the club. A woman asked to speak to him. Ivy told her he was working tonight with the band but she could pass on a message. The woman asked who she was, a hint of suspicion in her voice.

'The babysitter, Miss Bennett,' Ivy replied. 'Who's calling, please?'

'It's Agnes, Dora's friend. Would you ask Joe to ring me tomorrow before he goes to see her, please? Thank you.'

Ivy stared at the receiver in her hand and shrugged. She wrote the message on the pad on the hall table and went back to her knitting and Patti Page on the gramophone. She'd fallen asleep by the time Joe arrived home and he shook her gently by the shoulder. She opened her eyes and looked up and her heart leapt as she saw him gazing down at her, a smile on his handsome face and his light brown hair flopping down into his eyes.

She sat up and sighed. 'Sorry, it's so peaceful, I couldn't help myself.'

He laughed. 'Don't worry. I do it myself, often. Would you like a cup of tea, then I'll book you a taxi. Thank you so much for this. Hope she's been good for you.'

'Quiet as a mouse all night,' she said. 'And yes, I'd love a cuppa.'

'It's done me the world of good to get out,' he said, 'it really has. I feel human again.'

She smiled as he threw his jacket onto the armchair and removed his tie. He made two mugs of tea and carried them through to the sitting room and joined her on the sofa.

'Before I forget,' she said, 'Agnes called. Can you ring her tomorrow before you go to visit Dora? I made a note on the pad in the hall, but you might not see it.'

'Shit, yes! I was supposed to ring her today. I completely forgot.'

They drank their tea in companionable silence and then Ivy gathered her things together. 'Book a taxi for me now, Joe. Bet that bloody Dolly is at the window waiting to see if I stay or go. She'll have seen your car pull up, no doubt.'

Joe raised an eyebrow. 'Aye, and we'll be the talk of the canteen when she's finished bending Eric's ear. But it's hard for me. I've a kiddie to see to and a job to hold down, no wife to help me - okay, her mam does her best and Dolly helps with Carol. But I have no choice other than to rely on them. The alternative is to give up my job, then I'll lose my bloody home and end up begging with Carol going into care. I'm not being unfaithful to my wife, when all's said and done. I'm just taking help where I can get it. Sorry for banging on, Ivy.'

'Joe.' Ivy rubbed his arm. 'It's okay to let off steam. People need to keep their noses out of your business. And we'll ignore any gossip at work.'

Dora shook her head as Carol screamed at the top of her voice. She called for Joe who was trying to sort the washing out, cook the Sunday dinner and make a bottle for Jackie, all at the same time. Dora had remained on the sofa with Jackie on her lap almost all weekend. It had been a big mistake to agree to two full days at home. A few hours yesterday afternoon would have been enough for her as a trial run. She just wasn't ready for this. Joe hurried into the sitting room, gritting his teeth. He looked harassed and she wished she could do more to help him.

'What's going on in here?' he yelled. Carol was sobbing on the rug, kicking her legs in the air. He scooped her up into his arms and held her tight. 'Now shush, Daddy's here. It's okay.' He raised an eyebrow at Dora as she picked up Jackie's teddy from the floor. 'Well?'

Dora propped Jackie into the corner of the sofa and waved the teddy at him. 'She's pulled an arm off,' she cried. 'Frank bought that teddy for Jackie. She's a naughty girl. I asked her to give it to me and she just yanked the arm off.'

Carol looked sheepishly at the teddy and sucked her thumb.

'Did you break Jackie's teddy?' Joe asked, gently but with an edge to his voice that Carol knew meant business. She nodded. 'Then what do you say to Mammy?'

Carol looked away and shrugged. 'Sowwy,' she mumbled.

'Mammy can't hear you,' Joe said. 'Say it again.'

'Sowwy, Mammy.' Carol stared defiantly at Dora.

'Perhaps you can help me to mend it later, after dinner,' Dora suggested as Joe put Carol down and told her to go and play out in the garden for a while. She shot off, giving Dora a baleful glance over her shoulder. 'I give her attention but she ignores me,' Dora began. 'I've tried to read her a story earlier and suggested we do a puzzle together. I am trying, Joe.'

'If you didn't have hold of Jackie all the time it might help a bit more,' he suggested.

Dora remained silent and he went back into the kitchen to his chores. Last night had been difficult. She was no longer on strong sedation, just a very mild one and only when her mam felt she needed it. She'd not brought any with her for the weekend, so she'd had a small sherry once the kids were asleep. Joe had put some records on and invited her to dance with him. He'd moved the sofa back against the wall and they'd waltzed around the sitting room, laughing. It had felt good to have him hold her again and he'd kissed her. She'd responded to his kisses, but when he'd tried to steer her towards the bedroom she'd pushed him away in tears and told him he had to sleep on the sofa or take her back to her mam's. He told her he needed her and he'd make absolutely sure there were no pregnancy consequences. He'd pleaded with her to trust him, but she didn't want to know.

Joe banged on the kitchen window. 'Carol, come back inside please.' Carol ran indoors and looked at him expectantly. 'Take your Three Bears book to Mammy and she'll read you a story. Go on,' he encouraged as she pulled a face. 'She's waiting for you.' Carol ran into her bedroom and he nodded at Dora. 'Read it to her.'

'Okay. Will you take Jackie then?'

'Of course.' He popped Jackie into the high chair in the kitchen and stuffed a cushion behind her. Her blue eyes followed him everywhere and she smiled as he blew her a raspberry. She was such a placid little soul compared to Carol. Easy enough to look after, which was perhaps as well. He cocked an ear at the door. Dora was reading, with Carol interrupting every few seconds at places she liked to do the voices. He smiled and got on with the dinner, Jackie watching his every move.

Dora heard Joe setting the table and then he popped his head around Carol's bedroom door. She smiled as his eyebrows raised when he saw what they were up to. Carol was sitting on the bed and *she* was at the sewing table pinning the arm on Teddy.

'Pass me the thread, there's a good girl,' Dora said and Carol jumped up and handed her a spool of cotton. He smiled; it was a beginning, of sorts.

'Shall I just do Sunday next week?' she suggested. 'I think a full weekend is a bit too much for us all at the moment.'

'That's up to you, love,' he said. 'See how you feel nearer the time.'

Dora nodded. If she was totally honest with herself, at the moment she just couldn't see a time when they'd all live as a family again, but she could live in hope.

Chapter Thirty-Three

December 1950

Ivy was excited as she got ready for the ROF Christmas dance. Joe's band was playing and he was coming to pick her up in fifteen minutes. She wasn't courting Joe, in spite of the rumours she chose to ignore: he was still married to Dora. But he and Ivy had become closer as the months rolled by. Dora was still living with her mother and brother in Knowsley and came home to stay with Joe on Sundays. Ivy still helped him out on a Saturday night while he played with the band. She enjoyed looking after Carol while he earned a bit of extra money for his family.

A routine had been established, and as far as she knew, Dora had no idea that Carol was cared for by Ivy, or that she and Joe came to tea at her flat quite regularly. She had even invited Joe and Carol for tea on Christmas Day. He'd told her that he would need to have his dinner with Dora's family as it was Jackie's first Christmas, but would leave about half-four and come and see her. She was looking forward to it and for the first time in her life she'd bought a tree and decorations. Her landlord and his wife had invited her to eat dinner with them and she'd accepted. Flo was going to her sister's, so she didn't need to worry about her.

The doorbell rang and she slipped her jacket on and picked up her handbag. Joe had a big smile on his face and he looked good in his smart stage suit. Ivy made sure his shirt was always washed and pressed each week in case he didn't have the time to do it himself. He pecked her on the cheek and escorted her down the stairs.

'You look stunning,' he told her.

She beamed. 'Thank you.' No one had ever said that to her before, not even her late husband. She'd never be as pretty as Dora, she knew that, but she'd lost a bit of weight with all the worry over the last few months about Joe and the gossips, and she'd grown her hair longer; it was swinging on her shoulders now, dark and glossy and she felt good in her new red dress. She'd done her best to do him proud.

The festively decorated room was crowded as Joe led her to the table reserved for the band and their ladies. She spotted Flo sitting alone at a small table at the back of the room. 'Joe.' She pulled on his sleeve and inclined her head. 'I'll just pop over and say hello to Flo and when you're on stage I'll sit with her or dance with her.'

'Okay. I'll get her a drink while I'm getting ours. Sweet sherry?'

'Please.' How nice to have a man knowing what you drank without having to ask. She swanned across the room, ignoring the women who whispered behind their hands as she passed their tables. Such cold looks. She was officially with Joe at this do, he'd invited her and she was going to sit proudly with the band and their wives. She ignored the barbed comments: *wife snatcher* and *you should be ashamed of yourself*. The state of half of them, fat and untidy with no dress sense, they were lucky *their* husbands weren't sniffing around another woman. Not that it was like that with her and Joe. He treated her with respect and had only ever pecked her on the cheek or very lightly on the lips after he'd had a pint or two at a dance. But she lived in hope. His eyes had certainly lit up tonight when she'd opened the door.

Flo smiled as Ivy sat down beside her. 'You look very nice.'

'So do you. That dress really suits you.'

'It's the one poor Dora made for me. I've only worn it a couple of times before so it seemed a waste not to wear it tonight. Do you think she'll ever make dresses again, Ivy?'

'God, I've no idea. She might.' Ivy couldn't see it, but who knew.

'When she moves back in with Joe permanently she might do it then.'

Ivy frowned and looked across to where Joe was standing at the bar, talking to another band member, his back to them as he queued for the drinks. 'What makes you think that will happen? Has someone said something to you?'

'No, but she can't stay at her mam's for ever, surely.'

Ivy shrugged. 'It's not our business, is it? Anyway, here's Joe with a drink for you. I'll go back to the other table and I'll see you in a bit.' She smiled as Joe drew level and handed Flo her drink.

'Thank you, Joe. Merry Christmas.'

'You too, Flo.' He took Ivy's arm and led her back to their table as Dolly and Eric came into the room. 'Uh, oh, here's trouble,' he hissed.

'Just ignore them Joe. You're entitled to a life, for goodness sake.'

As she and Flo stood in the queue for the ladies, Dolly and another woman Ivy recognised as a wife of one of the workers came in. Ivy turned her back as Dolly snorted and opened her big mouth.

'She should be ashamed of herself, that one. Stealing a bloke from his sick wife. No decency, some folk. *And* she was after my Eric last year.'

Ivy ignored her. She wouldn't rise to the bait in case she said something out of turn that would lose her favour with Joe. The other woman joined in.

'I've heard tell she stops over when she babysits for him. He's as bad as her for encouraging it. No wonder his wife went mental, poor woman, and he won't have her at home, you know. She's still at her mother's. It's shocking.'

More women joined in with their pennyworth, but Ivy had heard enough. She could handle people talking about her, but she wasn't having anyone saying things about Joe that weren't true. She wasn't aware of just how much Dolly knew about Dora's condition as Joe had told her he only talked to the woman about child care for Carol.

She turned and pushed her face as close to Dolly's as she could. The smell of stale fags and alcohol on her breath almost made Ivy gag. 'You should get your facts straight, madam. You've no idea of what Joe has to cope with at the moment. He needs all the help he can get, not stupid women like you pulling him down and starting rumours all the time.' She took a deep breath. 'And believe me, Dolly; I wouldn't look twice at your Eric, even if he took a bath a week, never mind just on his birthday. I'm really not that desperate, chuck.' She grabbed Flo by the shoulder and bundled her outside before Dolly could react. Their exit was followed by hoots of laughter from some of the women who also wouldn't look twice at kindly, but bumbling and very sweaty, Eric.

Ivy marched Flo across to the band table and pulled up an extra chair. Joe raised an enquiring eyebrow and Ivy told him in a low whisper what had been said and that she felt Flo would be safer here with them.

He sighed. 'Bloody Dolly. I know she thinks she's on my side, but she needs to mind her own business. She's desperate to go and see Dora at her mam's, but she'll cause more problems with her loose tongue. At least I'm in on a Sunday when she pops into ours for five minutes. She wouldn't dare say anything out of order while I'm there.'

Ivy nodded. 'I'll dance with Flo now for a bit. Stop them yapping for a while.'

'We're back on stage in a few minutes anyway for the final spot. Catch up with you later.'

Joe drove Ivy home in silence. No more had been said by Dolly and her cronies, but there'd been an undercurrent and sly glances in his direction that took the edge off the night. He felt sorry for Ivy, because she really had been trying to help him. As they got into the car she'd announced that maybe it was best if they stayed away from each other for a while, but he didn't want that to happen. For one thing he needed her friendship and for her to be there so he could let off steam when things got on top of him. Then there was the help she gave him with Carol. He couldn't do without that. And she'd planned a little tea party for them on Christmas Day. Carol was looking forward to that and she knew it had to be kept a very special secret. He was amazed at how secretive she could be for a three-year-old, although it did take a bit of bribery, usually sweeties.

There'd been tears earlier as he'd taken Carol to Dora's mam's for the night. But Uncle Frank had swept his niece into his arms and said he'd got some board games to teach her. He'd placed a big boxed compendium set in her arms and told her it used to be his when he was a small boy. She demanded snakes and ladders before Joe left the house and seemed happy enough to be left there. Dora had been feeding Jackie and looked content enough and had greeted him with a smile. He'd dropped a kiss on top of her head. Hopefully once he was out of the way she might join in the games with their daughter.

He stopped the car and turned to Ivy. He traced a finger down her cheek and she smiled. 'I don't want to not see you,' he whispered. 'I value your support.'

'I don't want to not see you either, but there's Dora and she'll always be your wife, no matter what happens. The gossips will get to her eventually. You'll have to watch that Dolly.'

'And I will. Come on, I'll make sure you get safely inside on those heels.'

He helped her out of the car and into the house. Ivy took her shoes off and they crept quietly up the stairs to her flat.

'Would you like a nightcap?' Ivy asked. She switched on the table lamp and the electric fire. The curtains were already drawn against the cold December night and with her little Christmas tree in the corner near the window, the room felt cosy and welcoming.

Joe sat down on the sofa and sighed. He was tired, but there was only an empty house to go back to. 'Why not?'

'I've only got sweet sherry,' she said. 'Oh hang on; there might be a drop of brandy left from when I made the Christmas pudding and cake for my landlord.' She rummaged in the kitchen cupboard and produced a bottle. 'Is that okay?'

'Smashing.'

She poured their drinks, put them on the coffee table and sat down beside him.

'Cheers. Happy Christmas to us both.' She clinked her glass to his and took a sip. She was conscious of Joe staring at her and a change in the way he was doing it. His eyes were narrowed, as though seeing her for the first time. He took her glass, put it down on the table and pulled her into his arms. Her stomach looped as his lips came down on hers, gently at first and then crushing her to him. He kissed her like she'd never been kissed before. As he pulled away and gazed into her eyes Ivy was lost as he yanked her to her feet and led her into the bedroom. She held her breath as he unzipped her dress and let it fall to the floor. His eyes rested on her cleavage and he deftly removed her bra and buried his head in her breasts, lowering her to the bed. She helped him remove his clothes and like a man possessed he explored her every inch before pushing into her. There were no words of love exchanged, but by the time they fell into a deeply satiated sleep it was almost four in the morning.

Ivy stirred first as she lay in his arms. The clock on the bedside table said nine and she knew he had to go and collect Carol from Dora's mother's house. He looked so peaceful sleeping beside her that she hadn't the heart to wake him, but if he didn't get going soon there would be phone calls made to his bungalow and questions asked. She planted a kiss on his lips and he opened his eyes. A look of mild panic crossed his features, but her smile reassured him it was okay.

'I'll make you some breakfast while you have a wash,' she said. 'Then you need to get home and changed before you pick Carol up.' She slipped out of bed, pulled on her silky dressing gown and padded out of the room, conscious of his eyes on her.

By the time he was ready she'd made him scrambled eggs on toast and a mug of coffee.

'Thank you. It's ages since anyone made me breakfast. Except for you in the canteen, of course.'

She smiled and sipped her drink, sitting opposite him at the small table. Her heart felt heavy at the thought of him dashing off home. But he wasn't hers to hang on to and last night had been the best time of her life. She'd treasure the memory for ever. She knew she had to play it careful here and not give him cause to worry about the fact that he'd been unfaithful to Dora. 'Joe, last night was wonderful. But it has to remain our secret.'

'Of course.' He nodded. 'No one must find out. The only problem I can foresee is Dolly will have seen my car isn't at the house and will be patrolling, waiting for me coming home, putting two and two together and making five.'

Ivy had already got her answer in place for that one. 'What I'd suggest is that you go and get Carol first. Tell Dora you gave a lift home to one of the band and fell asleep on their sofa after a nightcap. Then you can tell Dolly the same tale when you arrive back at the bungalow. Because she'll be pouncing on you as soon as she sees you.'

Joe nodded. 'Good idea.' He got to his feet and picked up his jacket from the sofa. The car keys jangled in the pocket. 'Thank you, for everything. And right or wrong, what we did last night made me feel alive again.'

She smiled. 'Now off you go and enjoy your time with Carol. I'll see you on Christmas afternoon.'

Chapter Thirty-Four

Dora looked up with excitement as Joe and Carol came into the sitting room. She held out her arms and Carol ran into them. 'Did Father Christmas come?' Dora asked.

'Yes!' Carol shouted and thrust a dolly at her mother. 'He brought me this. And he brought me a bike, but Daddy said you can see it when you come to our house.'

'And I will.' She flinched as Joe dropped a kiss on her cheek and gave her a squeeze. She pulled away and led Carol to the small tree in the corner of the sitting room. 'I think he left some things here for you too. Shall we see what there is?'

Carol dropped to her knees and squealed with delight as Dora handed her several gaily wrapped parcels. She tore off the wrapping paper, exclaiming as she revealed amongst other things, a large teddy bears' picnic jigsaw puzzle, some dolly outfits for her new dolly made by Granny and a brightly coloured kaleidoscope from Uncle Frank. She held it up, a puzzled expression on her face. 'What does this do?'

Frank took her to the window and sat her on the deep sill. He showed her how to put the kaleidoscope to her eye and twist the end as she looked up to the sky. 'Can you see pretty colours and patterns?' he asked.

'Yes, yes.' She bounced up and down. 'Daddy come and see.' She thrust the metal tube at Joe, instructing him as Frank had done her. Dora smiled and threw the discarded coloured paper onto the fire and went into the kitchen to help her mam finish the dinner preparations.

Jackie was upstairs having a late morning nap so that she'd be fresh for the rest of the day. Dora felt happier today than she'd done in a long time and was planning to tell Joe something later that she hoped he'd agree to. She'd been off her sedatives for a while and felt she was coping well. Her state of depression was now behind her. She knew it wouldn't be all plain sailing, but she felt strong enough and ready to resume her role as mother to both her daughters.

Joe felt his jaw drop when Dora made her announcement as the family finished their Christmas dinner.

'I'm coming home with you.' Her cheeks were flushed and her blue eyes bright as she smiled at him. She looked almost normal and he thought back to the last time this had happened, when Carol was a few months old and Frank had bought her the new sewing machine. 'My bags are all packed and Mam and Frank think it's a good idea that we should try and get back to how we were again. I've been doing so well with Carol on the Sundays we've spent together.'

Joe spluttered and shook his head. 'I don't think I can allow that, Dora.'

'But, Joe, you can't stop me, it's my home and they're my children.' Her eyes filled with tears.

'I know that, love.' He pulled her to her feet and into the sitting room. 'This is madness, Dora. You know how you feel about Carol. I can't take any risks with her safety.'

'We are fine, if you'll just give me a minute to explain, instead of yelling at me.'

Joe shrugged and ran his hands through his hair. 'Go on then, explain.'

'I got Carol ready for bed on my own the other night when it was your works do and she was fine for me. Mam made me do it while she saw to Jackie. Then I played Ludo with her and we had fun when I let her win. She helped me wrap a few things for under the tree and I read her a story when I put her into bed. She was in my bed all night, Joe, and she snuggled close to me. In the morning she was okay too. I really want to come home and be a proper mother to both our girls.'

Joe felt a cold hand around his heart. While he'd been cuddled up to Ivy, his little girl had been sleeping next to a mother who'd admitted she couldn't really cope with her. He stared at her, this woman he'd once loved more than life itself. She was a stranger to him these days. One minute there was nothing in her eyes and now this sudden warmth. What if it went away again while he was working? What if she harmed Carol if she played up, as she was wont to do? Could he take the risk? Dare he? Everyone deserved another chance, but this was his daughter's life.

He pushed Dora gently down onto the sofa and sat beside her. He took her hands in his as she stared at him. 'Now listen to me. Today isn't the day to take you home with us for good. I need to prepare for that, gradually. I'm going to suggest something to you and I want you to think carefully about what I'm saying. I'm going home in a bit with Carol. Tomorrow I will come and get you and Jackie and bring you back with us for a few days. I'll see how you cope looking after both girls. I need reassurance, Dora, that I can go to work and you can handle them both. And don't forget this; your mam won't be in the next room to help you.' He saw a tear run down her cheek and knew he had to give her the benefit of the doubt, but it wasn't going to be easy, for either of them.

'Okay,' she whispered. 'If that's what you want, Joe. But it hurts that you're pushing me out. That you still want to keep me away from my daughter. I need *you* to see things how *I* see them. I didn't ask to be depressed. I've been through a lot, our baby's death, then losing Joanie and Dad so close together. All that affected the way I coped with things. Do you understand?'

'You know I do. But it's not just about us, is it? We have two little girls to put first.' He felt sick with worry. He still loved her and wanted to help her, but it was more the feeling of love for a sister than a lover these days. He cared deeply, he always would, but the passion he'd once felt had faded and from her reactions to him earlier, *she* didn't feel the same as she used to either. Maybe real love would return when they were back to normal, whatever normal was.

Sitting in the passenger seat, Dora felt the butterflies dancing in her stomach as Joe swung the car around the corner and pulled up outside their bungalow. Last night, packing her final things at Mam's, she'd convinced herself she'd be fine, but now the doubts were starting to crowd in. She took a deep breath and turned to smile at him. It would be difficult, but she was determined to try her best. Joe needed to feel confident in her ability to cope.

Inside the house she glanced around. It didn't look so different really. The walls were in need of a coat of emulsion to freshen them up. It seemed ages since she and Joe had distempered in here, just before they moved in. A lifetime ago, in fact, and a lot had happened in that short space of time. So much loss that still hung heavy in her heart. Her eyes immediately went to the framed photo of Joanie on the mantelpiece and she instantly felt calmer. 'Help me cope, Joanie,' she whispered.

Joe followed her in with Jackie in his arms, Carol by his side. 'Show Mammy the bike Father Christmas brought you, Carol,' he said, patting her on the head. Carol hung back, looking unsure, until Dora smiled and held out her hand. She followed Carol into the bedroom, where the little red three-wheel bike sat in pride of place.

'Aren't you a lucky girl?' Dora admired the bike and Carol got on it and immediately pedalled into the cupboard. 'Oh dear, be careful.' Dora bit her lip, looking at the scratch on the cupboard door. 'Maybe ride it in the garden later. Come on, let's go find Daddy and Jackie.'

* * *

Joe set Jackie down on the carpet and she crawled to the sofa and pulled herself up. Dora sat down and lifted her up to sit beside her. Carol immediately ran forward and Dora patted the seat next to her and Carol cuddled close. On the coffee table was a copy of *Peter Pan*. Dora picked it up and turned to the first page.

'This is a very good story, shall we read it?'

Carol nodded and at the sight of all three snuggled together Joe breathed a sigh of relief and went to put the kettle on.

He stood with his back against the kitchen door and lit a cigarette. Dare he hope for a future for them all? And would Ivy accept that he couldn't see her any more without kicking up a big stink and landing him in it? He'd been desperate the other night, frustrated as hell, and she'd been more than willing, but he'd kept a polite distance on Christmas Day and taken his leave right after tea had finished, claiming Carol was tired. Then there was Dolly. Would she use her discretion or her gob? Only time would tell.

By the time her dad's daffodils started to bloom in spring and Jackie had her first birthday, Dora was back home for good. Joe felt comfortable about leaving her in charge while he was at work, and in turn *she* felt like she'd never been away from her little family and the bungalow. They'd repainted the sitting room and kitchen. Joe took charge of the garden and the whole place felt like home again. She'd used her machine and made a couple of floral print dresses each for the girls to wear over Easter. Carol had helped her by passing things to her as she needed them. Dora had enjoyed seeing the self-important expression on her daughter's face as she'd been praised for handing over the correct colour of thread from the big work box in the cupboard. Living at her mam's place was fast becoming a distant memory, although Mam popped in regularly to offer a hand when she needed it.

There was just one great big fly in the ointment and it wouldn't go away. Joe was annoyed that she still wouldn't allow him to share their bed and that she refused to discuss it with him. She couldn't take the risk, even though he'd bought a supply of contraceptives when he'd had his hair cut at the barber's.

He'd pleaded with her, told her he'd wear two and then there was no danger of her getting pregnant. Agnes had worked out a calendar with her for the rhythm method that she and Alan used, with protection in the weeks when she knew she was most fertile. So far it had worked for Agnes, who didn't want more kids and was happy with the result. But Dora had hidden the calendar away in a drawer out of Joe's sight.

She dreaded the time after the girls had gone to bed and they were alone in the sitting room, relaxing and listening to the wireless or their records. All he wanted to talk about was them getting some help to deal with the problem and it was driving her crazy. He said he missed her and loved her and they couldn't go on like this. She loved him too and she knew she was being unfair to him. He was her husband and he had rights and needs. She no longer had those needs; they'd been quashed by fear of what may happen to her with another pregnancy. The thought terrified her and Joe sleeping on the sofa was the only way she could cope with the situation and be certain she was safe.

One week before Easter, Dolly knocked on the door and Dora let her in. Carol had gone to the shops with her mam and Jackie was asleep in her cot. She invited Dolly to sit down and made them a mug of Camp coffee.

Dolly had brought round a bag of clothes that Alice had grown out of, for Carol. 'There's a few bits and bobs that might do for playing out in. Nothing fancy, but too decent to give to the rag and bone man.' She took a sip of coffee and placed her mug down on the coffee table.

Dora put the bag on the floor by the sofa. 'Thank you very much. It's really kind of you.' She sensed there was another reason for Dolly's visit and the clothes were an excuse to get over the doorstep.

'How's your Joe doing now you're back together as a couple?' There was emphasis on the word *couple*.

Dora stiffened. Surely Joe hadn't spoken to Eric about their problems?

'We're fine, thank you. Taking it a day at a time.'

'And you're finding Carol easier to cope with?'

'Oh, yes. She has her moments, but they all do at that age. She's a good little girl most of the time. Thank you for helping Joe with her when I was unable to live here. It's much appreciated.'

'Oh, you're welcome. Any time, love. And it's better than the alternative any day.'

Dora frowned. 'Alternative? I don't understand what you mean.'

'Well that bloody Ivy one of course. Trying to get her feet under the table with your Joe while you was laid up at yer mam's. I had her measure all right, told her so at the works do. And swanning in here like she owned the place. Babysitting while Joe was out playing with his band on Saturday nights and then staying here till all hours after he got back. Mind you, she was good with your Carol, so I suppose any port in a storm, eh, chuck.'

'Oh, er, yes, of course. Joe said she was good with Carol.' Dora's head was spinning and she wanted Dolly to go. Jackie woke at that point and yelled loudly, signalling feeding time. Dora jumped to her feet. 'Right, I'll see you out, Dolly; I need to feed Jackie. Thanks for the clothes.' She practically bundled Dolly out of the bungalow and leant against the closed door, breathing deeply. Ivy had been here, in her home, with her husband and daughter. Joe hadn't even told her he'd been playing with the band again on Saturday nights while she was at her mam's. But then again, maybe he had said something and she couldn't remember because of the hazy state she'd been in. No - surely she would recall a fact like that, no matter how out of it she'd been. There'd definitely been no mention of Ivy whatsoever. Jackie's cries were getting louder and Dora hurried to the bedroom. By the time her mam and Carol arrived home she'd almost finished giving Jackie her dinner of mashed vegetables.

'I've got us a couple of nice egg custards and some Cheshire cheese. They'd just got a delivery and it smelt lovely, and some oven bottoms as well. I'll make us a nice sarnie. You okay, Dora? You look a bit pale, chuck.'

'Er yes. I'm fine, thanks, Mam. Just had Dolly here and you know how she can talk the hind leg off a donkey, as Dad used to say.'

'Oh aye, she can that.' Mam smiled and took the shopping through to the kitchen.

Dora wiped Jackie's face, lifted her out of the high chair and sat her on the rug. 'Carol, play nice with your sister for a minute while I speak to Granny.' Carol nodded and sat down next to Jackie with her box of coloured bricks.

'Mam, do you know if Joe played with the band at all while I was staying at your house?' Dora asked, leaning against the sink unit while her mam buttered two oven bottoms for their sandwiches.

'Yes I think he did, love. Said he needed the extra money badly as he couldn't do any regular overtime because of getting home for Carol.'

'Well, have you any idea who looked after Carol for him while he was out?'

Mam's brow wrinkled. 'A couple of girls from work, I think he told Frank. Why?'

'Oh nothing. Just wondered if it was someone we might be able to use again when we go out. If it was someone reliable.'

'No use asking me, love. Ask Joe, he'll know.'

'I will.' Dora filled the kettle, staring out of the window, her mind in turmoil. She wondered what else Joe had kept from her. Dolly said Ivy stayed till all hours after Joe got back. Why would she do that if she'd only been here to look after Carol? Had she sat with Joe here and had a nightcap with him, had they talked or listened to music and danced, like he used to do with *her*? Had he run his hands down Ivy's back and kissed her? And she'd been at the last works do at Christmas, Dolly said. What had gone on there that had made Dolly have words with her?

'Dora.' Her mam's voice brought her out of her thoughts. 'That water's going all over the place. Are you sure you're okay, chuck?'

'I'm fine. Just a bit preoccupied, that's all.' She put the kettle on the stove and made her escape to the bathroom. She sat down on the side of the bath, feeling like she'd been kicked in the stomach. Why hadn't Joe told her about Ivy babysitting? Even at the risk of her being annoyed with him, he should still have said something. The very fact he'd kept it from her made her feel he'd got something to hide. And although there'd been no intimacy between her and Joe for ages, she still loved him and the pain she felt at the thought of him even *kissing* another woman was too much to bear. She took a couple of deep breaths, tormenting herself with thoughts of what Joe and Ivy had been up to in her absence. Had he slept with her in their bed? The thought made her feel sick. Maybe they were still seeing each other on the sly. Joe had needs that she couldn't satisfy for him, but Ivy could, and Dora had no doubt the woman would do so quite willingly. How could she find out without asking him outright and causing a fall-out that would be impossible to take back? If he'd had sex with Ivy she didn't want to be with him. The thought of him begging her to make love made her cringe. How could he do that when he knew he'd slept with Ivy? How could she ever trust him again? She'd been at her most vulnerable and he'd betrayed her. Her mam was shouting that her dinner was ready. She pulled the chain and splashed her face with cold water.

Dora did her best to act normal that evening as Joe helped her to bath the girls and get them into bed, but she felt totally broken inside. It was hard to keep smiling as the girls giggled and kicked water everywhere. She couldn't even look Joe in the eye, although he didn't seem to notice and chased Carol squealing around her bedroom, growling like a bear, while Dora quietly got on with dressing Jackie. How could he be like that, knowing what he'd done? It wasn't easy to keep quiet and not yell and scream at him like she wanted to. She needed a plan in her head of what she would do if she ever found out the truth. The more she analysed what Dolly had said the more convinced she was Joe was having an affair. Although deep inside she felt heartbroken that he could betray her after all the vows they'd made on the day they married, she wasn't going to hang around and become an all-forgiving and downtrodden wife; she had more values about her than that, and if he'd betrayed her when she needed him most, what else would he do? She was perfectly capable of looking after herself and earning a living, so she knew she could take care of her family, even though it wouldn't be easy. She checked herself. Her thoughts were getting out of hand now and swung from divorcing Joe to wanting it all to be a silly mistake, a figment of Dolly's over-active imagination. There was no proof other than what Dolly had told her and everyone knew what a gossip she was. Why was she even letting her imagination run away like this?

Chapter Thirty-Five

On Easter Sunday Joe took them all to Sefton Park in the car he'd bought with the money his mother had given him. Dora had dressed her daughters in the new pink and white floral sundresses she'd made and each wore an identical white sunbonnet with a frilled peak. Jackie had just started to walk and Carol held her hand as they toddled along in front. Dora felt proud of her girls as people stopped to smile at them and admire their pretty outfits.

'Another little Miss Independent,' Joe said, catching hold of her hand and lacing his fingers through hers.

'She's not as bad as Carol was,' Dora said stiffly, unlacing her fingers. She couldn't bear any contact with his skin, knowing what she knew, or thought she knew. She tortured herself in bed at night thinking of Joe being intimate with Ivy. She'd found it hard to sleep the last few nights and knew she should tackle him before she got depressed again. It had to happen soon, for her sanity's sake.

Joe frowned and pointed across to the statues near the Palm House. 'Carol, go over that way,' he called. 'Peter Pan's over there.'

Carol nodded and gently led Jackie over to the statue. Joe got out his camera as they stood by the base of Peter Pan. 'Smile, girls. There we go. Go on, Dora, stand with them while I take another.'

As Dora took her place beside her girls and Joe pressed the shutter, Carol let out a shriek of excitement.

'There's Roly,' she yelled, jumping up and down as the little corgi pricked up his ears and waddled towards her, his tail wagging, pulling Ivy by the lead with Flo in her wake.

Carol dropped to her knees as Roly fussed around her, licking her face and yelping with ecstasy at seeing his little friend again.

She squealed with laughter as he knocked her over and Ivy picked her up and dusted her down, telling Roly to sit.

'Good afternoon, Joe, Dora. Nice to see you out and about,' Ivy said and Flo nodded shyly.

'You too,' Joe said as Dora stared at him, her eyes speaking volumes. 'Hello, Roly.' He squatted to stroke the little dog, who rolled onto his back.

'Can we go and see Ivy and Roly, Daddy, next time Mammy goes away?'

'Mammy isn't going away again, Carol,' Dora said quietly, staring at Ivy and looking for a sign of guilt on her face, in her eyes. But the woman was giving nothing away. 'I think we need to go home, Joe.' She started to walk away from the little group, her stomach churning.

'Joe, I'm so sorry,' she heard Ivy say. 'If I'd known you were coming here today, we'd have gone somewhere else. Go after her, we'll watch the girls.'

Joe sprinted across the grass and grabbed Dora by the arm. 'Slow down,' he panted. 'Why did you do that then, walk away, I mean?'

She looked at him, seeing no guilt in *his* face either. Was she mistaken about the whole thing? Had Dolly over-exaggerated? There was only one way to find out. 'Get the girls, Joe. I want to go home. We'll talk back there.' She watched as he walked back to Ivy and Flo, his shoulders slightly more hunched than before.

'Take the girls to Dolly's,' Dora ordered as they pulled up outside the bungalow.

'Why?'

'Please, Joe, just do it.'

She let herself into their home and waited for his return.

'What's going on?' he asked, rushing into the sitting room where Dora was pacing agitatedly up and down, wringing her hands.

'You tell me,' she demanded. 'I want to know what's going on with you and that Ivy woman.'

'Nothing!' he stuttered, his jaw dropping. 'She's just somebody from work, you know that.'

'I also know she's been coming to my home to look after my daughter while you've been out at night and that you were with her at the ROF do at Christmas. But for some reason you chose not to tell me. Why is that, Joe?' And then she saw the guilty look flash in his eyes. He didn't need to say anything. 'You slept with her, didn't you? Don't deny it; I can see it in your face.' She burst into tears and dropped down onto the sofa. 'How could you do that to me? I really needed your support and you were out with her.'

'You didn't need me, Dora,' he said quietly. 'You haven't needed or wanted me for a long time. I'm not saying what I did was right, I shouldn't have and I'm sorry. I've tried to put it behind us and make things up to you by always being there for you since you came home. But you still don't want me. I suppose Dolly told you? She just can't keep her bloody mouth shut.'

'You can't blame Dolly. She didn't say anything out of order. I had to pretend that I knew Ivy had babysat for you. I just don't understand why you didn't tell me you were playing with the band again. Why you tried to hide that from me. I can only assume it was because of your guilty conscience.'

'I'm sorry.' He got down on his knees in front of her and took her hands in his. 'Please forgive me. I love you and I always will. Let's start again. I'll have nothing more to do with Ivy. I'll change my job. We'll give up the house, move from here. Emigrate even. It's just you, me and the girls from now on.'

Tears ran down Dora's cheeks as she looked into his eyes. She *couldn't* forgive him and nor could they start again. 'I can't do it, Joe. It's too late. I'd never be able to trust you again.'

Joe's eyes filled and he struggled to speak. 'Do you want me to give you some space, a bit of a break? I can go and stay with a pal while you think about things.'

She nodded. It would further break her heart to see him go, but there was no other way forward at the moment for her. There was nothing *to* think about. She'd done all that in the weeks leading up to today. She'd grow to hate him even more if he stayed around.

'What about the kids? How will you cope with both of them?'

'We'll be fine.' She knew she'd feel a lot more relaxed too if she was on her own and he wasn't constantly trying to get her into bed. It wasn't quite how she'd envisaged her life, being alone with two kids to bring up and no man to love, but it was better than the alternative – living with a man she couldn't respond to or satisfy, and always at the back of her mind the worry of him cheating on her with another woman again. She couldn't live like that and there was no point in prolonging the agony. 'You can come and see them at the weekend.'

Joe took his bags out to the car and slung them into the boot as Dolly looked on, her face a mask of curiosity.

'Going somewhere, Joe?' She walked towards him, her arms folded.

'Like you fucking care,' he growled, slamming the boot shut. 'I hope you're satisfied now. Because as Dora's friend and confidante, I'll leave you to sort out the mess your bloody unruly gob has created.'

Dolly stood on the pavement and watched, her mouth a wide O as he started the car and drove off down Hedgefield Road. She hurried into Dora's house and called her name. 'Dora, where are you, queen? I've just seen Joe drive off at speed. Do you want me to bring the girls back yet, or shall I give them some tea at mine?'

The bedroom door opened slightly and Dora stuck her head out. 'Oh, Dolly, I didn't really want him to go, but I can't forgive him for sleeping with Ivy. I'd make both our lives hell. He's gone to stay with a pal to give me some space.'

'If you ask me, you're best shut of the cheating bugger. Sit down and I'll make you a brew and you can tell me what happened since I saw you go off to Seffy Park earlier.'

A couple of weeks after Joe's departure, Dora asked her mam and Frank to come over. She'd told them not to visit her until she felt able to talk about things and said she wanted to spend the time alone with her girls. It hadn't been easy adjusting to being alone, but Carol had been good, for a change, and Jackie was never any trouble. It was the overwhelming feeling of loneliness at night when Joe didn't come home from work and help her with the bedtime routine that had been the hardest to cope with. That and the sitting on her own, with the girls in bed and the wireless on, listening to programmes that she and Joe had enjoyed together. And then there was the wondering what he was doing that also plagued her. Was he with Ivy on Saturday at a dance? Did he take her home and spend the night with her? The very thought made her feel sick and she'd tried to block it from her mind.

He'd come over to see the girls on Sunday afternoon and taken them down to the park. Then they'd all had tea together back here. It had been a strained situation to deal with; he'd hardly spoken to Dora, and Carol had screamed the place down and kicked the front door as he'd closed it when he left. Nothing would pacify her. Dora had put her to bed after she'd fallen asleep on the rug, worn out from sobbing for Daddy. As Dora had sat on the sofa alone that night, she'd cried heartbrokenly too, until there were no more tears left to cry. But she was determined not to change her mind and take him back. Much as she still cared about him – he was the father of her children and they'd always have that bond – she knew in her heart that she'd never be able to trust him again.

'Now, are you sure you're doing the right thing?' Mam asked, looking worried. She and Frank sat on the sofa opposite Dora, who'd just explained the reason behind Joe's departure and how she couldn't live with him any more. 'It won't be easy, bringing up two kiddies on your own. Surely you and Joe can sort it out. He wouldn't be the first man to stray, and he was under a lot of strain at the time, love.'

'Yes, I'm absolutely sure. And we were *both* under a lot of strain, so don't sympathise with him. I've done nothing but go over and over things and I know I can do it. And with regards to the girls, I can cope easily enough now with the pair of them. With Joe not here I feel more relaxed. It's not fair to hang on to him when I can't love him like I should. We're better apart.'

Mam pursed her lips. 'And I suppose he's gone off with that Ivy woman?'

'No, he hasn't,' Dora replied. 'He's staying at his mate Don's for now.'

'Well, he can't stay there for ever. I don't suppose it'll be long before he gets his feet under Ivy's table. She'll be sniffing around, knowing he's not living here any more. And what will you do for money? Have you thought about that?'

'Joe will help me; he told me that when he came to see the girls. And I'm going to start my dressmaking business up again. I'll manage fine, Mam.'

Frank nodded. 'I'll always see you okay, Sis. You've only got to ask, you know that.'

'I know you would, Frank, and thank you. But I'm determined to stand on my own two feet. It was my decision to ask Joe to leave. I could have swept it under the rug and pretended all was well, but my head feels clear for the first time in months and I know I can do this. I'll stay here at the prefab for now, but by rights it's Joe's house with his job, so I'll look for a place of my own in time. I fancy living a bit closer to the city centre, and I'll probably get more work by doing that.'

She stood up and went to stand by the framed photo of Joanie on the mantelpiece. She knew that Joanie would want her to succeed in everything she did. She traced a finger down the glass and smiled. 'To be honest, I'll be glad to leave here. It doesn't hold the nicest of memories for me. I lost my little daughter here, and that pain will never go away. But whatever I do, and wherever I go, I know that I've got the best guardian angel in the world looking after me.'

Letter from Pam

I'd love to say a big thank you to the dedicated team at Bookouture who helped guide me through the experience of getting this first novel with them polished to perfection. Oliver Rhodes for taking me on, Natasha, Abigail, Claire, and Lauren for all their editorial encouragement and making my story something I feel justifiably proud of. Thank you to the lovely Kim Nash and all the Bookouture authors who have welcomed me into their online family. A nicer and more helpful group of people you couldn't wish to meet. I feel honoured to be amongst such illustrious company and to be part of a fabulous award winning team.

And to my loyal band of regular readers, thank you so much for sticking with me and waiting patiently for this new story. You all know who you are and your support is so much appreciated. An author's life can be a solitary one, and without you ladies and your daily contact on FB and the Notrights group, I'd be lost. If you enjoyed *The Lost Daughter of Liverpool*, I'd be so grateful if you could write a review and let me know what you think. Happy Reading. Much love to you all.

Pam.

You can sign up here to receive an email whenever I have a new book published: www.bookouture.com/pam-howes/

Or follow me on my Facebook author page and on Twitter:

 Pam-Howes-Author-260328010709267/

 @PamHowes1

Acknowledgments

For my man, daughters and grandchildren, for putting up with a completely vacant partner, mum and grandma over the last twelve months. I'm all yours again now, until next week!

Thank you to my FB friends on our little group - 60's Chicks Confidential - for their undying friendship and support. They keep me sane and tell me to go get some rest when I'm still up working in the wee small hours. Thanks also to my lovely friends and readers, Brenda Thomasson and Julie Simpson, who read a very early draft of this story and gave me encouragement to carry on and not chuck it in the bin.

Made in the USA
Columbia, SC
18 June 2020